BEYOND ALL FRONTIERS

BEYOND ALL FRONTIERS

Elizabeth Darrell

This first hardcover edition published in Great Britain 2002 by
SEVERN HOUSE PUBLISHERS LTD of
9–15 High Street, Sutton, Surrey SM1 1DF.
Previously published 1983 under the pseudonym *Emma Drummond*.
This first hardcover edition published in the USA 2002 by
SEVERN HOUSE PUBLISHERS INC of
595 Madison Avenue, New York, N.Y. 10022.

British Library Cataloguing in Publication Data

Darrell, Elizabeth, 1931–
 Beyond all frontiers
  1.   Afghanistan - History - 19th century - Fiction
  2.   Historical fiction
  I.   Title II. Drummond, Emma, 1931–
  823.9'14 [F]

 ISBN 0-7278-5656-1

Printed and bound in Great Britain by
MPG Books Ltd., Bodmin, Cornwall.

Introduction

In the late 1970's I was well into writing *Beyond All Frontiers* when my editor rang to ask what I was working on. When I explained, she said "No, that won't do. It'll never sell in the USA. The majority of Americans have little interest in Afghanistan or India; they are not part of their own history. Write something else."

Being at the start of my career, I did as she asked. In fact I had written two more novels before the Russians invaded Afghanistan creating headline news. My editor immediately called asking if I still had the unfinished manuscript and how soon could I finish it?

By pure chance, this re-issue of *Beyond All Frontiers* was already planned before Afghanistan became the focus of worldwide attention that it is today. Although this novel recounts events of over 160 years ago, you will find that time has little changed that harsh, wild country.

History has a way of repeating itself.

Elizabeth Darrell ©2002

*Dedicated to the memory of my friend
Major General George N. Wood,
CB, CBE, DSO, MC,
who was always so generous with
advice, encouragement and praise.*

Nor look thee 'ere beyond this kingdom
Beyond all frontiers of love and pain.
For thine eyes will tire and see no more
the truth. It will blind thee.

ANON.

Khiva

RUSSIA

CHINA

Bokhara

TURKESTAN

Herat

Kabul Jalalabad

Peshawar

Ghuznee

Khurd – Kabul Pass

Khyber Pass

AFGHANISTAN

Kandahar

Lahore

BRITISH INDIA

Ferozepore

Quetta

PUNJAB

Bolan Pass

R. Sutlej

Meerpore

Delhi

BALUCHISTAN

PERSIA

Hyderabad

(The location of Meerpore is fictional)

· *author's note* ·

ALL characters in this book, apart from well-known historical figures, are fictional and in no way represent anyone living or dead. The garrison of Meerpore and the fort at Malkhan have never existed, but the incidents depicted there and elsewhere are based on true accounts recorded in letters and diaries of those who were in India and Afghanistan during those turbulent years.

The first British occupation of Afghanistan lasted roughly three years before the army was driven out. The second attempt, forty years later, brought the same result. Only the future will show whether a permanent occupation of this proud, savage and intensely independent land can be achieved.

Beyond All Frontiers

· *prologue* ·

THE TWO MEN sprawled at ease on the spiky grass beneath a jasmine tree. Against the barren brown of the vast plain they had just crossed, the scarlet of their tight-fitting jackets provided a splash of colour. The plumes in the military shakoes on the ground beside them stirred in the hot sultry breeze, and each man had unhooked the stiff collar that plagued him in temperatures of over one hundred degrees. Mopping the sweat from their faces with silk handkerchiefs, they drank the warm water from the canteens they always carried with them on the march. Neither spoke during the first few moments of that welcome rest period. Each simply gazed at the range of hills ahead with eyes screwed up against the glare, and thought his own thoughts.

All around that small watering-place the Indian sepoys were slaking their thirsts with wise moderation. They had a long way to go yet, and they prayed those hills hid none of the brigands who had raided this village, killing the men, raping the women, and poisoning the water. That had happened four days ago, so there was every hope they would now be well away from this district.

Suddenly, the older man broke the silence to say reflectively, "This country will defeat us, in the end."

"Oh . . . what makes you say that?" asked the other slowly.

The first one turned to look at his youthful companion. "Don't you ever feel it?"

"I have hardly been in India long enough to form any solid impressions."

"Of course . . . I'd forgotten that." He sighed and turned his face once more towards the hills. "I have been in India since 1824—ten years, and it seems like my whole lifetime.

The mystique of this damned civilization eats into a man until he loses all sense of time and his own identity."

The younger man frowned. "Do you mean one's memory deteriorates in this climate?"

The other shook his head. "The heat does affect one's wits, at times, but it is more than that. It's a feeling of futility, of somehow growing less as time passes."

"Go on," came the gentle prompt.

"Well, look around you, Lingarde." A brown hand was waved in the air. "In every acre of its territories, in every hill and swamp, in each of its reptile-infested rivers is an ancient and indisputable culture that will outlive and outlast the brash East India Company. In each temple and shrine, at the heart of every exotic festival, in the rigid upholding of the caste system are the signs that should tell us the truth. But do we heed them?" He turned back to regard his companion with burning brown eyes. "Our sepoys are trained to behave like English soldiers, but the blood of India runs through their veins, and the history of past centuries shapes their actions when feelings run high. Fools forget that, Lingarde. When these men are loyal, show them you recognize what that loyalty has cost them . . . and when the day of reckoning comes, I hope to God I am not still here."

There was a short silence during which one man regretted having spoken so impulsively, and the other recognized in his companion a kindred spirit.

"India has not captured you, either!" It was said almost with relief at being able to confess his own disenchantment.

Edward Kingsley smiled gravely. "The East is no place for men from the West unless they are prepared to surrender, not only their lives, but their souls." He frowned then. "We have not conquered this country. It is the reverse, you know. Beneath the riches and glory, it is the reverse." He re-corked his water-bottle and sat up from his reclining position. The movement signified the end of his fey mood, and he adopted a bantering tone to say, "If the Russians are, in truth, wooing Afghanistan, then I wish them luck. I, for one, would not care to march into that wilderness even for a king's ransom. The barbarous devils are welcome to it."

"The Russians are not all barbarous, you know." It was snapped out with such force it took the other man by surprise. Then enlightenment dawned.

"Forgive me. No offence meant. I forgot Lady Lingarde was Russian." He smiled disarmingly. "Your mama is one of the most cultured and beautiful women I have ever met. I was presented to her once at a ball in Calcutta. She put every other female in the shade."

"She always does."

"But it was not merely her beauty. She has a kind of . . . *majesty*. There was not a gentleman there whom she could not persuade to do just as she asked, I am certain." His smile broadened. "I have heard it said it is more often than not Lady Lingarde who achieves the diplomatic success where Sir John might have failed."

Richard Gregori Lingarde smiled back. "Why should she not? Mama comes from one of the fine old Russian families and was used to the company of distinguished guests from an early age. Her intellect and understanding are equal to any man I know, her wit is superior, and her courage outstanding. She was with my father at Waterloo, you know, while he was on the Duke's staff. When his arm was shot off she tended him personally—along with several other seriously wounded officers. It takes more than mere beauty to do that, I think you will agree."

Edward Kingsley looked at his fellow officer shrewdly. "Mmm, it will take an exceptional female to capture your interest, I fancy." A wicked gleam entered his dark eyes. "Many a heart in Meerpore is destined to be broken, alas. A handsome fellow like you is certain to be besieged by a bevy of beauties from the moment he arrives. But none will bear comparison with Lady Anastasia Lingarde, I deem."

Richard tossed off the teasing remark carelessly. "At twenty-four, entanglements with the fair sex have no place in my plans."

"Oh?" commented the other amused. "What plans have you?"

"To study eastern languages, and to develop experimental engineering techniques that are presently in their infancy. Do you know, the military are using those same methods our fathers used in the Peninsula? Would you not think some advance would have been made in thirty years?"

The two fell to discussing campaign tactics—one a man of the Company's army, experienced in fighting numerous tribal skirmishes, the other in the service of the British Crown, skilled in sciences and mechanics but who had never yet used a weapon in combat. They argued intelligently and without anger until the subject of Afghanistan was broached once more.

"There is trouble brewing there, mark my word," said Edward wagging his head sagely as he got to his feet. "An unconquered stretch of land is an irresistible temptation, Lingarde. With the Russians on one side of it and us on the other, it will be interesting to see who resists that temptation the longest."

Richard stood up also, fastening his collar and brushing the dust from his shako in preparation for the continuation of their journey.

"I think the Russians are as discouraged by the terrain as we are," he said conversationally. "My cousin writes that it is generally agreed that a campaign into Afghanistan would end in disaster."

"Your cousin?"

Richard nodded. "Igor is a captain in the Imperial Russian Guard. A very intelligent, well-bred fellow. Not in the least barbarous," he added with gentle pointedness.

Edward Kingsley looked at him. "Have you many relatives there?"

"Numerous relatives," said Richard settling the shako firmly on to his fair head. "I spent a great deal of my childhood with them. Marvellous, vivid people, the Russians."

"So I have heard." Edward put on his own shako, but was struck by a thought so arresting he stopped in the midst of the action. "By George, if it ever came to a confrontation with them over Afghanistan, it would be dashed awkward for you, Lingarde."

Richard frowned. "Yes, I suppose it would, but it is not likely to happen, is it?"

They organized the men for an immediate resumption of their journey to Meerpore, then mounted their thirsty horses.

"Keep an eye open for a stream or pool, in case I miss it," called Edward as he trotted off to the head of the column, leaving his companion to take up the rear. "These beasts will drop under us unless they get a drink soon."

Although the hills had looked distant, just how distant had been deceptive. The sun was sinking by the time the column rode wearily into the shadows cast by them, and the horses were staggering. Richard followed the long line of men into the entrance of the mountain pass with a reluctance foreign to him. If ever there was a place ideal for a trap, this was it. It was stifling, sandwiched between the rocky heights that still held the day's heat with no breeze to alleviate it. He would give anything to be in sight of his destination, yet Meerpore was still four days away on the far side of another ridge of hills.

Then, before he could think what was happening, the quietness exploded into terrible unidentifiable sounds. The column of troops, already narrowed into single-file in the pass, broke up and scattered as the dim light revealed a horde in ragged clothes emerging as if from the very rock itself. Richard reined in automatically as the attackers fell shrieking on to the scarlet-coated sepoys. Then, as the struggling men parted, his stomach churned and his palms grew wet as he saw a living tableau of cruel arrogant features and long flashing knives close around Edward Kingsley on a bend up ahead.

The winding track now contained a savage mêlée of slaughter, and Richard's ears rang with inhuman cries. Next minute, his horse was leaping forward, his voice screaming commands to disorganized men. Without being aware of drawing his sword he found it there in his hand. All around him spun bloody images of brown faces with dark eyes full of hatred, mouths gaping wide in anguish, slashes across men's throats that emitted crimson froth, and grasping, writhing bodies seeking escape.

Then he was through the nightmare kaleidoscope, his

voice hoarse with shouting, his body drenched with sweat. But order was now emerging from chaos. The scarlet-and-blue-clad sepoys began to form up in organized defence, then attack, driving the tattered remnants of the enemy back up the hill. Desperately controlling his terrified horse, Richard bellowed further orders, forcing his troops to press home their advantage. They heard him and obeyed. But he did not recognize his own voice, the rage-filled curses uttered in all three languages he constantly used.

Then it was over. The last brigand had vanished into the darkening hillside, the soldiers were scrambling and sliding down the slope, the cries of the wounded men and horses echoed chillingly in the comparative quiet after battle . . . and on the ground nearby was a pile of bloody flesh, scarlet rags, and brown horse-hair that had once been Captain Edward Kingsley and his charger, Foxy. The paltry prize for the attackers: ten rifles and some boxes of ammunition.

As the soldiers dropped back into the pass and took in the scene it grew very quiet. Edward Kingsley had been revered by his men. Shaking, Richard somehow managed to climb from his horse and hand the bridle to a sepoy on the edge of the crowding circle.

"See to your men," he said huskily to a Jemadar, then forced himself to face what he had to do. As he neared the obscene pile he fought his growing nausea until sweat poured down his face and his legs threatened to buckle beneath him.

Digging a shallow grave in that hard-baked earth was not enough, even though he was reeling from reaction and fatigue. Neither was the task of trying to ensure that what he placed, with reverence, into a blanket to lay in that hole was, indeed, Edward Kingsley. Covering the rough grave with earth, he then manhandled a large stone on to it and recited in loud hoarse words the only prayer his stunned mind could produce. The burial over, he buttoned his tunic with fingers that shook, settled the shako on to his head and turned to face the men he must now lead. They were all watching him expectantly.

When the column set off Richard was riding at its head, out alone, back ramrod stiff. But the youthful subaltern showing every sign of outward control found his ears still full of agonized screams, his eyes unable to see anything but that terrible tableau, his mind tormented by uncertainty. Rigid military training had told him it was impossible for one man to save Edward Kingsley from his encircling murderers, and that it was his duty to rally an organized defence in men without a leader . . . or had it? However impossible or misguided such an action might have been, surely the natural instinct of a man would be to go to the aid of a dying comrade helplessly outnumbered? Had it really been rigid military training or the fear of becoming another certain victim of those slashing blades that had led him to stand away and shout orders to those who had responded instinctively to the voice of authority?

Possibly, the column had been saved: definitely, seven of the brigands had been killed and three wounded before they fled in disorder. But the thought that pounded in Richard Lingarde's brain as he rode towards Meerpore was that he had emerged from that attack completely unscathed, while the slaughtered Captain's body had lain a mere twenty-five yards ahead with not a single defender lying near it.

• *one* •

CALCUTTA ANNOUNCED ITSELF in many ways to the traveller approaching it up the River Hooghly. The thick, green jungle covering the banks was broken here and there by ghauts which revealed open parkland; orderly arrangements of cypresses and velvety lawns stretching in front of tasteful villas suggested urban tranquillity; a conglomeration of international shipping in the harbour told of thriving commerce and trade; while a backdrop of classical pillars and spires left one in no doubt of the greatness of this Indian city.

But the overpowering impression a newcomer received was spoiled by the terrible stench that wafted over the water. Not all the grandeur of the palaces, the wealth of its merchant trade, nor the verdure of its gardens could disguise the smell of open drains that spread disease like wild-fire through the city and its environs. Yet it was not only the drains that produced the odour. As the great sailing-ship approached its destination, garbage of every description floated past the wooden hull, and the passengers crowding the decks were horrified at the sight of a decomposing human corpse amidst rotting vegetable flotsam, and the swollen carcases of animals, that spiralled grotesquely in the current.

For one passenger, however, this approach to the greatest moment of her life could not be spoiled by *anything*. She had lain sleepless in her stifling cabin until the very first paling of the sky had called her irresistibly. At seventeen, Charlotte Scott was still enough of a child to rush on deck before any other passenger was astir, and cross from side to side in her intense excitement, hampering the crewmen trying to swab the decks, and dodging the pails of water brought up over the side from the river for that purpose. Twice, she almost cannoned into junior officers hurrying to their duty and, for a moment or two, put on a demure pretence of simply taking the air. Then, when they saluted and went on their way, she hung precariously over the rail once more, straining her eyes in the growing dawn for the sights she had dreamed of so long and so ardently.

All her life, Charlotte had been in the charge of people who were too Christian or high-principled to refuse to take her. Although she had two half-brothers in England, both married and well-established, neither had wanted to become the guardian of the small child of their father's second marriage. So Baby Charlotte had gone to Sir Rastin Scott's spinster sister, a woman who had compensated for her lack of a husband by immersing herself in the church and good works. Charlotte's two younger half-brothers had joined her at the small house in a quiet Shropshire village during their school holidays, until they had both joined their regiments and sailed off to India.

During all those lonely years there had been monthly letters from Charlotte's mama—never from Sir Rastin—but the extent of their interest had covered the girl's progress at her lessons, and her rate of physical growth. Kind comment had always been passed on drawings and poems sent to India, and on Christmas presents, begun a year in advance, that had been stitched with much diligence and unpicking. The presence of those monthly letters had denied complete lack of caring, yet the adolescent recipient had gained no impression of the woman who had written them, or of an affection any warmer than that given by Aunt Meg.

It had been Charlotte's two half-brothers who had provided the colour and reality of her distant family, writing her letters that contained vivid descriptions of the lives they led. Hubert, the dreamy one, had painted word-pictures of the country and its indigenous creatures. Charlotte remembered him as a kindly, rather serious young man, and her eyes now filled at the thought of his bones lying beneath the earth of this country she had just reached. She had loved him through his letters and had felt the anguish of his loss quite severely, even though the news had reached her half a world away and half a year after his going.

By contrast, Tom's letters had always enthused about his friends, his social life, and the army. Mostly about the army because he was a vigorous soldier. Neither young man had written much about his step-mother, and it had seemed to Charlotte that Lady Felicia Scott wished to remain a mystery where her daughter was concerned.

Yet, throughout those lonely years, Charlotte had had the conviction that if she could only reach India, that distant, vibrant land, she would belong, at last. She was the one true child of her parents—her brothers only claimed one of them—and this day, this moment, had taken on an almost magical importance that had grown from the moment her summons had arrived, all though the long voyage, until this last dawn.

As the morning advanced, and other passengers began to appear on deck, Charlotte was forced into a decorum that belied her exhilaration. This was when *adventure* began, and where better than in the mystic East, place of tigers and crocodiles, maharajahs and mahouts, splendour and poverty, barbarism and incredible beauty—and her very own family?

First, there would be the wonder of the journey overland to the northern station of Meerpore, which would allow her the opportunity to see the changing face of this vast continent. Then would come the wonderful reunion with Tom, and the chance to share, in person, all those activities and friends he had written of over the years. There would be excursions to places of antiquity and interest, fascinating and well-travelled people to meet, and maybe even a visit to one of the splendid, fabled palaces that housed treasures beyond price, for Sir Rastin was the Resident of Meerpore, and a man of high consequence. And there would be her mama beside her now, the friend and confidante Charlotte longed for and determined she would become. The thirteen years of separation would melt away and be forgotten once they met. Aunt Meg had lectured her on the importance of setting a good example as the daughter of two such eminent members of Anglo-Indian society, and Charlotte fully intended to give her mama no cause to be ashamed of her.

On the crowded deck, no one glancing at the drably-

· 3 ·

dressed young girl with a face that was no more than pleasant, and a shape that was only just deciding to become rounded, guessed that beneath the modest travelling-gown there rioted a personality glimpsing the light of freedom at the end of a long, dark tunnel of hidden longings. But a study of Charlotte's eyes as the ship slowed and began the sluggish manoeuvre that would eventually bring it alongside the jetty, would have betrayed the whole story of hopes about to be realized.

Knowing it was absurd, she nevertheless scanned the sea of faces on the jetty, even though distance still made them little more than a blur. With no experience of the filial bond, Charlotte could not rid herself of the foolish notion that she would know which of the eager, searching matrons was her own mama, by instinct. It was while she was waiting to do this that she was approached by the Purser—a kindly man who had answered her myriad questions during the voyage with patience and understanding. He explained that the pilot had brought aboard urgent messages for some of the passengers, one being for her.

She took it from him with careful composure and thanked him politely. But, as soon as he moved away, she ripped the envelope open with shaking fingers. The adventure was already beginning. An urgent message especially for *her*, Charlotte Scott, resident of India!

She read it two or three times to ensure that she had not misunderstood the message, then walked slowly to the stern of the ship, where the muddy wake could still be seen below. The garbage in the water looked like garbage, now; the stench was so strong she had to put her cologne-drenched handkerchief to her nostrils. Only now did she notice that the pillars and spires of the distant city looked shabby, the conglomeration of shipping was rusty and malodorous, the ghauts were slimy and covered with the maimed and the palsied. The glittering gem of her arrival had revealed a flaw. It was pointless looking for her mama; she would not be there on the jetty.

*   *   *

The gangplank had been lowered more than two hours ago, yet the lump of disappointment still blocked Charlotte's throat as she sat in her cabin surrounded by trunks and boxes. Above and around her were the shouts of the crew, mingled with those of passengers as they gave orders to the native porters swarming over the jetty in fawning competition for employment. Winches were squeaking badly enough to set her teeth on edge, deep thumps signified the removal of baggage from the holds, livestock grunted and squealed, while horses on the jetty added shrill neighs to the medley of sound that heralded the docking of a packet from England. Above it all rang the happy sound of companionship renewed.

For six months, the ship had battled its way towards India and, throughout the tedious voyage, Charlotte had ticked off the days with thankfulness. Yet, at that moment, she felt more alone than at any time with her aunt in England. She bit her lip. It did seem the very height of misfortune that a debilitating headache should assail her mama on that very day, to prevent her from meeting the ship carrying the daughter she had not seen for thirteen years. Yet the note in Charlotte's hand confirmed the fact, and the imagined proud, smiling matron, unable to hide her tears of joy at the reunion, remained an enigma.

A tap on the cabin door heralded the arrival of Miss Tamworth, who said her dear brother had hired porters and a carriage for their immediate departure. Charlotte swallowed her overwhelming disappointment and picked up her bandboxes, to follow the middle-aged spinster down the gangplank on to the land that was to be her new home.

She was quiet as they drove through the streets of Calcutta, her interest in the sight of the vivid, dirty, ramshackle, pretentious city being dimmed by a sense of embarrassment. The Reverend Tamworth and his sister had been sober but companionable chaperones throughout the journey, but had plainly expected to be rid of their charge on arrival at their final destination. Felicia Scott's headache had forced them to insist on abandoning the group of welcoming churchmen whilst they delivered Charlotte—like a parcel—to Lady

Scott's hotel. The sensation of being a parcel increased when the Tamworths left her at the hotel, regretting their inability to make her mama's acquaintance immediately, but promising to call on another day when indisposition did not preclude visitors. She stood in the hotel foyer, surrounded by trunks and boxes, the subject of intense scrutiny by passing guests, while the manager made the situation worse with flustered attempts to deal with a situation he had not expected.

Boys were sent scurrying—one with a message to Lady Scott's maidservant, another to pay the porters who had carried in all the trunks, and a whole army of them to convey those same pieces of luggage to a staircase shrouded with potted palms. By the time Lady Scott's gracious permission to conduct her daughter to her suite was brought by a bellboy, Charlotte was well on the way to believing the day was really an unpleasant dream from which she would soon thankfully awake.

Heads turned to follow the progress of the young woman in sprigged muslin gown of severe style, who held her head so stiffly as she followed the manager at the head of a long procession of servants and, by the time they had reached a shuttered door, the colour of embarrassment in Charlotte's cheeks had deepened.

The door was opened by a native girl of opulent charm, dressed in vivid green and gold Indian dress and gold slippers. Charlotte was taken aback by the fact that the girl's lips had been artificially reddened and her eyes emboldened by the use of black lines, giving her the appearance of an eastern goddess. But the maidservant was soon forgotten as the interior of the room took all the new arrival's attention.

Bowls of flowers were everywhere, filling the air with a heaviness of perfume that was almost more than her bewildered senses could stand. Potted ferns stood on tallboys and pedestals, spreading their lush fronds in a tangle of greenery alien to a sitting-room. Vivid rugs covered the floor in a dazzle of colour that brought to Charlotte a return of the swaying motion with which she had lived for the past six months, and three curtains of plaited reeds that swung rhythmically back and forth from the ceiling increased the dizziness.

Perspiration began to stand out on Charlotte's brow as she looked around for a chair to grasp. The Indian girl and the hotel servants had all gone, leaving her feeling she had entered the equivalent of the Garden of Eden.

"So, India has now claimed the youngest of the Scott family," said a low voice from the right, and Charlotte spun round.

In the doorway leading to a boudoir stood a woman of great beauty, black hair hanging to her waist in a soft silken fall that framed a face as smooth as that of the young girl who stared back. Sapphire-blue eyes, large and accentuated by thick black lashes, studied every detail of their subject as if searching for something they could not find.

Shock took away Charlotte's ability to speak. Framed in the doorway, as this woman was, it was possible to see the vague outline of her naked body through the floating lace wrapper, and practically the whole of her creamy bosom that rose in beautiful curves above the froth of lace and ribbons that constituted some sort of fastening to the garment.

Felicia Scott moved forward on a drift of heady perfume. "Can you possibly be my child? I would never have known you." She smiled faintly. "We must rectify that as soon as possible. I trust my wretched *malaise* did nothing to spoil your arrival."

Next minute, a soft cheek was brushing Charlotte's in a vague salute that left her conscious only of perfect shoulders emerging from lace beneath her bemused eyes.

"*Mama?*" The question was shocked, incredulous, and full of dismay.

With the going down of the sun the harsh glare that made its way through every crack in the tatties vanished very suddenly, but the temperature did not drop noticeably. Charlotte rose from her bed with complete lack of spirits, the shallow sleep of the past hour or so leaving her muzzy-headed and depressed. Had she been the type of female who resorted to tears there would have been a flood of them now, but she had been taught to subject her emotions and accept that the Lord knew best how His flock should serve Him. But her aunt's creed did nothing to help her accept this setback without an inner cry of protest.

That beautiful bubble which had been so multi-hued, beckoning and full of promise, had burst. The person who should be closest to a young girl on the brink of life—the mama full of affection and pride, the plump sympathetic woman to whom one could put confessions and fears—did not exist. Charlotte knew her father had taken as his second wife a girl in her first season—Aunt Meg had mentioned the fact in disapproving tones often enough—but a woman of thirty-seven was well into middle-age, and her daughter had pictured a buxom matron very much like the mothers and contemporaries of Aunt Meg's limited acquaintance. It still did not seem possible that a raven-haired, painted creature could be the wife of Sir Rastin Scott, and her own mama.

Sitting at the dressing-table to brush her long brown hair Charlotte told herself she was over-tired and had placed too much emphasis on that longed-for arrival in India. Yet her mind wandered wilfully into the realms of lost expectations once again.

Life with Aunt Meg had been comfortable, industrious, and predictable. Days had been occupied with domestic tasks: the making of preserves, pickles, and infallible remedies for country ailments; visiting the sick and aged; arranging flowers in the small village church and teaching a Sunday-school class; long walks through the countryside to gather ingredients for Aunt Meg's famous herbal mixture that cured croup. The evenings had been spent sewing for the parish poor, playing the harpsichord or reading aloud to her aunt, whose sight was fast fading.

All this had tended to make Charlotte into a capable, reserved girl with great compassion for those less fortunate than herself. But, deep within her breast, there burned a strong romantic bent that had blossomed in her little room beneath the eaves once she had retired for the night. Sitting in her bed by candlelight she had read the books forbidden by Aunt Meg but loaned to her by the elderly and somewhat dissolute squire who was always very kind to her.

From the pages of those books had leapt the great heroes of all time to dazzle and overwhelm her—the warriors, the explorers, the martyrs, the kings and emperors. She had studied the atlas to follow the routes of men who had sailed into the unknown, and of others who had marched to war against a savage distant foe. She had taught herself the ruling dynasties of all the major civilizations, and she understood and admired men who had died refusing to abandon their beliefs. Up in that bedroom she had fought battles against all odds and won, she had tamed hostile natives in hostile terrains, she had lain down her own life in defence of right or the truth innumerable times.

All that time she had waited for the letter from India that would open the door to life, at last. When the moment came, she had wanted to be completely prepared for the new adventure. Yet her mama had been visibly bored by her informed descriptions of places she had visited *en route*, had yawned behind her hand during Charlotte's admiration of the way their captain had handled the ship during a cyclone off Madagascar, and had suggested a nap right in the middle of a detailed account of the work the Tamworths had come to do amongst the wild people of India. Such apparent indifference, on top of her failure to meet the ship that morning, left Charlotte bewilderingly disappointed with the mother she had waited so long to discover, a mother who was so unlike any other she had met it seemed that some mistake must have been made. Life with Aunt Meg, however, had taught her to accept the unpalatable, and she told herself things would doubtless improve as time passed . . . and perhaps she was not quite as her mother had expected, either. It would take a while to grow to know each other.

Shored up by this optimism Charlotte washed and dressed in a white muslin gown ready for dinner. It was the most elaborate one she had, and she felt it would go a long way towards gaining the approval she had so far found missing. But it appeared Lady Scott took a long time to dress and

Charlotte, brought up to be unfailingly punctual, waited in the flower-decked sitting-room, growing hotter and hotter as the feeling of unreality returned. Half an hour passed, and still she waited. Her head had set in rigid lines on a neck grown stiff, so it turned slowly, in consequence, when the door of the suite opened to admit a gentleman who walked in without knocking and who appeared certain of a welcome from the female occupant.

Already wide-eyed with instinctive protest at his lack of manners, Charlotte found her eyes widening further as the intruder came into the sitting-room, for he appeared to be dressed for a costume ball. In amazement she took in the sight of black boots, spotless white breeches, citrus-yellow coatee in Indian style frogged and laced across the chest with crimson and silver, those colours being echoed in the wide sash that ended in heavy silver tassels. Dangling beside them was a jewelled scabbard sheathing a curved tulwar. His white gloves stood out starkly against broad cuffs encrusted with silver scrolls on crimson facings, and the ensemble was completed by a crimson turban embellished with silver and decorated with yellow plumes which the visitor held in the crook of one arm.

He put his heels together to execute a careless bow. "Good evening, I see I am still in time." He smiled, placed the turban on a nearby table, and leant against the wall with negligent grace. "We must suppose Miss Scott to have the same delightful disregard for time as her mama. Have you been waiting long?"

Totally at a loss over such a person walking so boldly into her mama's suite, Charlotte experienced a strange leap of excitement in her breast as she stared at the magnificent figure he cut. A Maharajah . . . here before her only hours after arriving in India? No, what nonsense! But who was he? Beneath his dark, questioning gaze she tried to speak, but had been so silent for so long that she had to clear her throat before words would come.

"I am . . . I am Miss Scott, sir."

The man frowned and straightened up with sharp interest.

"*You* are . . . *Mon Dieu*, you cannot be *La Petite Belle! You* are . . . I took you for the govern . . ." Two strides and he was beside her. "I beg your pardon. Forgive me," he said, merry brown eyes meeting hers in a glance that seemed to penetrate her gown and even the plain cotton bodice beneath. "But you do not resemble your mama one jot, Miss Scott."

His manners were deplorable, his scrutiny was acutely disturbing, he appeared to be superbly self-confident in a female's suite of rooms, yet Charlotte felt the unaccustomed sense of excitement increase as his eyes continued their insolent study of her from head to foot. It was so strong it swamped her instinctive disapproval of this astonishing man.

"Is my mama expecting you, sir?" she asked, in an attempt to keep the feeling of unreality at bay.

"I would hardly be here, otherwise."

It threw her. "She . . . I fear she did not mention to me a masquerade this evening."

He frowned in incomprehension for a moment, then realized what she was implying and broke into rich laughter as he stroked the costly brocade of his coat.

"You disapprove! My oath, I declare you disapprove of my attire!" The laughter continued. "Here is a piquant situation indeed. The entire garrison of Meerpore is expecting a . . ."

The sentence was never finished, for the boudoir door opened and Felicia took the attention of both man and girl as she walked towards them. The black hair was now piled into a combination of coils that emphasized the gracefulness of neck and shoulders above an extreme décolletage. Sapphire-blue silk moulded her body to the waist, then flowed over full petticoats to the ground. The gown brought the matching blue of her beautiful eyes to the notice of all who saw her, and diamonds flashed in her ears and round her throat in the form of a collaret. The effect was breathtaking, and Charlotte was dismayingly conscious of her own modest gown.

"Colley, how very civil of you to arrive early," she said in low, husky tones Charlotte found suddenly disturbing. "You have already made friends with my daughter, I see."

· 11 ·

"Hardly," was his amused reply as he went to her, kissing her fingers. "What do you mean by leaving the poor child to twist her thumbs in solitary state for an age?"

They turned together to study Charlotte. "My dear, you must learn to do everything at half speed in this country," advised Felicia absently. "The climate will soon force you to do so."

With the peculiar feeling that, beneath his frank gaze, her neckline had lowered quite as far as her mama's, Charlotte said awkwardly, "I did not know you were expecting guests, Mama."

Felicia laughed gaily, her headache of the morning apparently gone. "Major Duprés is not a guest. He is a close friend."

"Of Papa's?" she asked in surprise, knowing her father to be of very serious bent.

Felicia and Colley Duprés exchanged glances. "Of course," he assured her. "I am on Sir Rastin's staff. It is on urgent political matters that I am in Calcutta, and your papa naturally charged me with the delightful duty of escorting his wife and daughter on the dangerous journey up-country."

That news instilled in her a mixture of delight and dismay. "*You* are escorting us to Meerpore?"

"The knowledge is intended to reassure you, Miss Scott," was his response, made in a faintly teasing tone.

She felt her colour rise, and Felicia said, "Do not torment the child, Colley. She has only this day ended a tediously long voyage in the company of a missionary and his spinster sister. That circumstance is enough to addle anyone's wits." She looked at him in challenging fashion. "Do you take us to dinner, or not?"

"Your obedient servant." He offered his arm, then broke into flood of French too swift and accomplished for Charlotte to follow. But her mother laughed gaily up at him, and replied with equal fluency, the breathy quality of her voice enhanced by the vowels of the language. At the door they paused long enough to realize Charlotte was not with them so, after bidding her, much like a small child, to come along quickly, they went into the corridor still so engrossed in each other they were really not sure of whether she followed or not.

Walking to the secluded table, Charlotte was unaware of the other diners, too possessed by the difference between the reality of this first evening in India compared with her many happy dreams of the occasion. Could there be a greater contrast between Aunt Meg, the small hushed country house in England, and her present companions in this exotic Calcutta hotel? Her mama had been surprise enough, but Major Duprés. . . ! Every instinct urged her to distrust him, for everything about him, from his flamboyant dress to his negligent courtesy, aroused what almost amounted to distaste in her. Yet some alien compulsion kept her gaze on his broad back as he walked ahead, and put a confusion of ideas in her head. All this must have been plainly written on her face for, when they had sat down at their table, Felicia commented on the frown that should never be seen on a young girl.

Colley gave his easy smile. "It is my fault, I fear. Miss Scott must have received the worst of impressions of Anglo-Indian society with my casual greeting. If I am not mistaken, she has very correct notions of behaviour and propriety."

The whole speech was made in a tone that did not suggest he was in the least repentant, and made the possession of good manners and a sense of propriety sound almost like a fault in character. Her mother's unsurprised acceptance of his Indian uniform suggested he was often to be seen in it, and before long curiosity led her to question him directly during a break in their conversation.

"In what capacity are you employed on my father's staff, Major? I understood that only officers of the East India Company or the army of the Crown were admitted to the Political Service."

His dark eyes grew warmer as they studied her face. "Ah, a student of Indian diplomacy, Miss Scott? An unusual trait in very young ladies. You are correct, however. I am what they term 'seconded' to the Company." He gave their order to a white-coated bearer, then leant back with the lazy grace that typified all his movements. "How much do you know of the present political situation?"

"Please, Colley, spare us such dull conversation at the dinner-table," protested Felicia, the warm huskiness gone from her voice.

He flashed her a smile. "The day you can truly prove my conversation is dull, at the dinner-table *or anywhere else,* I shall close my mouth never to open it again." Turning back to Charlotte, he said, "Well, Miss Scott?"

Ill at ease over the incomprehensible atmosphere created by her mother and this man who could be as Indian as his dress—an atmosphere that left her feeling disquieted, yet longing to be part of it—Charlotte nevertheless embarked on a subject on which she was fairly knowledgeable.

"The history of the Company and its conquests are well known to me, Major Duprés, but more recent events will have escaped my attention due to the length of my sea voyage. Please enlighten me, sir. If I am to be a useful member of Meerpore society it will be necessary for me to be fully informed."

Felicia raised her eyebrows. "I think it will not matter if you are not entirely *comme il faut* with the intricacies of government, Charlotte. The population of Meerpore is not expecting it of you. Quite the reverse, in fact."

Charlotte did not understand, and said so. But the Major turned the conversation smoothly back to its original line.

"For the moment, I shall make it as simple as possible. Later, your . . . friends . . . can satisfy any further interest you may have in the subject, if they have a mind to."

Hors d'oeuvre were brought, and Charlotte selected sparingly from dishes that appeared to contain enough for an entire meal such as was served by Aunt Meg. Meanwhile, she tried to concentrate on what her extraordinary companion was saying.

"This great land upon which you have today set foot is divided by countless races and creeds, which makes it the ideal target for unscrupulous besides well-meaning foreigners," said Colley by way of introduction. "To further complicate the situation, the custom that allows royalty to take as many wives plus as many more . . . ah . . . *unofficial* ones as they wish ensures that each ruler produces up to twenty or more heirs who will cut each other's throats without a qualm in order to gain the throne and its accompanying wealth."

He dabbed his mouth with the corner of his napkin and reached for the wine glass beside his plate. "So, the situation within each kingdom is complicated enough," he continued, "without the additional problems that arise when one ruler covets another's territory and sets about obtaining it. By fighting amongst themselves they weaken their combined strengths, and larger powers then turn their eyes in that direction."

Quails were brought to the table but, although the Major refilled his own and her mother's glass, Charlotte left her full one untouched. Aunt Meg had not approved of intoxicants, and the Reverend Tamworth had skilfully steered both ladies away from young men on board who had shown signs of merriment and flushed cheeks. She now watched the Major toss back the pale liquid with careless enjoyment. His cheeks remained unflushed and excessive merriment did not appear to be overtaking him.

"The situation facing us today is a result of all these conditions," he said. "Afghanistan is a country in internal turmoil. Power is changing hands with dismaying rapidity, and the neighbouring Sikh empire is taking great bites into it as a reward for the supposed support of rival rulers. In consequence, there are opportunities for invasion from the other neighbour, Persia, and through them, the far more dangerous Russia. We must prevent that from happening, at all costs."

"Why?" asked Charlotte, trying to follow his speech. "We do not rule in Afghanistan, I believe. Tom says it is a very wild and independent land."

The Major nodded. "And so it is. You are right: we do not rule there, but neither do we wish the Russians to do so. In fact, we have a treaty of non-aggression with the Afghans and seek only trade outlets with them. However, should their country be overrun by others, we would find our new neighbours too close for comfort, Miss Scott. The Russians in Russia are acceptable. On our frontiers with rifles, they are not."

Charlotte was deeply impressed. "You truly believe they would do that? That they would fight *us*?"

"Even *us*," he said in a serious tone that belied the merriment now apparent in his eyes. "That is the reason for my presence on Sir Rastin's staff. I have lived in Russia and speak the language fluently. Also, I have spent the past eight years in Persia and the Upper Provinces training the armies of native princelings. I am still nominal general of Mekhar Khan's troops, but I felt the East India Company would value my services more, at present. My many friends in Persia and Scinde, plus the intimate knowledge I possess of native tongues and customs, enables me to travel back and forth to obtain information a British officer would find difficult to come by. Sadly, in return for these invaluable services, they have declined to give me a rank higher than major. Do you not consider it rather shabby of them?"

With a great leap of her heart Charlotte stared at the splendid native-style uniform, the black hair and moustache, the swarthy handsome face, the broad physique, and realized incredulously that she was looking at a soldier of fortune—a man with allegiance to all, yet none; someone whose loyalties flowed with the tide or changed hands with gold pieces. Governments used such men ruthlessly without undertaking responsibility for them if they failed and paid the price. Charlotte had read of the horrific fates suffered by men like Colley Duprés, who died agonizingly and alone in savage corners of the earth, their bones bleached by the sun and marked by no commemorative stone, disowned by society.

She swallowed hard as she found herself unable to wrench her gaze from his face. Was he truly what he claimed to be? Could she possibly be sitting at the dinner-table with such a man? Had this flamboyantly-dressed officer ventured alone into the heart of enemy territory? Had he ridden out to risk danger and torture at the hands of the wild natives of India? Did he laugh and snap his fingers at the perils of his profession?

A sensation astonishingly akin to pain grew in her breast as she knew he *had* done all those things; would continue to do them for men like her own father. The pain reached her throat and made her swallow again. All those nights by candlelight in that far-off bedroom in Shropshire now merged into one unbelievable reality. She, Charlotte Scott, was face-to-face with someone even more overwhelming than her book-heroes. Colley Duprés had explored uncharted areas, had battled with savage tribesmen, had endured all for what he believed in. And he was on a par with exotic princes! All those things, yet he consented to discuss with *her*—a seventeen-year-old girl from a tiny English village—the political situation that confronted him. It was more than she had ever hoped, more than she could believe. Thank God she had studied so hard, had read so many books, had remembered all that had stirred her spirits so much halfway back across the world!

"Have you quite finished the quail, Charlotte? We are both waiting."

Blinking she turned to encounter a sapphire-blue glance that now glittered with the cold hue of seas that washed the coast of England. With something of a shock Charlotte felt there was rejection in that glance, rather than approval for her daughter's knowledge of India.

"Your conversation is growing dangerously near the point of boredom, Major," Felicia continued in a tone as cold as her glance. "My daughter has not been brought to India to join the Political Service."

"Ah yes," was his soft comment. "Why *has* she been brought to India, did you say?"

"The people I wish Charlotte to meet will not be impressed if she discusses with them the Russian threat to Afghanistan."

A knowing smile lit the darkly tanned face. "My oath, they will not! I anticipate a situation *sans pareil* that tempts me to postpone my mission to Kabul on our return."

Felicia's voice changed subtly in a way Charlotte could not interpret. "I think that would be most unwise, under the present circumstances."

"Alas, the decision does not rest with me. I take my orders from Rastin . . . or do I?" came his reply in an equally disturbing and inexplicable tone.

As the pair sat looking at each other silently, Charlotte had the peculiar sensation that they were playing some kind of game with their eyes and voices that precluded her entirely. She had been forgotten by the remote and beautiful woman she must call "Mama", and by the man who had, but a moment ago, been deep in conversation of a serious and important nature. The strange pain in her breast she had experienced earlier sharpened unpleasantly as she realized her mother had once again brought to an abrupt end a discussion on, something in which she had no interest. But, this time, she had also brought to an end the attention of Major Duprés. He now only had eyes for the lovely woman across the table. Such neglect after total interest was hard to accept, but Charlotte could think of no way to restore it. She sat erect and tongue-tied while the optical game continued as if she were not there.

Suddenly a wave of homesickness swept over her. The alien atmosphere of that Calcutta hotel, the roomful of strangers surrounding her, the disappointment of her arrival that morning, all combined to make her wish herself back in England with her dreams intact. The sensation of being at sea overtook her again as the room with its elegant tables and chairs appeared to be rocking up and down to a distressing extent. She closed her eyes, but the sensation grew worse. Her lids flew up again just as Felicia said, "I suggest you signal the bearer, Colley. This meal has grown too lengthy, and Charlotte must be wishing to retire."

"As you wish," he said easily, snapping his fingers to command attention without taking his glance from her. "If the conversation has to be restricted to social chit-chat, Miss Scott will surely be glad to escape to her room. I feel she has a poor opinion of frivolity."

Curved eyebrows rose delicately. "A snap judgement, sir! Are you so expert at reading a female you can form an opinion after so short a time?"

He leant back looking at Felicia across the top of his wineglass. "Do you not feel that is something of a rhetorical question, ma'am?" he asked in a silken voice that, for some reason, made Charlotte grow hot. That heat increased as she watched the muscles of his throat move as he swallowed his wine, and then stretched out a brown hand to take up the crystal decanter with lazy familiarity. Everything he did held a fascination for her, but he was no longer aware that she was present, so engrossed was he with the interchange of words that had Charlotte puzzled and uneasy.

The bearer came with a chit to sign, and Felicia turned to the young girl irritably. "For heaven's sake, child, drink your wine or we shall be here half the night."

Tired, overcome by experiences new to her, and resentful of being shut out of the conversation for no apparent reason, Charlotte avoided her mother's eyes by looking at the tablecloth. "I never take wine. Aunt Meg says it is the fount of the Devil."

There was an explosion beside her as Colley Duprés choked on the contents of his own glass and seemed in danger of never regaining his breath as he buried his face in a silk handkerchief, shoulders heaving. But Charlotte's swift concern turned into a new emotion when his eyes, brimming with laughter, appeared above the handkerchief and he gasped, "By that reckoning, my dear Miss Scott, I must be on very intimate terms with Satan himself."

Charlotte could stand no more. "Then I wonder you have not turned Devil's Advocate, sir. The payment might not be attractive, but I am persuaded *he* would not be so shabby as to make you a mere major."

The first stage of their journey to Meerpore was along the Ganges in budgerows—flat-bottomed boats with shuttered windows that could be raised during the day to allow what air there was to circulate. When an advantageous breeze sprang up a sail could be rigged but, in the main, a crew of natives pushed and pulled the small vessels over the sandbanks, quite often struggling up to their waists in water in the effort to negotiate the tortuous reaches. It was an extremely slow method of travel, but the method they would have to employ after Cawnpore entailed being carried in coffin-like boxes, which took even longer.

Charlotte and her mother occupied one budgerow, Colley Duprés another, with several more carrying a laundry, kitchen, and baggage store. In lazy fashion they passed each day, tying up at night to allow the natives to rest and eat. The cooler evenings afforded the passengers the opportunity to stretch their legs along the river banks, which they did thankfully.

At first, Charlotte found the journey intensely interesting, bearing out all she had read about the country. There was so much to see—the women in vivid clothes pounding washing along the banks, naked children using the river as a latrine, playground, and source of refreshment at the same time, crocodiles lying in sinister immobility in the mud or in the shallows of the river. It was a noisy progression. The women exchanged gossip at the tops of their voices, children laughed and squabbled with equal provocation, monkeys in the overhanging trees chattered in scolding manner, peafowl communicated with harsh cries, parakeets screeched constantly. At night, jackals set human blood curdling by adding their threats to the jungle noises created by unseen animal prowlers.

Initially Charlotte commented on everything they passed, until her mother begged her to cease forever chattering about things she could see perfectly well for herself. Then the girl hugged her excitement to herself and continued to marvel at terrain, creatures and ways of life so very different from those encountered in Shropshire. But it was Colley Duprés who dominated her thoughts and interest during those early days. India was a country in which he appeared supremely at ease. He shot game, which improved their diet; he killed snakes and other vermin, which improved their peace of mind; he dealt with local chieftains and officials in assured manner, and rode the large black horse that travelled with him with an élan Charlotte had never seen in young men of her village. He disturbed her whenever he came aboard their budgerow, yet left her inexplicably restless when he was not there. On some days he leant on the rail beside her and thrilled her with his confidences, his total attention for her views on serious topics, his opinions of her great heroes such as Clive and Wellington. On other days, he hardly noticed she was there and, if she volunteered an informed comment, silenced her with a response that suggested he was amused at such temerity from a mere child. As a result she fluctuated between elation and embarrassment in his presence, but the fascination he aroused in her remained constant. It had even increased since the day on which he had told her of his past. It was as colourful and romantic as she had known it must be.

He was of French aristocratic descent, he told her, his grandparents having dressed his father as a little girl in order to smuggle him from France during the Terror. The Marquis and his wife had been caught and guillotined, but a soldier had taken pity on the "little girl" and allowed the child to slip away. He went to England and eventually married the daughter of an exiled Russian count. The pair were drowned whilst returning to France. Colley, left in England until he was sixteen, became the subject of a struggle between relations in England and those in Russia. Finally, he went to Russia to take over estates restored to his mother's family. He had lived near Petersburg until another noble family, vowing vengeance for past insults, sent an army of men to burn down the house and kill everyone in it. Colley had been the only one to escape alive. Dressed as a peasant he had made his slow way into Persia, and thence to India.

Charlotte had listened spellbound to this narrative, her head full of pictures as dramatic and colourful as the man beside her, but they faded abruptly when he asked for details about her own life.

"I doubt they would stand the test against yours, Major," she had replied shyly. "Females do not normally indulge in adventure."

He had smiled, increasing her heartbeat. "Perhaps not females from the heart of Shropshire. But you are now in India where adventure is its life's blood. Who knows what may lie before you?"

Those words had stayed in her mind ever since, and

buoyed up her hopes when things went wrong. And they often did. Felicia had lectured her on the way in which she had spoken to Major Duprés on that very first evening, and, instructed on how Sir Rastin's daughter would be expected to behave on arrival in Meerpore, Charlotte resignedly accepted her mother's advice to watch and learn from her during the months they would take to reach their destination. By the end of two weeks, she was made aware that there was *everything* wrong with Charlotte Scott.

"Meg has taught you only what you must *not* do," Felicia told her one afternoon as they sat beneath the shade cast by an awning fastened to the top of the cabin. "It has been left to me to instruct you on what you must do, on how to be a woman."

She sat with beautiful straight back, one hand tranquilly along the arm of the chair, her face serene, her skin smooth and creamy. Charlotte, fidgeting beside her, felt her own face damp and probably pink from the heat, while even in the harsh sunlight no wrinkle or flaw could be seen on her mother's countenance, and the deep blue eyes observed everything that went on around them with a strange kind of abstract interest.

"A woman has to have one of two qualities, Charlotte— beauty, or the ability to produce sons. Without them she is nothing, can hope for nothing. Your papa already had four sons, so it did not matter that the child I bore him was a daughter. But I have been blessed with beauty. It is a big responsibility while it lasts. Beauty of features will often survive old age, but a perfectly formed body will only remain that way through absolute dedication to it."

Charlotte found herself critical of her mother once more. Aunt Meg was not beautiful nor, being a spinster, had she produced any sons. But her mind was well-informed and many people had been grateful for her charity and medicaments when ill. Miss Tamworth was from the same mould. Were they "nothing" as her mother had just suggested? Reason protested strongly, but she did not voice her thoughts as Felicia continued.

"In India it means a completely different way of life. Never accept an invitation from anyone—and I mean *anyone*, my dear—unless you can be certain of remaining to the end as *soignée* as on arrival. Never attend a ball during the hot season, refuse all dinner invitations from hostesses who press heavy greasy meals upon their guests. Always invent an excuse when asked to entertain at a *soirée* unless you possess the voice of a nightingale or play the pianoforte like an angel, and always plead a longing for refreshments when approached by boisterous subalterns or bouncy majors."

She put up a white hand to brush away a fly, then quoted a further list of behaviour that had Charlotte dumbfounded. "It is most unwise to participate in more than one third of the dances at a ball. A well-timed visit to the ladies' retiring-room can deal with unwanted partners, gentlemen who are pleasant but clumsy on their feet can be sent for a glass of ratafia, and any partner particularly favoured will be glad to take the air instead." She smiled with a spark of gaiety. "That leaves one with sufficient energy to dance with those gentlemen who execute the steps with enough elegance to complement one's own, and those whose uniforms do not clash with one's own gown."

Charlotte was unable to remain silent any longer. "But, Mama, does not such behaviour make one appear extremely ill-mannered to others?"

Eyebrows rose in surprise. "On the contrary. Hostesses strive harder to perfect their dinners, guests are impressed by a charming modesty that prevents their hearing what they are persuaded is an unsurpassable talent, and the few appearances one does make upon the ballroom floor are remembered long after the evening has flown—in pleasing contrast with the damsels who have danced the night away and departed with a streaming face, shaggy curls, and a gown crushed and limp." She smiled in faraway manner. "I am certain I have no need to warn you never to go riding if there is the slightest chance of becoming drenched by a sudden shower, not to enter the carriage of any gentleman who cannot control his horses, refuse to go walking in anything but a zephyr, and never, *never*, attempt to eat dishes in the least complicated when on a picnic. I have never yet seen any female manage strawberries and cream successfully whilst seated on a rug on the ground. Eating is a subtle art. It should be done decorously—*always*."

Movement on Major Duprés' budgerow took her attention for a while, then she returned to her theme, seemingly unaware of the way Charlotte was staring at her.

"Rest in a darkened room with pads on one's eyes and cream smoothed into face and neck is essential after tiffin. If one is dining alone, an hour is sufficient time in which to prepare for it; two, if one is being entertained or expecting guests. For a ball, one needs a great deal longer, of course." At that point she suddenly became struck by her daughter's expression. "Why do you look at me like that, child?"

"Your . . . your timetable . . . seems to leave no allowance for anything of an important nature," said Charlotte aghast.

The sapphire eyes widened. "What could be of more importance to a woman than making the best of that with which she has been endowed?"

Although she had resolved to defer to her mother, Charlotte felt she had to argue further in this instance. "There are so many ways in which a female can make a useful contribution to society, Mama. She does not have to be just a beautiful ornament. Aunt Meg believes it is immodest to spend more than the minimum time before a mirror, and Miss Tamworth is firmly of the belief that self-adornment is sinful."

Felicia was highly annoyed. "*Mon Dieu*, Meg has gone broody in her old age I deem—and if you do not wish to earn your papa's complete disparagement you will cease forever quoting your aunt. I am persuaded Major Duprés is already quite out of patience with foolish and presumptuous remarks from you. As for the Tamworths, I suggest it is extremely sinful of that man to drag his poor sister to this country on the pretext of converting the heathen. I assure you he will not succeed. He will more likely suffer torture and death at the hands of those he believes he has come to save, and Miss Tamworth will, I fear, suffer an even worse fate. It would have been kinder of her brother to marry her off in England before he left. If she *has* to be ravished against her will, better by far one of her own race than those black devils who will cut her throat when she is of no further use to them."

Charlotte was shocked by such a speech, and could not get the implied horror of it from her mind for the rest of the day. So troubled was she, she resolved to question the Major on the subject of missionaries when he joined them for dinner that evening. But it was some time before she could bring herself to start a direct conversation with him. She had no wish to sound foolish and presumptuous again.

In white breeches, a white tunic embellished with light blue and silver, and hung with a row of decorations for gallantry bestowed on him by princes of native blood, he banished all notions of indiscriminate killing for gold pieces and enchanced only the bravura of his enigmatic profession. His cavalier manners, his rich uninhibited laughter, his bold eyes that seemed able to see through the material of a gown—and even beyond that into one's inner feelings—aroused their usual guilty fascination in Charlotte during the first part of the meal.

In the wake of her mother's conversation that afternoon on how she should go on in this country, she was startlingly swept by a wish to be exactly like Felicia Scott as she gazed at Duprés drinking freely of what she had termed "the fount of the Devil." She found herself growing hot as, against her will, she studied the way his spotless white tunic sat without a crease across his broad back and, more covertly, how the breeches so exactly moulded his strong thighs when, the meal finished, he leant back in his chair and crossed one leg negligently over the other. She was caught at a disadvantage, therefore, when he cast a glance her way and commented on her faraway expression in provocative tones. Covering up quickly she told him she had been thinking of her friends, the Tamworths, and felt some anxiety over their fortunes in India.

His eyes narrowed slightly as he studied her face. "Very worthy people, no doubt, like all missionaries, Miss Scott.

Sadly, they devote their lives to a lost cause. Indian races, not unnaturally, believe their own religions to be the true ones and defend them fiercely—with knives, not words."

"But the *Bible*," she protested. "Can they not read the indisputable truth?"

His mouth twitched. "Ah, the Bible! They will show you their own holy books, which also claim the indisputable truth. They might well be your friends, Miss Scott, but do you truly believe the Tamworths have the right to attempt to impose their beliefs on others?"

She was disappointed in him. It had been her hope he would champion Christian martyrs. "We must all of us do what our consciences dictate, sir."

To her dismay she saw he was openly amused as he took up his wine glass again. "Quite . . . which is why I dispensed with mine some years ago."

That remark, coupled with his glance at Felicia that seemed to hold further secrets she could not share, made her retort, "A man who surrenders his conscience is halfway to hell, so I have been taught."

The salvo brought a shout of laughter from him. "*Formidable!* If your friend Tamworth speaks to the natives of hell and devils, they will understand him readily enough. It is about God that they will not agree. We are all unanimous about what is sinful, are we not? It is when we come to goodness that we all have our own ideas—and you have a great number, if I am not mistaken." He glanced over to Felicia with a smile that showed his fine white teeth. "Have you considered Richard Lingarde? There is no more virtuous man in Meerpore—apart from the Rector, and I even have my suspicions of *him*."

Felicia smiled in vivid response. "*Diable,* a man of the cloth! Where is your sense of piety, Major?" She drank from her glass, her eyes laughing at him over the rim.

"I have none, as you are very well aware," came the soft reply.

Her mother grew thoughtful and, after a moment or two, said, "Richard Lingarde? I cannot believe that *Charlotte* would succeed where every other girl in northern India has failed."

"That, surely, is challenge enough to a woman like you."

They exchanged one of the unreadable looks that always made Charlotte feel like part of the furniture, then Felicia said softly, "*Mon Dieu*, what a triumph it would be, though!"

Bewildered by a conversation made as if she were not present, which apparently concerned her, Charlotte began to burn with anger at the way in which Colley Duprés had turned her serious concern over the Tamworths—and all those like them—into an amusing game which only two could play. It happened so often, the switch from total attention to complete dismissal, and there never appeared to be any cause for it. With determination she attempted to rejoin the conversation.

"Tom has written to me of a Mr Richard Lingarde who shares his quarters. They are great friends, I understand."

Major Duprés turned with amusement still twitching at the corners of his mouth. "The most fortuitous of circumstances, surely."

Not understanding his remark, she frowned slightly. "But I am told Lieutenant Lingarde is an engineer and accomplished sportsman. Were you not speaking of another missionary, Major?"

The signs of amusement grew. "I have often felt he missed his true vocation," was the murmured comment that brought a gay cry of "Shame on you" from Felicia, before she turned to Charlotte.

"Richard Lingarde, my dear, is an extremely eligible bachelor who has been besieged by every hopeful matron with a marriageable daughter—so far to no avail. If we could capture *his* interest it would be the triumph of the season. Oh, do not regard me in that manner, child," she said, with vague irritation. "If you heed my words, and also rid yourself of the unfortunate habit of quoting Meg and the scriptures, there is no reason why we should not look there for a match. You are his social equal, after all."

As her mother grew speculatively silent, Charlotte felt goose pimples begin to rise on her arms and scalp. "A . . . match?"

"Of course," came the brisk answer. "I could not do my duty with you in England. Why do you imagine I sent for you?"

Clenching her hands tightly together beneath the table she fought the thickness growing in her throat. "I thought . . . to be with you all. To join the family, at last."

"That as well, naturally," agreed Felicia in throw-away tones. "But the priority is to see you advantageously settled. You are fortunate, Charlotte. In a military garrison females are scarce, so it should be possible to find someone suitable who also pleases you. Tom has been told what is expected of him, and will instigate the essential introductions."

Feeling suddenly sick Charlotte stared at her mother's beautiful face across the table, enhanced to the full by the soft glow of the candles. That a husband would be found for her one day had always been accepted by her, but to be handed on—like a parcel—to a stranger the minute she arrived amidst the family she had always been denied was something she could not immediately accept. Then, she caught sight of Colley Duprés' dark face lit by an expression of relaxed enjoyment, and a feeling of shame swept over her. That her mother should have broached such a subject in *his* presence! To think that she had questioned him on the political situation, the conversion of heathens by missionaries, the virtue of men like Clive, Wellington, Nelson, and the current hero, Alexander Burnes of Bokhara fame, when all the time he had known she had been brought to India simply to be handed over to the first suitable bachelor, to ease his lonely grind in the Company's service and bear him children who would go back to England to suffer the same abandoned childhood as herself. After telling her of his exciting past, he had hinted that adventure awaited her in India. Yet he had known all along that she was just to be dangled before the male population of Meerpore like an item in an auction.

As she studied the face that had haunted her dreams since her arrival in India, she knew the full extent of humiliation.

He had been amusing himself at her expense from the first moment. How would she face him now? How would she endure the coming months in his company? How *could* she have been so foolish as to imagine a man of his stature would find her interesting?

Getting to her feet she went to her cabin before her growing emotion made her humiliation even worse. Once inside, she stood rigid and icy cold against the flimsy woven wall as her new glossy world fell around her. Then she became aware of voices that floated with disastrous clarity across the short distance.

"Your timing is generally faultless, my dear Felicia, but you misjudged your moment badly, it seems."

"Nonsense! I cannot believe Rastin's sister did not make the situation quite clear before she packed the child off to me."

"Rastin's sister, I am forced to think, is a woman of eccentric personality. It was probably quite beyond her to even mention the word 'marriage' for fear of sinning."

There was a low husky laugh from Felicia. "Shame on you, wretch!"

A long silence was followed by Colley saying in vibrant tones, "If you have truly set your sights on young Lingarde, I cannot wait for the outcome. The thought of you and the 'Incomparable Anastasia' becoming mamas-in-law is exquisitely intriguing."

Felicia's response was more than frosty. "Do you not already find enough to entertain you on this voyage that you must amuse yourself at my expense?"

There was another long silence, then, "I must tell you that what does amuse me is that a bird of paradise could produce a small brown sparrow. Here is the whole of Meerpore awaiting a ravishing beauty, and you are taking them a Bible-thumping blue-stocking. Do you not find it *très émoustillant?*"

· two ·

MEERPORE WAS A large station but, situated in the remote northern extremity of the East India Company's territories as it was, life was not easy for those isolated there.

The pressing heat, the dust, the smells, the *foreignness* had to be pushed to the back of the mind somehow, lest one should become prey to madness or the temptation of a quick bullet in the temple, and what better way to remain in control of one's wits than to pretend one was still in England: that green, gentle land last seen long ago and never to be seen again by a great many?

Towards this end, the cricket competition was held each year as just one of the ways in which the Company's civil and military servants, together with their long-suffering ladies, beguiled themselves into surviving their exile. In the first few months of a new girl-queen's reign, there had been balls, banquets, reviews and parades, and royal salutes fired by the artillery, against which the annual competition had paled somewhat, so to add a little spice to the event Sir Rastin Scott had given a handsome silver trophy to be known as the Victoria Cup and to be presented to the man who most distinguished himself in the series of matches. It was the general opinion that Richard Lingarde must already have cleared a space for it on his mantelshelf.

All around the playing area elegant spectators were seated beneath awnings or in their carriages with fringed shades, the gentlemen languidly applauding the progress of the game, the ladies secretly thrilled over the display of manly muscular vigour by players in tight-fitting trousers and thin shirts. A flush of excitement tinged their cheeks, and the heat of their bodies that made the muslin dresses wilt was not entirely due to the temperature.

Richard Lingarde had only half his mind on the cricket as he sat beside Tom Scott, watching the progress of the match through eyes narrowed against the glare.

"Well, I'm dashed if I agree with you," said Tom, a brown-haired firebrand who attacked a cricket ball with the same reckless enthusiasm as he conducted an argument. "There is more behind Burnes' presence in Kabul than commerce. Everyone knows the Russians are wooing Persia with a view to the eventual rape of Afghanistan. What price our possession of India then? She would become a doxy to the first sword that took her."

Richard squinted sideways at him. "Your method of expressing yourself leaves much to be desired."

"Stow it, Richard," was the cheerful rejoinder. "Amy is not within sight or earshot."

"Just as well, since you hardly covered yourself with glory at the wicket a few minutes ago."

"It's not the quantity but the quality of my runs that counts," he said in injured tones. "I might not help my side to victory, but I always ensure them a *stylish* defeat."

Richard laughed, and thought once more how fortunate he was to have such an uncomplicated man as Tom to share his quarters.

"I know I'm right on this Kabul business, however," Tom continued. "If Burnes has not been charged to play it sweet with Dost Mohammed, I'll kick a monkey. We are not likely to let the Russian bear dance over our territory and do nothing about it."

"A minute ago, Russia was a lecher; now a bear," observed Richard dryly. "Can't you adopt plain language?"

Tom sighed. "All right, but you won't like it. Russia has a fancy to take over our rich trade in India, and to do so will negotiate a treaty either with Persia or the Afghans direct. Once they are on our borders there will be bloody war." Seeing the shake of Richard's head he went on hotly. "Look at the facts, man! Father has told us there is no doubt that Russian agents have been received in the Persian court, and they have been seen in Afghanistan, also."

"Those men were a party of explorers."

"Pouf!" exclaimed Tom disparagingly. "You are too intelligent to believe that, Richard. They were encountered on a hillside *apparently* making a survey of the territory, yet several days later they were installed in great comfort in the Bala Hissar, Dost Mohammed's palace. And why has Burnes, of all people, gone to Kabul? He is a political officer, not a trader."

"Alexander Burnes is a courageous, intelligent and esteemed explorer, as apart from his military talents. He met Dost Mohammed during his famous expedition to Bokhara, and formed a warm relationship with him. Is it not sensible, in view of the Afghan's hostility to any stranger, to send a man known and favoured by the Amir?"

"Yes, yes, I know all that," was the impatient reply, broken by a short burst of applause and an enthusiastic, "Splendid shot! That's his fifty, you know." Then he turned back to face Richard. "I do not deny Burnes' achievement on that famous trip to Bokhara, but he is not the only fellow we have with the ability to make himself pleasant to native overlords."

"Did I say he was?" asked Richard mildly.

Tom broke into a rueful smile. "Dash it, you make it hellish difficult to conduct an argument."

Richard smiled back. "I confess I do not have your bloodthirsty tendencies. Think man, if your sanguine prediction of war is realized, what of Miss Shilton?"

Tom had the grace to look guilty. "She would not relish the situation, naturally, but she is a splendid girl, you know. I think she would not faint away at my departure, nor turn pale and clutch a vinaigrette at the sound of gunfire. There is no more level-headed female than Amy."

Richard kept to himself his opinion of Miss Shilton. He could not, somehow, picture that spoilt, wilful girl emulating his own mother on the battlefield at Waterloo. Nor could he believe she would accept her betrothed's departure for an uncertain number of years of battle with anything other than extreme pique at having her plans ruined.

Seeing Corporal Raker cleverly run out, he leant forward to pick up his own bat and got to his feet. But he had one more point to make before walking out on to the field. "I have heard you in the mess enthusiastically advocating war as a means of quick promotion in dead men's shoes, Tom. But has it never occurred to you that you could be the same means of another man's promotion? Would Miss Shilton be understanding of *that*, you hot-head?"

With an affectionate punch on the other's shoulder he walked over to start his innings, but the thought of conflict other than that with bat and ball lay heavily on his mind. He was well aware of the growing complexity to the north-west of India, aware that ill-founded alarm was growing in the ranks of those governing the East India territories. He knew, better than most, the true situation. The latest correspondence from his Russian relatives reiterated the reluctance of their military leaders to undertake any kind of campaign in Afghanistan—this from men accustomed to fighting even in the wildest of terrains! There was certainly no suggestion that his kinsmen wished to take up arms against the mighty East India Company on its own borders. His own letters to them must have suggested it would be very foolhardy.

However, Dost Mohammed, Khan of Kabul, and Amir of all Afghanistan was appealing for financial aid to fight the bids by usurping blood relatives that were devastating his country, and Russia was very willing to provide it. Richard believed this was being interpreted wrongly by scare-mongers, because the Company was prevented from making a similar offer through a treaty of friendship with the Sikhs, who were at war with the Afghans. It was merely a diplomatic tangle that should be handled with coolness and tact. He feared the dunderheaded alarmists would shout down the voice of diplomacy. He did not care to think of the outcome, were that to happen.

The afternoon wore away as he tried to concentrate on the pleasure of matching eye, brain, and the whole of his body in his favourite pastime. There was something about the peace of an open field, plus the physical satisfaction of using muscle and balance to send a ball flying in the precise direction he wanted time after time, that totally relaxed him. That morning he was tense, but it did not affect his skill.

As was confidently expected by all those who watched, the game was won virtually single-handed by the man who was certain to receive the Victoria Cup, and Richard was surrounded by well-wishers as he tried to leave the field. Doing his best to offend no one, yet edging toward his horse, he spotted Mary Summerford homing in on him. That settled the matter. Putting departure before graciousness he left everyone standing and vaulted on to the grey gelding held by a groom. Only when fifty yards away did he let out his breath and congratulate himself.

Mary Summerford was the bored wife of a captain of irregular cavalry who was presently at an isolated fort holding it against a small rebel army. Richard sympathized with her loneliness, but not to the extent of deputizing for Captain Summerford. Even were he head over ears in love with a woman he would draw the line at making a fool of another man who had legal claim to her. Perhaps it was due to the trait of possessiveness running through him that made him certain the female he eventually chose would have to be entirely his, heart and soul.

When Richard emerged from his room clad only in a towel after taking a bath, Tom had arrived and appeared to have the subject of females very much on his mind, also. He instantly broke into an angry complaint about two cavalry officers who had told him they had applied for leave to go down to Delhi.

"They have some idea of meeting Charlotte and attaching themselves to the party for the last stage of the journey," he said in disgust. "I know those two. They try to press their attentions on every female in sight. They actually admitted that they hoped to fix their own interest with her before she was besieged by every other bachelor on the station. I can tell you, it did not please me one jot to hear those two discussing my sister in such terms."

Richard rubbed at his wet hair with another towel. "Have you never played fast and loose with some fellow's sister, Tom?"

"Eh . . . well, that is not quite the same thing," he protested. "And in any case, I was not jiggered enough to discuss the fact with him."

Richard flopped into a cane chair and took the cool drink handed him by the bearer. The Indian departed softly.

"I recall you spent much of your time trying to *avoid* brothers—and, in some cases, fathers."

Tom laughed suddenly. "Aye, so I did. But that is all at an end now."

"Good thing, too. I doubt Miss Shilton would take a level-headed view of *that,*" commented Richard dryly, knowing how that young woman had his friend eating out of her hand.

"You had your share of female attention today," Tom said, wisely deciding to switch the attack. "I saw the Martin sisters twittering at you as you left the field, and Miss Mapleford almost swooned away when you hit that ball into her carriage."

Richard grinned. "Remind me never to do so again, in that case."

"You should settle down," came the nonchalant observation. "Twenty-seven is a responsible age, and you are a steady, reliable fellow with a distinguished career ahead of you. Oh, I know you have foreign blood in your veins, but the ladies seem to find the fact fascinating, and none of us holds it against you."

"My thanks for that," said Richard, used to Tom's lack of tact.

"And I don't hold it against you that Amy had hopes of being Mrs Lingarde before setting her sights on me," his friend continued generously. "Every young female in India has sighed over you at some time or other. You cut a dash on the sports' field, you make every other fellow on the dance floor look clumsy by comparison, you have the art of dalliance to perfection, and no man looks more impressive in uniform than you do. Deny it as much as you will, Richard, but you have broken hearts from here to Calcutta. It must be that wicked smile, those Russian eyes, that air of Slavic mystery attached to your background, and the challenge you have become by declining every damsel offered you on a plate. Dash it all, Richard, there must be *someone* who could stir your masculine blood."

"There was. Luana," he retorted.

Tom scowled. "I am not speaking of a native woman. But I know for a fact you can be dashed lusty, and sooner or later you will have to take a partner."

Richard grinned at him, highly amused by all this. "From the eulogy of my charms you have just given, am I to understand *you* are also sighing over me?"

A deep flush covered Tom's face. "Stow it!" he grunted, in acute embarrassment. "I was thinking of my sister."

Richard choked on his drink, and glared at Tom. "So *that's* what is behind this ridiculous song of praise, all of a sudden. *That* is why you have been reading me her letters, telling me what a sweet, gentle, and intelligent girl she is, and sounding me out about the state of my purse."

"No . . . no, word of a gentleman, old fellow."

But the embarrassed protest went over Richard's head. An even worse thought had occurred to him. "You dismissed Luana, deny it if you dare."

"You know Luana left because she did not like it here without her sister and, dash it, Richard, I could not keep Tahli, under the circumstances. It was you, if you remember, who pointed out that Amy would take a poor view of her continued presence."

"So you paid them *both* off," cried Richard angrily, surprised at the strength of his feelings. "How much did it cost you?"

The young lieutenant was spared from answering by the sound of heavy footsteps approaching along the verandah. Within seconds a tall moustachioed cavalryman of their acquaintance entered and stood blinking in the sudden dimness.

"What, has your wife sent you to invite us to one of her excellent dinners?" asked Tom hopefully.

The man grinned. "The news I bring will be of even greater interest to you than that, believe it or not. I have it on excellent authority that your father received a vital dispatch within the past hour."

Richard waved at a chair. "Take a seat, John. What can we offer you?"

"Nothing, I thank you. We are off to dine with the Braceworthys."

"I thought you looked well primed and polished," observed Tom with friendly candour. "Dinner with the Braceworthys is as harrowing as a review parade."

John Preston assumed a woebegone look. "It is one of the penalties of matrimony. Goodbye to convivial evenings in the Mess with plenty of wine and hearty companions. Instead, it is dinner with the Braceworthys and cards for penny points. I should withdraw from your attachment to Miss Shilton before it is too late, Thomas."

"That's enough," he replied gruffly. "So, what is the great news?"

Growing serious their visitor gripped the back of a chair. "It appears the worst has been realized. The Persians—with Russian backing—have gathered an army which is now marching on the city of Herat. By now, it has probably reached the gates."

"By George, did I not tell you?" was Tom's elated cry. "Once Herat falls they will push on to Kandahar, then Kabul." He turned to Richard. "Did I not say only this morning that there will be war over Afghanistan?"

"You have not yet heard the whole," John went on. "It seems there is one of our artillery fellows—by the name of Eldred Pottinger—presently in Herat on an expedition through Afghanistan, and he has offered his military services to the Khan in defence of the city."

Tom made a face. "If a fellow with a name like that turns out to be any help, I'll kick a monkey. They need someone like Duprés. He has led native armies for most of his career."

"I know of Lieutenant Pottinger," put in Richard quietly. "He is one of several brothers in the Company's service— nephews of Colonel Henry Pottinger—and is a man of some worth, I believe." He rose and walked over to the other two. "The Heratis are fortunate to have such a man passing through, but only if their artillery is in any kind of shape. If it follows the usual pattern, it will simply be the sacrifice of an admirable soldier. The best gunner officer in the world can do nothing with ineffective weapons."

"As to that, I hear the Persian army is no better than a rabble," said John. "Do you think they stand a chance of victory, Richard?"

He considered a moment. "It is difficult to say. Our own knowledge of Afghanistan is so sketchy. No one has had the opportunity to visit the cities extensively except Burnes, who knows Kabul well enough. It depends how vulnerable the fortifications are. From the details I have seen of Kabul that particular wall would seem to be easy enough to breach."

"You judge everything by the ease with which it can be blown up," complained Tom. "Do you never consider scaling ladders and superior numbers of infantry, Richard?"

"How did you come to see sketches of the fortifications of Kabul?" asked the cavalryman in curiosity.

"I asked Sir Rastin if I might," was the simple answer. "But there is no certainty that Herat is of similar design and state of deterioration. This city could be well endowed. Let us hope, for Pottinger's sake, that it is, or he is a dead man."

Tom was indignant. "Do you mean we are not to send a small force to his assistance?"

John shook his head. "Out of the question. We have no treaty that obliges us to go to the aid of the Afghans—only an agreement not to attack her ourselves. Pottinger's only justification is that he is as much under attack as his hosts."

"But we do have a treaty of friendship with the Sikhs, who are the sworn enemies of Afghanistan," Richard reminded him. "If we are seen to be helping Herat, we not only take on the Persians but also our immediate Sikh neighbours. That is the last thing we want."

"Then why has Burnes been sent to Kabul, the major city of Afghanistan?" persisted Tom.

"To negotiate trade concessions. I told you that this morning."

"Nonsense! Politicals are not sent to negotiate on trade. I tell you, we are dabbling our fingers there."

Richard frowned. "If we are, it is very unwise. Have you read Burnes' book on his expedition to Bokhara? The tribes across those mountains are hostile and fiercely independent. They would never accept a foreign conqueror."

"Wild untrained tribesmen?" sneered Tom.

"Have you never considered superior numbers of infantry?" Richard asked him slyly. "*And* fighting in a terrain they know and we do not. A sword can cleave a man in two whether wielded by a ruffian or a trained sepoy."

Tom held up his hand. "All right, all right! But I should like to see the troops that could worst my sepoys."

"So you might, if we ever make the fatal mistake of marching into Afghanistan." He glanced at the clock and sighed. "This is no time to be standing around in nothing but a towel. If we are late in Mess again, Tom, you will have no sepoys to your name—you will be broken. Farewell, John, and thank you for that news, albeit disturbing news."

He headed for his bedroom, and Tom followed him with the words, "Well, I would not be in Pottinger's shoes tonight, I might tell you." Turning into his own room he called, "If I *am* ever in such a situation, swear you will come to my rescue, Richard. I promise to do the same for you."

"You will be a very welcome sight," he called back, "so long as you do not bring your sister with you."

The Mess was buzzing with speculation when they arrived, and every man was full of his own ideas on how to handle the complicated situation at Herat. In consequence, Richard's head was full of unsettling thoughts as he strolled back alone to the bungalow he shared with Tom, who had gone to visit Amy. Already the nights were cooler. In a month or two there would be frosts during the hours of darkness, and clear invigorating days. The change of temperature cleared his head of wine and tobacco fumes, and wooed him into slowing his steps.

Where his fellows were all excited by events beyond the frontiers, Richard viewed them with foreboding. He was disturbed by the apparent support given the attacking Persians by the Russians. In his last letter, Cousin Igor had vowed there was no Russian intention to gain territory from her neighbour. But letters took a long time to arrive, and policies could be changed overnight. If they had, it suggested a situation of great gravity which could lead to bloody conflict on the frontiers between two nations who had no wish to fight each other but were forced to do so through allies.

Suddenly he recalled the words of Edward Kingsley three years before on the edge of that brown plain. *If it ever came to a confrontation with the Russians over Afghanistan it would be dashed awkward for you, Lingarde.*

Suddenly, he was back in that dusk-filled pass, and the familiar serpent of guilt wriggled in his stomach. He could see again the obscene pile that had been left on the path ahead of him. Sweat began to break on his body and his hands began to shake as he asked himself the question that had plagued him since that day. The answer still eluded him.

Taking in a deep breath he tilted his head to look at the stars—the same stars that would be shining on Eldred Pottinger in Herat. It would take a special brand of courage, he reasoned, to make a man volunteer to remain inside a fortress with one band of barbaric cut-throats whilst an enormous rabble of similar brutes advanced upon it. Pottinger had not been *ordered* to perform his act of gallantry. Richard went on to torment himself by wondering what his own decision would be, under similar circumstances.

Seeking escape he hurried indoors, but then lay restless on his charpoy, longing for the gentle charm of Luana, the Indian *bibee* he had kept until a few weeks ago. What a good relationship it had been! She, gentle and sensitive to his moods; he, grateful and protective. Luana had been the perfect partner in passion. When he was restless, as he was now, he would draw her against him, and her very acquiescence acted as a balm. Later, she would soothe his tense body until he was seduced into desire.

Flinging his arms above his head in impotent anger against Tom whom, he realized, must have paid the girl to follow her sister back to their village, Richard thought about Charlotte Scott, who was on her way to Meerpore. His friendship with Tom would grow strained if he really intended to set up as matchmaker.

A *bibee* was one thing, but before he would be willing to give up his blessed freedom for domesticity and the stifling social round of an Indian out-station, a female would have to be found for him who incorporated all Luana's qualities, plus lively intelligence, a thorough education, unbounding energy, and the gift of remaining silent for long periods while he studied. He could not believe that any daughter of Lady Felicia Scott, beautiful, calculating, and completely self-centered, would answer to that description.

He rolled on to his side. The physical gratification of playing superb cricket that day, plus the trend of his thoughts, had brought on a severe case of "John Company's Plague" known to all bachelors on lonely stations. Feverishly attempting to take his thoughts from torment of the body, he fell to tormenting his mind by letting memories from the past rise up like bloody ghosts. It was all the fault of an artillery subaltern called Pottinger, who had created such a stir with his heroism.

By the end of that month news had arrived that Herat and its defenders were under siege by the Persian army which was encamped outside the city walls. On that same day, the party that had been slowly travelling up from Calcutta was a bare twenty-two miles from Meerpore. But their imminent arrival had almost been forgotten by the station members in the face of greater events.

Charlotte felt no excitement at the thought of the northern station with its adjacent cantonments. It had taken so long to arrive, and she had seen stations galore along the route. Even the excitement of meeting Tom again that had consumed her at Calcutta had died the slow death of four-and-a-half months' extension, and hopes she had kept fresh in an English village had wilted beneath the impact of her two constant companions. Between them, they had wrought havoc in the young lonely girl who had had no experience of life and love other than the sheltered, rather prudish, existence of a maiden aunt much involved in good works. As a result, the Charlotte Scott who arrived at Meerpore looked, spoke, and acted in a way that would have astonished those who had known her before.

Sir Rastin Scott's house was very large, taking Charlotte

by surprise. She had not realized the extent of her father's importance in his country of adoption. Aunt Meg had lived in a small manor with half the rooms constantly under dust-covers and the other half with no pretensions to gracious living. This white-pillared residence was richly furnished, with floors of mosaic and graceful staircases illuminated by chandeliers of crystal drops. Ground-floor rooms included two large reception rooms, a study and an office-cum-library where Sir Rastin worked, and two dining-rooms—one for entertaining large numbers, the other for family use. Upstairs were a dozen or so bedrooms, plus suites for Sir Rastin and his wife. In the centre, above the entrance-hall, was a pretty salon where the family gathered or entertained close friends.

Everywhere were great bowls of flowers, in alcoves or on pedestals of white marble. The walls were hung with paintings and lengths of jewel-embroidered cloth of vivid foreign weave, costly enough to be presents from maharajahs. There was more than a hint of military association in a selection of guidons, swords, and native knives embellishing the inner walled curve of the staircases. The whole place was filled with treasures of oriental wealth which Sir Rastin had collected during his years with the Company, and Charlotte thought she had never seen any place more beautiful, elegant and grand than this one which was to be her home. Only when she remembered that she was to be sent from it as soon as possible to live with a stranger husband did her enthusiasm fade.

It was with relief that she heard Sir Rastin was closeted with several men of diplomatic importance and would not be free to greet his wife and daughter for several hours. If only the meeting could be delayed permanently! Knowing now what he was expecting—like everyone else at Meerpore—Charlotte dreaded seeing proof of her fears on her father's face. This meeting would be her first test.

When the summons finally came, her heart sank. Would he see beneath her new veneer and recognize a Bible-thumping blue-stocking? But as she went along the corridor half an hour later she was satisfied she had done all she should. If an inner voice told her she had looked equally neat in the first dress she had tried and with her curls arranged the way they had been when the note arrived, she turned a deaf ear. And she entered her mother's sitting-room with determination to face the man who had fathered her but not seen his child since she was three years old.

The large yellow-faced man who turned at her entry could well have been a bishop. In sober frock-coat, hands behind his back, and unsmiling scrutiny of his daughter from beneath heavy brows, Sir Rastin Scott would not have surprised her if he had said *May the Lord bless you, my child.* Instead, he frowned and produced a hand from behind his back as if bringing a rabbit from a conjuror's hat.

"You are Charlotte? Well, you have not inherited your mother's looks, but you appear to have the same deplorable unpunctuality. I do not care to be kept waiting, let us get that straight from the start. I shall make allowances this time for the possibility that you wished to present the best side of yourself. How do you do?"

Charlotte stood nonplussed. Was she meant to shake the hand, or take a seat that it possibly indicated? Could she ever bring herself to call this stern stranger "Papa"?

"Rastin, she is your daughter, not a visiting subordinate," put in Felicia in cool tones.

Sir Rastin's lips tightened, but he drew nearer the girl and put his hands on her shoulders. "Beg pardon. I'm not used to daughters. Your brothers outnumber you four to one—or they did until poor Hubert was lost. Overwhelming odds, eh?"

Her heart plummeted. He was no warmer than the ecclesiastical guests of Aunt Meg. "Yes, Papa."

"Well, you have come a long way to join us," he went on awkwardly. "I'm sure you'll do all that is expected of you."

"Yes, Papa." Then she remembered what was expected of her, and ventured, "There is no doubt I shall find much that is *très amusant* in Meerpore. After the dullness of village society—not the most brilliant in England—the gaiety of a military garrison will be excessively refreshing."

His hands dropped from her shoulders, and he glanced

· 43 ·

across at his wife. "You are in excellent company, I deem."

Felicia's white hand hovered over the sofa. "Sit here, child, whilst you tell your father news of his sister. I have ordered tea."

The ordeal was spared her. Sir Rastin headed for the door. "If you are to take tea, I will have an hour or so at my desk."

"You cannot do that, Rastin. We have hardly seen you."

"Then why order tea when you know I never take it?"

The blue-ice gaze Charlotte had come to know accompanied Felicia's next words. "When someone has been away for almost a year is it too much to show a little deference to her wishes? I should be pleased for your company while we refresh ourselves."

His mouth twisted. "With a daughter who so obviously complements but will never outshine you, you have no need of someone bowed down with matters of great importance." He gave a half-bow. "If you will excuse me."

In that moment, Charlotte sensed an astonishing circumstance. Here was the first male she had come across who appeared completely uninfluenced by the woman beside her. It was all the more surprising when Felicia looked superb in a mulberry-pink gown of lace over silk that enhanced her colouring and made an impressive contrast against the ivory brocaded sofa. How was it possible to have a dashing, experienced soldier like Major Duprés at one's beck and call while an elderly husband, stiff and yellow as parchment, wished to retire to his study after only a few minutes?

Struck by such a thought she sat silently staring at the door that had closed behind Sir Rastin. Her reverie was broken by a knock on that same door as a servant brought a tea-tray. It was then that she realized how still was the person beside her. The paleness of Felicia's face and the sharp burning blue of eyes grown lustreless shook Charlotte to the core. In the five months she had known her mother she had seen many expressions on that beautiful face, but never one like this. The servant left, and Charlotte could stand the silence no longer.

"Has something disturbed you, Mama?" she asked hesitantly.

Slowly Felicia moved forward from the past and came to a halt in the present. The ghosts in her eyes faded to make way for the mummers who would act out a million charades. A smile presented itself on reddened lips.

"I never allow myself to become disturbed. It is far too fatiguing, besides increasing the heat of the blood." The shapely eyebrows rose as she looked at the tea-tray. "Here is a test, indeed. Unless you are certain of your ability to eat a raspberry fondant without accident, you had best ignore them. Well, do you take the test?"

In an instant, Felicia had returned to the person she knew, but Charlotte remained puzzled. Her papa had shown not the slightest interest in his only daughter, yet it seemed as if he had only been driven away by the beautiful woman he had married. Could a man dismiss his offspring purely because he had no love for the mother? It seemed a very unchristian thing to do.

Ignoring the raspberry fondants she took up her cup and sipped in perfect imitation of the older woman, as she tried to concentrate on what Felicia was telling her about the routine existing in the household.

"We dine at eight, unless we give a reception first. Your papa dislikes waiting for his meals, so be sure to start your preparations an hour beforehand. When we have important guests you will take your meal in your room, unless your presence at dinner is especially desired by your father. On such occasions I advise you to take exceptional care with your appearance, which will, of course, take longer than an hour to perfect. Of course, you will not be allowed to . . ."

This speech was interrupted by the noisy opening of the door to admit someone with a great deal of energy. Charlotte's head shot round. Striding into the room was a wiry young man with brown curly hair, dressed in scarlet regimentals. A broad grin lit his pleasant features.

"I heard you were arrived. This is the first chance I have had to ride across."

"Tom!" shrieked Charlotte with utter joy, and flew up from her seat into his outstretched arms, where she was twirled around in the air with skirts flying up above her starched drawers.

Laughing and trying to speak in turn, brother and sister lost themselves in the happiness of childhood bonds renewed. Finally, after much laughter over trying to get some sense from each other, Tom held her steady and studied her with brotherly affection.

"You look exactly the same as when I left England—well, perhaps a *little* more grown up."

Laughing, breathless with excitement, she put up her hand to tuck in a long strand of her hair that was part of her ruined coiffure.

"You have grown so handsome, Tom, and your uniform is so very dashing." She clasped his hands tightly. "I missed you a great deal after you left England . . . you cannot know. When you did not meet me at Calcutta, I . . . and poor Hugh, too . . ." She was suddenly overcome with feelings that had been controlled for too long.

"Here, you goose," mumbled Tom, quite moved himself, "we cannot have tears at such a happy occasion." He pulled out a handkerchief and pressed it into her hand. "Dry your eyes. We are going to have such jolly times."

She sniffed and blew into the handkerchief, pushing the rebel curls away from her flushed face once more. Smiling through her tears, she said. "It *will* be just like old times when you used to come for the holidays—say that it will."

"It will be much better than that." He grinned. "Lord, how Aunt Meg used to scold me for involving you in my adventures! But you led such a dashed dull life there—nothing but the church and good works. I often thought you would turn into a blue-stocking, but. . . ." His voice tailed off as he saw her stiffen. "What is it?"

As if under some strange compulsion Charlotte slowly turned to the woman they had both forgotten in their enthusiasm, knowing what she would see written on her face. It was there in full strength, and the large blue eyes took in Charlotte's tear-stained cheeks, the hair in disarray, and a crushed skirt that was still hooked up to reveal beribboned white drawers. However, Felicia did not address her icy remarks to her daughter.

"I had thought you had been taught good manners, Tom, but it appears I was grossly mistaken. I can only be thankful that you made your inexcusable entrance alone, and that no *gentlemen* accompanied you."

Brother and sister flushed to the roots of their hair: Tom, at the slur on his manners; Charlotte at the swiftness with which she had forgotten all her hard-learned lessons. If Major Duprés had been present and witnessed the last few minutes, how his lip would have curled, how those dark eyes would have mocked her. He had dubbed her a little brown sparrow, and that was all she really was.

• *three* •

BEING SIR RASTIN'S daughter entailed more than a few social obligations, one of which was the necessity of meeting all the senior ladies of Meerpore before any form of social visiting could take place, or any invitations accepted. When, therefore, Tom called to collect Charlotte the following day to take her riding, she understood that she must give no greeting to anyone nor would anyone acknowledge her presence. Until due deference had been shown to the ladies of rank, she had not officially arrived.

It seemed to Charlotte the height of absurdity to ride the small chestnut mare beside her brother, seeing people hail him whilst carefully looking right through her, and to find him exchanging greetings with acquaintances as if he were riding alone. Was it possible, she thought, for adult persons of any intelligence not to see how ungodly it was to encourage a few puffed-up ladies into inflicting such veneration upon their fellows? Once she would have indignantly voiced her opinion, but not now. Yesterday's lesson had gone deep. But she could not help remarking that she had not encountered such strange behaviour in stations on the journey.

"Of course you did not," reasoned Tom. "You were simply passing through, and Felicia was with you."

She pounced then. "That is another thing I find shocking, Tom. It does not seem right for you to address Mama by her name."

Tom flushed, probably remembering the attack on his manners the day before. "Dash it, how could we call her 'Mama' when she is not? Hugh was only seven years younger than she . . . and it was by her own request, if you must know."

"Oh . . . I see."

He brightened. "Look, there is the Shiltons' house. I cannot wait to show Amy to you. You are certain to love her."

"How could I not?" she agreed warmly. "Tom, I am so happy for you."

"My father put in a word for me with the Colonel. He does not, in general, approve of subalterns marrying, but made an exception in my case with Father to stand surety against any debts I might incur. As if I would do that once I had obligations. A bachelor may be as free and easy as he likes, but I have had my wild days." He gave a gay salute to a captain and his lady, then turned an eager face to Charlotte. "Now you are here, the betrothal can be announced. Father insisted that we wait until Felicia could preside over the celebrations."

"I am glad you waited, too. There is no doubt we shall get on famously. Amy must be a female with extreme good sense to wish to marry you," she said smiling at him. "But . . . but I hope it will not mean that I shall not see you, as we had planned."

He shook his head. "After waiting so long for this reunion? But of course I shall have my responsibilities towards Amy and her family, which will take a great deal of my time as well. Still," he continued, waving to a dashing young matron in a red and green riding-dress, "do not be thinking I shall neglect my duty in your direction. There are some excellent fellows of my acquaintance whom I can present to you, and I can also warn you about one or two adventurers and practised flirts. Be sure I shall not let them play fast and loose with my sister."

He did not appear to notice Charlotte's silence as he led her away from the civilian section of the station towards the military cantonment a mile or so away. She had begged to be taken to see where Tom lived and worked, but all the anticipation and pleasure had been taken from her by Tom's words. It was now all too obvious that even he, the lovable brother of past days, was simply dedicated to the overriding business of finding a suitable husband for her as soon as was possible. He had his Amy and another family to embrace. The little brown sparrow must find her own garden hedgerow: the other birds had flown!

Heading into the sun that would soon be dipping behind the distant hills they entered the gates, and the whole aspect changed dramatically. Instead of pleasant rambling roads and gracious houses, shops and church, racecourse and gardens, there was regimentation. The roads all ran straight and parallel, with others crossing them at precise right angles. The domed bungalows constituting officers' quarters followed similar design, with stables at the side and a verandah running right round. A painted board at the gate provided the name of the occupants. Away to their left lay the bulk of the cantonment in a series of huts and long stone buildings. There was a strong smell of horses and warm hay, boiling meat and pungent Indian dishes, and a mixture of saddlery, polish and human sweat.

The sounds were different here, too. Bugles rang out, shouted commands could be heard as men fell in for evening parades, and hooves thudded on the dirt roads as brightly uniformed officers and cavalrymen trotted past. Boots clattered on wooden verandahs, harness jingled, rifles smacked into brown palms with drilled precision, horses snorted through their nostrils at the prospect of getting on the move for a short while.

Charlotte began to revive slightly. The army, it seemed, did not give a fig for the lofty ladies of Meerpore. Every officer who passed followed her with his glance—some with bold laughing eyes, some with a brief nod, one, even, with a swift closing and opening of one eye as she had seen village lads signal to milkmaids. She looked away immediately, of course, but could not help feeling the young man must have a more generous disposition than those who had looked right through her outside the cantonment.

The sight of so many colourful uniforms, the marching lines of sepoys, the glitter and impressiveness of the cavalry, the regiments' colours fluttering bravely in the breeze, the bugles, the shouting voices, all brought a strange response in her. All this was for the sake of England and her new queen, even though both were thousands of miles across the world. Her eyes blurred with sudden emotion, and she was filled with a pride that had never touched her until that moment. The meaning of all she had seen on her journey was suddenly impressively clear.

At that moment, Tom uttered an exclamation of annoyance and checked his horse. Charlotte drew rein alongside and asked what was wrong.

"What dashed infernal luck!" He looked around quickly. "If we turn down by the Guard-House we can avoid him."

She saw then, against the dazzle of the sun, a figure riding towards them. "You cannot do that, Tom. It will look most ill-mannered, surely?"

"I . . . well, I did not precisely wish him to meet you under such circumstances as these," muttered Tom, turning rather pink.

"I cannot see how you can turn off now without it looking most particular," she argued. "We have passed more than a dozen gentlemen already . . . and he will not speak."

"Will he not?" growled Tom. "You do not know Richard."

"Richard?"

"Richard Lingarde—the fellow who shares my quarters. I must have written of him to you. Oh, that's the end of escape. He has spotted us."

Charlotte sat helplessly in her saddle as the rider approached. Of all people to encounter it had to be the man whom Major Duprés had recommended as the perfect husband for her! The most virtuous man in Meerpore would welcome a Bible-thumping blue-stocking, would he not . . . and Mama would bask in the glory of having captured for her plain daughter a man whom every mama in northern India had tried to ensnare.

"Hello, Tom. The hares were running well. We shall dine famously tonight, I promise," said Richard Lingarde as he arrived before them.

"Splendid!" cried Tom in forced tones. "Well, I must be off."

His friend ignored him and doffed his cap. "Good afternoon, Miss . . . ?"

"Stow it, Richard," put in Tom angrily. "You know very well Charlotte is my sister. I wish you would go away. Dash it, she has not yet met the Nine Muses."

"Your *sister*? I had no idea. Forgive me, Miss Scott. You must think me sadly dim-witted."

The lowering sun was full in her eyes, but she managed a faint smile in the newcomer's direction.

"I am merely showing Charlotte the extent of the station, so be a good fellow and go about your business," begged Tom.

"But you particularly wished to present me to your sister," persisted the Lieutenant. "You have spoken of little else for the past few months, my dear Tom, now you wish to throw away your perfect opportunity."

Charlotte gained the impression that he was teasing, as there was a hint of laughter in his attractive voice. She relaxed slightly. He sounded very pleasant and was taking a commonsense view of the ridiculous practice of ignoring new arrivals. Her interest in him grew. Colley Duprés' description did not seem to tally with this man before her, although the sun did not allow her more than a vague impression of a build that suggested athletic pursuits, and an easy manner without affectations such as some young men adopted.

Her mama's description of the most sought-after bachelor in the area suggested a polished and immaculate beau verging on the dandy. But Richard Lingarde's hair, bleached almost white by the Indian sun, was tumbled and shimmering like pale threads of silk as it lifted at his crown into a crest, and dust from the track had settled on his brown face, accentuating thick, fair eyebrows and layering motes on eyelashes half-closed in amusement.

Charlotte felt infinite relief. Tom's friend, in dirty boots, breeches stained by foliage, and a shirt that was decidedly limp beneath his jacket, in no way suggested a suitor. In fact, as he turned a laughing face towards Tom, absently flicking at a fly with his whip, he seemed much more like a brotherly figure with whom she could have a pleasant friendship.

With that thought in mind she kept her glance on him as he brought his horse around alongside hers, and the sunlight no longer restricted her sight of him. Then, she saw that his eyes, thick-lashed, oblique, a vivid greenish-blue, and dreamy with far-off goals yet to be reached, were looking at her in a way no brother would. She felt herself grow hot with humiliation. He knew, as much as everyone else, just why she was in Meerpore. Why else would he be giving her that open scrutiny?

"Miss Scott," he began, "I am prepared to run the terrible risk of being dropped from the lists of the ladies of Meerpore—something tantamount to social ruin—by making conversation with you." A smile broke out and was echoed in those startlingly unusual eyes, showing Charlotte why so many hearts had reputedly been broken. "Have no fear of personal retribution, however, for you can say I was ill-mannered enough to force my company on you. Did you have a pleasant journey from Calcutta? I heard Major Duprés was on hand to escort you."

The sound of that name was enough to remind her of that shattering night on the budgerow, and the day was spoilt. "Yes, was it not fortunate?" she responded. "I quite thought I would die of *ennui* and despaired of ever again enjoying civilized company. The Major eased the long hours on the river with *racontares* and kept one from starving with his excellent

· 52 ·

hunting. When one is used to gourmet dishes, one cannot be satisfied with anything less."

The Lieutenant was slow in answering, then spoke as if he had been prodded in the side by Tom. "Er . . . no, one certainly cannot. I trust Meerpore will not disappoint you. You will have to make some allowances for our somewhat narrow outlook. But we do not lack entertainment. There are frequent band concerts, military reviews, theatricals, and several grand balls. There are also the usual amount of dinner-parties and morning-calls—the latter so beloved by ladies." He put up a wrist to wipe some dust from his eyes. "I think you will find no lack of gossip, either, Miss Scott. I feel sure you will feel eminently at home before long."

"On the contrary, I deplore gossip, Mr Lingarde," she told him in as haughty a tone as she could manage. "You will never find me in a circle of *poules*. As for amusements, I only attend balls in the cool season, and theatricals not at all. I have to know my hostess well before I will be tempted to dine anywhere, and you will not find me circling the bandstand if the weather is at all inclement."

The blond officer appeared to have no observations to make on her words, merely looked at her as if in a trance. So she continued.

"Naturally, I shall be pleased to speak to you if we should chance to meet at any function. It is refreshing to come upon one person who will not let himself be ruled by a circle of ladies who are under the impression that they are in some way superior to any others. Your determination to make my acquaintance is *très apprécietement*. *Mon Dieu*, I do not care for the opinions of *femmes* who would ostracize you for observing the common civilities. A *bientôt*, Mr Lingarde."

She turned her horse's head and rode off leaving Tom to make a hasty farewell before following her. When he came alongside he appeared to be breathing unusually heavily.

"*Charlotte*, I was never so embarrassed in my life."

She turned to see he was red in the face. "I cannot see why," she told him in a trembly voice. "You could hardly have ridden between us with a sword, forbidding us to converse."

"I wish to God I had," he declared vehemently. "Richard is the son of Sir John and Lady Lingarde."

"I am the daughter of Sir Rastin and Lady Scott."

He groaned. "That is not the point. I felt like sinking through the ground when you began to put on that air of deplorable affectation. Whatever came over you? Then, as if that were not enough, you started punctuating everything with *French,* most of which was incorrect. Was it meant as some kind of inexplicable joke?"

Knowing the whole meeting had been a disaster, knowing Felicia's words did not sound the same on her own lips, Tom's blunt criticism was the last straw. The brown sparrow brought ridicule; the bird of paradise chick was now doing the same. From her beloved brother it was almost more than she could stand.

"Be quiet, Tom," she whispered hoarsely.

"How can I be quiet when you have just . . . Dash it, Charlotte, Richard is a friend of mine and a man of great intelligence. I had intended to present him at a suitable time, but I dare not think what opinion he will have of you now. I have never heard a young girl make such a goose of herself as you have just done."

Trying to hold on to some shred of pride, she said through stiff lips, "Then you cannot have the acquaintance of many on which to base such a declaration."

But her brother, not a sensitive man at the best of times, would not let the matter drop. "You have always been so sensible. I have told him a dozen times that you are the sweetest of girls, and what must you do but chatter in the most nonsensical way about not liking balls and theatricals as if you had any experience of either. And in French, which you were never taught, as far as I knew. Richard will gain the impression that you are eccentric, that the rustic life with Aunt Meg has addled your wits."

She turned on him then, unable to bear any more criticism, and said wildly, "I do not give a fig for Mr Lingarde's opinion of me, or that of anyone else. And if you have no other conversation than a list of my faults, I wish you will go this minute and join him. It will not matter if you do not escort me home, for anyone I pass will pretend I am not there—and you will be saved the bother of suffering my company any longer."

With tears beginning to sting her eyes she rode off leaving Tom open-mouthed and completely mystified.

Richard rode to his quarters telling himself he had just met the first female he had ever felt inclined to take across his knee and administer a hearty slap. It was surprising, but there had been something about the preposterous Miss Scott that had aroused the strangest feelings in him.

By the time he reached his bungalow a smile was beginning to spread across his face. When he handed his horse to a groom he was laughing. What a stimulating situation! The raven-haired beauty expected by everyone who knew Lady Scott had turned out to be a chit of a girl with no sign of voluptuousness, whose hair was dull brown around a face both pale and artless. Even the most generous could not say her green eyes were a redeeming feature for, although large and thickly lashed, there was little warmth or expression in them. He had had no chance to discover if she rode well, but the elaborate frogged habit and tall black hat, tied beneath her chin with veiling, swamped her beneath its severity, leaving her looking like a child wearing her mama's clothes.

In view of that, her haughty, preposterous dismissal of him had left him with the desire to set her down very smartly. If she were not Tom's sister he would have done so, but there was another reason why he had let her ride off so very well pleased with herself. The girl he had just met did not in any way tally with the description of her Tom had given on many occasions, nor did it seem possible that she could have written the letters her brother had received. They had been full of sensitivity about the world around her, conjuring up an idea of a lonely child seeking affection. The extracts Tom had read him—not that he had paid too much heed, at the time—had certainly not contained any of her atrocious French. At the thought of it, he began to laugh again softly to himself. How on earth would she fare in this closed Anglo-Indian community?

When Tom came in, rather red in the face, he made no mention of his sister, as if the meeting had never taken place. Instead, he kept up a ceaseless monologue on his forthcoming engagement celebrations to be held at the end of the following week. Richard listened with only half an ear. He was taking his preliminary examination in Persian around that time and knew he was still shaky on some of the formations. It would mean some long hours of study before then, and he hoped his friend would be well occupied with Amy Shilton during the coming days. Tom was an excellent companion most of the time, but did not have a lot of perception when it came to sensing the wishes of others.

"You have not listened to a word I have been saying, Richard," he now complained.

Richard looked up in feigned innocence. "I heard three of them. MISS . . . AMY . . . SHILTON."

Tom threw a cushion at him. "I cannot wait for the time when you find a female who will make you realize you have a heart. You have been offered all the marriageable girls in India and refused them. I think there is not one alive who would please you."

"Yes there is . . . but you paid her to go back to her village with Tahli."

Tom scowled. "I do not mean a *bibee*. One does not lose one's heart to women of that kind."

"Perhaps I have no heart," suggested Richard, giving a final tug to his jacket and picking up his shako. "Come along. We dare not be late tonight. A visiting general is dining with us and I have heard from the *poules* that he is *très formidable!*" Smiling to himself at the arrow he had just shot, he went out into the night knowing Tom had been effectively silenced, for once.

They walked the short distance to the Mess with no word between them. Richard had already forgotten the raillery and was lost in thoughts of Luana. For the rest of his life, wherever his military duties might send him, he would only have to smell jasmine blossom to think of her and return him, in spirit, to India.

As on many other occasions, the wide sky and faint sound of discordant native music filled him with a sense of frightening destiny in this country. It was so large, so wild, its people so hideously savage behind their charm. Yet again, he wondered if his own deep determination to learn their tongues was not born of a fear of the people rather than a desire to understand them.

In that moment his stomach churned and his palms grew damp as he remembered the living tableau of cruel, arrogant features and long, flashing knives above a mound of scarlet, blue, and brown, and the fanatical shrieks as the attackers ran off, blades crimson with blood. Richard had been commended for his actions that day, and there had never been any suggestion that he had not behaved as any other man would have done. Yet the subconscious question remained. Faced with a situation when he *could* save a man's life, would he still hold back from danger? As an officer in the Queen's army, he could exchange into another regiment at any time—leave India never to return. When every part of him longed to do so, to shake from his boots the dust of a country he hated more as day succeeded day, he could not decide whether it was reluctance to disappoint his parents' hopes for him, or some kind of penance for Captain Edward Kingsley.

Perhaps some sixth sense had brought on his mood, for when he and Tom entered the Mess it was to hear something that was almost a continuation of Richard's thoughts. George Refford, a young captain in Tom's regiment, hailed them and came over.

"Have you heard the news? Poor Summerford is dead."

"Fever . . . cholera?" asked Richard, thinking immediately of Mary Summerford who had chased after him in her loneliness. How would she feel about her behaviour now?

"No, poor devil. The fort was overrun by mahrattas. They killed the sepoys and took Summerford prisoner." He looked at the brandy swirling around in his glass. "The relief force buried what remained of him when they re-took the fort. God, I hope if ever I am in that position I have time to put a pistol to my brain before they lay hands on me." He took a pull at the drink. "Mrs Summerford is in a state of collapse, and small wonder."

"Damnation, can they never get a relief force there in time to save those who ask for help? It is always the same story," stormed Tom. "Those safely distant quibble and argue about sparing men to go on such a mission then, when they do decide to send a force, it always arrives in time to bury those who gave their lives whilst living in hope that someone was caring enough to try to save them."

Refford nodded. "I do not envy the man who has now taken command of the fort. It will be an uneasy tenure. What can a mere handful of us do against a horde of tribesmen? I believe the garrison held out very bravely for three weeks until the camp-followers, who were on starvation rations, decided they would be better off with the invaders. They stealthily opened the gates at night, and let the mahrattas in." He gripped his glass tightly. "They received their just desert and were slaughtered along with our men. So much for traitors!"

"Hardly traitors," said Richard, surprising himself as well as his two listeners. "Should we expect them to be loyal to the death to mere employers—and that is all we are, however one looks at it? A sepoy is different. He swears allegiance to his officers and regiment, but the lowly peasant who drives the camels and cuts grass for the horses has no such sworn bond. He does it in order to live. When his livelihood is threatened, is he a traitor to wish to join his own countrymen?"

Refford, a choleric man at the best of times, was instantly aggressive. "Of course he is! Dammit, the majority of our camp-followers would die of starvation at an early age if it were not for us. They get no help from their own kind, who would let them drop in the gutter and walk past unconcerned. How can you possibly defend their betrayal the moment things get difficult?"

"I do not defend them," Richard said quietly. "I merely protested because you called them *traitors*. Yes, they get a living from us because we need them. I trust you do not believe we do it from charitable instincts. The need is reciprocal, and I challenge you to deny the majority of Englishmen would walk past a dying native in the gutter and feel little concern, either."

Refford, maudlin and full of the tragedy of the dead Summerford, not liking the way Richard was treating the drama, lost his head.

"You are a damn funny fellow, Lingarde. Here is Summerford been tortured to death by those barbarians, and you champion *them*. As a Queen's man you have done nothing towards the Company's achievements in this country in the three years you have been in it . . . and, by God, if it *does* come to a war in Afghanistan instigated by your Russian blood-brothers, we shall know whose side *you* will be on."

The brightly-lit ante-room full of scarlet-coated officers vanished in the surge of white heat that raced through Richard in that moment.

"You will take that back, or I will choke it out of you," he heard himself say in tones that left no one in doubt that he meant what he said. Conscious of Tom's hand on his sleeve, he shook it off. "Keep out of this, if you please. Well, Refford, I give you thirty seconds in which to apologize and withdraw your last statement," he said in ringing tones.

A hush fell on the entire room at the sound of the challenge, but the two aggressors remained confronting each other, one with a white face and speechless with rage, the other flushed and thunderstruck.

The seconds ticked away in that silent room until a man appeared beside Richard and said in an urgent undertone, "What is this all about, gentlemen?"

Richard answered without being aware of or caring who the speaker was. "Captain Refford doubts my loyalty to Queen and country. I demand an apology and a complete withdrawal of those doubts."

There was a stir around them as others made brief comments to each other. There seemed to be a clear path between them, as if they had parted to allow Colonel Smethwyck and the visiting general a clear view of the scene. Richard was aware only of the full ruddy face of his adversary.

"Do you not feel you might have mistaken what was said, Mr Lingarde?" asked the man beside him.

"No," snapped Richard. "Captain Refford knows quite well what he said, and Mr Scott is a witness to it. If the insult is not withdrawn, I shall have only one alternative."

There was a buzz around him, but Richard would have taken on a whole regiment, in that moment.

The mediator said, "Captain Refford, Mr Lingarde demands the withdrawal of an insult and a full apology. Does he have the right to demand that?"

Slowly Refford nodded. "I offer my sincere apology and withdraw in full a statement I made in the stress of the moment. I have never, for one moment, doubted his loyalty to the uniform he wears."

"Thank you. Are you satisfied, Mr Lingarde?"

Richard let out his breath painfully, then gave a curt nod.

But the affair could not end there. It had blown up on a night when a general of great distinction was the chief guest, and all the leading men of Meerpore society were also present. The mediator, whom Richard now recognized as the Mess President, requested the two officers to make public apologies to their guests and their fellow officers before excusing themselves and going to their quarters for the remainder of the evening.

Standing stiffly to attention Richard recited the necessary words through lips that were cold and rigid, and would have left immediately if he had not overheard Colley Duprés, standing with a group of politicals, remark in soft lazy tones, "What, a fall from grace for young Lingarde! The lovely Anastasia would have been heartbroken if it had led to blows, and her boy slain. Fortunately, Refford values his career too much to throw it away by offending the 'Duchess of Calcutta.'"

The rage still governing Richard rose to uncontrollable proportions, and he strode across to grab Duprés by the shoulder of his elaborate brocaded coat. The urge to hit a man he despised was so great, he swung his victim round to face him, his fist already clenched. But that was as far as he got. His arms were securely gripped by men on each side of him, and they marched him very determinedly from the room.

He had been in his quarters for over half an hour before the white heat filling him had subsided enough to allow him to think straight. He now felt empty and shaken, reflecting on the suddenness with which his temper had flared.

Twice before had he had evidence of the extent to which anger could drive him, and both occasions had been an attempt to defend someone he cared for. As a boy in Russia, he had once set about a gypsy with his riding-whip, lashing him unmercifully because he had pestered a girl cousin to let him read her palm. The second instance had been when completing his training at Chatham. A puffed-up cadet had sneeringly suggested that Igor, who was in England with a military mission, was no more than a pretty toy soldier with more fancy uniforms than a female had dresses. Richard had knocked the boy down, and it had taken four of the victim's friends to pull him off.

The consequences of tonight's affair would be complicated, and his fists clenched at the thought of that rogue Duprés coming out of it with his usual guile while it would be all hell to pay for himself. He sat staring from the window thinking back over the whole incident.

Did men like Refford truly have no notion what they were doing in this country? Were they really not aware that they were training Indians to fight other Indians? Did they, in all conscience, feel that the filthy, ragged camp-followers, who comprised the lowest of the low in this country of immense riches and unimaginable squalor, should owe unswerving allegiance to those who had conquered their land and used their services because they had no alternative? Would Refford serve a foreign master to the death when his own countrymen were outside the walls? Any man of intelligence must surely acknowledge the truth of it. It did not mean he was disloyal to those he served, or in any way condoned the murder of a British officer doing his duty.

He sighed and turned away from the window. What was he doing here? Indians would never become Englishmen, dress them in western uniforms and teach them as many fancy manners as they would adopt. How often he saw the truth in Edward Kingsley's words to him at that watering-place before he was murdered.

Next minute, he broke into a sweat at the thought of Basil Summerford's agony. What were the poor devil's thoughts when he found himself a helpless captive of cruel sadistic tribesmen? Remembering the torn flesh and flashing knives beneath hot sun, bile rose in his throat and his stomach tightened with physical pain. Would Pottinger suffer a similar fate in Herat as a reward for his noble gesture? The Afghans and Persians were quite as viciously barbaric as Indians . . . and if the British ever marched into Afghanistan, as everyone appeared to believe they would, the army would be made to suffer. The wild mountain dwellers would resist the yoke of conquest without mercy.

When Tom noisily entered the bungalow several hours later, Richard was still in introspective mood. "Was it a good dinner?" he asked absently.

Tom stood looking at him with the remnants of bewilderment on his face. "Good God, has everyone gone mad today? First my sister, and now you! You came so near to a court martial I offered up a prayer. What possessed you to blow up like that? Never in my life would I have said you could become so completely irrational. Did you have a brainstorm?" Leaving Richard no chance to answer he said, "You are so reasonable and placid a fellow, it makes no sense. I have seen men angry before, but never as you became in a mere instant. Refford was stunned. You were being provocative, admit it."

"I was being realistic, admit *that*."

Tom was still baffled. "What if he had not apologized?"

"I should have demanded satisfaction in the usual way."

"A *duel* . . . and been cashiered for it?"

He nodded. "I suppose so."

Tom clutched at his hair. "Richard, do you know what you are doing or saying tonight? You would probably have got away with a dusting-down from Smethwyck in the morning, then you must needs fly at Duprés like a man possessed. I thought you were going to knock the man down."

"I was."

This staggering admission so shook Tom he could only sink into a chair and groan. "Why, man? *Why?*"

Richard looked at him from the neighbouring chair and said through his teeth, "Duprés typifies everything that is bad about our occupation of this country and its damn double values. When I am face to face with adventurers like him, I wonder how much more of it I can stand."

Morning brought retribution in a way that astonished and perturbed Richard. He was called before the Chief Engineer of the Meerpore garrison, a major of great professional knowledge but ineffective as an administrator, and found Colonel Smethwyck also present in the sweltering office. It angered Richard from the start. Admittedly the incident had taken place in the Mess of a regiment of which Smethwyck was colonel, but Major Symes was the only man who should carry out disciplinary action where engineers were concerned. However, it was soon apparent that this interview was not to follow expected lines.

It started with an apology from the infantry colonel that Refford, one of his own officers, should have been the cause of the unfortunate incident in the presence of an important guest. Major Symes then surprised Richard by asking him when he was due to sit his examination in Persian.

"Er . . . in two weeks, sir," he replied, wondering what that had got to do with the matter.

"Mmm, that is very soon after the advanced examination in Pushtu that you have just passed with flying colours, is it not?"

"Perhaps, but I think I stand a good chance of gaining the required standard, sir." He looked from the grizzled hair surrounding features of mournful uncertainty, to the round ruddy-cheeked face of the Colonel, still wondering what they were all there for. Not a word had yet been said about his attack on Duprés.

Major Symes coughed and rolled his eyes in Smethwyck's direction, before fiddling with some papers on his desk and mumbling, "I have studied this somewhat . . . er . . . lengthy treatise on a system for breaching fortifications by a sequence of explosions placed in an exact pattern. It is . . . er . . . it is very . . ." he coughed again, "interesting. Yes, indeed, very interesting."

Which means he does not begin to understand the first principles, thought Richard in disgust. It will never be passed on to the proper quarters.

"Colonel Smethwyck was impressed, and saw at once that you were just the right man for him."

Richard's surprise grew. Instead of the reprimand he was expecting it appeared he was being offered a special assignment.

"Yes, sir, in what way?" he asked with interest.

The Colonel pulled at his moustache as he studied Richard with bright beady eyes. "My good lady is much concerned with the conditions presently existing at the hospital. Been down there several times and come back full of schemes, you know. Says it is unsavoury, uncomfortable, very dirty, and in need of alterations in the kitchens." He blew through his moustache in embarrassment. "Thing is, she is getting together a small group of ladies for the purpose of . . . well, of putting things to rights. Surgeon–Captain Michaels doesn't hold out much hope of their success, but is happy enough to let them try out their ideas, if I support the scheme."

He walked to the window and looked through it at the cavalry trotting past in splendid rows, as if unwilling to go on. Then he turned back to Richard.

"Michaels has his work cut out with the medical side, but the ladies cannot be allowed the run of the hospital. Some things not fit for their eyes, d'ye see? Major Symes has agreed that you are the ideal man for the job. Escort the ladies, see they get all the things they want, but keep them away from anything . . . well, you know as well as I do what a soldiers' ward is like, Mr Lingarde."

Escort a party of old tabbies bent on good works! Good God, that was a duty for the most junior and most useless subaltern! This was worse than a reprimand; it was a public humiliation.

"What about my company of sappers, sir?" he protested hotly.

"They will be looked after by young Fanshawe," mumbled Major Symes. "He has been here more than a month—time enough to get to know the routine."

"But there are several junior ensigns who could very well escort the ladies," he pointed out, trying to keep calm.

"It needs an engineer, Mr Lingarde," said the Colonel. "A man who understands buildings, drainage, field kitchens."

"Then send Fanshawe. He is fresh from Chatham."

Colonel Smethwyck frowned. "Mr Fanshawe is not in need of a rest, Mr Lingarde. You are. Major Symes and I agree that you have been pushing yourself too hard, of late. Too many difficult examinations, several involved papers on engineering practices. You should relax more, work off your energies in social pastimes . . . enjoy the company of ladies."

Richard stared at the two senior officers who were confronting him with great seriousness. They thought he was heading for Bedlam! He addressed Major Symes, because he still felt Smethwyck had no right to be in on the interview.

"Sir, I had six months' leave last year when my parents were in Delhi; there are men in India who have taken more examinations than I have, and in quicker succession. As for social relaxation, you cannot have failed to notice that I spend as much time as any man on this station in the company of females, and more than most. Unfortunately, I have discovered that politeness seems not to deter most young ladies, and I cannot see that it would do me—or them—any good to be forever at their beck and call. In short, sir, you are mistaken in thinking that I am in need of a rest."

"And the hospital scheme?" asked Colonel Smethwyck, determined not to be ignored.

Richard turned to him. "With the greatest of respect to Mrs Smethwyck, sir, I can only believe that a party of ladies wandering around the hospital will do less to improve the conditions than hamper what little is already being done for the patients. Their intentions are very worthy, but doomed to failure, I fear."

The Colonel raised his eyebrows. "So I said when Mrs

Smethwyck returned from Delhi recently. But the idea was suggested to her by Lady Lingarde, who has already instigated similar schemes in other stations with moderate success."

Richard was at a stand. He could not now insist that a campaign launched by his own redoubtable mother was ridiculous and doomed to failure. Neither could he say that only a woman of Anastasia Lingarde's worth would make it work—and he had not yet come across another.

Taking advantage of Richard's silence, Major Symes said jerkily, "Well, that is settled, then. You may hand over to Fanshawe, then go up to the house, where Mrs Smethwyck will wish to outline her proposals. I understand she is taking tea with some of the ladies this afternoon."

The battle was lost. Richard had made his protest and been met with surprise tactics. The order stood, and he wished very heartily that he had had time to hit Duprés. There would have been a court martial, but he would have received a more manly punishment than being condemned to take tea with Mrs Smethwyck and her do-gooders before conducting them around the cantonment beneath the amused eyes of his fellows, like some obsequious lackey.

Oh, Mama, what have you done to me? he groaned silently as he turned to go, but it was not until he had reached the door that Colonel Smethwyck stopped him.

"You will apologize to Major Duprés, of course."

Richard stiffened. He would certainly not repeat to these two men what he had overheard, neither would he apologize for his justified attack on Duprés. He turned to look at his own superior officer.

"If that is an order, Major Symes, I must refuse to obey."

The long dismal features looked extremely apprehensive. "An order . . . oh, no." His eyes rolled in an appeal to the senior man. "We . . . we just thought . . . the gentlemanly thing, Mr Lingarde."

Richard's anger over the previous evening returned. "One only does that to another gentleman."

Both men looked thunderstruck, and Richard, deciding he had nothing to lose, added, "Duprés—if that really is his name—is an adventurer, a charlatan. He claims to be of noble birth, yet the few words of Russian I have heard him utter are peasant expressions. His French is good, but has been taught to him by a citizen of the new regime, certainly not by *émigré* relatives. He purports to have owned estates in an area of Russia where it is impossible to farm, and his estimates of distances he travelled to reach Persia whilst pursued by a bloodthirsty mob are ludicrous. There is no record of such an estate being burned down by a neighbouring family as part of a vendetta, nor is there any daughter of a Russian boyar called Drovski, who married the exiled orphaned son of Marquis de Vernai-Duprés." He paused for breath as disbelief crossed the faces of both officers. "I am in the unique position of knowing the truth—and Duprés knows I know. From the moment we both met there has been mistrust between us, and he has made no secret of his attempts to decry all I stand for. Would you not agree that is the action of a man unsure of himself?" When there was no reply offered from either officer, he said with a slight note of scorn, "I'll wager Duprés has not demanded an apology!" One glance at their faces was answer enough. "As I thought. He is nothing if not concerned with self-preservation."

"Mr Lingarde!" exploded Colonel Smethwyck coming from his stunned silence with force. "You are maligning a fellow officer, a man of much higher rank than yourself. Have you lost all sense of honour?"

"A courtesy rank, sir, since he is not a member of the forces of the East India Company, or of her Majesty, Queen Victoria. We are told he also holds the courtesy ranks of General of Mekhar Khan's army, Commander-in-Chief of Ranji-Lal's troops, and Aga of some Turkish ruler's cutthroats. These titles suggest he has the power of leadership, but they do not make him a *gentleman,* Colonel." Warming to his theme, he added, "And when one considers that Mekhar Kahn and Ranji-Lal are presently locked in combat, I suggest *Major* Duprés found it expedient to offer his services to the East India Company."

The atmosphere became tense with the incredulous shock of the truth Richard had just highlighted. The slow rhythmic squeak of the *punkahs* above their heads made a mockery of the sweat-stained uniforms and wet brows. When feelings ran high, the blood refused to be cooled. The three men stayed as they were for some minutes, then Colonel Smethwyck said in a quiet shocked voice, "What you have just said is *infamous*. Be thankful Major Symes and I were the only people present this morning. You are relieved of all military duties, and may take all your meals in your quarters, for the present, until Surgeon-Captain Michaels has had a good look at you. Your case is more serious than I feared, Mr Lingarde."

The sound of that distinguished name must have recalled to the Colonel whom he was addressing, for his attitude softened somewhat. He came across to put a hand on Richard's shoulder.

"You have been working far too hard. We already think very highly of you. There is no need to make yourself ill by driving yourself beyond your limits. Take a rest, my boy." He propelled his victim to the door. "We know you are one of the most even-tempered of men. Rest assured Major Symes and I will forget all you have said here this morning." He frowned at the Major until the harassed man grunted in assent. "After all, Richard, Major Duprés is Sir Rastin Scott's right-hand man on affairs beyond the frontiers . . . and it was Sir John, in Calcutta, who gave the approval for his secondment to the Company's army."

At the door Richard halted. "My father had not then met him . . . and neither had my mother. She is an admirable lady, sir, who is not easily blinded by a gaudy uniform and a glib tongue. I trust, for all our sakes, there are not too many among our ranks who are."

He walked out into the heat of mid-morning wondering if they were right, and he was half-way to Bedlam. He had an instinctive dislike of men like Duprés, who abounded in India, there was not a single female he had ever met who had aroused slavish devotion in his breast, and he stubbornly remained in a country he hated when he could apply for a transfer whenever he wished, as a member of the Crown's forces. Added to that, he had just unnecessarily set his career

back alarmingly, and landed himself with the duty of conducting a parcel of busybody females on good works.

Poules, he thought to himself suddenly, and a reluctant
smile touched his lips. Now there was one female who
aroused *something* in him, if it was only the desire to laugh. In
some strange way he felt his mother might take to Charlotte
Scott, and she would most certainly approve of what he had
done this morning, half-way to Bedlam, or not.

• *four* •

THE ENGAGEMENT BETWEEN Lieutenant Thomas
Henry Scott and Miss Amy Theodora Florence Shilton was
to be announced at an evening party given by Judge Shilton
and his lady. For Charlotte, who had now met eight of what
the younger men on the station irreverently termed "The
Nine Muses", the evening was to be an important one. The
introduction to Mrs Shilton would complete her social obligations so that she would then have officially "arrived" at
Meerpore and be free to send and accept invitations. Tonight,
she was to meet the cream of Meerpore society. All those
faces that had studiously looked away from her before would
now scrutinize her avidly from head to foot; the eyes that
had seemed blank would now be searching for faults, making
comparisons; the silent mouths would now bombard her
with questions.

Half an hour before the time they were to set out,
Charlotte sat in her starched drawers and camisole, gazing
mutinously into her mirror and wishing she could break out
in spots, have an apoplexy, or even die prematurely. How
could she face the worst aspect of the evening—being put on
show before all the young bachelors who knew she was to be

handed over to the first one lonely enough to take her? It would be like the fatstock market in Aunt Meg's village, where the poor animals were driven round and round in an enclosure, while interested buyers looked them over.

Applying all she had been taught since her arrival in India, she had begun her preparations over an hour before, but only a few minutes had passed before she knew her heart was not in it. The white gauze dress with a deep flounce and knots of pink rosebuds everywhere made her look like a misshapen birthday cake, and the demure string of pearls was not shown to advantage against her skin that was still the healthy pink of new arrivals from England. Her cheeks were the same, but the lotion Mama had given her to disguise the rosy country blush made her look as if she had just risen from a sick-bed. If only she could collapse on to one and remain there until morning!

The servant girl approached once more and begged to be allowed to make a start on the arrangement of her mistress's long brown hair. Charlotte's feeling of desperation grew as the girl began twisting long strands around heated rods until they became shining ringlets. The white gauze dress hung before her in all its dismal glory. If only she could have a dress of deepest apricot satin, like Mama's. Or the emerald silk. Better still, the amber-coloured lace worn with the topaz collaret. In such dresses how could she fail to draw every eye in the room tonight? Other guests would fall back to allow her through, gentlemen would vie with each other to bring forward a chair for her, and the whole garrison of Meerpore would gasp with admiration for Felicia Scott's daughter.

The visions vanished, and the leaden feeling returned. It was already too late even for a miracle. She was a failure! The evidence had been gathering during the past two weeks. The ladies of Meerpore had been gracious to her only because was Sir Rastin and Lady Scott's daughter, but she had seen the rejection in their eyes and heard it in their well-bred voices. No matter that she had worked so hard at it, that she had so slavishly followed the shining example, that she had used iron will not to return to her old self, it had not averted a failure. The whole station had expected a bird of paradise fledgling, but she had remained a sparrow despite her borrowed plumage. Lady Felicia Scott was on a pinnacle of her own: it was useless trying to join her.

Charlotte now felt tired of the struggle, heartsore over what her life had become. Mama lived in a world Charlotte did not begin to understand, Sir Rastin was always too busy, and Tom was either tied up by military duty, or engaged at the Shiltons'. She was lonelier here than she had ever been in England, and time had hung heavily with nothing to do all day but change her dresses and alter her hairstyle. She had not dared ask to use her father's library for fear of being thought a blue-stocking.

But that was what she was, and there seemed no way of changing the fact. Mama's choice of clothes looked wrong on her, Mama's elegant manners impressed no one when she copied them, and the fascinating habit of breaking into French made Charlotte a subject for scorn when she applied it. Oh yes, she knew the experiment had been a failure, but had no idea what to do now. There was no one she could ask, no one to listen to her. Tonight, of all nights, she felt desperate to know what to do for the best. The one great blessing was that Colley Duprés would not be there to witness her exhibition in the bull-ring. She had not seen him since arriving in Meerpore, because he had gone on a mission to Kabul. An inner voice told her life had only been unbearable because of that fact, but she silenced it with the thought that he would be one less bachelor to assess her tonight.

Just as she was deciding that if she was a big enough failure no one would offer to marry her at all and she could go back to Aunt Meg, a servant arrived to summon her to her mother's room. Charlotte let out a wail, then scrambled into the white gauze dress and satin slippers while the maidservant attempted a coiffure with an arsenal of pins. It did nothing for her confidence to find Felicia looking incomparable in a deep apricot gown that hung off her shoulders in the most breathtaking way. Diamonds flashed at her throat and in the shower of apricot silk flowers that adorned the high-piled raven hair. Charlotte gazed at her in despair. How could such a mother have produced a child like herself?

On arrival at a house very much like their own they went up the long flight of marble steps to where the Shiltons were waiting to greet each of their guests. Tom was already with them, and Charlotte followed behind her parents, a small, lone figure in an unflattering dress, knowing she was about to face the worst evening of her life. *A little brown sparrow. A Bible-thumping blue-stocking.* Never had Colley's words rung more clearly in her ears as she climbed those stairs.

Judge Shilton seemed a kindly man, prematurely aged, with the yellow-brown complexion of those who had spent many years in that country. His blue eyes twinkled with a suggestion of humour that belied his stern judicial stance. Charlotte gave him a hesitant smile and replied in subdued but friendly manner.

Mrs Shilton was entirely different. From the cold, autocratic stare down to the very best kid slippers Charlotte detected disapproval and a smug satisfaction that the new arrival did nothing to outshine her own daughter. As a result, she made a clumsy curtsy and a stilted reply before passing on to meet, for the first time, the girl who had taken Tom by storm.

Amy Shilton looked radiantly pretty in white spangled net over apple-green satin, and with her auburn curls tumbling provocatively over one shoulder of milky paleness. She was dainty, vivid and very self-assured.

"I have waited so long to meet you," she told Charlotte in a high sweet voice. "Tom has never ceased singing your praises. I declare, if you were not his sister I would be burning with jealousy." Her glance travelled beyond Charlotte to return the smile of a handsome young man waiting in line to be greeted. Then she looked at Charlotte, the smile losing its dimpled warmth. "We must have a long chat when I am free to move amongst the guests. But I promise not to monopolize you. I know there are others here tonight who will wish to claim your attention. How fortunate you are to have a brother. I was obliged to rely on my own efforts to make

. . . friends." Her large blue eyes turned towards the centre of the room. "We have never known such a crush at one of our parties before. All the world is here!"

Charlotte followed her glance, and her heart sank. The crowd seemed to consist of nothing but young men in bright uniforms, all of whom were making no attempts to hide their frank study of her. Rebellion burned brightly inside her. She would *not* be assessed like the cattle at the fatstock market! But the haughty glare she was about to give, never materialized. Beyond a large group of youthful officers she caught sight of a tall, muscular figure in a white coatee decorated with blue and gold, who was in conversation with a woman in puce.

Her heart leapt and her knees grew weak. Torn between delight at finding him here when she had thought him in Kabul, and dismay that he would witness her ordeal tonight, she forgot the girl beside her as she gazed at the man who had created such havoc in her life. As if he was aware of her scrutiny, his gaze moved from the woman to meet and hold hers for a paralysing second. Then, unbelievably, he turned back to his companion without giving any sign of recognition. Charlotte felt the blood drain from her cheeks. It was like a physical blow. After four months of being daily in his company, after the confidences he had given her, after the efforts she had made to become the bird of paradise he apparently admired, he had turned away from her as if she were invisible.

The incredible hurt she had suffered on that night on the budgerow returned in full measure. Then, it had instilled in her the desire to win his approval, become what everyone at Meerpore was expecting. Now, it set inside her a burning desire to show him she had no need of his approval, and demonstrate to the entire garrison of Meerpore that she was not an embryo Felicia Scott, but a person in her own right. She had seen the animals at the market charge the spectators, on occasion, and that was what she prepared to do.

Mumbling something in reply to Amy without having the least idea what it was, she moved away with her glance still on that dark head that had turned away from her. But she found her arm caught, and Tom standing to confront her.

"Dash it, Charlotte, what is come over you tonight? There was Amy being perfectly civil to you, and you dismissed her with hardly a word. I dare not think what impression she received of you."

She came out of her trance to stare at him. Further criticism from the one person for whom she felt great affection in her family was more than she could take just then.

"Your duty tonight is not to lecture me, Tom, but to find me the first available husband," she told him in a voice that shook. "You must be in possession of the fact, for I have had it impressed upon me until I am weary of the subject . . . and Amy has just reminded me of it in case I had forgotten."

She swept off in Felicia's wake, leaving behind a young man with a face as red as his coat.

It was half an hour before Amy dutifully approached Lady Scott and Charlotte, who was sitting numbly beside her. After Tom's fiancée had said all that was correct, Felicia drifted away leaving the two young girls together.

Charlotte turned to Amy. "I beg your pardon if I was a little offhand to you just now. I did not mean to be, for I have been longing to meet my new sister. It was simply that I caught sight of someone I had not expected to attend tonight."

Amy gave a knowing smile. "Well, I had guessed something of the sort, for you betrayed the fact too well. It does not do, you know, to make a gentleman aware of one's feelings."

Resenting the slight reprimand from a girl she hardly knew, Charlotte said, "Oh, do you not make Tom aware of your feelings for him?"

Amy's smile faded. "That is a different matter altogether. I had many beaux before your brother, you must know, and it was only after quite a few months that I betrayed my preference. You must make a rule to do the same. However, Tom's friends can wait awhile to meet you, for I have so much to discuss with you. And impatience increases a gentleman's eagerness, do you not agree?"

"I fear not," she replied, thinking of her father. "In my experience it makes them out of reason cross."

Amy cooled her face with a painted fan. "But you have had little experience, I understand. A Shropshire village, Tom says. And a spinster aunt."

"That's right," agreed Charlotte, bridling at the girl's derogatory tone. "It was vastly different from this, I assure you."

"Poor Charlotte! I am all sympathy and understanding, and trust you will not hesitate to ask my advice on how to go on in society."

Instantly leaping to her aunt's defence she said, "Aunt Meg is my father's sister, you know. A spinster she might be, but she knew well enough how to go on in society."

Amy widened her eyes in protest. "Of course, but hardly this kind of society, as you said yourself. And a female's mama is really the only person who can arrange certain things essential to her future happiness." She waved the fan with increasing vigour. "It is so much easier in a military garrison. There is no shortage of escorts for picnics, explorations, or visits to the native bazaar. I have found there are not enough hours in the day to fit in the invitations I receive," she continued, eyeing roguishly a dark-haired ensign who passed them. "But somehow I always do. Young gentlemen come to one with the most lamentable tales of broken hearts and pistols at dawn that one is hard put to refuse them. I never can. They are so very persuasive . . . and so very lonely."

"Whatever will they all do now you are promised to Tom?" asked Charlotte, thinking Amy sounded too practised a flirt to give up her conquests easily.

Amy's lips lost their upward curve. "I understood *you* had come to Meerpore for that purpose." Her glance took in the unflattering white dress with pink adornments. "Or perhaps we have all been wrong, and you will not console our lonely bachelors, after all."

Charlotte felt her cheeks begin to burn. "It is certainly not my intention to exhaust myself by entertaining every young man who is foolish enough to say he will put a pistol to his head if I do not. I should hope he would find something of greater worth to fill his days. We are all of us lonely, at times, and solitude is part of a soldier's profession," she added, remembering Colley Duprés descriptions of the lone forays he had made into hostile terrain. "They should be man enough to accept it."

Amy turned pink. "I wonder they have not thought of that before. I trust you will make the observation to them at the earliest opportunity."

Charlotte had no chance to comment further, for a voice behind her made her heart almost stand still.

"Miss Shilton, you must allow me to compliment you on the success of your party," said Colley Duprés with a careless bow to the pretty recipient of his attention. "Knowing your impeccable taste, I believe the choice of flowers to be your own . . . with yourself as the centrepiece of incomparable blooms."

Amy neither blushed nor stammered. "A compliment from you, Major, must, I believe, be treasured and entered into a scented book. Is that not what you expect?" she demanded provocatively, looking up from beneath her lashes.

He laughed. "Dear young lady, why will you never be serious with me?"

"Because you never are with me, sir." She leant forward so that her bosom was shown to advantage to any person looking down upon it. "But I would not dream of leaving your name off my guest-list, for your splendid uniform sets off my floral art to perfection."

He appeared charmed by her, and Charlotte could only watch silently. "I am delighted my attire pleases you. I regret it meets with less approval in some quarters." At last, he acknowledged Charlotte's presence. "Miss Scott thinks it more suited to a masquerade."

Amy laughed with soprano prettiness, and Charlotte knew she was the animal in the market enclosure, after all.

"I cannot understand your presence here tonight, sir," she said through stiff lips. "Did you not tell me of a dangerous mission to Kabul?"

"The plan was changed," he responded, interested in something on the far side of the room. "I am amazed that you recalled the matter."

"You went into it in some detail, if you remember."

His gaze returned to hers. "Did I?"

It was one of her most treasured occasions of that journey up-country, and the fact that he had forgotten diminished it.

"So, you are now entered into Meerpore society," he said. "Have you found the experience harrowing?"

She lashed out at him. "Harrowing? Indeed no. If anything, I find Meerpore society highly amusing and quaint. But one must bow to the rules when one enters a narrow community."

Thick eyebrows rose in amusement. "Must one? I never do . . . and I had thought you were seeking adventure, Miss Scott. Was that not what you confided to me in secret one evening? Why did you not begin by making a few rules of your own?"

"But she has, Major," put in Amy, her eyes brimming with laughter. "The bachelors on the station are to be told that loneliness is part of a soldier's profession and they must be man enough to accept it. You must see what a comfort *that* text will be to them. Even Canon Braceworthy could not better it."

Charlotte turned on her. "Well, it is certainly time someone told them, my dear Amy. If they are all about to put pistols to their heads because you will now be obliged to refuse their invitations, there will be no army left in India. It will be left to Major Duprés to take on the enemy single-handed, which he would not hesitate to do but which would surely ruin the beauty of his pretty coat. That would be a bigger disaster than losing the battle."

She got to her feet and walked away from them both and, with the same feeling of meeting her Waterloo, defiantly took a glass of wine from the tray of a passing servant. As she took her first gulp she felt she had made a start on following a few rules of her own. At that point, Tom approached her with a dark-haired cavalry officer whom he presented as Cornet Huntingdon-Forbes. She hardly saw the young man because, over his shoulder, she glimpsed Colley now taking the arm of a beautiful woman in apricot satin and dazzling diamonds, and leading her to a corner, deep in fascinated conversation. He looked totally unaffected by what she had meant to be a wounding remark.

Her attention was drawn back by Tom, who reminded her that she had just been asked a question by his friend. She looked at the young man and saw assessing grey eyes, a petulant expression and a weak mouth. Taking another gulp of wine she wondered wildly if her mama would think him "suitable". No, she could not spend the rest of her days across the table from that face!

"Are you lonely, sir?" she asked in a voice that did not sound like her own.

He stared back goggle-eyed. "At times, Miss Scott."

"Then I suggest you occupy your time relieving the poverty of those around you. Heaven knows, there is enough of it in this country!"

Several more young men joined the group in time to overhear this remark, and Tom presented them somewhat awkwardly. But Charlotte did not hear their names because the sound of her mother's deep, husky laughter rose above all else to torment her. She took another glass of wine, drinking from it quickly, and giving Tom back a glare as good as the one he sent her way. What did he know of a female's feelings on occasions such as this?

A bespectacled clerk asked if she played the pianoforte, and she replied that she was better at the harpsichord but never gave public performances . . . or sang, for that matter. Busily watching the way her mother was looking at Colley over the rim of her glass in that secretive way that seemed to shut out anyone else, she automatically told another nearby voice that she never went riding if there was the slightest chance of a shower.

The room was getting very hot, and the growing circle of faces around her were blurred and indistinct. She was glad of the fact, for she had no wish to see any one of them. Tom had been cornered by a large lady in purple, and her view of Colley had now been cut off by tall young men in scarlet-

and-blue, who bombarded her with questions that confused her wits even further. It was like being under attack—cut off from all help like that poor man who had been cruelly slaughtered in a far-off fort this week. Thinking of it made her want to cry. It also reminded her of the Reverend Tamworth, who was destined to be murdered by heathens. And Miss Tamworth, who would suffer an even worse fate. They were fighting for a lost cause. They could not win. The last of her wine went in a despairing gulp. Perhaps they were wrong. She clutched at her empty glass. Perhaps *she* was wrong—about everything!

She stared at the indistinct faces around her. "In Russia, noblemen dash their glasses into the hearth when they have pledged a toast," she announced, thinking of all those books she had read in the solitude of her room. "It is to ensure that the symbolic property of the glass will never be sullied by other lips. Do you not think that splendidly stirring?"

There was a snigger alongside her. "I should not try it here, Miss Scott. The Judge would not appreciate the symbolic property of one of his best goblets brought, at great expense, from Venice."

"I have never seen Richard Lingarde indulge in the practice—and he is supposed to be a Russian nobleman," said an affected voice on the far side of the group.

"*Half* a nobleman," giggled a thin figure that should have been dressed as a girl, in Charlotte's opinion.

"No one can be *half* noble," she protested, finding difficulty in forming the words. "You would not say that of Lieutenant Pottinger who is so bravely defending the city of Herat at this moment."

The thought of his courage brought a return of immense sadness, but the unknown officer turned into Colley Duprés in her visions of a distant fort and a lone Englishman holding off savage hordes. Through the haze in her mind something he once said returned in perfect clarity.

"The Persian army is backed by Russia, who has designs on India. We must prevent them taking Afghanistan, not because we want it for ourselves, but because it will mean one step nearer this country. Our valuable trade is at risk." She looked around at the silent blur of faces and played her ace. "The Russians in Russia are acceptable. On our borders, with rifles, they are not!"

In the ensuing moments there was an inexplicable stir of activity. Then, she became aware that those surrounding her were all suffering from various forms of uncontrollable laughter. One was stuffing a handkerchief into his mouth, one was departing hastily for a large potted palm, another was shaking with silent helpless laughter, yet another was giggling with fatuous paroxysms. The cavalryman was choking on his wine and being slapped on the back by a colleague.

"By God!" he spluttered. "A blue-stocking, to boot!"

The brutal pain of hearing those words that Colley Duprés had used to destroy the girl she had been that night on the budgerow, broke through the wine-induced haziness in her brain. In a frenzy she pushed through the circle of helplessly amused young men, searching for a dark corner where she could hide and no one would ever again find her. Blinded by the anguish of all her hopes trodden beneath uncaring feet, and knowing her pride had not withstood the test that evening, she came up hard against someone who was crossing her path. The empty wine glass slipped from her fingers to smash on the floor.

"Miss Scott, I beg your pardon!" exclaimed a voice she recognized. "Have I hurt you?"

Hands steadied her and she looked up to see a brown face full of concern, with eyes of a vivid arresting greeny-blue that gave it a Slavic look.

"*Mr Lingarde!*" she whispered, beginning to tremble uncontrollably.

The concern on his face was emphasized by a frown, and he made a sighing exclamation as he led her swiftly from the room into the dimly-lit sanctuary of the verandah. When he would have placed her on to a chair, she moved away from him and went to stand at the end of the walk decorated with paper-lanterns for the party, staring out at the darkness where the hills rose unseen. It would be the ultimate humiliation for this man to witness her bursting into tears. Aunt

Meg always held that nothing was resolved by weakness: strength and prayer was the answer. Right now, her whirling brain could not remember her prayers, and all her strength seemed to have deserted her.

For a long while she stood gripping the rail as her lashes grew wet and her throat dried up. But although the drops trembled on her lashes they did not drop to roll down her cheeks, and the fierce grip she maintained on the verandah rail kept the anguish in her chest from escaping in sobs.

Finally she became aware that it was very quiet, and she half-turned, thinking he had gone. His smile of encouragement was only evident by the faint whiteness of his teeth in the half-light. He had made no attempt to follow her, just stood waiting by the chairs with relaxed patience, as if he found this a not unusual occurrence.

Feeling that he would not break the silence until she did she said, "Mr Lingarde, I should like very much to return home."

There was a short pause, then he said quietly, "No, you really cannot do that. Tom would be very disappointed. He has delayed this moment until you arrived from England. You must be there to drink to the health of the happy couple."

"I . . . I think no one will notice if I am not there," she said unsteadily.

He moved nearer. "They will notice if we are both not there, and I shall not go in and leave you out here alone."

She stood uncertainly, still unable to face going back into that house and still feeling uncomfortably giddy.

"Are you feeling ill?" he asked, as she put out a hand to steady herself.

Shaking her head, which only increased the giddiness, she told him, "It was the wine." Then, for fear of further ridicule now from this man, she added quickly, "It did not taste like the usual sort."

"Then I shall make a point of avoiding it," he said gently, taking one of her hands in his.

She started at his touch, but he smiled reassuringly. "Miss Scott, I once risked becoming a social outcast by speaking to you before you had met the Nine Muses. Do I not deserve some recognition for my courage?"

The most virtuous man in Meerpore! Well, there was no one else in whom she could confide . . . and he was there before her. Pulling her hand gently from his, she half-turned to look out over the garden washed by moonlight.

"Mr Lingarde, I have made a goose of myself in front of you on two occasions now," she admitted. "What must you think of me?"

His answer was surprising. "When I have met the real you, I will answer that question."

She swung round to face him, and he leant back against a pillar, arms folded across his chest as if prepared for a long discussion. "You did not surely imagine I was taken in by your imposture a week or so ago."

It took her aback, and her head began to clear in the face of such sane conversation. "I . . . I see it is useless to pretend to you, sir."

"Quite useless," he agreed. "You see, your garrulous brother has spoken to me so often of a young girl he had left behind in England, and read me extracts from your letters to him, so that I formed an impression of someone with sensitivity, intelligence, and a great deal more compassion than the average female whose thoughts go no further than the colour of a gown or the arrangement of curls. Your letters seemed to reveal a lively interest in social problems both in England and India, and suggested a knowledge far beyond the other young ladies of my acquaintance." He let that register with her for a moment or two, then went on. "When I came across you riding with Tom that day, I was extremely disappointed . . . until I realized you were possibly trying to be what the residents of Meerpore expected you to be."

She was astonished by his perception, and confession then came easily. "You will have heard the gossip, undoubtedly, and know that I am a failure."

In the darkness she could just see him shake his head. "No one is a failure, Miss Scott. It is simply that some people are less successful than others."

She turned back to speak out over the garden, as if by

doing so it would not seem so personal. "My life in England was vastly different from this. I soon saw that I had no idea how to go on in a society with standards and habits ruled by the climate, the tremendous distances, and long absence from the mother country. I tried hard to learn, but it did not seem to come easily to me and, to be truthful, I do not approve of half the things people say and do in Meerpore. When I speak my mind I am told not to be foolish; when I copy those who set an example I become a figure of fun." She angled her head to find him watching her intently. There was no sign of derision or amusement on his face, although it was half-hidden by darkness and she could not be certain. "Mr Lingarde, you are spoken of a great deal in Meerpore—and other places," she added with feeling. "I hear you are an expert linguist. Tom says my French is atrocious. Would you agree?"

"Regretfully—yes."

It was said in such a mild tone, she found herself smiling. "Well, you are honest, sir, at all events."

"In the hope that you will be the same with me," came his reply.

Out of that disaster of an evening there suddenly came a ray of brightness. In no more than a few minutes Richard Lingarde had instilled in her the confidence to reach out and take the hand of sympathy he offered. It was more than the tall, sturdy figure, the assured manner, the knowledge that he had seen through her pitiful attempts to be what she was not. It was even more than the relief of finding just one person in the wilderness of her new existence with whom there was some kind of rapport. It was the feeling that he had experienced the same loneliness and understood. Unlikely though it seemed, she sensed a kindred spirit in him.

"Well, I will be as honest as I can, sir, and tell you that I have just now made such a laughing-stock of myself it will keep the gossips busy for weeks."

"Ah . . . *les poules,*" he said softly, then added, "But I suspect you did it deliberately. That is not half as bad as being a laughing-stock unwittingly."

"Well, that is as maybe, but all I have done is set Miss

Shilton against me, and caused the young men of Meerpore a great deal of merriment." She gave a wry smile. "Amy told me they had little to brighten their lives, so I suppose I have, at least, relieved their boredom for a while."

"If you had been the person I believe you really are, they would have been more than a little brightened, I assure you."

She shook her head sadly. "If I had been myself I should have been even more of a fail . . . even *less* successful," she amended.

"Oh no, that is where you are quite wrong," he said with surprising fervour. "If there is one thing at which everyone is eminently successful, it is as being himself. I promise you, no one is better at being Richard Lingarde than I am."

Her smile was wider this time. "Now you are being quite as nonsensical as Tom can be . . . only more understanding, I think."

"Friends should be so."

She hesitated, then asked, "Are you my friend, Mr Lingarde?"

"If you will allow me to be," came the answer from the darkness. "I hear supper being announced so, if you have not already chosen a partner for it, I beg you to ask me very swiftly. Duty kept me from my dinner, and I am positively starving."

He held out an arm, and she slipped her hand through it with a spurt of pleasure. She had been right at their first meeting. Here was someone almost like another brother, someone with whom she could have an enjoyable and relaxed friendship.

They walked into the crowded salons, chatting lightheartedly, and Charlotte was so full of the delight of feeling restraint fall away, she hardly noticed the mild sensation they caused. The young officers who were still high on the wave of derisive laughter over Felicia Scott's absurd daughter, found their smiles fading as they saw the subject of their ridicule walk in, glowing, on the arm of one of India's most eligible and distinguished bachelors, and apparently holding him fascinated by her conversation. The young women present, who had all had cause to feel smug satisfaction that the exotic Lady Scott had not passed on her beauty to the newly arrived contestant for the marital stakes, were given a shocking setback in their self-congratulations. The quaint little creature in a dress more suited to a pert, sophisticated beauty was drifting in from the darkened verandah with the one man they would all love to be with. His eyes, that melted their bones with just one glance, were smiling down into hers, his face that hinted of mysterious facets to a personality he would not fully betray to any one of them, was alive with interest, and his tall, supple body that had them all tingling with excitement when he swung a cricket bat, or bent over his horse in a steeplechase, was half turned towards hers in an attentive, almost protective attitude. But, worst of all, little Charlotte Scott came in on his arm in the most casual manner possible, as if she was not in the least aware of her incredible good fortune. The appetites of the unmarried girls and their mamas vanished in an instant.

Amy Shilton saw their entry with incredulity. Richard Lingarde had resisted her own all-out attempt to capture him last year, and she had had to settle for Tom Scott. Now, his little dab of a sister had achieved what she had set her own heart on doing, and appeared to be completely unconcerned over her triumph. The evening was ruined. Her own engagement seemed sadly flat in the face of this. Tom received a sharp set-down when he commented that he was glad his sister seemed to have recovered from her indisposition.

The only guests who remained unaffected were Lady Scott and Colley Duprés, who were deep in conversation. But Charlotte saw nothing of them, or the expressions of those around her. She was asking her escort about the romantic practice of dashing a glass into the fireplace like the Russian noblemen in books she had read. When he replied laughingly that such things were only done by the more absurd and eccentric of his mother's countrymen, and that he most certainly had never indulged in the wholesale destruction of fine crystal goblets, she felt her first disappointment in him. But the supper-table was so tempting, she brushed that feeling aside in the youthful pleasure of selecting delicacies for her partner to put upon a plate for her.

A week later, Charlotte entered her home happier than she had been since she first arrived in India. Richard Lingarde had just escorted her to her door after a delightful picnic with Tom and the Shiltons. Although she could not say Mrs Shilton—or Amy, for that matter—had been exactly friendly, they had been polite enough, and the Judge had made her feel welcome amongst their number. Dear Tom had been like his old self, having forgiven her for the way she had spoken to his friends at the engagement party. She had a shrewd suspicion that Amy would have said nothing of *their* conversation, since it would hardly do herself credit, either.

But it was Richard she had to thank for it all. He had saved her from the humiliation of that party by returning with her to eat supper, and remaining by her side for the rest of the evening. Thankfully, Colley Duprés had left after the supper announcement of the engagement, and Charlotte had been able to survive the scrutiny of the other guests, knowing she had by her side someone who understood what she was suffering.

Life had suddenly grown brighter, more interesting. Loneliness was retreating. Everything she had heard about Richard Lingarde was true. His dependability was evident, his gentleness manifest, and everything he did was designed to please. A sharp humour surprised one from making the mistake of thinking him serious, and his athletic prowess softened the impression of studiousness. There were no dark challenging looks from his vivid eyes, no smooth slurring words of disparagement, no cruel teasing. She could relax and speak naturally of her thoughts and feelings. Today, they had laughed and chatted together, climbed, breathless, to see a waterfall, then challenged Tom and Amy to a pool-skimming contest with little flat pebbles. It had been a day of youth, and sunshine, and companionship: a reminder of school holidays with her two brothers in Shropshire. It was then she realized Richard Lingarde could well be a substitute for her older brother, Hubert, who was buried in some lonely hill station far away.

The thought put lightness in her heart and she hurried up the stairs and along the corridor with feet that wanted to skip, until she came to a painful halt against someone who turned a corner unaware that she was approaching.

"*Diable! Qui est-ce-qui?*" Strong brown hands gripped her and held her at arm's length. Then, the rich amusement in his glance chased her butterfly happiness away on the wing. "My dear Miss Scott, was it your intention to bring me to my knees before you?"

"Major Duprés! I beg your pardon," she cried, her breathlessness due to more than running.

He continued to hold her while he took in the sight of her tumbled curls and muddy hem. "I was told you were on a picnic with Lieutenant Lingarde. From the excitement of your return I conclude the outing was successful. Confess it, was I not right about that young man? The perfect candidate for the purpose. Although I am distressed that he so far forgot himself as to allow you to become *en désordre*."

Charlotte recalled the muddied hem and the kid boots, then her hair that had become dampened by the spray from the waterfall. The engineer officer might not mind having a brown sparrow for a friend, but the exotic Major Duprés admired something vastly different.

But even as the old uncertainties began to return they were banished by something that occupied her whole attention. The man before her, usually so resplendent, was dressed with a simplicity that was even more arresting because of some kind of sinister overtone. He wore white baggy trousers, a white loose-fitting tunic, and a white turban, with a long swathe of material attached to it that he had thrown across his shoulder in the manner of native merchants who travelled the country. Instead of his usual colourful sash he wore a leather gun-belt with the pistol very obviously in its holster, and the long knife he preferred to a sword attached to the belt by a leather thong. He was spurred and booted ready to ride, and she now saw there was a kind of exhilaration about him that passed on to her in the form of apprehension.

"Why are you dressed like that?" she blurted out sharply.

His eyebrows rose. "You ask with such disapproval I quite despair of ever pleasing you. My everyday attire you find more suited to a costume ball, yet my field dress—simplicity itself—does not meet with your approbation, either."

"Field dress?" Her apprehension deepened.

He began walking to the head of the stairs, placing a hand on her back so that she found herself being led back the way she had run so joyfully a moment ago.

"I am off to Herat—should have been on my way an hour ago."

"*Herat!*" she echoed. "But that is the city under siege. The Persians are fighting to take it, and everyone says it will fall despite the heroic defence commanded by Lieutenant Pottinger of the Company's army."

His hand went up to pat her head in paternal fashion. "Very good, Miss Diplomat. We shall have you in the service yet!" They reached the top of the stairs and he descended two, which brought his face on a level with her own. "I am going to attempt to persuade the Persians to withdraw. Herat cannot hold out much longer and, once it falls, the victors will not be content until they also have Kandahar and Kabul. As I once told you, Russians or their allies on our borders with rifles, we cannot allow. Since we have no wish to fight a war with them, Sir Rastin is sending me to speak to my Persian friends in the hope that they will see where their folly might lead us all."

She looked at the face that had teased, tormented, and challenged her from the moment she had first seen it. His smile had derided her, his eyes had mocked the girl she was at heart, his words had nearly defeated her. It was a face full of charm, mystery, and arrogance. She despised his air of self-consequence. Yet, she could not help remembering the times she had been thankful for his presence on the journey from Calcutta, glad of his protection and expertise, saved from venomous creatures by his timely shots.

Through her mind rushed all she had ever heard of soldiers of fortune, the dangers they faced, and the way many of them died, alone and unacknowledged by those who had used their services. No shots were fired over the graves of such men; no regiment mourned them and added their names to the roll of honour.

She looked again at that face she had seen every day for four-and-a-half months, and felt her throat constrict. This man was preparing to ride off, risking an unimaginable fate on behalf of her own countrymen and her own Queen, to try to prevent a bitter war. Did not such heroism excuse all else?

"You are not going alone?" she breathed.

"A single man travels faster." He put his hand beneath her chin and stroked it carelessly with his thumb. "I do believe you are concerned for my safety."

Trembling from his touch that signified an intimate farewell, she said, "I shall pray for your safe return."

He laughed softly. "The Devil looks after his own, *ma petite*. I should have been dead long ago, if not, believe me."

He ran lightly down the stairs, the clatter of his boots and the chink of his spurs sounding a desolate farewell in her ears. She stood at the top of the curving staircase watching his broad figure until it vanished into the blazing afternoon outside.

For a long time she stayed where she was, her skin still burning from the caress of his hand, her heart pounding. She had never seen a man go off to die before. The emotion of such an experience drove away all thoughts of pool-skimming with little pebbles.

When New Year's Day heralded in 1838 it was becoming clear to even the most languid of observers that real trouble was brewing in Afghanistan. Eldred Pottinger in Herat was doing the seemingly impossible by keeping the Persians outside the city walls. But the ruler of Herat was as greedy and mercenary as most of the lesser Afghan royalty, and was tempted to take the bribes offered him by the Persian leaders, since Pottinger's requests to the East India Company for money brought nothing but enthusiastic praise for what had already been achieved, and hearty encouragement to continue along the same lines.

In Kandahar, the Khan was already succumbing to Persian

monetary persuasion. That left Kabul, where Dost Mohammed, Khan of the city but Amir of the whole of Afghanistan,
was also being wooed with gold. In this instance, it was Russians envoys who promised him the much-needed aid to prevent his country being sold piecemeal by his treacherous
half-brothers.

Despite the murderous and bloody path Dost Mohammed
had carved in order to reach the throne, he was much revered
by the people of Afghanistan, whom he ruled with a strong
hand. The future peace of the country depended very much
on his remaining as Amir. This was desired by the East India
Company, who had no wish for warring neighbours.

To this end, Alexander Burnes lent his considerable diplomatic flair and personal charm to advise Dost Mohammed,
who regarded him highly. The Amir was only too willing to
put his trust in the people represented by Burnes, and agreed
to send the Russians away, sign a treaty of loyal friendship
with the British, and grant the all-important trade concessions sought by the Company. All this generosity, naturally, required something in return. But it was the one thing
the British could not do. In a recent war between the
Afghans and the Sikhs, the city of Peshawar, pride of the
Afghans, had been captured and was still occupied by the
Sikhs. Dost Mohammed was willing to do all Burnes asked,
provided the British helped him regain Peshawar, with force,
if necessary.

Burnes sent the request to his superiors with a heavy heart,
knowing the case was hopeless. The Company had a treaty
of friendship with the very powerful Sikh nation that stood
on its immediate frontiers in the north-west, and it was out
of the question to begin aggressive overtures suggesting the
Sikhs should hand back a greatly prized city to one of their
longstanding enemies. Not only that, even to be known to
be sending financial aid to the Afghans would be viewed as
an act liable to strain the treaty of friendship to dangerous
limits. So British hands were tied.

Even so, Burnes was shocked when the reply to his vain
request arrived, and he began to wonder at the sanity of his
superiors. The dispatch was not only couched in extremely

tactless terms, it sounded almost dictatorial. The Amir must forget about the city of Peshawar, a legitimate prize of war which the Sikhs had every right to keep; the financial aid requested would come from the trade with the East India Company as soon as arrangements were made, and the Amir must make no agreements of any kind with Russian envoys without first consulting the British. It was only Burnes' personal friendship with Dost Mohammed, and his diplomatic expertise that prevented the Amir from flying immediately to the amenable Russians presently guests at his court along with Burnes.

So, with Herat battered and starving, with a ruler who could not be trusted, Kandahar already pledged to the Persians, and Dost Mohammed being sorely tempted by Russian offers to do anything and everything he wished, Afghanistan lay weakened and open to plunder. The British, on the sidelines, were tied in impossible diplomatic knots knowing the situation could only worsen. When it did there would be a blood-bath, and God alone knew who would emerge the victor.

For Charlotte there had been a period of metamorphosis during those last months of the old year. Unable to forget the impact of seeing Colley Duprés depart alone and so dramatically for a city surrounded by an army of savage thousands, where another lone British soldier was facing unknown peril with the greatest heroism, her youthful sense of the romantic was aroused with sudden passion. She therefore followed avidly all that was said on the subject of Afghanistan and Herat, her quick intelligence enabling her to follow the extremely complicated diplomatic nuances that were making nations nervy and suspicious of each other.

Charlotte soon realized the best person to approach in her search for information was her father. Firstly, he was at the hub of political affairs in Meerpore and, secondly, Major Duprés was a member of his own staff. At first, she had approached Sir Rastin with diffidence, finding little encouragement from him. But as he grew gradually aware that she could speak informatively on such subjects, it was not long before he even greeted her with a kind of bluff welcome when she knocked on the door and peeped into his study.

If Charlotte suspected, after a while, that the old gentleman regarded her more as another of his sons than his daughter, it did not seem to matter. The fact that she had established some kind of understanding with the dry, aloof man who had begotten her was a great satisfaction in itself.

The other influence on her attempts to become immersed in the vital and thrilling affairs beyond the frontiers was Richard Lingarde, although he had such decidedly opposite views to her own that she found their discussions turning into arguments, more often than not.

Yet Richard had come to be regarded by her as her closest friend, because he answered every need she sought. He treated her with kind thoughtfulness, asked her opinions with genuine interest, and provided her with that feeling of belonging to a large human unit that she had lacked in England. He made her laugh a lot, bolstered her confidence and, by his frequent companionship, introduced her into the boring but essential social round of Meerpore with such ease that Charlotte was the only person unaware of the true reason why she had suddenly become so popular.

It was Richard, also, who was the reason for the greatest change in Charlotte as an adolescent girl thrown into a life so completely different from the one she had always known. Only a few days after that picnic with the Shiltons, Mrs Smethwyck called upon Lady Scott and her daughter, eventually turning the conversation round to the fact that she had heard from Lieutenant Lingarde that Miss Scott had had some experience with good works in England. She had then gone on to eulogize on the scheme she was running with the help of a few other concerned ladies to improve conditions for soldiers in the hospitals. It did not, she had hastened to add, involve any kind of work that was unpleasant or indelicate, no nursing of patients, or anything of an exhausting nature. Just a study of conditions, a discussion on how the hospital could be made more efficient and comfortable, and lists for the higher authorities of necessities which the ladies of the Hospital Mercy Group felt should be supplied. Her face had assumed a grim smile when she revealed that a large number of ladies who had volunteered had now found they were unusually occupied with other things and were never to be seen at the meetings. Others confined their help to the stitching of heartening texts to hang on the walls of the wards.

Charlotte had been immediately fired with enthusiasm and pleasure at being able to find useful occupation to fill the long days, especially one with which she had had such a great deal of experience. Felicia had looked almost horrified at the prospect, at first, but when the Colonel's wife had explained that Lady Lingarde was mounting a similar campaign in every station in India, and her son was officially liaising with the military on behalf of the Meerpore ladies, she rapidly relented and was pleased to give permission for Charlotte to lend her services, if she wished to do so.

Everyone concerned benefited, but none more than Charlotte. With her years alongside Aunt Meg to stand her in good stead, she found herself the only female in the group who had any real understanding or experience of the poverty-stricken sick. But, used though she was to tenants' hovels, the sight of the hospital horrified her from the moment she entered it. The white-painted walls outside had suggested a pleasant airy place, but inside the scene was very different. With lazy *punkah-wallahs* who were not chivvied into keeping the air moving freely, the stench was so overpowering Charlotte had to press her handkerchief to her nose as she walked through the long rooms strewn with all kinds of refuse. But she did not succumb to the vapours, rush from the place, or stumble to the far exit with her eyes closed and horror written all over her face as some previous volunteers had done. Her heart welled with sympathy, anger, and the burning determination to put her feelings into words at the very first opportunity.

This she did, without mincing matters, and those few residents of Meerpore who were present, were treated to the spectacle of a personality they had not dreamt possible in the little quaint shadow of an incomparable mother.

Amongst that number was Richard, who had still not been

let off the punishment of "escorting the tabbies around" as he described it to Tom. He stood with them, if not exactly as open-mouthed as they, deeply astonished at a small girl of not yet eighteen who, after enduring half an hour inside a building full of the mixed stenches of boiling meat, unemptied urine tubs, vomiting of a heat-stroke victim, and the suppurating stump of a man who had lost his foot in a tribal skirmish, spoke with assurance and intelligence on what she called "disgraceful neglect of common cleanliness."

Charlotte went on to point out that the first essential to recovery was hygiene. "It is no wonder those rooms are so full," she declared, eyes flashing with anger. "What I have seen is enough to persuade the patients to die of their sickness rather than endure another day in there. I have seen the filthiest shacks in England, but they are palaces compared with this hospital."

The next essential, she told them, was a suitable diet. Simple measures to remedy the appalling food at present served up could be put into effect easily, she informed her spellbound audience. But she supposed other essentials would take more organization. She had no ideas on drainage or things like seepage through pressed earth floors, but it took no great intelligence to know that insanitary conditions were the greatest enemies of the sick. At present, the kitchen where the patients' meals were prepared—if one could call them meals—stood right next to the amputation room and night-soil beds.

She had then turned to an amused Richard and completely nonplussed him by saying that he, as an engineer, could investigate the drainage system and see that a better type of floor was laid. He could also draw up the plans for a new kitchen that should be built at the opposite end of the hospital and contain new equipment for the preparation of invalid foods.

Half the sickness and deaths, even, she told him with great severity, could be accounted for by incorrect feeding. From what she had just seen, all the patients were given the same boiled mutton running with grease, unless they were so ill that they were on a spoon diet, and that, she told them with disgust, was simply the water in which the meat had been cooked! It was essential that extra provisions were included such as calves' foot jelly, arrowroot, and a little port wine.

When Mrs. Smethwyck pointed out in a somewhat strangled voice that she doubted such a request would receive even her own husband's endorsement, Charlotte had been undeterred and turned a smiling face towards Richard.

"Mr. Lingarde, you are in the unique position of being able to do for us the impossible, are you not? Since Lady Lingarde is at the head of this whole movement to improve hospitals, and has the ear of everyone of influence in Calcutta, a word from you to your mama will bypass the wastebaskets of a great many gentlemen, will it not?" She smiled even more warmly." It will almost certainly get us what we want."

Stunned, Richard had heard himself murmur that he would be very willing to mention whatever she wished in his next letter to Lady Lingarde.

With the hospital work to fulfil her very real desire to be of some worth, her improved relationship with her father, and her friendship with Richard, whom she saw as a substitute for her love-sick brother, Charlotte was less influenced by Felicia, who of late was more often than not resting in her room. Gradually, the young girl resorted to the plainer gowns she had brought from England, and wore her hair in the simple clusters of curls that took away her look of hollow-eyed over-sophistication. If she had once more become a serious-minded ingénue, abandoning the pretence of a fashionable enchantress, the guise suited her better. There was laughter now in the large green eyes, soft roundness in her cheeks, and sprightliness in her step.

Although it could not be said she had become the latest rage, she was certainly never short of an escort, and those young men who had derived such sport at her expense on the night of the engagement party were never to do so again. The unthinkable had happened! Richard Lingarde, the undeniable prize of the matrimonial market, was the girl's constant companion! The entire population of Meerpore knew the son of two such distinguished parents would not pay such marked public attention to the daughter of two equally distinguished people unless he knew very well what he was about. It was incredible, inexplicable, *infuriating*, but undeniable. Felicia Scott must be on her knees in fervent thanks that her strange little offspring had managed to do what all the beauties in India had failed to do.

The only person unaware of the speculation, envy and gnashing of teeth was Charlotte, who continued to talk to Richard as a good friend, to question him about the growing talk of war in the hope of hearing news of Colley Duprés, or that young man Pottinger in Herat, both of whom she saw as romantic figures offering their lives for a far-off queen no older than herself.

But her conversations with Richard somehow tarnished the glitter of her girlish fancies. His peaceable manner and his dismissal of the threat growing beyond the frontiers left her disappointed and irritated with him. He did not appear to her to be in the least like an eager heroic warrior!

She spoke of her friend's attitude one evening when Tom had joined the rest of his family for a quiet private meal together.

"Mr. Lingarde is of the opinion still that too much is being made of the Afghanistan question," she told her father. "He said only this afternoon that the unrest has largely been created by over-panicky politicals who have turned one Russian explorer in Kabul into an army dragging cannon."

Sir Rastin paused in the act of dabbing his mouth with his napkin, turning dangerously red with indignation. "Did he, by Jove! And what was his condescending opinion of the affair in Herat?"

Felicia looked across the table at her husband. "Rastin, you should not encourage Charlotte to discuss such things."

He surveyed her with acute distaste. "And why not? If my daughter cannot show a little commonsense at her own table I should like to hear good reasons. I am only too delighted she has rid herself of the silly ways she affected on her arrival!" He turned back to Charlotte. "Well, what of Herat?"

Acutely conscious of the bridling discord between her parents, she answered hesitantly. "He feels . . . well, he *says* he feels Lieutenant Pottinger is being asked to do an impossible task, unless we give him a bottomless coffer with which to buy the treacherous Khan's friendship."

Sir Rastin smiled grimly. "Ho! Perhaps your friend Lingarde would care to transfer into the political branch?"

"Oh no, Papa, I should not think so, for he has remarked on many occasions that they are nothing but a parcel of . . ." she broke off, flushing as she realized how Richard's scathing words would sound to her father.

But he laughed, a short shout of sound that made her guilty nerves jump. "The damned impertinent puppy! So he has the effrontery to air his disapproval of the Political Branch to me own daughter? Well, he includes his father, Sir John, in his comments. Has he thought of that, hey?"

Tom spoke up quickly. "I think it is just that Richard feels that decisions of political importance ought to be taken on the advice of those who have to fight the subsequent wars. It is all very well for political men sitting safely at desks in Calcutta to make sweeping statements; Pottinger is surrounded by the devils and never sure whether they might not slit his throat at the first opportunity."

Sir Rastin frowned. "Pottinger is a soldier, sir. That risk is part of his profession . . . as it is yours and that Lingarde fellow's," he added, bending a stern look on Charlotte. "Are you both saying he does not relish a fight?"

Charlotte felt obliged to defend Richard in the face of her father's attack. "Of course not, Papa. But Lady Lingarde is Russian, and it cannot make the situation easy for him when . . ."

Her voice tailed off as a chair scraped on the floor and Felicia rose with graceful dignity, her beautiful eyes flashing.

"Since the two gentlemen present are under the impression that the ladies have now left the table, we shall do so. Then, they may continue this discussion without a breach of good manners." Moving towards the door with a soft sway of her crimson skirt, she added languidly, "Come, Charlotte . . . or have you decided to imitate the male sex to the extent of taking port and cigars?"

Wincing beneath the reprimand, Charlotte hastened in the

wake of her mother as the two men got to their feet in silence. She attempted to soften the atmosphere as soon as they reached the salon.

"I beg your pardon, Mama, if I have acted in a way that has upset you."

She was standing in the center of the surrounding chairs watching as Felicia arranged herself gracefully on the sofa. But her mother's blue gaze was raised to her as if nothing were wrong.

"I never become upset, Charlotte. Agitation is very damaging to one's nerves, besides putting unsightly lines on one's face. Sit down, child. Wringing one's hands in the center of a room does not present a pleasing picture . . . neither does a female who discusses subjects better left to gentlemen, and which bring an unattractive redness to her cheeks."

Charlotte sat down with resignation. How could she tell her mother that she found gentlemen's conversation so much more interesting than a discussion on perfect eyebrows?

Felicia gave her a bright glance. "In the midst of all this political dabbling, I trust you are not forgetting our main purpose."

Her heart jarred uncomfortably. "No, Mama, but . . . but I have been here no more than four months, as yet."

Almost as if she had not spoken Felicia went on, "Of course, I had not hoped for such instant success, but have no objections to this obvious eagerness. He is young, of course, but I am certainly not going to push you into the arms of age and wealth when there is a chance of happiness with a young man in full possession of the ability to . . . *please* you," she finished delicately. "Age is a frightening thing, Charlotte, and should only be encountered when one is old." There was a slight pause while she banished ghosts from her eyes, then lifted her head with a smile. "Such a brilliant alliance will be met with complete approval on all sides. Richard Lingarde is so eminently suitable. I have invited him to dine with the Shiltons and the Braceworthys on Thursday next. He accepted with flattering promptness."

Charlotte felt suddenly chilled from head to foot as she stared at her mother. Might as well suggest she marry Tom!

Then she grew even colder as memories of that night on the budgerow returned. *There is not a doubt Richard Lingarde is the ideal candidate for the purpose. There is no more virtuous man in Meerpore.* And her mother's soft exclamation: *What a triumph it would be, though!* Shame ran through her. Richard was her dearest friend, her close confidant, the one person in Meerpore with whom she did not have to pretend or flatter. Whatever would he think of these matchmaking attempts? Surely he would not imagine they were with her own approval!

"Mama," she cried in protest. "The Shiltons and the Braceworthys! Why, he will think such particular attention . . . I mean, it will surely be plain . . . No, no I could not face him across the table."

Felicia laughed softly. "Perhaps that has been the attraction all along. Who knows? My dear child, he would not have accepted my invitation, knowing what it signified, if he was not very sure of what he was doing."

Staggered by what her mother was suggesting, she protested further. "I cannot believe you have the rights of it, truly I cannot. Richard is always so very frank. He would not . . . would not . . ."

"Of course he would not speak of it to you until he has your father's permission to do so," put in Felicia.

Cornered, Charlotte cried, "But he is just a friend, not unlike a brother. Besides," she added desperately, "he is so very unexciting."

"Compared with whom?" It was an icy, silken question that brought a strange jolt to the young girl's heart. All she could think of was a distant figure in white riding out alone into the unknown.

"You have a great deal to learn about gentlemen, Charlotte," continued Felicia in the same abstract, silken tones. "The step into womanhood is a gigantic one—and sometimes a very painful one. That which appears exciting can often turn out to be tragically misleading—even dangerous! Gentlemen would have us believe they are strong and infallible, demigods with infinite wisdom for whom we should have eternal respect and admiration." She almost held her breath beneath the weight of her words. "It is a myth, my dear. They can be cruel, vain and worthless. They can be pompous and selfish. They can be greedy and blind. They can also be enticing and infinitely thrilling. But beware them all, Charlotte, and put yourself into the hands of someone like Richard Lingarde."

Charlotte was filled with embarrassment and lack of comprehension. She always disliked it when Felicia spoke in such an uncomfortable manner.

"Mama, I have my work with the hospital—it is coming along very well, you know—and so many friends to keep me occupied," she began with some attempt at determination. "I had thought . . . I mean, there is plenty of time for . . . for. . . ."

The dark, graceful head slowly shook a denial. "I doubt Mr Lingarde would agree on that. No one has ever called him a rash young man, but he is moving faster than I ever dared to hope. He will want a match of it before the year is out, so if you do not have a warm partiality for him I advise you to see that it grows very rapidly." Her eyes flooded with meaning. "Do not allow yourself to be dazzled by the gems of the Orient when sterling silver is in your grasp. Gems may flash fire, but they can very easily burn. And one has to look very deeply into that brightness to find the heart."

Charlotte sat in stunned silence. It seemed the family she had come from England to join were conspiring to marry her off as quickly as possible to a studious, dependable, unwarrior-like man whose only claim to glory was his skill at hitting a cricket ball! The dreams of a romantic figure riding off alone into the savage unknown became an ache in her breast.

Richard was standing in the sunshine of early afternoon trying to keep his thoughts lucid in the crushing heat. Some fool in the Artillery had swung a gun across the channels piping water to the horse troughs, and fractured them. Gallons were being lost, and he had been called out to effect repairs. With the pick of his sepoy sappers he was making hasty temporary channels to restore the supply before doing a permanent job.

His men were disgruntled at being called from their rest period, and he was being unusually sharp with them because of his present mood. Standing over the men as they worked, he bombarded his brain once more with the problems that seemed to be facing him. He had reached a crossroads in his life: which direction should he take?

The trouble beyond the frontiers had gone further than he had expected, and he could no longer maintain that the Russians did not have their eyes on the boiling-pot in Afghanistan. Yet he had been thinking more and more often of returning to England. He hated India—the heat, the smells, the boredom of station life, the foolish animosity between Company officials and those of the Crown. He hated the rows of tiny gravestones in the churchyards, where children and babes lay, killed by pestilence and disease. But, most of all, he hated those of his own countrymen who lorded it in India, who strutted through that alien land enchanting and mesmerizing the simple natives into slavering submission, and using their strange sadistic powers to satisfy their own craving for some kind of divinity. There were many such men—some holding posts with the East India Company in lonely outlying districts where they became a law unto themselves, others who had sold their services to native princes, jumped from captains to generals overnight, and lived like princes themselves with zenanas of dusky mistresses, and the power to order floggings, the lopping off of hands, or the boiling in oil of any who displeased them.

Men like Colley Duprés, he thought bitterly, remembering how Colonel Smethwyck had defended that rogue against all Richard had said about him. There was a strange trait in many of the men who came to this country that led them to exalt those of Duprés' stamp, to be impressed by the mixture of native opulence in dress and manner, yet reassured by the white skin and English language, so that they were almost as ready as the Indian people to accept that they had superlative skills and infallible wisdom. But when there came along another who, in truth, could dispute their claims, he was derided, regarded as a "bad sort" . . . or told he was suffering from fever of the brain!

Richard watched his sappers hauling the heavy pipes and slithering in the mud caused by water gushing from the fracture, and thought again about leaving India. Now was the time to go. He had spent nearly four years here and given away no sign that each year had been regarded by him as a penance for the death of Edward Kingsley. Four years was reasonable, surely, to account for that moment when he had to decide whether to stand fast, or rush to give impossible aid.

Now was the time to go. If the Afghanistan situation *should* take the disastrous turn of setting British against Russians, any request by him for a transfer then would be seen as lack of loyalty, if not downright treachery. He knew, only too well, how some pudding-heads with a bottle or two of wine inside them would soon have him a spy for Imperial Russia. But no man in his position would wish to march against his own kinsmen, would wish to tell his mother he was off to slaughter her countrymen, if he could possibly avoid it. Better by far to go now before such a predicament faced him.

Turning away to glance across toward the civilian section of Meerpore, he sighed heavily. Now was the time to go . . . and *now* was the time he found the one girl who could completely captivate him. How many times had he wished it had been some other man with whom she had collided at that party: how many times had he cursed his own suggestion that Charlotte should join the Hospital Mercy Group! They had been thrown together so much more than they would normally have been, and the emergence of her delightful, determined and quite innocently dictatorial personality had knocked him off balance. Watching her sweeping purposefully through the hospital rooms ticking off all the items that needed investigating, hugely enjoying her unconscious assumption of control as the only person amongst those of greater age and rank who really knew what she was doing, and enchanted by the revelation of a female who could throw off her unsuitable frippery façade to become a girl with intelligence, purpose, and the makings of courage, Richard had been a willing captive before he could stop himself. Even her outrageous suggestion that he should write to his mother and bypass official sources, or that he should design new kitchens and drainage systems had been accepted by him with a sense of delighted enslavement.

He had found the girl who proved he had a heart, as Tom had once hoped, but despite her commonsense and capability, it would appear she was a novice to love; her heart had never been touched. To Richard the knowledge was infinitely exciting and aroused his own deep desire for her, but he was a man of twenty-eight, experienced in passion, and knew he would have to teach his unique little Charlotte the lessons very slowly if he did not wish to frighten her away.

Now was the time for him to leave India, but she would remain behind. Time, time, he needed *time,* he thought desperately. There was no doubt the Scotts would give their consent to his request—Lady Scott had made her feelings perfectly clear with the invitation to dinner that night with the two most influential couples in Meerpore as the only other guests. His immediate acceptance had made his intentions almost irrevocably clear to her. As to his own parents, they could have no objections to Charlotte's background, and his mama would surely appreciate those qualities in his love that she possessed herself. No, they would give wholehearted approval—even if he were not hopelessly in love.

The real problem lay with Charlotte herself. He wished he felt she was ready for a declaration from him. She surely could not have mistaken his attentions to her comfort, the compliments he had paid her, of late, or the way he had tried to convey with his eyes what he felt deep inside? Yet he sometimes doubted she had notions of courtship on her mind at all. Now was the time for him to leave India, but he wanted to take her with him, and it could only be as his bride.

He sighed and turned back to the fractured water-pipe. She was so full of enthusiasm about the possibility of war and glory—had even once told him he was "as dull as ditch-water" because he was not anxious to be riding off to relieve Herat. She followed the developments with as much avidity as the menfolk of Meerpore, and was deeply involved in hastening the hospital improvements in case of large numbers of wounded, and Richard ruefully acknowledged that she was far more likely to be swept off her feet by a declaration of love from a knight in shining armour, than a multilingual engineer who proposed taking her back to England away from all the excitement and danger.

A shout brought him from his reverie, and he started forward instinctively towards a group of sepoys that had left their work to gather around two of their fellows. The scene was an ugly one. A man he knew as Mohan Lal, proud and unsociable, was on the ground in imminent danger of being cleft by a pick-axe held aloft by his long-standing enemy from the same village. There was some kind of family feud, but Richard had refused to separate them in the company, stating that they were now soldiers, and soldiers had to put aside personal feelings in the interest of their profession. There would come a time when every man in the company might depend on the other for his life, and there was no room then for resentment that dated back so far no one remembered what had caused the original quarrel. But, as Edward Kingsley had once told him, beneath their English-style uniforms and discipline, they were men of India, and feelings soon ran high. However, their few previous outbursts had never reached such a dangerous level as this present one.

"Juddar, stand away!" he roared, striding toward them, then repeated the order in the man's native tongue. But Juddar was beyond listening and kept the pick in the air above his head, ready to send it slicing down at any moment.

One look at the Indian's face was enough to tell Richard this man would never put aside his enmity as long as he lived, and meant to skewer Mohan Lal to the ground the minute the whim overcame him. Knowing the other sepoys would not interfere, Richard threw himself at Juddar, grabbing at the handle of the pick above the man's head and putting all his strength into preventing the implement from being smashed downward, whilst shouting to the man on the ground to roll away as fast as he could

Juddar was a strong man, but so was Richard, and it was a long sweating battle of strength and wills that sent the handle of the pick-axe swaying back and forth over Richard's head until his own desperate thrust overcame the Indian's balance, sending man and pick harmlessly to the ground.

It was quickly over. Juddar was put under arrest and marched away; the working-party continued the repairs. Richard stood supervising the work, outwardly calm, but inwardly sick to the stomach. During that long, long minute he had looked closely into a black native face full of hatred— hatred redirected against himself for robbing the man of his heritage of revenge. That Juddar would have brought that pick down on him and killed *him*, Richard knew without doubt. During that minute he had seen again the cruel faces and long flashing knives closing around Edward Kingsley, and he had been afraid . . . desperately afraid.

The knowledge made him churn with self-disgust, even as he stood receiving the thanks of Mohan Lal. The fear haunted him for the rest of the day, leaving his assurance undermined and his soul sore with guilt over that incident four years ago. He cried off the Scotts' dinner-party that evening, and knew himself a coward for having done so.

· *five* ·

WHILST THE SIEGE at Herat dragged on beyond anyone's expectations—due only to Pottinger's inexhaustible patience and moral courage—affairs in Kabul worsened. Alexander Burnes pleaded with his superiors to make *some* gesture of goodwill towards Dost Mohammed, since the Amir desperately wished to form an alliance with the powerful East India

Company, rather than anyone else. He was human enough to wish the signs of friendship to be reciprocal and, not unnaturally, hoped for word that the British were prepared to protect Afghan interests, even where the Sikhs were concerned.

Those who listened to the voice of the experienced man-on-the-spot were men with intelligence and far-sightedness. Those at the top had ideas of their own . . . and Burnes was only a captain, when all was said and done. One of those at the top was the Chief Secretary, Sir William McNaughten, a man with vast experience of India which he had gained mostly from behind a desk. He was a polished diplomat, perfect in the niceties of protocol, and had little patience with political juniors who spent their time raking about the country as Burnes and Eldred Pottinger had done.

Despite Burnes' recommendations concerning Dost Mohammed—a man he knew and by whom he was trusted—McNaughten felt the Amir was devious and cunning. There was no foundation for this belief, but McNaughten's bones told him to beware the man, and his bones had never let him down yet. He felt certain that the solution to the problem in Afghanistan was simply to replace the Amir with a man who would do what the British wanted without asking for anything in return . . . and Sir William had the ideal man in mind.

Shah Soojah had been Amir in Afghanistan until deposed by Dost Mohammed during bloody battles several years earlier, and he now resided, together with his family and zenana, under the combined protection of the British and Sikhs. Shah Soojah was, naturally, anxious to regain his throne and the power that went with it, and had the supreme advantage of being full of gratitude to those who had given him a haven in which to lick his wounds after defeat. With such a man on the throne as a puppet-king, the British would be certain of holding sway in Afghanistan, and the Russian threat would fade away.

McNaughten was a single-minded man. Once he had conceived what he believed to be a brilliant plan, nothing and nobody would persuade him against it, and he began to infect everyone with distrust. Politicians in Calcutta and London had succumbed to a bad attack of Russophobia which was not truly justified, and agreed that something decisive must be done. The rabble of Persians outside Herat had suddenly turned into highly efficient Cossacks, in their eyes, and the panic grew. The Council in Calcutta argued ceaselessly about what ought to be done. McNaughten's plan was the subject of heated arguments, but since none of the objectors came up with an alternative, it became adopted before anyone was aware that a vote had been cast.

In the face of his superiors' wildly foolish and impolitic moves Burnes was obliged to abandon his efforts and leave Kabul. But Dost Mohammed bade his English friend goodbye with genuine regret, even though it was the *Russian* envoy who now occupied the favoured suite in the Amir's palace. Burnes set off for India still with the firm intention of persuading his superiors that they were losing their best chance of success in Afghanistan, but he did not know Sir William McNaughten had recklessly set off to Lahore, where he determined to negotiate a treaty with the exiled Shah Soojah and the land-hungry Sikhs in the first step of his plan.

The garrison of Meerpore did not know this, either, or Richard would not have taken the step he was considering, and Charlotte's life would have followed a vastly different pattern.

On the night of the Spring Ball there was a great deal of coming and going in the Scott household. A small dinner-party comprising the Shiltons, Tom and Richard was to precede the departure to the ball, and the army of servants was busy preparing both meal and residents for the evening.

Up in her room Charlotte was humming to herself. Although Richard joined them this evening as her partner, there had been no further mention by her mama of marrying him. Indeed, he had been unable to attend that very significant dinner, after all, and Charlotte began to think Felicia had mistaken the situation of close friendship for something stronger. Her fears and awkwardness with Richard had subsided, and she again enjoyed the confidence he always inspired in her. They talked of everything under the sun, but where Afghanistan was concerned they still differed. To Charlotte, Richard appeared to be sadly lacking in the fiery anticipation shared by Tom and others like him, as they followed affairs in Kabul and Herat. The voice of cold reason touched no chord of excitement in the girl who had always had her heroes.

Where Tom drilled and practised bayonet fighting with his men, and others of her friends galloped headlong at turnips on posts to cut the "enemy heads" in two with a sword, Lieutenant Lingarde was busily drawing maps and learning Persian. Such occupations did not seem to Charlotte half as dashing as . . . as riding off to Herat to face a whole army alone!

Sir Rastin had revealed that Major Duprés had been halted in his mission at Peshawar by a message from Pottinger, and was returning to Meerpore with important information from a spy within the Persian ranks. So there seemed every hope that Colley Duprés would survive. Charlotte felt it in no way detracted from the courage of his mission, and there was now the hope that he would soon be back in the garrison.

The Spring Ball was traditionally held by the military, and their ballroom had been decorated in appropriate style. Having run many times through all the variations of English flowers, baby chicks, and gambolling lambs as themes, the committee had decided on March Hares this year. But the subalterns, whose lot it was to organize the ball, had gone as mad as the furry creatures were reputed to be and made gigantic models to sit in each corner. Richard laughingly confessed he had been responsible for drawing the animals, and the committee had been so incensed it was only lack of time to prepare anything else that prevented the models from being banned. So the great grinning hares were set up. No fault could be found with the dance-cards, or the banks of potted ferns and if, by the later stages of the evening, small cut-out rabbity faces mysteriously appeared in hordes amongst the ferns, the members of the committee were past knowing or caring who might be the culprits. There were arbours set around the verandah lit discreetly with Chinese lanterns, for those who wished to take the air a while, for lovers wishing to exchange shy kisses, or for the thrilling embraces of those who should not be there together.

Richard Lingarde had been invited to dinner with the Scotts and Shiltons prior to the ball, and was therefore Charlotte's accepted escort for the evening. It did not suit Amy, who had not yet fully recovered from the shock of Charlotte's apparent success where she had failed. The girl was petulant with Tom, and offhand with Richard during the first part of the evening.

Charlotte felt her attitude did her no credit, and was hardly flattering to Tom, whom she was supposed to adore. Her brother appeared blind to his love's faults and was slavishly devoted to her, but Charlotte sometimes wondered how much of his devotion was due to his own feelings and how much to Amy's telling him of it. Determination and a large helping of selfishness were a combination of qualities that demanded the getting of one's own way—and Amy had them in good measure.

The commencement of the first quadrille, which she naturally danced with Richard, took away all introspection, and Charlotte remained light-hearted until young and clumsy Ensign Carson arrived to claim his polka some three-quarters of an hour later. Bearing in mind one of her mama's maxims, and thinking of the toes of her satin slippers, Charlotte sent him off to fetch her some lemonade in the hopes that it would take him the length of the dance to get it. While he was away, Judge Shilton engaged her in light conversation until, glancing up, she felt a severe pain in her breast and let out a sigh of relief so great it must surely have been heard by all present. Standing in the doorway, in white breeches, a dark-blue coatee decorated with silver-and-crimson cross-sash, and a scarlet order of honour around his neck, was Colley Duprés.

The Judge broke off, looking at her with concern. "Is something amiss, Miss Scott?"

"No . . . I . . . it is rather hot in here, that is all."

He glanced around him vaguely. "Perhaps, if I could find Mr Lingarde."

"*No* . . . please, there is no need . . . it will pass."

She had never felt so sick with giddiness, so heated by the acceleration of her heartbeat. Surely the whole room could hear it? She wished the Judge would go away, and the last person she wanted beside her now was Richard Lingarde.

"Would you care to take a little air?" persisted the elderly man with concern.

"Yes . . . *no*," she reversed quickly, not wishing to leave the ballroom. "Perhaps a drink."

The Judge left on his errand, and she was left alone to concentrate on the man who had bidden her such a poignantly heroic farewell. The memory of his tall figure striding across the hall on his way to danger was as fresh now as it had been on that day.

At that moment, he glanced up and saw her. For some seconds he held her immobile with anticipation, then she felt her heart jump as he excused himself to a young writer and started to cross the ballroom toward her. The couples danced as before, the matrons continued to gossip, the orchestra played, old men bragged of ancient battles to each other, yet it seemed to the young girl that there should have been a roll of drums, a length of red carpet before her, and silent watching crowds lining it.

He bowed before her and looked up from beneath his dark lashes. "Miss Scott, once more I find you sitting on a chair waiting."

"Ensign Carson has kindly offered to fetch lemonade," she managed through sudden lack of breath. "I find it a trifle hot in here."

His glance took in what she knew were flushed cheeks, but she could only gaze into those dark eyes and wonder at what he had seen out there alone in the wilderness, what thoughts he had had during his solitary mission.

"Young Carson was hopping back and forth trying to make himself heard as I passed the refreshment table just now. He will be another ten minutes, at least. A few moments on the verandah is what you need." He placed a hand beneath her elbow. "Come!"

In a world of her own she allowed him to lead her from

the ballroom on to the verandah and along to one of the arbours—the one furthest from the sight and sound of the ballroom. She was vaguely conscious of soft laughter or rustling skirts in the secluded bowers, but his presence beside her overrode any other thoughts as she went, hand tucked into crooked blue-sleeved arm, wherever he might choose to lead her.

They reached the end of the verandah and stopped beside a stout pillar hung with lanterns. It was breathless and still, with only the clicking of insects, the plaintive brays of mules and the distant sounds of a polka to disturb the silent night. To Charlotte it seemed the whole world was holding its breath along with her.

Colley took her hand from his arm and held it in his strong fingers. "You are still fever-hot. I had hoped you would benefit from the cooler night air. What can have created such a fire in you?" His dark head bent over her as he studied her upturned face in the dim lantern-light. Then, his voice softer, more tantalizing, "*Mon petit moineau,* I believe your foolish heart has been anxious for me."

Her head swam with his close proximity. "How could it not when you have been facing such danger?"

"Did I not tell you the Devil looks after his own?" he murmured teasingly. "But perhaps my safe return had *something* to do with your prayers."

She sighed with pleasure . . . pain . . . it was difficult to tell which. "So many prayers. You cannot guess how fervently I have asked the Lord to guide and protect you."

A strange glow entered his eyes. "And so he did, my dear." His hand slid up to tilt her chin so that his mouth could close softly and briefly over hers. "There, it is all over now."

He drew away, and she remained in shock, near to tears yet more exultant than life had ever before rendered her, as he leant back against the pillar with the great jewel on that ribbon of valour around his neck dazzling her. When another voice broke against her ears she found it difficult to make any sense of it.

"Ah, Miss Scott, I see you decided to take the air, after

all," exclaimed Judge Shilton arriving at the end of the verandah with a glass of lemonade in his hand. "Evening, Major
Duprés. Good of you to look after this young lady."

Colley waved a careless hand. "Not at all. It was decidedly
hot in there, and Miss Scott was a little *desperate,* you know. I
think she has benefited from a spell out here."

"Oh . . . I see you already have some refreshment," said a
hot and disappointed Ensign Carson arriving close on the
Judge's heels with his glass of lemonade. "And the polka is
just ending."

"*Alors,* Miss Scott," said Colley suavely, "here are three
gentlemen at your command. How wicked of you to set us
one against the other in the hope of having the honour of
escorting you back to your seat in the ballroom. Will you put
us out of our misery and make your choice?"

Judge Shilton smiled. "I think Mr Carson should have the
privilege. It was *his* polka, and I am sure Miss Scott would
prefer youth to maturity, Major."

Charlotte, floating on clouds of ecstatic numbness, moved
off on the arm of the young Ensign. She did not see, a minute or so later, Tom and Amy emerge from one of the arbours, he reeling with the extent to which his fiancée had
allowed him to demonstrate his passion, but Amy with far
more on her scheming mind than Tom's reckless advances.

Richard escorted Mrs Smethwyck back to the Colonel,
thankful that his second duty dance was over. After a polite
bow he walked away, taking his dance-card from its place
tucked in his sash. Three more until the supper-dance. Why
was he so nervous? He had never been so in Charlotte's company before . . . but he had never asked her to marry him
before.

There was no name against the next schottische, so he
made his way through the arch on to the verandah and
walked down the two steps into the gardens. Silly to get into
such a state over something most men managed successfully.
Tom, hardly the most eloquent of males, had won a sought-
after damsel with ease, and his own relationship with

Charlotte had never been fraught with hesitancy or embarrassment. He flattered himself she trusted him with her true personality, and he had always been completely honest with her.

Unable to remain still he walked through the scented shrubs with his eyes on the distant sky. Out there, out in the vastness of night lay the whole world . . . and his whole life. The former had already been shaped by the hand of the Almighty; the latter was ahead, waiting for his own shaping of it. Apart from the call of duty to God, country, and family, he could do exactly as he liked with Richard Lingarde. His life was his own gift, given just once.

The world lay waiting to be explored, discoveries lay waiting for his mind to alight on, freedom lay waiting for him to take it by the hand and follow step-for-step. Every decision he now made was a single-minded one, dependent on things that influenced him alone. For twenty-eight years he had been undivided; his own master.

Marriage brought a division, took away that single unit. He would have to share himself, and everything that was his. The responsibility for the safeguarding and happiness of another human soul would rest upon his shoulders like a permanent yoke. There lay the crux of it. Once he had taken the fatal step, he would never be free and undivided again.

There was so much he wanted to do, so much he wanted to see. The pleasure of conquering foreign tongues required hours of study in silence, the joy of athletic pursuits usually precluded females, and his profession could send him to the wilder, more exciting, parts of the world where wives could not follow. At twenty-eight, with his career before him and so many goals he longed to reach, it was madness to consider marriage. It meant domesticity, children, responsibilities and ties, dinner with the Braceworthys, and cards for penny points as entertainment.

But he knew very well why any young female was brought to India. If he did not take her into his own keeping soon, Charlotte would be given to some wealthy crank three times her age, or to a lonely, insensitive brute who would break her body and spirit. Such thoughts set unbearable burning within his breast and limbs. Freedom would be a small price to pay for riding in harness with a girl he loved so deeply as Charlotte Scott.

Easing the tight collar with his fingers he stared at the cantonment buildings that had stood for years, inviolate. *This country will defeat us, in the end.* Edward Kingsley had probably been right. India had certainly defeated Richard Lingarde. He planned to leave for England as soon as possible. He expected no difficulties over a request for a swift marriage and, with luck, they could be on a packet and back in England by this time next year. His heart leapt. It would be wonderful to be back in that green and gentle island with a sweet bride to whom he could teach the delights of passion.

His dreams had a quick setback. Inside the ballroom the music was concluding, and he was forced inside to search out the elder Miss Clancy who was his next partner. But before passing beneath the arch he looked back into the night. He would bring Charlotte into the garden. The night was high and wide, and she would find his words of love more persuasive in the half light.

Throughout the next two dances his nervousness returned. Should he lead her outside *before* or *after* supper? Searching the room for the girl in the ivory-coloured dress caught up with knots of buttercups, he was knocked completely off balance when he finally caught sight of her. She looked absolutely radiant. The blush of a bride was in her cheeks to give her a beauty more delicate than the prettiness of Amy or the voluptuousness of Lady Scott. Her large green eyes glowed with the fire of desire, and in the way she held her head and the pliancy of her body there was an indefinable quality of sexual awareness that was clear to him right across the room.

He frowned, and had to apologize to his partner for missing a step. He had not imbibed unwisely, yet he was seeing a girl who was the embodiment of his own desires. She was dancing with Major Fielding, a dry old bachelor with a bungalow full of pet monkeys, and a penchant for young male Hindus. *He* could not have created such a change in her.

Puzzling over it and growing more impatient as the minutes ticked away towards the announcement of the supperdance, he finally bowed before her fully determined to waltz her on to the verandah at the first opportunity.

She went into his arms at the commencement of the music as if in a dream, and all his thoughts of patience fled. There was a soft melting submission in her body that raced his pulse, and he recognized the glow in her eyes as something that set up a blazing response in him. She had never been like this before. He was used to women flirting shamelessly, pressing their bodies immoderately closely to his, but this was something different. There was an unconscious yearning, a promise withheld that was begging to be wrenched from her, a dreamy seductive air his experience translated into the shy surrender of a virgin who does not know her own powers of arousal.

He thought quickly as he began the waltz. She knew . . . she must know! The Scotts had made no secret of their approval of his courtship. Had Felicia guessed he would declare himself tonight and warned her daughter? Was Charlotte waiting as impatiently as he for the dark seclusion of the garden?

Steering her purposefully towards an archway he twirled her right through it and on to the verandah where, seized with sudden exultation, he took her hand and ran down the steps into the shrubbery.

"Richard, whatever is the matter?" she cried breathlessly. "Have you gone quite mad?"

He pulled up and threw back his head with a triumphant laugh. "Yes, I think I have." He led her to a clear space where the whole spread of star-hung sky hushed all those beneath it. "See that?" he asked softly, gazing upward. "*That* is tonight . . . and it is all ours." He turned to face her and took her other hand in his, longing to hold the beauty of her against him, to kiss the lips that had suddenly become soft with surrendering wonder tonight. But he forced himself to wait until the conventional words had been said.

"Charlotte, from the moment you bumped into me at

your brother's party, my life has never been the same. Your friendship makes everything here bearable, and has become so precious I cannot bear to lose it." He pressed her fingers with his own as he pleaded his case. "I am not as wealthy as some who have amassed a fortune in India, but I have a sizeable income, a shooting-box in Hereford, and a *dacha* in Russia, left to me by a fond great-aunt. I shall also inherit my father's large estates in Kent, and several farming properties near the Urals that are owned by my mother.

"I intend to pursue my study of languages with the hope of qualifying as an interpreter in the diplomatic branch, or to apply my skill as an engineer in more exciting experimental directions. But anything I do manage to achieve will be for your sake, dearest Charlotte."

He swallowed hard. "I cannot believe you do not know what I am trying to say, with all my heart, and what I am offering you along with all I own."

She pulled her hands very gently away before he could do or say any more. "How could I not know, Richard, when you have made it plain from that very first day? I cannot tell you what your friendship means to me, and what a deep debt I owe you for all you have done and taught me. When I arrived here I felt desperately alone, but my affection for you equals that I feel for Tom. In fact, you have taken the place of my poor lost brother, Hugh, without a doubt, and I know you would share anything you have with me, should I ever be in need. I shall never have a better friend in all the world than you, dearest Richard."

He reeled under the blow of her words. Independence seemed like failure, the wide starry sky now looked desolate, and freedom sounded the loneliest word he knew in any language.

Despite the exertions of the night before, Charlotte was up soon after dawn to join the dedicated riders and, in company with Amy, set out along the tanned avenue with the hope of seeing the dashing figure that had remained in her mind all night.

That kiss, that enchanted moment, had been relived a thousand times until, to the awakening girl of eighteen, it had become romantically immense in significance. That a man like Colley Duprés had walked right across a ballroom straight to her after his return from a dramatic, dangerous mission had kept her awake with dizzy incredulity. Everyone must have seen; everyone must have noted that the man who had once dubbed her "a little brown sparrow" had seen only *her* in all that glittering crowd. Her plain feathers had dropped away: this morning she wore the brilliant plumage of youth's *naïveté*.

Amy's light frothy gossip about the ball took little of her attention until a name stood out in heavy emphasis to draw Charlotte's hopeful gaze away from the distance.

"What was that you were saying about Major Duprés?" she asked sharply.

Amy gave her pussy-cat smile. "I thought *that* might retrieve your straying attention."

Charlotte said casually, "I am not always desperate to hear every latest *on dit*, Amy. I shall hear it all again from the hospital ladies, I assure you."

They rode slowly on. "I merely commented on the fact that Major Duprés grows too absurd for words. Do you not agree?"

"No, I certainly do not," said Charlotte quickly without looking at her companion. She waved to an acquaintance, then continued, "He is a man of great courage."

"I would not argue with that . . . but perhaps we are thinking of his daring in vastly different terms."

An inner voice warned Charlotte not to pursue the point, but the temptation to defend the man who ruled her thoughts was too strong.

"Perhaps you do not know his tragic history as I do," she said with dignity.

Amy suppressed a giggle and had to steady her mare because of it. "Do not tell me he impressed you with that tale of his escape from Russia! Really, Charlotte, you are a great deal more foolish than I took you for."

Dislike of the girl, and the derision in Amy's voice sent Charlotte headlong into an angry defence immediately. "How very smug you sound, Amy. But it is you who are the foolish one. You forget Major Duprés is on Papa's staff. He knows Russia well, for he has spoken of that country's affairs many times with my father. I think that proves my point, without question."

They turned a corner at walking pace, so intent on their confrontation they ignored all those who passed by.

"I think he probably does know Russia well, but I would prefer to believe his departure from that country was more obligatory than heroic. He is an *adventurer*, Charlotte."

This was said with such haughty superiority, Charlotte was driven to saying things she should have kept to herself.

"You cannot refuse to acknowledge that I must know more of Major Duprés' character than you," she cried heatedly. "I spent four and a half months in his company en route from Calcutta, with only Mama as chaperone, when he spent nearly every minute of the time with us. It is possible to learn a great deal about a person, under such circumstances—especially when he confides the secrets of his tragic past to someone he *knows* will sympathize and understand. I have seen a great deal more of people's sufferings than you, Amy."

The other girl's colour was extremely heightened by now, and she cried, "Lieutenant Beamish declared you were bookish, Charlotte, and I see now he was right. I declare you will have Major Duprés on a white charger and wearing the cross of St George before long." She tossed her head arrogantly. "If you understood a man of his nature in the slightest degree, you would never have arrived from Calcutta looking like a clownish imitation of your mama, in the hope of claiming his attentions." Drawing rein she fired her big guns. "Neither would you have allowed him to be so very intimate with you last night on the verandah. You may thank providence it was Tom and me in the next arbour, or your name might now be on the lips of every gossip in Meerpore."

Charlotte pulled up, also, bosom heaving. Such violence

of feeling was new to her, and she had not the sophistication to control it.

"How dare you speak to me in that manner! You are impertinent and deceitful. If anyone's behaviour is in question it is yours, for being a Tom Pry in arbours built especially to provide privacy. I had not realized what a very spiteful nature you had."

"And what of your nature?" retorted Amy incensed. "A virtuous God-fearing little innocent intent on good works. That is what you would have us believe, you sly little creature! It is beyond everyone how you have managed to bring to heel a man like Richard Lingarde, but it is quite plain there is something of the Delilah behind that puritanical exterior. No doubt you were also on the verandah with *him* last night, and equally generous."

Beyond controlling herself now, Charlotte flew into a frenzy. "Sly! A Delilah! You wicked, wicked girl to suggest such things! I can only make the excuse that your vanity is so very hurt because *you* did not bring Richard 'to heel' . . . and . . . and because Major Duprés made it so very clear to everyone last night that *I* was the one who had been in his thoughts and to whom he immediately came on his return from danger. You are jealous!"

Amy's mood changed to one of ruthless destructive bitterness that began with harsh laughter. "You cannot . . . no, no, you *cannot* believe that, you silly little vain creature. Is it possible that you spent four and a half months in their company without discovering the truth?"

Something inside Charlotte stilled, making it painful to speak even when her lips formed the words. *"What truth?"*

"Colley Duprés is your mama's lover!"

The iciness of winter settled over Charlotte as she felt the colour fade from her face and the blood freeze in her veins. When the other girl reached out to touch her arm, she remained like a frozen equestrienne statue, staring in horror at the mouth that had spoken such words.

"I . . . I am sorry," whispered Amy, white-faced. "I did not mean to . . . I swear I have not mentioned it to another

· 119 ·

soul—not even Tom. I went to visit Lady Scott one after-noon when Sir Rastin was at Simla. She did not expect my visit and . . . and . . . dear heaven, the number of times I have wished I had called at some other time, that I was not the possessor of such knowledge." Her hand shook Charlotte's arm urgently. "I did not mean to tell you. I had no wish to . . . but you made me so very angry it was out before I knew. I see I have . . . I did not guess the extent of your regard for . . . oh please, Charlotte, do not look at me like that!"

Seeing nothing, hearing nothing but those terrible words, Charlotte dragged cruelly on her mare's mouth to turn back in the direction of her home. Heedless of her surroundings, the thudding hooves drummed home what she longed to cry with desperation: *lies lies lies!* Yet, in her heart she suddenly knew they were not. Why had she not seen the truth in their secret glances, their swift mysterious repartee, the smiles across the table as if she were not there, the deepening of their voices that made seemingly simple remarks more per-sonal? Rushing through her memory like the wind now rushing through her tumbled hair came the echoes of soft, beguiling laughter, glances highlighted by candle-glow, and bare shoulders beneath his burning glance. They had played their game beneath her nose, and she had been too innocent to guess, too bewitched to see the truth.

Galloping still, she raced along the wide avenue to the sur-prise and alarm of those who witnessed her wild progress. She saw no one, heard nothing but the pounding hooves that matched her pounding heartbeat. Hysteria was rising in her throat, tears of painful acceptance were blinding her. Those secret looks across the dinner-table spun round and around in a wheel of candle flames and burning brown eyes. She moaned through her sobs. In her dreams, it had been her own bare shoulders in breathtaking gowns that had claimed his fiery glances, her own husky voice speaking in French so intimately, her own laughter that held his entire attention. Worse, far worse, she had imagined those long fingers caress-ing her as they caressed the stem of a wine glass, those arms holding her protectively as they rode together through the wild country regions, those eyes gazing with fascination into hers as she held him captive with her words. And all the time they had laughed at her, dismissed her as the child she really was. Yet how could she have guessed, how could she have believed that he . . . and her own mother . . .?

Colley Duprés is your mama's lover! She had lived on her dreams of his dramatic departure when she had been the last person to whom he had spoken before he rode off, and his deliberate approach to her last night, across a ballroom filled with people had seemed . . . "No, no, no" she moaned in protest, humiliated by her own thoughts, her own imaginings that had just been ruthlessly destroyed by a girl who had seen plainly what her yearning spirits had not.

At her front door she slid to the ground before the syce had time to catch at the bridle, and ran up the steps on legs that threatened to buckle beneath her. On up to the first floor she went, her breath coming in agonized gasps and her cheeks streaked with tears. The door of Felicia's sitting-room flew open beneath her hands, and she ran on into the bedroom sending the double doors crashing back against the wall.

Her mother was sitting in bed in a slip of a nightgown covered in lace and ribbons, the long black hair rippling over her shoulders. Even in the depth of her personal nightmare Charlotte had time to register shock at the difference in a woman she had tried to love, but secretly envied. In the harsh light of morning, the naked face looked yellowed and faded—hard, even. Without artificial aids to add bloom to her cheeks, the black hair looked false. In her early morning privacy, Felicia Scott was a matron nearing forty, with the shape of a girl. The effect was almost vulgar; the lace confection she wore gave a touch of the bizarre to a woman desperately holding on to her youth. Charlotte stood just inside the door, seeing everything clearly now it was too late. Her beautiful mama did not exist: she had once tried to imitate a painted doll!

Felicia stared at her with the usual large blue eyes reduced to unimpressive slits, and ordered the Indian girl from the room without taking her gaze from her daughter. The doors closed softly behind the servant.

"Tell me it is not true," whispered Charlotte, the terrible transformation of the woman before her making the implied betrayal even worse. She felt sick and degraded. He had put his mouth over her own last night in a gesture of the most intimate feeling, yet he had kissed the colourless lips she now saw, caressed that yellowing throat, held ageing nakedness in his arms. Instinctively she put trembling fingers to her mouth. *"Say it is not true,"* she pleaded, but it was to him she was now making her desperate appeal.

"Charlotte, you are nothing but a child. You understand nothing of the needs of a woman." The voice that could be so changeable and fascinating was now incredibly weary. "Love has many faces and you are too young to have seen any of them. You must understand it is sometimes . . ." she put up a languid hand in an attempted appeal, then let it drop to the bedclothes again. "I tried to warn you that you should not be dazzled by a jewel that shines too brightly."

"Dazzled!" gasped Charlotte, her voice breaking. "I am destroyed . . . by you both!"

She backed to the door and fled blindly downstairs again. She could not stay in that house, could never face either of them again. Rushing outside and down the stone steps, panic filled her. Where could she go? Aunt Meg was halfway across the world, and there was no one else. At the bottom of the long flight of steps she stopped, clutching the balustrade with frenzied hands, as her shattered brain tried to return to reasoned thought. Where could the parcel be deposited next? The Tamworths? She did not know where they were. Then she was off, racing round to the back of the house where the syce was still leading the mare to the stables. There *was* a haven, an escape for her. Throwing herself into the saddle she galloped back along the broad avenue heading toward the cantonment.

Richard was on morning parade, thankful that his duty gave him something to do when his thoughts were so black. It was a good thing his men were well drilled. They almost dispensed with the need for commands. He looked at the ranks of regimental faces before him and longed to see the last of them. Soldiering was a monotonous grind, and his years in India had been a long, lonely penance with no reward at the end.

He sat in the saddle with the sweat already gathering on his forehead and neck. His shako felt too tight, and so did his collar. He thought of England, so green and soft on the eyes, as he screwed up his against the glare of sun on bayonets. He thought of boating on the lake, and strawberries and cream in the shade of oak trees. He heard the shouts of his fellows on the lush cricket green, and the "view halloo" on a crisp October morning. God, if only he were there now!

He would apply for a transfer, go on half-pay, sell-out—anything to get away. He had had enough of heat and dust; cholera and disease; black faces and chapatis . . . and long knives that slashed and slashed at living flesh. He was sick of learning Persian and methods of blowing up fortifications. He wanted to see the back of Meerpore, where he had offered his heart and life but been accepted as a substitute brother. He would send in his papers as soon as possible.

"Sir, there's . . . there's *someone* wanting to see you."

He turned to see a cavalry sergeant on a large black horse beside him. "What do you mean by coming out here during morning parade?" he snapped.

"Beg pardon, Mr Lingarde, but . . . well, *she* won't take my word you're on duty and can't be disturbed."

Richard followed his glance across the parade square to see a girl in pale blue on a brown mare.

"It's Miss Scott, sir," said the sergeant, holding back a knowing grin. "Seems *very* anxious to speak to you. I'd excuse meself, if I was you, sir, or she's liable to come out here."

Shaken to the core Richard thanked the man and urged his horse forward to Major Frost who was commanding the parade. It was an embarrassing situation, but Sir Rastin's daughter was of sufficient consequence to demand the assistance of the military if she needed it. Richard was allowed to hand over to his ensign with only a caution that he should remind the young lady that duty meant *duty*.

He rode off the parade-ground feeling that all eyes were following him. Why, *why* should she come to him in such a manner after last night? If there was some emergency regarding her family, Tom was there to handle it—or any number of people. Why must she see him so particularly that she would interrupt a parade?

It was plain to him even from fifteen yards off that there was something drastically wrong, and he spurred his horse forward to leap from the saddle and go to her.

"Charlotte, what is it . . . what has happened?"

She had to fight to speak at all. Her face was deathly white, her eyes blank, and her hands shaking as they held the bridle. "I . . . I went to . . . your quarters. They . . . they said you were here."

He put up his arms to lift her down, and she almost fell into them. "Is Tom not available?"

"It was *you* I had to see."

Putting an arm around her to support her wilting figure he led her to a shady tree where they were less conspicuous to those on the parade-ground.

"I am at your service, you know that," he said with difficulty. "You can trust me, whatever it is."

She gazed at him as if he were the only person left on earth, and he wondered how he would be able to do whatever it was she wanted of him without betraying the way he felt about her.

"Richard, were you trying to ask me to marry you last night?" she asked in a rush of frenzied words.

He steadied himself with a hand against a tree, and tried to keep calm. "Yes, yes I was."

"I did not realize . . . I just did not realize," she told him, almost breaking down. "Do you still wish to?"

Warning shots fired, trumpets sounded the alarm, and he saw the way ahead strewn with explosives, but heard himself answer, "Very much indeed."

"Then . . . oh Richard, the answer is yes. And please can it be as soon as possible?" she cried with as much fervour as he could have wished to hear.

· *six* ·

THE REPERCUSSIONS OF that day split the Scott household asunder. As Charlotte emerged from her initial coma of personal humiliation and disillusionment she began to think of how her knowledge affected others. Amy had sworn she had said no word to anyone else, and it must be true or the whole of Meerpore—of Anglo-Indian society, for that matter—would have shunned Lady Felicia Scott. But what if it should be discovered in the future?

Charlotte's distress spread to encompass her father, who was being cruelly deceived under his own roof by his wife and a man he trusted professionally. Being the kind of girl she was Charlotte found another's hurt even worse to bear than her own. In a rush of compassion for her father she tried to lavish on him all the affection that had, for years, remained unspent. He did not want it. The businesslike relationship that had grown between them collapsed beneath the onslaught of femininity. All the time she had behaved like a son, the bond had held. Endearments and maidenly solicitude broke it.

Denied access to her father now, Charlotte was isolated in loneliness inside a house that had never been a home. Felicia had made only one attempt to speak to her daughter since that fatal morning. Charlotte had walked from the room immediately.

Tom Scott had a different temperament. The quarrel between his sister and financée threatened his happiness and his friendship with Richard. Amy had called to see Charlotte and been sent away again. One rebuff was enough for the red-haired girl, who told Tom she had tried to make amends and her conscience was now clear.

Tom stormed to his father's house to see Charlotte and charged her with ill-manners and an unforgiving nature. All his attempts to get to the root of the quarrel were thwarted by both young women, and he turned despairingly to Richard. Success in that quarter was no better. A stubborn refusal by Richard to discuss his future bride brought a stalemate, and put a strain on the two men who shared quarters.

In truth, they were both puzzled over what could be drastic enough to cause a quarrel of such proportions between the two girls. Richard, knowing the manner in which his proposal of marriage had been accepted, could only imagine Amy had baited Charlotte over her own forthcoming wedding, suggesting that her friend would remain a spinster if she did not soon follow her example. As ignorant as most men over the reasons why a female's attitude sometimes changed so mercurially, he gladly accepted the girl he loved without delving too deeply into her motives. He was too happy in his love to spoil his peace of mind by worrying over what could have happened overnight to make Charlotte understand what he had been trying to ask her in the garden on the night of the ball.

He tried to ignore the fact that he had seen no repetition of the glowing girl she had been then. In fact, she had been curiously quiet and withdrawn, but her lack of liveliness was compensated for by a flattering dependence on him. If she did not exactly look like a girl glowing with love, she most determinedly wished to be by his side at every opportunity and her repeated requests that the wedding should take place as soon as he could possibly arrange it, deepened his tender passion for her. He knew she was innocent of love, but was prepared to take her gently across the threshold of deep and enduring devotion at whatever pace she set. Passion could be delayed until the perfect moment, and would be all the more heady when it came.

Affairs appeared to be working for Charlotte. No sooner had she become engaged than very strong rumours were heard regarding the invasion of Afghanistan, and it seemed all too likely that the men from Meerpore garrison would receive marching orders within the next few months. Tom Scott's wedding was advanced from November to July and Sir Rastin gave in to pleas from Richard for a rushed alliance under the emergency situation, even though it meant Sir John and Lady Lingarde could not arrive in time from Calcutta.

A double military wedding was a highlight in a place like Meerpore, and the two young bridegrooms found the event mushrooming into something that threatened to empty their pockets of more than they had bargained for under ordinary circumstances. Meerpore society gushed and cooed over the event, too excited to notice that the pair of brides were no on speaking terms.

A week before the wedding a dispatch from Calcutt added poignancy to the event, and had all the ladies sighing The Bengal Army had been ordered to provide a contingent to join that of the Bombay Army which was already embarked on ships that were moving up to Karachi on the first stage of their journey to Kabul, capital of Afghanistan. It would be only a matter of days before the selection of regiments was made, and the numbers were far, far larger than had been expected.

Sir William McNaughten had launched his plan, and it had rebounded on him. Instead of the *Sikhs* marching to Kabul with the exiled Shah Soojah, supported by levies paid for and officered by the British, the wily Sikh leader, knowing the British tendency to wish to take charge of things, had somehow engineered an advantageous alternative which meant the *Company* army was now going to march in with the exiled Amir, supported by a few Sikhs. This meant the British had been forced into absolute invasion of a non-aggressive country—a country with which they sincerely hoped to trade!

The more intelligent of the military men were completely dismayed, but promotion-hungry subalterns cheered. A brisk march into Afghanistan with a battle or two on the way was exactly to their liking. It meant they might be away for six to eight months, see something of the country beyond the frontiers, and come back covered in glory.

Richard was in despair. He believed the decision to force an exiled Amir on people who were well pleased with the one they had already was a great mistake. Being a firm advocate of listening to the voice of experience, he preferred to accept the views of Alexander Burnes, who had left Kabul to join McNaughten and the Sikh leaders clustering around their puppet, Shah Soojah.

But, like an avalanche, once having been started the invasion plans not only could not be stopped, but gathered force as they went . . . and word was received that the Persians had launched an overwhelming attack on Herat, which was about to fall. Panic prevailed. Scaremongers already had the Russians marching on India. It was then that Richard realized it was too late. To leave India now would brand him a coward!

Because of all the confusion and drama the residents of the northern station were determined to make the most of the wedding. Two handsome young officers, the picture of fine British manhood about to be sacrificed on the altar of war, and two pretty girls in dreamy white gowns and veils, about to be offered on the altar of love! The ladies of Meerpore, from eighteen to eighty, all went completely daffish over the affair. A bride *always* looked beautiful, and even the ungenerous allowed that Charlotte's pale lethargy pointed to purity of thought and modesty of conduct at such a sacred occasion.

The garrison church was filled to capacity; there was a guard of honour of fellow officers who made an archway of swords when the couples emerged as husbands and wives. The large marquee was banked with flowers that added overpowering scent to an atmosphere already stifling under canvas, and the scarlet, blue, and green of military uniforms mingled with the pale muslin of ladies' dresses while champagne flowed, and venison, ham and pheasant were consumed in large quantities.

It was an evening wedding to escape the intense heat of the day, and lanterns had to be lit during the reception which made it even hotter and attracted insects to flutter around them, but the guests were used to that and wrung every ounce of enjoyment from the occasion. They were all too busy enjoying themselves to notice that Charlotte Lingarde spoke no word to her mama and acted as if Amy Scott were a stranger and not her new sister. If one or two frustrated mamas with unmarried daughters noticed that she clung limpet-like to her new husband, it only emphasized their belief that she had somehow tricked him into the marriage and would have to work hard to retain the interest of so eligible and handsome a man.

The hot season and the present critical times prevented the couples going to the hills for a honeymoon. Tom and Amy were to spend a week in the home of one of Judge Shilton's advocates who was in England on extended leave, and the other couple had been offered the use of a rather grand place on the far outskirts of Meerpore, which had once been a wealthy nabob's hunting-lodge. It was a little off the beaten track on the edge of the jungle. Richard thought it ideal; Charlotte did not care where she went so long as it was away from Felicia's house.

Finally, the bridegrooms decided enough was enough and indicated that it was time they took their brides off. Since neither had more than a twenty-minute drive to undertake, the brides went off still in their wedding-gowns. Sitting beside their scarlet-coated husbands in the two carriages they made a wonderful, touching picture by lantern-light.

Their destinations lay in opposite directions, so the two carriages were drawn up side-by-side facing different ways, and the subalterns had planned a rousing departure for them. Having had their horses secretly waiting near the marquee they stole away, mounted them, then, at an agreed moment, fired their pistols in volleys into the air. The two bridal carriages shot off in different directions, pulled by terrified horses and each escorted by a whooping, yelling, excited crowd of young men who fired their pistols all the time to ensure that a reckless pace was maintained. Not until their newly-wed fellow officers were well away from the canton-ments did they ease up and fire a last volley as a salute to the brides and grooms.

It was past ten when Charlotte and Richard reached their house. She saw it with an air of thankfulness that the whole difficult business was over, the pretence, the false smiles, the feigned shy delight . . . the escape from a house which con-tained an adulteress.

Richard alighted and came around to her side of the car-riage with a vivid smile, reaching up to lift her from the seat and carry her inside held closely in his arms.

"At last," he breathed, tightening his hold. "I can kiss my wife as I have been longing to do since she arrived beside me at the altar."

It was sweet and gentle, as all his kisses had been since their engagement, but it shook her, nevertheless. All through the ceremony and reception her thoughts had only been of thankfulness for the escape of the intolerable pain of seeing her mama, day after day. The real significance of the day only now caught up with her.

Richard set her down on her feet, but kept his arm around her waist as he untangled the thrown-back veil from one of his buttons with infinite care.

"You look beautiful," he murmured. "I shall never forget how you looked in this dress that signified your final prom-ise to be mine. I am not very good at putting emotion into words, my dearest, but I must be the happiest man alive at this moment."

She could do nothing but stare at the face she had come to know so well, and feel herself growing desperate.

He led her across to the stairs with an arm behind her, and his voice had taken on a husky quality when he said, "Your maid is waiting upstairs. You must be tired. She will refresh you and make you comfortable." Kissing her fingers fiercely he added, "I will join you shortly, my love."

She went slowly up the stone staircase, filled with some-thing approaching dread. The house was full of the steamy smell of the jungle that surrounded it, and the light of flam-beaux in sconces cast flickering shadows over the unfamiliar walls and corridors. The room where the Indian girl was waiting with a branch of candles in the open doorway was huge and high-ceilinged, also smelling of the dankness she had encountered in the hall. It was furnished tastefully but with faded grandeur as a double boudoir and dressing-room, but old ghosts flitted there in the place that had stood unoccupied for ten years or more. It seemed desolate, as if the room was telling her it did not want her, as if the nabob's colourful past was rejecting a "Bible-thumping blue-stocking" in a place where scenes of erotic splendour had taken place.

Charlotte shivered as the Indian girl carefully removed the silk gauze bridal dress and fine petticoats. Across the vast room was an archway through which could be seen a four-poster bed that looked large enough for *ten* people. Her heart began to thud. What had she done? This evening she had pledged her life to Richard for as long as it might last. She had vowed before God to be obedient, submissive, and faithful only to him. She had vowed to care for him, supply him with creature comforts, tend him when sick . . . *bear his children!*

She stared at that bed until it all became too much for her, and she sent the girl away in her agitation. Dear heaven, what *had* she done? She had seen Richard as a means of escape, a rock to which she could cling in her ocean of unhappiness, a friend in her moment of direst need. But downstairs in this remote, haunted house was a stranger waiting to claim her, to take charge of her and order her life from now on. The parcel had been deposited with yet another kind-hearted guardian.

Tears began to slide down her cheeks as she sat clutching the wrapper around her shivering body in that huge shadow-filled room. This time, the guardian was different. It was not a spinster aunt, nor a missionary and his sister, nor an uncaring adulterous mother. But Richard was no longer a friend, he was a husband—a man who legally owned her and who would dictate all she did from now on, a man who had the right to . . . to demand certain things from her. The pleasure of his company, the arguments they had had, the gentle teasing and frank discussion on everything under the sun was at an end. Richard was her lord and master . . . until death parted them. The tears flowed afresh.

At that moment, there was a tap on the door and Richard entered almost immediately, jacket unbuttoned and holding a bottle and two glasses in his hand.

"I took a lot of care selecting this," he said as he came up to the half-moon table. A smile lit his face as he poured some wine into one of the glasses. "I think you will find *my* wine tastes like the usual sort, Mrs Lingarde."

He held the glass towards her, then his smile faded and he put the glass carefully back on to the table before coming round to take her hands in a hold that drew her to her feet and into his arms.

"Dearest, oh my dearest, there is no need for this, I swear." His lips moved over her cheeks, kissing the tears that sat on them and bringing more by his very gentleness. "I will never do anything you do not want, anything to hurt you, you should know that. My only desire is to see your happiness."

The buttons of his jacket pressed into her flesh, the pain helping to bring to full flood the tears that soaked into his shirt as he held her tightly against him for comfort.

"I know it has not been easy for you, my love," he murmured against her hair. "I understand more than you think, my sweet little innocent. I shall never demand from you anything you cannot freely give, nor shall I ever want you to be anything other than the girl I loved from that first moment."

He moved to a nearby chair and drew her on to his lap, stroking her drying cheeks. "I *love* you, Charlotte. Never forget that for a moment, for that is your lifelong protection and security."

She stirred and looked up into his familiar face. It seemed very brown in the candle-light, and his eyes shone more vividly than she had ever noticed. They were like the glow of a distant homestead when one is battling through a blizzard. His hair was clean and silver-gold, with that little funny strand standing up like a crest on his crown, where it had become ruffled. Her fears began to vanish. He was no stranger—only the dear friend he had always been. She was safe in his keeping. He had just promised, and she believed him. He did not think of her as a parcel.

"Richard, I think I could not ever bear to be parted from you," she whispered hesitantly, and he let out a long contented sigh as he leant back with her in his arms.

They sat in silence for a moment, his hand stroking her loose hair as she nestled against him. Then, she wriggled and complained that his buttons were digging into her most uncomfortably.

He laughed, and removed his jacket, drawing her back against his chest after reaching for the wine glass on the table. "And you still have not tasted the wine I chose for you. We shall share it—as we shall share everything, from now on."

He held the glass to her lips, and she sipped daintily then watched the movement of his throat as he tipped back the glass himself. His eyes were laughing down at her, then his finger raised her chin so that he could touch her wine-wet lips with his own, an experience so unique she caught her breath.

"Well, ma'am, what do you think?" he asked softly. "Was it to your taste?"

He looked so dear, so familiar, so full of happiness, she felt waves of gratitude and relief wash over her. With him beside her the ghosts in the house vanished, and her fears of loneliness were groundless.

She put up a hand to touch his bare throat. "The wine was beautiful and, if gentlemen can be described as beautiful, so are you tonight, Richard. No wonder all the mamas were after you for their daughters."

He laughed exultantly. "Never change, my dear sweet Lottie, for I adore you to distraction when you say such things."

So, recklessly sipping wine and exchanging gentle experimental kisses with him between each sip, Charlotte received Richard's overture to consummation without being aware of it. When he later carried her across to the bed, her fears and fancies were all forgotten in the wine-glow relaxation his tenderness had wrought in her.

She sighed with pleasure when he stroked her shoulders with butterfly caresses, and was sleepily aware that his chest and arms were now bare. It was exciting after the roughness of his jacket, and her lips moved against the cool sweetness of his skin in involuntary salutes.

Through a drifting haziness she became aware that he was murmuring beautiful words against her breasts, and that was exciting, too. When her nightgown slipped completely from her body she found a joyous freedom in lying naked in his arms. His body was strong and invincible; she, with no covering and with her hair down, was as defenceless as a woman could be. When he finally grew impatient in his ecstasy she melted against him, knowing he closed his defences completely around her. Even the swift pain he inflicted on her was a triumph, for it was nothing to the inner pain she had previously suffered and it was his final and irrevocable protection. No one could ever hurt her again: he would not allow them to do so.

They had been married a month when the orders arrived to dash Richard's happiness. He had hoped and prayed the trouble would blow over. The great Persian assault on Herat had failed and on the advice of Eldred Pottinger and others of his ilk, the invaders were preparing to withdraw to their own country. Pottinger's courageous tenacity had won through and put paid to any fears that Afghanistan would be overrun by Persians or their Russian allies. Yet, incredibly, McNaughten's invasion plans were still going ahead.

Even more incredible was the rumour that Alexander Burnes, since his advice had been ignored, had now decided to support the scheme to depose his friend Dost Mohammed, whom he had just left. Those who did not like Burnes or who were jealous of his achievements, said he was courting further honours. Others were prepared to allow that a mere captain was expected to follow orders whether he approved them or not. If every man who disagreed with higher authority withdrew his services, there would be few men in the Company's army.

However, there did seem to be a good chance that an acquiescent Burnes could be given the coveted post of British Envoy to Shah Soojah in his bid to regain the throne, and who could blame an ambitious political officer if he tried to make the path to promotion easier? But Burnes' hopes were dashed. Sir William McNaughten himself was given the appointment, and Burnes had to be content with the promise of becoming his successor once Shah Soojah was safely installed in Kabul.

The expedition was on. The Army of the Indus, as it was to be termed, was to assemble at Ferozepore for a grand durbar in the presence of Shah Soojah, Ranjit Singh—the Sikh leader—and the British Governor-General, Lord Aukland. The durbar was to be a very lavish affair meant by the participants to impress each other, and to give any Afghan spies a sample of the might of the invaders. Selected regiments of the Bengal Army were to march up to Ferozepore fully-equipped for war, and arrive there by the end of November. Amongst these were Tom Scott's infantry regiment, and Richard's detachment of sappers and miners.

Richard heard the news with a heavy heart. What he had dreaded had happened, and he had no choice but to go. Doubtless, Cousin Igor would also march, if the need arose, but Igor's parents were both Russian and he would face no question of split loyalty. Deep inside, Richard was also convinced a terrible mistake was being made in thinking it was going to be an easy task to walk into a foreign country and tell its people they would be far better off with a ruler they had only several years before thrown out. There would be resistance, blood was going to be spilt, feelings would run high. He thrust back the inner voice that asked him what he would do now the testing time was upon him, and he would have to watch men being killed.

He also dreaded the months of parting the expedition would involve. Four weeks of marriage was no time at all in which to achieve his full desire. He was happier than he had ever been in his life, and only now realized how lonely bachelordom had been, especially after the departure of Luana. But, although Charlotte was sweet and loving with a trust in him that swelled his heart, she was still a child to passion and he had had to curb himself drastically. Her submission was in the style of a reward for his kindness to her. He did not want a reward, but a demanding wanton! Waiting was a strain on his lusty nature.

Preparing for war was a long and expensive business, for an officer, and left him no time to woo a child-bride. He had horses to buy that had stamina and speed for campaigning rather than hunting, and he had to equip himself with weapons, uniforms and accoutrements to last through an indeterminate campaign. They were to march off from Ferozepore at the turn of the year, and Afghan winters were harsh. The regimental tailors were kept busy making flannel shirts and thick, waterproof cloaks, while the cobblers turned out hundreds of pairs of tough boots.

Richard was kept everlastingly busy, for he also had to supervise all his equipment. Infantry did not require much beside their rifles. Engineers needed saws and hammers, spades and picks, gunpowder for bombs and mines, cordage for fuses, measuring devices, compasses and timepieces, telescopes, buckets, and winches. To his own personal equipment were added sketching pads and pens, blocks of ink in all colours for map-making, drawing instruments and compasses, a telescope and sextant, measuring-tape, calculator and mining manual, darkened goggles to facilitate the studying of instruments in the full glare of the sun, a map case, and a choggle for carrying water as he rode.

He spent a great deal of time studying maps of the routes to be taken, knowing he would be in constant demand to clear a way through obstacles, and the more he saw the more he sighed. His profession enabled him to translate a map into a complete mental picture of the terrain in a way that untrained men could not and he grew even more sceptical of the success of this invasion. The only routes into Afghanistan were tortuous, narrow defiles with gigantic craggy sides and rivers running through them. Men would have to go single-file, guns would have to be pushed, pulled and levered, and store-waggons would be lucky to get through with even *one* wheel left unbroken, much less four. As if that were not enough, the passes were known to be infested with hostile bandits who were completely at home in the mountains and repeatedly attacked anyone attempting to pass through. *Long crimson blades stabbing and stabbing at human flesh.* His stomach turned, and he shrank from the test he knew would come. This time he would be surrounded by hundreds, who would see whether he proved to be a coward or not.

There was also the problem of Charlotte. He had toyed with the idea of asking Brigadier Spanforth, who was commanding the Meerpore contingent, if his wife might travel with him at the head of the column, but there was no reason he could give for the request without appearing a lovesick fool . . . and it would certainly be turned down as Charlotte was amply catered for in her parents' retinue. He worried over it for some days then, in the end, decided to leave things as they stood and somehow smuggle her into his tent whenever they halted. Officially she would travel with the ladies; in reality she would travel with him.

The departure from Meerpore of those selected to join the Army of the Indus was attended by great ceremony. This was the first opportunity the British garrison had had to see soldiers march away to fight for their young Queen Victoria, and the sight filled their throats and eyes with tears. There seemed to be an added touch of chivalry in men going out to face death for the sake of an eighteen-year-old girl in distant England.

The column, detailed to move off at four a.m., did not get started until past nine, and the sun was well up in the sky. It promised to be one of those leaden brassy days when the heat drove down to knock men over like nine-pins. The sepoys were born to it, but the British officers and troops in stiff high collars, head-hugging shakoes, and tight woollen tunics were feverish and sun-struck after three or four hours.

Nevertheless, they marched out bravely enough to the stirring sounds of military bands, providing a sight guaranteed to make the spectators swell with pride. In full marching order they looked efficient and businesslike, the glint of sun on bayonets and lances hinting at slumbering might that could be instantly awakened, and the rhythmic tramp of boots accompanied by squeaking leather, jangling harness and muffled hooves of heavy cavalry intensified the suggestion of heroic conquerors going out to cover themselves with glory.

It was as well the station residents did not follow them, for boots began to drag after ten miles, and the horses plodded with weary downbent heads, not liking the extra weight they were carrying. The smart ranks began to straggle, and one or two fell down beneath the fever to which they had refused to admit for fear of being left behind. The gap between infantry and cavalry widened. At the rear, the tremendous column of guns, waggons, ammunition-carts, pack animals laden with everything from forage to cigars for the officers, and camp-followers with their entire families in tow tailed back for five miles, struggling along through the dust raised by those who marched ahead.

The ladies, who were allowed to accompany their officer husbands as far as Ferozepore, were lucky. Sir Rastin's party had been given pride of place at the head of the column just behind the advance guard, so the track was relatively clear of dust.

The first march of eighteen miles had to be abandoned after they had covered only twelve of them. At midday the sun boiled men's heads within their shakoes, making their vision play terrible tricks, their brains swarm with inconsistencies, and their tongues swell to twice normal size. Animals were beginning to sink to their knees, or stagger pitifully about the track, and some of the camp-followers were already talking about turning back. Brigadier Spanforth was a man who was rigid in his obedience to order, and was likely to plod on until they all dropped dead in order to reach the allotted camp-site, but his officers all protested with such vehemence he finally gave the order to halt and make camp.

Charlotte was then witness to the most amazing sight of an army on the move preparing to rest and eat. The ladies, who had travelled in lighter clothes and without accoutrements, were able to dismount in the shade of a tree and watch the spectacle with a fair amount of interest.

Firstly, the halt being of necessity near water, there was the highly entertaining sight of exhausted parched men in tight uniforms trying to lead horses to drink in orderly fashion beside them. The animals smelt the water and the only thing in their minds was to get at it, in it, over it . . . anything so long as they had the relief of its cool blessing.

Cavalrymen were being dragged at the end of reins right into the stream up to their middles, or were chasing their mounts that had pulled free and were charging at the milling mass of bodies at the water, determined to get some for themselves. Even more hilarious to the female spectators was the sight of mounted officers who were chastising their men for not keeping control, then finding themselves racing against their will into the water that was now thoroughly churned up and swirling with mud. Thankfully, the baggage train was so far behind, thirsts had been quenched by the time they straggled into camp with mules, bullocks, camels and goats, who started a fresh bellowing, grunting stampede to the river.

Also by that time, tents had gone up all over the open plain and fires had been lit for the cooking of dinners. As old soldiers knew, the inevitable last arrivals were the commissariat with the supplies, so the boiling pots were waiting a long time for their contents. Outlying piquets and sentries had to be posted and horses fed before riders could relax, so it was a long time before Richard came to Charlotte, drenched to the skin and his hair plastered wetly to his head.

He grinned broadly. "Forgive my state. I have just been tossed a second time into the river by that brute of a stallion I bought last month. I think I now believe he will go to water when *he* wishes, not when I decide upon it."

Already amused by what she had seen, she thought this the final laugh. "Oh, Richard, you do look so very funny all covered in mud and soaked to the skin. I do so wish I could have seen him toss you in. What a sight it must have been."

Sobering slightly she added, "Still, I daresay you do not mind it too much after today's terrible heat. I almost envy you feeling so cool."

To her astonishment he began to advance on her with a strange gleam in his eye. "Oh, do you? Then allow me the boon of assisting you to share my experience."

Glancing quickly around to see who might have heard, she felt her pulse quicken and her limbs start to weaken in a most amazing fashion.

"Pray stop being so foolish." Seeing his expression her pulse quickened more and she jumped to her feet in a feeling of inexplicable pleasure-fear, and she began to back away from his advance. "Have you been affected by the sun?" she asked in unsteady tones. "*Richard,* stay where you are!"

He grinned even wider. "Only if you promise to come here," he said in a tone she had never heard him use before. It was soft, lulling, yet full of exciting command.

Struggling against something she could not even begin to understand, she ventured in as normal a voice as she could muster, "I should think you would wish to put on dry clothes and have something to eat."

"Naturally, but before that I want to kiss you . . . and if you do not come here this instant, I shall be across to take what I want from you."

Trembling with the need to run yet also the need to stay and be caught, she cried fiercely, "I think you have lost your wits. We are in full view of everyone here."

"What if we are?" he asked with soft, laughing torment, his vivid eyes sending a message she only half understood. "It is my privilege to kiss you. It is not as if you were another man's wife."

His words hit her hard, bringing a return of that moment Amy had said *He is your mama's lover.* She turned and began walking away, filled only with thoughts that washed her with shame.

"If you do not change from your wet clothes they will never be dry for the march tomorrow," she said in a toneless voice, that hardly travelled across her shoulder to the man she had forgotten.

He came up beside her, and they walked in silence to his tent on the outskirts of the camp. She did not notice the change in him; her own thoughts were too absorbing. They were both tired after the gruelling day, and turned in early knowing they must be up at two a.m. ready to move off. Richard had only one folding camp bed, which he gave to Charlotte, then made himself as comfortable as he could on the ground wrapped in his cloak. A tent in the midst of an army is not very private, and Charlotte, that night, missed the comfort and safety his arms provided. She lay tormented by the thought of losing his protection, his constant presence beside her, his gentle understanding. It did not occur to her that he might be missing anything.

With the lesson of the day before well and truly learnt, the column was underway by three the next morning with the dawn coming up on their right. Charlotte wished she had not to join the entourage of the day before, but Richard was busy from the moment he arose and said he could not possibly let her ride beside him with senior officers breathing down his neck. She went off with little relish for the coming day.

It did not start well. Amy made a point of riding up to her and soon pounced on Charlotte's offhand answers to her comments.

"Do you not think it is time you recovered from your pique over something I did only for your good?" she enquired in a low voice. "With our husbands away we could be of great comfort to each other in the coming months."

Charlotte rode looking straight ahead. "I am surprised to hear *you* offer comfort, I have to say. Do you not think it is a little late for that?"

"I think it is a little too late to go into a decline over something that happened before you ever came to India, and which you cannot stop," was the sharp reply. "You might have rushed to poor Richard as your only means of consolation, but when he goes you will be quite alone. How do you propose to pass the time until he returns?"

"I shall do quite well," she told the girl with a touch of bleakness.

Then Amy dropped her bombshell. "And what if he never returns?"

Charlotte swung her head round at that and stared at the girl as if she had struck a blow with her riding-whip. She was shocked by the putting into words of something she had not ever considered. Of course he would return! Everyone said the expedition would merely be a triumphal procession through to Kabul with the exiled Amir. The shining bayonets, the lances and swords, the rumbling gun-carriages were simply to impress those who watched them pass with the might of the East India Company. Richard did not entirely agree with that view, she was well aware, but she had suspected before that he was not as enthusiastic about the prospect of battle as Tom and some of her other friends. But, in any case, Richard was an engineer, and would not have to fight.

Amy had been watching her face shrewdly. "I have to consider that I might also soon be a widow. It seems astonishing that your aunt did not teach you to face realities. She seems to have done an over-zealous job in teaching you all the virtues."

Charlotte flushed with anger. "I would be glad if you took your company elsewhere. One of the things my aunt did teach me was to appreciate good manners. I cannot say I have had them from you."

Amy tightened her lips. "I hope you will not regret your decision to isolate yourself from everyone but Richard. The truth is often very cruel, however it is revealed. One has to learn to accept it."

Charlotte rounded on her. "And if it had been *I* revealing such things about *your* mama—betrayal of your father beneath his own roof? Would I have seen blissful acceptance of it from you, I wonder? I very much doubt it, Miss Wisdom!"

Amy was silenced, and dropped back from her place beside Charlotte. She did not attempt to speak to her any more on that journey. But the incident upset Charlotte, so that she rode deep in thought oblivious of the villages of clustering mud-walled huts, the dark distant lines of thorn forest and purple-blue shadow, even further distant, of the Himalayas. She did not see the dust track beneath her that wound in a brown snake across the plain crossed by nullahs, dried out and rocky at the end of the hot season. The sounds of man and animal that were continuous during that march fell on her deafened ears. The thud, thud, thud of dusty boots, the snorting of horses, the groaning creaking waggons, the incessant jabber of the camp-followers faded into silence as she grappled with what Amy had said.

Even if it turned out to be more than a simple matter of placing a new Amir on the throne of Kabul, even if there should be a battle of some kind, it would not affect Richard. He would not be fighting. Engineers put up bridges and built walls, they studied instruments and worked out long calculations. His luggage contained pens and fine brushes for sketching. Richard made maps and diagrams. He did not rush at people with sword and pistol like the infantry, he did not charge headlong into the fray like the cavalry. Engineers lit fuses and blew things up from long distances, in safety. She was certain of it—so certain she could put all thought of Amy's question from her mind. Of course he would return. Who would take care of the "parcel" if he did not?

They halted for a quick snack by the roadside, and to water the animals at a tank beside a village, but Charlotte felt so restless she could not wait for Richard to come up with them. Leaving her horse with a groom she walked alongside the track on a swathe of yellowy grass, holding her skirt up as she stepped over the humps and uneven ruts. It was quite pleasant to be walking and stretching her legs, even though the tail of the column was still pouring in, raising dust over everything.

She knew Richard was detailed today as officer-in-charge of the escort to the treasury—a necessary part of any army that hoped to bribe implacable rulers to allow its boots, hooves and wheels to cross their territory in order to invade a neighbour. But the treasure-waggons rolled by with a young cornet supervising their last few hundred yards or so. Richard was nowhere to be seen.

Cornet Tomkinson saluted at her question and said Mr Lingarde was a short way back talking to some natives, but would be along at any minute. She went on, loath to return to the company of Felicia and the other women, and anxious to see him after her gloomy thoughts of the morning.

Spotting him in the distance, she was surprised to see that the natives were two women in bright colours. Their conversation appeared very absorbing, for Richard had dismounted and was standing in the most casual way with one booted foot on a low wall and his elbow on that knee as he bent forward to them.

Charlotte had drawn near enough to see that the women were both young, when he glanced up and saw her. His wave greeted her, but she was further surprised to see him straighten up, take his purse from his pocket and give each woman something they obviously prized. They salaamed gracefully and stood watching as he led his horse towards his wife, all his attention on her from that moment.

"This is delightful." He smiled and laid an arm across her shoulders. "When I was detailed to escort the treasure I did not know it would turn out to be my own dearest wife." His arm tightened around her. "If only we could ride off to that distant forest, away from everyone and these trappings of war. Imagine being alone together in the shade of trees by a cool river—a place for confessions that can only be made in secret places such as that."

"Why did you give those native women money?" she asked, not recognizing his mood because of her own uneasiness.

He sighed slowly and heavily. "We . . . Tom and I . . . we used to . . . employ them. They are sisters and come from this village. I had no idea until I saw them by the roadside."

"You mean they were your servants? Is that not a little unusual?"

"Not really. It . . . it is a custom in some parts of India. Now, my love, have you already refreshed yourself?"

She shook her head. "I had a cup of water, but preferred to wait for you." She walked on a few steps, then looked up at him. "Richard, is your pistol loaded?"

He raised his thick fair eyebrows in comical fashion. "Do you wish me to fight a duel on your behalf? Name the scoundrel and I will challenge him at once."

Her forehead became marred by a tiny frown, and she looked away from him. "Since we left Meerpore, you seem to be altered, in some way. I cannot put it into words exactly, but you speak so much nonsense and do nothing but tease me."

He stopped walking and let go his horse to turn her to face him, with his hands on her shoulders. His face was burnt even browner and covered with a fine layer of dust, as was his red coat, and she was reminded of the first day they had met, when he had been hunting. But those unusual eyes were full of much more than they had been when he had looked at her on that day. He tilted her chin up with his rough gauntlet.

"Lottie, do you never *ever* wish to tease *me?*" he asked huskily.

Completely foxed, she had no idea what to answer. She did not even understand what he was asking her. This new Richard made her feel unrelaxed in his company. It was as if he had secrets, and she was shut out from them.

"I wish to be *with* you . . . always," she assured him, yet sensed that the answer disappointed him, for some inexplicable reason. "But you have not answered my question about the pistol. *Is* it loaded?"

He began walking again, but did not put his arm around her this time. He seemed almost angry. "*Of course,* it is loaded. What is the use of a treasury escort if he cannot defend the treasure?"

"There is no need to shout at me, Richard," she said, hurt at his manner. "It is just that, although I know engineers do not have to fight, I thought it curious that you should always carry a pistol."

"I also carry a sword, but it does not mean I shall fight, naturally. It is simply to slice my fruit after dinner." His voice was cold, bitter and cutting.

Since his stride had increased she found herself having almost to run to catch up with him as they approached the others ahead who were eating slices of meat and bread-and-butter. She realized they were on the brink of their first marital quarrel, and *he* was instigating it. Having no idea what she had done to upset him, she tried soothing.

"Doubtless you are hungry," she told him with sympathy. "Aunt Meg always says a man must have sustenance for the body as well as food for the soul."

He rounded on her without slowing his stride. "Your Aunt Meg, madam, was nothing more than an ignorant old tabby, in my opinion. She knows as little about the things a man requires as . . . as . . ." He sighed and halted. "Oh, for the Lord's sake stop looking at me like that, Charlotte."

Upset and disturbed by the change in him lately, she replied, "Well, you frighten me when you become angry in a moment like that—just because I asked you about your pistol."

Pulling off his shako and heading for the spot where his bearer had placed a rug and light refreshment, he said heavily, "Let us forget all this talk of pistols. By the time we reach Ferozepore they will most probably have seen sense and called the invasion off."

With that she had to be content, but the tiff unsettled Charlotte for the rest of that day. The march was resumed with the utmost promptness, and the camp-site reached only a bare hour later than had been planned. It had been an extra long leg because of their curtailed march the previous day, so everyone was easing aching muscles and rubbing stiff necks when they finally dismounted.

The ladies found a shady spot and sat down on a layer of cloaks spread by the gentlemen in the party who were on Sir Rastin's staff. But Charlotte chose not to join them. She knew Richard would be busy for an hour or more yet, and she was still under the influence of that unsettling scene with him earlier in the day. Deep in moody thought she strolled away to a small hillock overlooking the village, and thought back over all she had said to her husband in an effort to find the cause for his uncharacteristic anger.

The rustle of skirts behind her made her turn and, when

she saw who had followed her in her attempt at solitude, she prepared to move off quickly.

"No, Charlotte," said her mother, "you cannot avoid forever what must be said between us."

Felicia looked beautiful, despite the rigours of the journey, and Charlotte wished she had never seen her mother during that early morning time.

"I do not wish anything more to be said on the subject," she told Felicia.

The older woman drew nearer, the skirt of her yellow gown dragging the leaves across the dry grass. "But I have wishes, and you will listen to me, Charlotte. I was your age when I married Rastin Scott. He had not been knighted then, but the event was already foreseen by my parents." She looked across towards the village, but it was plain she was looking back into the past as she continued. "The life of a woman is dependent on gentlemen. If she does not 'take' when brought out, she will be an old maid, pitied and abused by all those who imagine she will be grateful to be given the odious tasks of minding their children, running their houses, and receiving their unwanted guests. Your Aunt Meg is a prime example."

Charlotte was startled. She had never considered Aunt Meg in that light—lonely, unwanted, under an obligation to others. Her life had always seemed so full and satisfying to her.

"A successful season, on the other hand," continued Felicia, "brings a girl offers of marriage, and she will be persuaded into accepting that which will bring her wealth or a title. It is almost certain that the young man who makes her heart beat faster and who adores her with desperation, will be penniless, of lowly stock, or forced to leave the country over some disgrace."

She smiled a sad, haunting kind of acknowledgement. "My parents were right. He died penniless in Genoa of consumption when he was only twenty-six . . . but I have never forgotten him."

The sad eyes turned back to Charlotte. "So, you see, I do

· 147 ·

know what it is like to be eighteen, my dear. Well, romantic poverty denied her, the young girl is taken into marriage by a suitable gentleman who might love her very sincerely, or regard her as just another of his possessions. Whichever the case may be, once married, she has to depend upon him for the rest of her life—and that life might last many, many years.

"She must go where he dictates, do exactly as he bids, obey his wishes with meekness, enhance his consequence with his fellows by being the perfect partner. If he loves her, it is possible for her to wheedle or cajole so that life is pleasant enough. But if he does not love her, her life can become more unendurable than that of old maids, for there is one way in which *they* can never be humiliated."

She tried to take Charlotte's hands, but the girl stepped back in revulsion. The pale, graceful hands dropped wearily to the sides of the yellow gown.

"Charlotte, a woman can suffer humiliation for years without giving away any sign of it. Her pride keeps her going until, one day, she can take no more. She sees the chance of release—not happiness, perhaps—but a salve for loneliness and neglect. If there is no prospect of any other person being hurt by it, she is hardly human if she can turn her back on it."

Charlotte stood in the dappled shade staring at the woman before her. What did she know of loneliness and neglect? Nothing, or she would never have left her child so bereft of love in England for seventeen years, with only a stilted monthly letter to provide a reminder that there was a family at the other end of the earth.

"Do you understand what I am trying to say?" asked Felicia.

"What of Papa?" came her cold accusation.

Felicia laughed bitterly. "You think he would be hurt? So long as there is no whisper of it he would not care one jot! If it had been anyone but Colley you would never have guessed. I saw what he was doing to you and warned him. I tried to warn you, but you did not wish to hear. You have run away from it, but now your refuge is to be taken from you for a while—who knows how long?"

Charlotte began walking away. "I have to find Richard."

The voice floated after her. "You are one of the lucky ones, Charlotte. He deserves more than your gratitude."

The words fell on deaf ears, but the encounter made her strangely afraid. Without Richard there would be nothing. For the remainder of the journey to Ferozepore she rode at her husband's side, as did the other officer's wives. They would have to part all too soon and return to Meerpore for a lonely, anxious solitude, and no one any longer bothered about official rules.

• *seven* •

WHEN RICHARD RODE into the army camp on the banks of the River Sutlej at Ferozepore, he realized all his hopes of a last-minute change of plans were ridiculous. An army of twenty thousand men had not been brought from all over India to impress the Sikhs and their leader, Ranjit Singh, only to be sent back to their cantonments again.

The fear of Russian invasion of Afghanistan had now been supplanted by the heady and headlong plunge into self-aggrandizement by those who maintained the Anglo–Indian empire at the expense and envy of other nations. Herat had been relieved: the Persians had marched away. There was now no reason for entering Afghanistan, but the machine of war-making had begun and would now cause as much damage if it were stopped as if it were allowed to run on.

The sight of the enormous encampment that stretched some miles along the left bank of the Sutlej in a conglomeration of men, beasts, and artillery, plus the marching force of Sikhs on the other side of the river in all their vivid trappings, silken tents, golden banners, and caparisoned horses filled Richard with anything but pride. He was still convinced the British were making a costly mistake to interfere with Dost Mohammed's rule of Afghanistan, and as for the Sikhs themselves, his only thought was that today's friend was often tomorrow's enemy when dealing with native princes.

His intense dismay at the inevitability of the gathering was augmented by his growing anxiety over Charlotte which, taken together, was interpreted by a few of his fellows as reluctance to go to battle, to face the fierce tribesmen of Afghanistan. It did nothing for his peace of mind that *he* questioned his reasons, also. Was he using professional and emotional convictions to hide the truth from himself—the truth he had been questioning ever since that day four years ago when he had ridden away from a shallow grave dug with his own hands as some kind of penance?

Tom Scott, having to leave his young bride also, was nevertheless fired with the enthusiasm of possible battle, and commented on his companion's cool response to the coming months. With their relationship still under something of a strain because of their wives, and worried to death over his marriage, Richard told Tom very shortly to keep his confounded tongue between his teeth, whereupon Tom had walked off greatly disillusioned with a man he had once admired.

Throughout the two-week march to Ferozepore Richard had tried to perfect his relationship with Charlotte by all manner of means, none of which had been successful. In the role of guardian—protector—call it what she wished, he had been very patient. Her dependence demanded from him what he had been very willing to give, whilst she had been with him every day, but it was only human to hope for something more to take away and hold in his heart. He wanted a mistress as well as a wife, a submissive tormentor, a girl to whom he could be a passionate master besides a tender guardian. He wanted someone who could tease him into desire with her hands, who could light his nights with fire in his limbs, who could make him conqueror rather than mentor.

Wary of frightening her with full-blooded passion, he had tried to arouse her with stimulating teasing, by physical contact whenever possible, by romantic situations. But still she merely clung to him like ivy to a wall, all the early self-possession and promise of courage which had so attracted him to her gone. It seemed as if, with marriage, she had abandoned herself as a person in her own right, to become a limb of himself. He had told himself, at first, that all her qualities would return as she became used to the state of marriage, and once he had aroused that passion he had been certain was within her.

Depressed, tired, and uncertain of himself, now, he began to think that he had seen a creature of his own imagination in her and fallen in love with her, but he could not forget the night of the Spring Ball when she had been transformed into a vital, glowing girl who had taken his breath away. *That* had not been imagination, and he had somehow to work the miracle that would bring a return of *that* Charlotte. But there was so little time, and his desperation grew when the advance party of the Governor-General's staff rode in, amongst them Sir John and Lady Lingarde.

The arrival of his mother caused Richard further disillusion and a great deal of anger. In the higher echelons of the British contingent there was a small number who felt personal outrage over the fact that Lord Aukland had approved the inclusion in his party of Lady Lingarde, who was a Russian—*the enemy*. These people did not keep their opinions to themselves, but began a whisper of protest that grew and multiplied until many officers and, particularly, their ladies made it abundantly plain that they thought the presence of such a woman on that occasion was in very bad taste. Worse, they maintained it was typical Russian effrontery that had led Anastasia Lingarde to accept the invitation. Of course, it was a tricky situation with Sir John being so distinguished an English diplomat, but the woman should have had the sense and decency to invent an excuse to stay in Calcutta.

Nevertheless, all the women present were full of the titillating speculation on the meeting of the two most accredited beauties in Anglo-India, who were now mamas-in-law. The two had seldom been seen together, so descriptions of their beauty varied. At last, the matter would be settled, and it was not surprising that all hopes were pinned on Felicia, that true English belle.

Although no one actually spoke of it to Richard's face, they all made little attempt to lower their voices or change the subject when he approached. The fact that he had other problems on his mind, plus the knowledge that the best way he could treat such an attitude was by ignoring it, stopped Richard from venting his anger in defence of his mother. When he saw her ride into the camp with all her usual panache, as if she did not know very well what was being said, he was filled with love and pride.

Well used to her beauty, Richard saw only that she looked thinner and there were dark hollows beneath her renowned mysterious blue-green eyes that slanted upward and were fringed with dark lashes in contrast to her fair colouring. Early enquiries of his father revealed that she had been suffering from a recurring fever for some time, and that she had resisted all persuasions to go home for a rest—England or Russia, it did not matter which—saying that, with the situation as it was, it was quite the wrong time for Sir John Lingarde's foreign wife to do anything but stay at his side.

It so happened that Felicia Scott had succumbed to heat exhaustion after the journey to Ferozepore, so the dinner-party that would conventionally have been held by the two sets of parents of the newly-weds had to be delayed. Richard was delighted to be able to present his bride to his mother and father without the Scotts present, and the meeting was an unqualified success.

Charlotte, initially timid towards the one-armed Sir John, soon discovered he was not in the least like her own father and was laughing and at ease with him, talking of everything under the sun. But it was Anastasia who wrought the greatest change in the girl. All Charlotte's warmth of personality, her wit, her intelligent understanding of things normally ignored by females, and her unconscious but deliciously humorous honesty were drawn out by a woman whose national volatility, combined with all Charlotte's qualities and a natural compassionate charm, made her loved or envied. No one ever felt half-hearted about Anastasia Lingarde.

The evening could not have been a greater success, but it went on for a long time, and Richard had had a hard day organizing field works under the blazing sun. The relaxed pleasure of seeing his parents again combined with the effects of his father's excellent wines to send him very quickly to sleep after a brief embrace from his wife, who glowed with his praise.

But, early the following morning, when Richard had slipped from his tent without waking Charlotte, he was delighted, but very surprised, to encounter his mama riding her spirited mare in exactly the direction he had to go. Spurring his horse he came up alongside her, laughing with admiration.

"After so late a night there is no other female I know who could look as stunningly beautiful as you do this morning," he greeted in Russian, kissing the hand she held out to him.

She put back her head in the dark-red hat of Cossack style, and laughed delightedly, answering in her mother tongue.

"There will come a day when you can no longer truthfully say such words, my dearest boy. And you must not then lie, because I shall see it in those wicked eyes of yours." Her own, which had captivated many a hapless admirer, shone with love. "But all the time it is still true, please continue to say it. There is not a woman alive who does not thrive on compliments."

He looked away from her and across the nearby River Sutlej, where the Sikh encampment lay. He knew a girl who did not even recognize his compliments.

"It is a wondrous sight, do you not think?" she asked softly, riding beside him and following his glance. "Your grandfather had a painting on the wall of his study that I used to love, as a child. Perhaps it was the bright colours, or the

suggestion of wild open lands with freedom for restless unconquered people. It was a picture of a famous Tartar encampment, and those dark-skinned people over there remind
me of my childhood wonderment at that painting."

He looked at her again, erect, tall, and slender in the dark
red riding-habit that so flattered her faintly golden skin and
flaxen hair. Her face was calm and so exquisitely dainty in
features, her next words seemed inappropriate.

"It is in our blood, you know—that wild restless desire for
freedom. Your ancestors were ruthless boyars who stopped
at nothing to keep their lands and possessions . . ." She
smiled with all her wicked charm, ". . . and especially their
women. They never surrendered to an invader, and became
aristocratic bandits rather than bow to conquest."

She put a hand over his as it rested on the pommel. "We
have what your father calls 'black sheep' in our family, but
they were all possessed of fierce and indestructible pride. Do
not let yours be broken by this thing you have to do."

He reined in, and she did the same. They were on the outskirts of the camp where they could not be overheard, even if
a listener understood Russian, and the pale rose of morning
touched their faces like the flush that comes after a hard canter.

"If my pride were broken I would not be here now," he
said with deep emotion, "but you do not know what it has
cost me to do so."

She gave a half-smile that turned her eyes into luminous
softened mirrors of understanding. "Oh, but I do, my splendid son. Do you think my thoughts have not been with you
during this tragic business, that I have not been in constant
contact with Dmitri and young Igor, to whom you have expressed your affection and burning regrets on all that has
happened?" Her glance travelled over him as he sat his horse
as erectly as she. "The mixture of the fiery blood of two
proud races is in your veins. It has given you a magnificent
body, a splendid brain, and many talents . . . but it has also
given you qualities that are at war within you." She took his
hand again and kissed it in extravagant fashion. "My son, my

· 154 ·

own splendid child, I shall always love you. Even when we are so very far distant you are close to my heart. But . . ." Here, she gently put his hand back on the pommel . . . "you made your choice eight years ago, and you must not waver. It is the uniform of the army of the English queen you wear, not that of the Imperial Russian Guards. Your actions must not be influenced by anything other than that."

He sighed, loving her for her ability to read his thoughts, grow close to him through gentle honesty, still express her love and pride for a child who was now a grown man. He loved her for giving what he still so badly needed from someone else.

"*Mamotchka,*" he said heavily, using the boyhood endearment. "I came to terms with my loyalty, and it has nothing to do with the uniform I chose to wear. It is concerned with right and wrong, honesty or deception, justification or trumped-up glorification." He glanced meaningfully across at the vivid silken tents of the Sikh encampment and at their own white canvas ones on this side of the river.

"If I truly believed I was about to set out in defence of a people that were being cruelly and wrongfully oppressed by a nation seeking to conquer the whole of the eastern world, I would draw my sword against Cousin Igor himself." He gripped the pommel hard. "But I know in my heart that this is wrong. My father knows it is wrong, a hundred intelligent men know it is wrong, but it rolls forward like an inexorable destructive tidal wave while we stand by as helpless as Canute."

He frowned at her, knowing he could speak to her of all he had been unable to confess to the other woman he loved. "They doubt my loyalty because of my mixed blood. They suspect that cowardice, not reason, is behind my unwillingness to go to war. All the same, I . . . I sometimes doubt my own . . ." He broke off, unable to speak, even to her, of his fear of failure when faced by dark-faced enemies with knives.

"Yes, my dearest boy?" she prompted. "What is this you doubt?"

He tried to evade it by laughing and saying, "I sometimes doubt I shall ever reach the Diplomatic Service like my father. I do not have his tact."

Anastasia spurred her horse so that it began to move off. Richard moved forward with her.

"Tsk! John has no tact whatsoever," she said with amusement. "It is I who prevent him from offending everybody and anybody who upsets him. Tell me that you do not already know this, and it will be the second lie you have given in succession, my wicked handsome son."

He cast a quick glance at her beautiful profile, but she kept her gaze straight ahead as they rode past the piquet-posts and towards the rising sun.

"It is a great pity your delightful child-bride does not read your thoughts as easily as I do, my dear."

He was thrown by the sudden change in the conversation, and refused to say anything in reply. They rode on in strained silence, until she suddenly laughed and turned her horse across his path, forcing him to stop.

"Fierce and indestructible pride, I said, did I not? My beloved boy, your glowering expression, your stormy, beautiful eyes, and your white knuckles as you grip the bridle show it in full, at this moment. Bravo, Richard Gregori Lingarde!"

Her face softened with compassion, her voice grew low with loving pleading. "But not with *me,* my one and only child." She put up a hand to touch his cheek softly, and he was shaken to see tears in her eyes. "These might be our last private moments together in this life. You know that I have always been absurdly and outrageously fond of you. But, despite a mother's prejudice, no female has ever denied you are irresistibly attractive, destined for brilliance, and virile to the point of a woman's desperation. You have been offered the pick of the beauties for miles around, and declined them all. Then, you married in haste, a chit you had known a few months only. Your Charlotte is intelligent, lively, compassionate, and quite delightfully ingenuous, but . . . but why, oh why, my darling boy, does she not love you to distraction? No . . . no, do not speak, or you might regret your words before many weeks are out," she said swiftly, placing her fingers over his mouth as a tide of angry colour rushed into his cheeks.

"Forgive me. *Forgive me,*" she whispered. "But I am hurting you only in the effort to help. I cannot bear to think you must go off wanting that girl so much it tears your heart out. *I* see it, but she cannot, that much is obvious. Why are you letting yourself be tortured like this? Can it be that you do not understand females even after surviving the assault of every unmarried girl in India? Or is it this particular one you do not understand?"

His anger went, and it was suddenly a tremendous relief to express his own doubts. "I understand all too well when a female is on the attack. Perhaps I do not understand defence. She . . . she has a wall around her which I think she does not even know is there. I wrote to you of her background, and you have seen for yourself that she is not in the least brazen or hoydenish. She is very young and has had no experience of . . . of *life.* I was prepared to take time over . . . but it is running out faster than I had expected, just at a time when I am more occupied than ever before with duties. She is . . . generous . . . but, I cannot believe that is all there is within her heart." He sighed heavily. "A tent in the midst of a military camp, and the excesses of a durbar are not the ideal conditions for . . ."

"Seduction?" she suggested gently. "My darling boy, seduction is a slow, tender, beautiful process which should take place in *chambre séparée* with red velvet, roses everywhere, and champagne in buckets of ice."

She drew her mare back from across his path, and moved off again, speaking over her shoulder.

"I hear there are many great fortresses on the way to Kabul. No doubt, your engineering skills will be much in demand. How do you take an impregnable fortress, my dear?"

Bewildered by her change of subject, he began to follow, murmuring abstractedly. "It depends on the way it is built. First search for weak spots, place explosives, breach the walls, then take the defenders by storm."

Anastasia's face was laughing and triumphant as she

looked back at him over her shoulder, and her eyes were full of their legendary enchantment in the early sunrise.

"Just so, my clever invincible warrior." She flicked the bridle and spurred her horse. "Come, let us meet the dawn with suitable gratitude."

Richard's heart leapt as he realized how she had managed to tell him what he could not ask her, and exultation set him off in pursuit of the woman who rode a horse as well as any of her wild ancestors.

Finally, they curbed their headlong, exciting gallop and looked at each other, laughing and breathless, the tented camp a distant vision of white triangles in neat rows. Anastasia gradually slowed her mare until it came to a halt, and Richard drew up alongside her. But when she looked up at him then, he was shaken by the change in her. The elegant erect figure, the beautiful Slavic features, and those eyes all seemed to emanate sadness.

"Sometimes, it is necessary to have a little madness before we return to sanity," she told him. "You have your duty from which I have just taken you, and I have mine. Balls, receptions, *soirées,* dinner-parties when they all look at me and see 'that Russian woman.' That is when I must be sane, my dearest one. Out here, I can be with the spirits of my wild boyar ancestors." She edged her mare nearer. "This morning you have shared that madness with me. You do not know how very precious that has been to me. Now we shall say our goodbye—our very own private goodbye."

"But I shall see you before we march off," he protested swiftly.

Her smile was wistful. "Surrounded by an inexorable destructive tidal wave and a few helpless Canutes? No, my darling son, I shall say goodbye to you here, then stay with my boyar spirits while you go about your duty."

As he took her hand to his lips, she reached up to kiss him gently on each cheek, then on the fingers that held her own.

"I have been a vain, doting, triumphant mother, my dear one, but I am ashamed of none of it. God bless you, and spare you from the torments of life. *Do svidaniya,* Richard Gregori Lingarde."

"Do svidaniya," he replied through a throat thickened by emotion, then turned his horse back towards the tents where Charlotte would just be awakening.

Richard's plans were not destined to be as straightforward as he had hoped after that morning meeting. A durbar was a lavish exhibition of wealth, power and ostentation, and this one was no exception. The British officers were kept on their toes in full dress uniforms to impress the Sikhs with displays of military manoeuvres, parades and weapon demonstrations throughout the days, and all kinds of evening entertainments by the Sikhs, to which ladies were not invited, kept them busy and hot under the collar, to say the least, until the early hours.

These nights of eastern delights and sensuality did nothing to help Richard's frustration in the slightest, and his desire to awaken Charlotte's slumbering passion began to centre almost entirely on the sexual drive that tormented him to the extent of losing his concentration on anything else. Finally, after four nights in a row of rich orgies in silken tents, nautch girls in diaphanous garments, performing dances that were suggestive of copulation, and the offer of private tents into which the honoured English guests might take their choice of the girls—two or three, if they so wished—Richard arrived back at his own tent very definitely drunk and very definitely lusty.

Making no attempt to be quiet on entering, luck appeared to be with him when he found Charlotte already awake, for once. In a state of heightened virility and insobriety, he went straight to her bed and sat on it with such force that it tilted and sent him sprawling on to the ground.

Charlotte sat up clutching the blanket to her bosom. "Richard, are you feeling all right?" she asked with apprehension. "Do not say you are going down with a fever."

"Yes . . . yes, that is just what I am," he muttered thickly, and pulled himself up into a sitting position to lean across and make a grab at her.

She drew away and wrinkled up her nose. "Oh, you are covered in smoke fumes and the reek of Indian dishes!"

More intoxicated than cautious, he replied with a sleepy-eyed smile, "And perfume, no doubt. The dishes were served by black-eyed damsels wearing very little by way of attire."

At the back of his mind he thought jealousy might have been a good introduction to passion, and tried to seize her in his arms and kiss her again. She turned her head away, so the passionate seeking of his lips found only her ear and a swathe of brown hair.

"The persuasion to remain for . . . further entertainment . . . was very great," he hinted slyly against her cheek. "But the married men all left, of course."

"Of course," she said severely.

Getting to his knees he pulled her close against him and began to nibble her neck. "That is why I came home, my dearest. What need have I of dusky damsels when my sweet wife is waiting for me?"

"It is only by chance that I was awake," she said. "It really is impossible to sleep in a place where men are stumbling noisily about for most of the night."

Trying to inch the blanket low enough to kiss her breasts he rambled on in as lusty a tone as he could manage, "Our gallant Major Duprés will, I am certain, partake of all their amusements. He had a girl in each arm when I left. She who waits tonight in his tent will be vastly disappointed, I'll wager."

Finding his attempts to remove the blanket frustrated, he abandoned gentleness and threw himself on top of her with every intention of stripping not only the blanket, but the nightgown from her as quickly as he could. But he was astonished at the furious strength with which he was soon pushed away and on to the floor on the other side of the flimsy camp-bed.

"What do *you* know of that?" It was a whiplash of a question in the guise of an accusation.

Roused to instant anger, he said, "I know as much as anyone about that scoundrel—in fact, a damned sight more than most. He has never made a secret of his native amours. Over port and cigars he becomes excessively boring." Not in control of his tongue, he added loudly, "And I should like to know what you know of such things, madam! Do not tell me *les poules* have now taken to discussing gentlemen's *chères amies*, their latest prime pieces of sullied virtue?"

He was amazed to see how pale she had turned, how fearful, almost. But he was too drunk to work out why, and, realizing that everything was going wrong, became more recklessly aggressive.

"Well, do they?" he demanded. "No doubt, you have heard all about Luana—who never behaved like this, I can tell you."

She sat very still, wrapped to the chin in her blankets. "You are not in command of yourself, and will soon have the entire camp awake. Such remarks as you have just made should be confined to the company of gentlemen. Perhaps you should have stayed with them."

"Perhaps I should," he retorted furiously, stumbling to his feet, then cracking his head on the lantern and setting it swinging dangerously from the pole.

"Hell and damnation," he swore violently, putting one hand to the back of his head, and trying to steady the lantern with the other, burning his palm in the process. "Aaah! Curse the bloody thing to perdition!" he yelled to give vent to his feelings.

"Richard, whatever has come over you?" whispered Charlotte furiously as she gazed at him over the blankets.

"Nothing has come over me," he snapped. "I have simply returned to my home . . . *tent* . . . after a lavish feast, great quantities of potent liquor, and a dancing display of . . . well, *les poules* will doubtless have described that in full detail to you, also. I have been doing my duty for God knows how many interminable days in this damned place, and had hoped to find a loving wife awaiting me with consolation. Instead, I find a shrew."

"Richard!"

It was an indication of how potent was the liquor forced on the British officers by the Sikhs as a test of their manhood, that he could start such a quarrel and not care that he had. Not only was he very drunk, he was aching in every limb from sitting for hours on a pile of cushions in an extremely tight-fitting uniform with his legs crossed, and he was full of sexual desire after the titillating gyrations of the nautch girls, who had reminded him of Luana.

"Yes, a *shrew*," he repeated doggedly and very loudly.

"Please," she implored. "Captain and Mrs Cunningham will hear every word. Their tent is next to ours."

"Ha, is it? Then have no fears, for Cunningham has just been deposited at his door by Tom and me," he went on equally loudly. "I doubt he will hear *anything*, and she is probably too busy being shrewish, also." He glared at her. "Females are all the same, you know. They act like a shrew if a fellow is away too much, and just the same when he is there. Well, I will tell you this, madam, a scolding tongue and a blanket pulled to the chin is very likely to drive me back to join that devil Duprés. Doubtless, *he* is now very well satisfied with *his* evening."

"*Please*, Richard," she begged, "the whole camp must by now be aware of every word you are saying."

"I doubt it," he said savagely, "for they are all much too pleasantly occupied to hear how my wife treats me. One would not think I shall soon be marching off to war. You do not know, madam, what you are doing to me. I sometimes wonder if you know me at all," he slurred with bitterness. "Or if you will ever attempt to find out."

Unable to stand any longer, he buckled up on to the blankets spread on the ground for his bed, and covered himself with his cloak, telling himself there were some fortresses that could never be stormed.

Lord Aukland arrived in Ferozepore on the twenty-seventh of November and two days later officially greeted Ranjit Singh at a magnificent ceremony that even those used to India found impressive. Charlotte, who had seen nothing to compare with such pomp, was overwhelmed. The Maharajah crossed the Sutlej with his escort and rode into the British encampment on his elephant surrounded by his own household cavalry. The British had turned out in all their unsurpassable ceremonial best to show their allies how things should be done, but had reckoned without the volatile natures of their guests and almost had a fight on their hands.

So large and immaculately drilled was the display of troops lining the route, and so crisp and warlike their movements when presenting arms, that a general impression of aggression was planted in the minds of the Sikh soldiers who did not relish being hemmed in by thousands of well-armed men. A certain amount of edginess crept into their expressions as they closed in on their ruler. Their unease increased as they moved further along. The shouted commands ahead and behind, the smacking of rifles against hands in unison, the bands playing martial music, the awesome colours of regiments famed for their conquests in India fluttering in the breeze, the British officers in the dread scarlet jackets that many believed gave the wearers superhuman powers (why else would men wear such garments in the heat of India?) and the ranks of horsemen on magnificent tall beasts that stood as still as those sitting astride their backs gave such an impression of superior might that all flavour of friendship seemed to have gone from the occasion.

Into the tumult of roaring officers and N.C.O.s, stamping boots, swords scraping against scabbards, pulsating drums in the bands, and bugles ringing out calls to arms, it needed only the first few thunders of artillery embarking on a royal salute to convince the Sikhs they had been led into an elaborate trap and were about to be annihilated. With sudden ferocity they drew their weapons and prepared to defend their ruler to the death.

The British carried on in their inexorable manner even though more than one private said to himself, *Gawd, they're goin' to cut our throats* and several officers licked their lips and thought *By jove, they look as if they mean it!* The sepoys took no notice. If Allah decided it should be so, it was useless to panic. They were great believers in leaving decisions to Allah—or whoever took his place in their religions.

The dangerous moment passed and the Sikh leader, a shrunken, debauched old man with only one eye, was greeted by Lord Aukland and his staff in true diplomatic style used by the British for years—deference with an air of superiority. In impressive uniforms encrusted with gold, and cocked hats covered in feathers the staff officers all seemed twice as tall as the Maharajah in his plain dress and turban, but he had been an iron ruler of the Sikhs, as viciously cruel and tyrannical as any of his brethren, doubling his kingdom and building an army trained by European mercenaries like Colley Duprés that was second to none but the one he was presently visiting. The British did not underestimate him and respected the alliance that kept their border safe under his friendship. Had they been able to see into the future they might not have undertaken the task they were set upon in an effort to further win the friendship of the Sikhs. Within a few years they would be bitter enemies in two wars to settle the ownership of the Punjab.

After the ceremonial came the displays of martial arts in which the British executed brilliant manoeuvres to dazzle those watching. One reckless high-spirited cavalry officer led his men in a dashing charge straight at the Sikh audience, pulling up when only a few yards short of their terrified faces as they scrambled to their feet. He wheeled his horse, grinning beneath his giant moustache and muttering *That gave the bastards a damned good fright,* but he soon stopped laughing when confined to his tent for the rest of the celebrations, and had to be content with the lewd accounts of his friends who had no sympathy with him in his forced abstention.

The Sikhs had their turn next and managed to take a little wind out of British sails when it came to ceremony and manoeuvres. Their army was trained by Europeans and, therefore, quite disciplined, and if it was restricted to simple drill movements, they were carried out with an air that surprised and impressed those watching. Where ceremony was concerned, what they lacked in spit and polish, regimentation and inbred flair for timing and organization, the Sikhs made up for with pure unadulterated ostentation.

The ladies of the British party had been invited to sit in the shaded enclosure with all the high-ranking officials. Ranjit Singh had a fondness for English ladies in their absurd bell-shaped skirts, and was forever fascinated by the reverence with which they were treated by the white men. In his endeavours to discover how they accomplished such sway over the superior male, he mixed socially with them whenever possible and, as Lord Aukland's two unmarried sisters were with him in Ferozepore, it was possible to invite quite an assemblage of the pale-cheeked creatures. The Sikh leader's own erotic interest in females—to the extent of having a corps of mounted amazons to perform for his pleasure—was famed over India, yet the haughty covered women of the British who had their menfolk bowing before them, earned his great admiration. It was as big a mystery as the famous scarlet jacket!

It was due to this that the ladies took to boats to cross the Sutlej for this display of renowned Indian pageantry. But also of great interest was the fact that Lady Scott and Lady Lingarde would both be present, and a great deal of discord had arisen because of it. As the wife of Sir John, who was on the staff of the Governor-General, Anastasia Lingarde took precedence over Felicia Scott on such occasions, and much anger was felt between the others attending that a Russian should be allowed to queen it over an Englishwoman of equal rank and beauty—especially at a ceremonial between two nations preparing to go together to war because of Russia's greed.

No one bothered to hide their bitter resentment, and those who felt most strongly about the subject were now not even speaking to those ladies who counted themselves friends of Anastasia Lingarde. The whole issue had grown out of proportion, perhaps due to the stress of the coming departure of the men, but some were now implying that Anastasia had been behind Sir John's opposition to the invasion plan, as was her son, Richard. Others even went so far as to suggest that she was an agent of the Czar.

Many of the men admitted that they felt Sir John would have been wiser to leave his wife behind on this occasion, and Lord Aukland should have insisted that he did so. But the Governor-General's two sisters, both superior and intelligent women, went out of their way to treat Lady Lingarde with every courtesy and friendship, so bitter feelings had to be officially put aside and gossip confined to the privacy of tents.

Even so, there was speculation on how the two beauties would compare on this occasion, but since it was a morning display, convention demanded dress of modest nature, and both wore pale silks with shady hats that put them equal in the fashion and beauty stakes. But there was to be a reception on the night before the army departed, and that would be the real testing time, all the women knew.

Charlotte, as daughter of one and daughter-in-law of the other, took no part in this particular gossip, of course. She had seen little of Richard since their nocturnal quarrel two nights before, duty having claimed him for long hours at a time. But it had given her a chance to get to know Anastasia better, for her mama-in-law had spent as much time with her as possible talking about everything under the sun, especially the hospital situation which was dear to both their hearts. It was Anastasia's description of the battlefield after Waterloo that put the first faint fears into Charlotte's mind. Although she told herself she was being fanciful, they would not disperse, no matter how hard she tried.

But the prospect of seeing the Sikh procession was just the thing to take her mind from morbid thoughts, and she went off happily with Richard when the boats came across the river for them. They pulled into specially constructed ghauts where sepoys stood waiting to assist them ashore after their short voyage. Richard climbed out and extended his hand to his wife, laughing at her fears that the boat would swing away before she was safely out of it. He who had spanned torrents with bridges saw no fear in climbing from a boat, and he teased her by saying she would have to jump in on her own on the return journey, for he was required elsewhere. He was still teasing her, and holding her tightly against him as they climbed the bank, when a voice hailed them.

"Good day, Lingarde . . . *Mrs* Lingarde."

It was a smooth voice with a bubble of amusement in it, and it made her legs turn weak. It was the first time she had come face-to-face with the man since the night he had kissed her, and she could only look back at Colley Duprés' dark challenging eyes with a face that felt frozen and bloodless. He was in the full glory of crimson and silver with a white turban decorated by a flashing order in diamonds and rubies. Standing before him as Richard's wife, knowing what she now knew of him, was one of the most degrading moments she had ever known. She could now read the secrets in his eyes, hear the true meaning of the smooth tone of his voice, and recognize his derision when he had said there was no more virtuous man in Meerpore than Richard.

"This promises to be exciting, does it not?" he commented. "Felicitations, by the way, on your nuptials."

"Exciting, if one cares for the wail of native bands and the smell of elephants," said Richard with strange coolness. "But, of course, you are used to such armies, Major."

"Yes, experience is a valuable asset—as I am sure you will agree when you have acquired it, Lingarde." He turned to Charlotte. "How are you enjoying these hectic days of a soldier's life, ma'am? I warned you in Calcutta, that this might happen, did I not—and many things besides?"

In two seconds she was past him as if he were not there, walking with a back so rigid it could have snapped with ease. The pulse-beat in her ears was so thunderous it drowned all other sound. Never had she cut anyone in that fashion, although she knew such a thing had been done by haughty high-society ladies with ease. For her, Charlotte Lingarde, it had been the hardest thing, yet the only thing she could do.

Richard came up to her with long strides. "*Charlotte!* Good God, you cut the man direct!"

She marched on with a set face, wishing he would keep silent, wishing he were not so well-mannered, wishing he were not so . . . so . . . good! He would not then be the butt for men like Colley Duprés.

"*Charlotte!*" cried Richard gripping her arm to halt her. "You will listen to me. I have never seen you so lacking in composure, except . . ." He broke off looking keenly at her face. "Except on one other unforgettable occasion," he said slowly. He was frowning and flushed beneath his tan. "You will tell me what possessed you to behave in such a fashion. If Duprés has offended you I shall demand his apology."

He was making things worse, for she could only imagine Colley laughing in Richard's face at such a request. She tried to walk on.

"There is nothing . . . I do not care for Major Duprés, that is all."

He held her back. "That is no excuse for such drastic ill manners. Besides, I have seen you treat him with the greatest civility in the past. What has he done? I demand to know!"

A storm was beginning to gather inside her. "*Richard!*" she hissed urgently. "I wish you will stop making such a fuss, in public. It is of no importance."

He flushed even darker, and grew more aggressive. His fingers dug into her arm. "It is of the utmost importance, and you cut him in public. You are in a state of the greatest agitation—trembling and pale—yet you would have me believe it is *nothing?* I tell you, Charlotte, if a casual word from that man has put you in this state, I have a right to know why . . . *and you will tell me.*"

Desperately aware of the other passengers climbing the bank in their direction she tried to lie her way out of what had become a disastrous situation which Richard was treating with uncharacteristic forcefulness.

"I was feeling ill after crossing the water."

"I do not believe a word of it," he snapped. "But, even were it true, I could not have my wife cutting someone who is my superior in rank without a note of explanation and an apology. Are you prepared to write such a note to him? *Are you?*"

To her horror tears began to gather on her lashes, and she lowered her head so that Richard would not see them. "Do not insist that I apologize . . . or him. Richard, *please,* it is a matter that I cannot explain . . . oh, do let us go on, for we are drawing eyes in our direction. *Please,* do not put me through even more public distress, I beg you."

He gave in, but reluctantly, it appeared. "Very well, we shall leave it for now. But when I mentioned that man's name two nights ago you grew upset—oh, no, I have not forgotten that night, even though my head was not too clear. I mean to know what is behind this, Charlotte, so be ready to tell me the truth when the time comes. It will not be the first time I have had cause to confront Duprés . . . and this time I shall make certain there is not the whole of the Officers' Mess looking on! For the rest of this morning I shall ensure that we avoid him."

Having no doubts that he meant what he said about demanding the truth, Charlotte began the day in something like despair. Daunted by the knowledge that he would march away and leave her alone in two days' time, this recent change in him was almost too much to accept. He had become aggressive and domineering, treating her like . . . well, not the way he had always treated her before. As the time for parting grew nearer he grew more moody, snapped answers at her, found fault with everything she did. His embraces were much rougher and less comforting. He was no more her dear, gentle Richard . . . neither was he the most virtuous man in Meerpore! Two more days and she would be alone. Richard had agreed to retain the bungalow and had hired two bodyguards to ensure her safety. The thought of such loneliness filled her with dread, but nothing would persuade her to move back into her father's house, so she had no choice. Surely Richard would not make his last two days with her as miserable as this morning had been? But the sights that passed before her soon after made her forget her misery, for a while, and revel in the pageantry of India.

The cavalcade began with a long line of elephants covered in cloths of silk that hung almost to the ground and decorated even their trunks, with only holes for their eyes. These panoplies were richly embroidered with gold thread, and the elephants' toe-nails were painted with gold leaf. The howdahs each contained a youth of outstanding beauty, clothed in Indian dress that glowed with jewels. One was a study in emeralds, another in rubies, yet another in diamonds, all as weighted down as the others, since the precious stones covered the cloth with hardly a gap between. The men watching knew the boys were another of Ranjit Singh's vices, but the ladies admired, in all innocence, the many handsome sons of the Sikh ruler.

Following behind the elephants came the Maharajah's personal bodyguard wearing gleaming steel helmets and chain mail jackets over their vivid tunics, and riding small capricious horses caparisoned in long pointed cloths of scarlet and yellow. Those two colours were predominant throughout the procession, the cavalry being uniformed in silk tunics and loose trousers of the same hues.

All the horses had shabraques of elaborate design beneath saddles high in the pommel and beautifully tooled with gold and vivid colours, and Charlotte thought them and their riders a stirring sight as they passed in a great seething mass of glittering spears and rippling golden banners.

There was a detachment of Akalis—maniacal fighters through generations past—in high pointed blue turbans encircled by quoits, and silken coats that blew in the breeze. They were a law unto themselves, these men, and rode with supreme insolence before the men of the Company of the White Queen.

The infantry, in scarlet tunics, blue trousers and turbans, marched past barefooted looking very smart and quite happy without boots to smack upon the hard earth.

It was all much less precise than the display mounted by the British, with the bands setting up a cacophony of brass blowing that wilted the European ear, and miscellaneous salvoes from artillery with no apparent meaning, but it was a glorious, glittering, exotic surge of men and beasts that could only be achieved by eastern tribes to whom *might* meant thousands in number and excess of everything.

The British officers were impressed, despite themselves, but the seasoned campaigners reserved judgement until they had seen the Sikhs in battle, and Richard commented to his neighbour that he would like to know how well they could throw a bridge across a chasm or undermine a fortress.

Charlotte was a little overawed by such hordes of tall, fierce, brown-faced warriors, and secretly felt glad Richard would not have to face the Afghans, if they were at all like the Sikhs. Her apprehension for Tom was very real, however, and she glanced across to where he sat beside Amy.

Already, the day of parting was so near to lay a heavy hand across her heart, and now she realized how far her quarrel with Amy had driven her and her brother apart. He only exchanged the plainest greetings with her these days, and the two couples never exchanged visits. Tom and Richard remained the same towards each other—as men always managed to do under such circumstances—but their friendship had had limits set upon it. In a moment of infinite sadness Charlotte wondered if she would ever regain her brother's love, and reflected once more that affection was a very elusive commodity. If Hubert had still been alive . . . but she had Richard in his stead and must not dwell on sad thoughts of that nature when she had but two days before being deserted by them all.

By a cruel twist of duty rosters Richard was Officer of the Guard that night, and engaged very heavily in entertaining Sikh chieftains to dinner and a firework display the following evening, from which he returned in a deep depression in the early hours. Charlotte pretended to be asleep, the fear of his broaching the subject of Colley Duprés being greater than the need to snuggle against his reassuring strength.

On the last evening before the Army of the Indus marched off, a grand reception was to be held as a farewell to the dignitaries and officials of both sides. Soon after midday rain of monsoon proportions began falling and it was not long before Richard was sent for to give advice on the best way of draining the ground surrounding the huge tent. Having been out on duties all morning he had hoped to attend to his personal equipment as soon as possible, then have a quiet hour or two with Charlotte before further social duty that evening. Cursing quite audibly, he instructed his servant to check that everything needed for the morrow was in perfect condition, kissed Charlotte briefly, then went out into the torrents with a black expression.

She was left in the tent surrounded by all kinds of instruments and trappings that appeared to be necessary for an engineer on the march. With a slight feeling of guilt as she watched the soldier servant begin piling the items into groups whilst ticking a list, Charlotte realized her short marriage to Richard had left her no time to discover much about his duties as a military man. No time—or no inclination? She now realized her knowledge of what he did was very hazy. Whilst the others seemed to be practising martial arts he had been at his table with books and maps, lost in study, and it was natural to suppose he was not expected to be very active. But, if that were the case, why was he taking two pistols and a great number of bullets; his own sword and that which he had told her was his grandfather's; a stout knife of native design; and something that looked remarkably like a small iron anchor at the end of a coil of rope?

So worried was she by the sight of such aggressive weapons it was the first subject she tackled when he returned drenched to the skin and legs plastered in mud. He was not in the best of tempers and answered her questions very curtly.

"How can I fight without weapons? Have you forgotten we are mounting an invasion, which is not likely to be accepted without resistance?"

His words frightened her. "I thought *you* would not be expected to fight."

He stood with rain dripping from his hair, and the tips of his fingers as they hung at his sides.

"I am a *soldier*, Charlotte."

"But . . . but you do not practise sword–drill like the cavalry, and I have never seen you fire a rifle at the targets."

A hint of savagery entered his voice. "You have not seen me as anything but a . . . Charlotte, I sometimes wonder if you look at me with your eyes closed." He flung out a hand in an angry gesture. "I do not gallop about whirling a sword above my head like the cavalry because that is not my rôle— but I can run a man through, if necessary. As for shooting, have you really never read the inscriptions on a dozen trophies in our home? I am accredited the best marksman in northern Bengal. Can you be unthinking enough to imagine engineers build bridges, survey hostile territory and blow breeches in fortifications while the enemy stands by giving them their blessing? *Of course we fight!*"

For a few seconds he stood looking at her with pain and desperation in his eyes that were normally so dreamy. Then he moved towards her.

"We have so little time, Lottie, and there is so much . . . *oh damnation!* How can a man talk to his wife when he is a walking waterfall?" Leaving her staring he walked behind the screen to strip off his saturated clothes, aided by his bearer.

A sudden coldness that had nothing to do with the wet Bengal night filled her from head to foot. The things he had said had no trace of reassurance or consolation in them. Was he telling her there *was* a chance he might not return—ever?

"I wish you had not to go tomorrow." It was a chilly echoing sentence he apparently felt needed no answer. She heard the rustle as he rubbed himself dry and donned the shirt his bearer would hold ready for him, and the grunt as he eased himself into the skin-tight overalls so that they fitted without a crease. The reception was due to start around now, and he was late. All his thoughts must be on getting ready to join her, already in her pale lavender gown.

But suddenly his voice came from behind the screen, making her tense nerves jump. "I must tell you I have asked John Preston to help you with any serious problems you might have, and you will find any of the Meerpore officers at your service while I am away. Unfortunately, my father and Mama must return to Calcutta almost immediately, but if you should ever need anything from them you must not hesitate to let them know."

He continued speaking about his father's heavy commitments and his concern for his mother, who looked so exhausted, asking Charlotte to write regularly on his behalf, and all the while she grew colder and colder. The day had been threatening and unreal from the moment she had awoken. Richard's equipment piled all over the tent put a warlike, masculine emphasis on the morning, his absence all afternoon had left her prey to fears, and now he was wrenching himself from her with frightening pitiless sentences. As if

· 173 ·

that were not enough, the leaden skies and pelting rain made the interior of the tent as dark and comfortless as limbo—as if all light had already gone with Richard's imminent departure. Only now did she really realize it *was* going to happen, that she was going to lose him, that tomorrow he would ride away into the distance leaving her completely bereft.

Then he came round the corner of the screen, fastening the hooks of his high collar, clean, neat, pale hair gleaming in the lamplight. It was no different than it had been on many other formal occasions, yet she felt a curious intense ache begin in her breast as she looked at his fine figure in blue and scarlet dress uniform. Suddenly, that uniform had become the trappings of a warrior, suddenly she saw a man who was physically splendid about to go off to offer his youth and strength on the altar of sacrifice.

The feeling was so shattering and unexpected she could only stand and gaze at him as he came towards her, grappling with the tight-fitting collar. But something about her stillness must have transmitted itself to him, for he glanced up at her, abandoned the collar, and came forward, the muscles in his throat working.

"Lottie . . . oh, Lottie," he breathed. "You look beautiful tonight . . . *beautiful.*"

She was amazed to notice that his hands were shaking as they lifted hers to his lips, and she looked up into his eyes with breathless awakening curiosity.

"I shall never be beautiful," she whispered to this exciting stranger. "Just a small brown sparrow."

His bright head bent so that his mouth could travel the smooth curve of her neck and shoulders. "If you are a bird, my dearest love, you are a lark who sings a man so sweet a song he soars to heaven with her."

Catching her breath with the wonder of his words and the incitement of the soft, kissing caresses on her bare shoulders, she put her hands up to curl her fingers into his shining hair.

"Richard, I . . . I wish we had not to go tonight," she whispered, marvelling that she had not noticed before the depth of changing colour in his eyes that rivalled his mother's for vividness.

"By God, you do not wish it more than I," he vowed fervently, pulling her against him in a movement so sudden, her heart leapt with a message she had previously ignored.

"I have tried to be patient. I have waited . . . Lottie, this is the eleventh hour. I want you with all my . . ."

The moment was shattered by hearty voices outside calling Richard's name and urging him to be quick.

"Hell and damnation," he groaned in despair. "The Devil take Harry Mortemore for his ill-timed arrival. God, was duty ever more demanding than at this moment?" He held her away and spoke of mundane things she could not instantly absorb. "The ground is like a mire, so we have arranged waggons to take us all to the marquee. Ours is outside, and we have no choice but to go."

It was too sudden. The budding emotion was suspended at the critical moment of unfolding, and remained within her as an ache that heightened every aspect of that evening. Suddenly, it was real. The morrow would truly take Richard from her, and she would be all alone again. Tomorrow, the brave young men were going to war; their women were being torn from their arms.

All through that journey in a jostling waggon with three other couples, Charlotte was silent, sitting close to Richard. Phrases like *laying down his life for his country and gallantry in the face of the enemy* spun around in her head. She remembered all Lady Lingarde had told her about the battlefield after Waterloo, she thought of Pottinger surrounded by Persians—one Englishman against a horde—she recalled that poor Captain Summerford, who had been savagely murdered in a fort six months ago. Those weeks of Richard's comforting protection had ended. Reality was upon her. *The eleventh hour*, Richard had said just now, and it truly was.

The driving urge to burden herself with emotion turned the social gathering into a noble farewell to those knights of chivalry in scarlet jackets, who laughed and drank with brave nonchalance on the eve of danger. But for many others, the main interest and drama of that evening was the confrontation of the two beauties of Anglo-India who, at a glittering formal occasion such as this, would be put very severely to the test. All the ladies had had gowns especially made for the evening, and hardly had there ever been such a dazzle of satins and jewels covering bosoms full of envy, pique, and pure hatred as the marquee gradually filled up.

Charlotte watched and felt the tension for a unique reason. She knew most of those present were championing Felicia wholeheartedly and that, in some strange way, there was more at stake than merely proving who was the more beautiful of the two. For herself, admiring one tremendously and now despising the other, there was also more to this ridiculous charade than beauty, and her mood of extremes set her throbbing with anticipation as the guests arrived one after the other, and the general tension rose.

But when Sir Rastin Scott and his party arrived an hour after the commencement of the *soirée*, the buzz of speculation rose to an overwhelming gasp of relief. Felicia Scott, the incomparable, had done the impossible! Amidst that gorgeous throng of colours and gems, she walked in looking superb in plain black velvet of the severest cut and style that made her much-envied creamy skin look unbelievably beautiful. Without a jewel in sight, the only adornment she had was a spray of blue camellias fastened in the elaborate swathe of her coiffure—flowers that no one could guess by which method they had been obtained and kept fresh for the occasion.

The effect made every other woman feel overdressed and decorated like one of Ranjit Singh's "sons," and their only consolation was that Felicia Scott had undoubtedly won the crown that night and the sight of Anastasia Lingarde's face when she arrived would compensate for all else. This Russian defeat augured well for the coming invasion, and it would teach Sir John a little more diplomacy where his wife was concerned.

So avid was the eagerness to see the downfall of the foreign "queen" that the reception did not seem to settle into the normal relaxed groups, all eyes watching for the first sign of the arrival of the main party. Charlotte had to acknowledge that her own mama had undoubtedly created the sensation of the evening, but knew who would be the reigning queen of Anglo-India, as far as she was concerned. How well she remembered that overheard conversation on the budgerow when Colley had said the thought of Felicia and Anastasia becoming mamas-in-law was highly stimulating. During their few meetings at the camp they had both treated each other with unaffected pleasantness, with no suggestion of being rivals, but Charlotte had seen immediately that Anastasia's beauty was more in her volatile personality, her many expressions, and her most unusual eyes. Felicia was physically more perfect . . . but Charlotte remembered that morning when the powder and colour had not been applied.

With the mood of sadness that was upon her that night, Charlotte found sympathy welling up inside her for the woman everyone awaited with such malicious impatience. In the bizarre situation she found a comparison with her own feelings on the night of Tom's engagement party, when she had known she would be on show and certain to fail.

So it was, when the main party eventually arrived, causing a ripple of anticipation from those nearest the entrance, Charlotte found her throat tight with unshed tears for Anastasia Lingarde who was on her own against the whole assembled company. But the ripple slowly died, and there was complete silence as the Governor-General and his large following of attendant staff filed into the stifling atmosphere under canvas. When Charlotte saw the reason for the complete silence, the drama and import of that last evening reached a peak within her, and she felt she would burst with emotion. It was courageous, completely breathtaking, and undoubtedly the one thing that would be remembered in the minds of those attending that reception. It would become a legend long after the coming years had fashioned the great land masses into nations of completely different natures.

Anastasia Lingarde was a Russian, and that was how she attended a reception where Sikhs dressed as such, and English people wore their own style of clothes. In a three-quarter dress of cloth-of-gold over a full-length one of flame-coloured silk, with long floating sleeves and a jewelled belt around her tiny waist, the tall, slender figure glided in with all the stateliness and dignity of her ancestry. Her golden hair hung to her waist at the back in a series of long braids, whilst a jewelled pill-box headdress, with flame-coloured chiffon that passed tightly beneath her chin to drape over her shoulders to the length of her hair behind her, completed the image of a princess of the boyars. With her golden skin and upslanted brilliant eyes she presented a beauty that challenged anyone to pretend she was anything but just that.

Hardly able to articulate her words, Charlotte glanced up at Richard, and whispered, "She is absolutely magnificent!"

"Yes, yes . . . she is," he replied, his eyes, so like hers, bright with embryo tears, as he watched his mother being presented to the high-ranking Sikhs, who were completely enchanted and amazed by beauty that combined the exoticism of the East with the commanding dignity of western women. Anastasia Lingarde had answered and silenced her critics!

Being the wife of a mere subaltern threw no heavy burden on Charlotte other than smiling graciously at the Sikh officials when all the English ladies were presented. The important guests, however, remained in a special enclosure encircled with crimson ropes, doing their duty with skill and diplomacy that was suffering a little under the strain of so many other such evenings and occasions whilst on the banks of that river. The Scotts and the Lingardes were there with other high-ranking dignitaries, and Colley Duprés, that friend of princelings and sirdars, was naturally also there.

For Charlotte there had been one paralysing moment when the Major, standing beside Felicia, had caught her glance and bowed. She had turned away immediately, but her legs had remained rubbery for a long time afterwards, and she had been glad Richard had not seen the incident. He had, unfortunately for her, been dragged from her side some while before by a staff officer who said Richard's interpretive skills were needed in the main enclosure. With a look that spoke volumes, he had apologized to her and gone off to obey a summons that could not be ignored. She had been left with his fellows, who did their best to entertain a young woman who was well and truly married, hardly beautiful, and obviously wishing to be with her husband on his last night. She hardly said a word to them, still caught up in the tempest that had been aroused in her by all that had happened that evening. It was gathering in force by the minute, and, by now, she was almost aching with it.

So it was not surprising that, when the natural movement of groups brought Tom and Amy nearby, Charlotte knew she could not let her brother march away without giving him her prayers and blessing. Seeing her wistful expression, he excused himself and came across to her with the diffidence each had adopted since the quarrel with Amy.

"Good evening, Charlotte. Are you enjoying the spectacle?" he asked lightly.

Her eyes filled with ready tears. "Tom, you cannot go off without . . . I had hoped we could . . ."

Seeing her distress he offered his arm. "Shall we go outside for a moment? It is devilish hot in here."

His kindness only increased her heavy sadness, and she walked blindly beside him into the darkness where planks had been covered with sacking and drugget to make a rough verandah along the longer sides of the marquee, where an awning was pegged to protect walkers from further rain, if it should come.

"It is going to be fine tomorrow," remarked Tom nodding at the stars that had now appeared. "I see poor Richard was soaked to the skin today trying to get this place suitable for elegant guests."

She looked up at him quickly. "You do still speak, then?"

"Oh, yes . . . but we shall have much more opportunity in the coming months." He paused and turned an unhappy face towards her. "We have been friends a long time, Richard and I."

"I know," she said miserably.

"Charlotte, it would have been splendid if . . . I mean, there was no one I would rather had married my sister than Richard. I was certain he would make life better for you than it had ever been, but this stupid business . . . I'm deuced if I can make it out. You have never been a girl to be spiteful, and Amy is the one female with whom you should have a close bond. But it is you who will not kiss and make up, Amy tells me, and I do not think she would lie over it." He

· 179 ·

sighed heavily. "If you would but tell me the cause of the quarrel, I am certain I could mediate."

Knowing she could never tell him the truth, she tried to brush it aside. "I have no quarrel with Amy. It is just that we are different kinds of people."

"Stuff and nonsense!" he replied spiritedly. "You have always got on with other females well enough. I will admit that Amy's temper is a little hasty, but she is most generous with apologies." A slight flush betrayed his knowledge of her generosity in making-up after a quarrel.

He took his sister's hands and swung them back and forth with awkwardness. "The thing is, Charlotte, Amy is *enceinte*."

She was almost shocked. They had been married so short a time—only as long as herself and Richard. "Oh, Tom, what a thing to happen!"

"I think it is the most wonderful thing in the world," he said with hot defence. "It is just that I wish it had not happened just as I am going away. It does not make our parting any easier."

His pleasant face, normally full of happy enthusiasm, was clouded by the shadow of responsibility, and Charlotte's poignant mood that night led her to say, "Dear Tom, there is no need to be anxious, Mrs Shilton is at Meerpore and will do everything that is necessary for her daughter. She is a sensible, competent woman. It is not as if she was like. . . ."

"Felicia?" finished Tom for her, then took the bull by the horns. "You never visit my father's house now. Has your quarrel with Amy something to do with your mama?"

Her throat began to thicken. "Amy is the best person to answer that." She put a hand on his arm. "Tom, I am sorry if you have been unhappy—but I have been even more so, believe me."

He looked up sharply. "Unhappy—with Richard?"

"No, oh no. He has been my rock to cling to, but when he goes tomorrow I shall have no one."

"Then why cannot you and Amy support each other," he pressed eagerly.

In her present mood she could not send him off without

some kind of assurance, some olive branch. "I will undertake to do anything to help her during the coming months, if she should need me. And if you wish, I will write every week of how she goes on until the baby is born. You will surely be back soon after that event."

"Yes, of course." He kissed her heartily on the cheek. "I always knew you were the best of sisters. It will all work out, you see."

"Yes," she agreed swallowing hard. "Now go back to Amy. She needs every moment of your company tonight."

His nod was brief. "The same applies to you. I shall rescue Richard, whatever the nabobs say, and send him out here to you."

After he had gone she fought the flow of emotion saying goodbye always brings, and walked along the makeshift verandah, feeling the breeze drying her cheeks. The stars looked so far away, so infinitely remote. They shone down over Afghanistan. Dear Lord, after tonight she would be beneath them alone. There *was* no one else to look after the parcel! Hearing footsteps approaching, she turned quickly.

"Oh, Richard, I am so thankful. . . ."

Colley Duprés stopped several feet away and looked her over from head to foot. The study was insolent, fiery, and supremely challenging.

"I am not the gallant Richard, as you see."

Shaking violently she turned to go, but he gripped her arm and forced her back to face him. "No! You have cut me twice in public. I wish to know why."

Looking at him with contempt she cried, "I do not *have* to speak to men like you."

"Yes, you do—for the sake of your honest, upright husband. Unless I have given you cause for such treatment—in which case, you tell him so that he can manfully demand satisfaction from me—you will accord me the same breathless civility you have always shown. What has occurred to make you turn away with palpitations and wide eyes from someone you have always treated with suppressed admiration? I recall the warmth of your welcome on my return on the night of the Spring Ball."

That smooth arrogant voice with overtones of mastery was all she needed to complete the unfulfilled physical ache that whole evening had aroused. Highly emotional after her parting with Tom, she found it impossible to stop herself from throwing daggers of her own hurt as hard as she could at the man who had caused her so much disillusion and anguish.

"*Suppressed admiration!*" she cried bitingly. "What a vain peacock you are!"

He laughed, but with a touch of anger in it. "So marriage has put some spirit in you, has it? Well, you have not caught it from *him*, for I have heard it is more of a friendship than a marriage."

"You *dare* to speak of friendship when you abuse it in so monstrous a manner," she flung at him, ignoring the taunt about Richard. "She told me you were a friend—of Papa's also—and I believed it. Oh yes, I believed that," she added in icy fury, "and put your cavalier manners down to the fact that you had spent so much time with native armies. I also believed you were a man of courage and integrity. How could I have known, at that stage, just what you really were?"

"And what am I?" he grated out, gripping her arm tighter.

"A soldier of fortune in every way. You might have strength and a certain kind of courage, but integrity is not a word you understand. You *sell yourself* to the highest bidder," she said, leaving him in no doubt of the contempt she felt for that. "You do not care whom you hurt or betray so long as you achieve your goal—and when that happens, you ride off leaving those you professed to serve to take up their lives as best they can." The agony of her emotion had her swaying back and forth, and husky with the force of her words. "Beneath that ridiculous fancy costume you are a jester who makes the fool of everyone, a traitor to all those qualities that make a man a gentleman."

He gripped her other arm, holding her a few inches away from his dark, angry face in helpless immobility. "Just what are you really trying to say?" he demanded in a voice no one had ever used towards her before.

"You and . . . and *her!*" It came out in choking agonized words. "My father—your own superior and supposed friend—you humiliated and betrayed him beneath his own roof. You and *her!* While we travelled from Calcutta . . . all that time you . . . you are both *despicable*. I will not acknowledge you . . . or her . . . ever again—adulterers! *Adulterers!*" she repeated on a sob.

With unexpected speed he turned into a highly dangerous adversary. Charlotte gasped when he pulled her roughly into a dark recess on that verandah, and shook her without mercy.

"*Mon Dieu!* What a righteous little prig you are. A pillar of the church, defender of purity and saintliness! How dare you behave in this manner you selfish little orphan of ignorance! Has she not suffered enough without being treated to a ridiculous exhibition of virginal piety by a child who knows nothing of the needs of a woman? I should have done this long ago, for it is plain that young fool who married you has not yet plucked up the necessary virility to achieve it."

The exhilarating pain of bruising strength as he held her arms behind her, forcing her body against his, re-awakened the flowering of sexual desire that Richard had brought into bud earlier that evening. But Colley's mouth set her throbbing in every limb as it drew up from deep within her the heady rush of full summer without waiting for spring.

As his mouth left hers to travel down across her throat, she shivered and sighed with complete surrender; as his teeth bit against her bare shoulders she pressed closer against him, gripping his upper arms with convulsive delight; when his lips reached the soft rise of her breast above the dress her body began to move insistently against his, yearning for the relief she must have from the unbearable ache in her thighs.

"*Colley, Colley,*" she whispered, begging for the final capitulation.

It was then he let her go, pushing her away with such force she was thrown against the rail along the makeshift verandah where the flambeaux highlighted her shocked, panting body at the moment of her greatest weakness. His dark eyes were cold as he looked her up and down. "Before you

· 183 ·

point your virtuous accusing finger again, you should remind yourself that you are also a potential child of the Devil, *Mrs* Lingarde!"

He strode off leaving her shattered, holding one of the wooden uprights.

Richard excused himself on the grounds of his wife's sudden indisposition shortly after he found her where Tom had said she was waiting for him. Although she had recovered sufficiently to speak to him with reasonable coherence, it was more than she could do to go back into that marquee now. It was only necessary to tell Richard that saying goodbye to Tom had upset her too much to be able to stay, and he acted at once.

Commandeering one of the waggons he carried her to it in something of a triumphal fashion, then held her tightly against him as it jolted and jerked through the camp towards their tent on the outskirts. He said nothing to her, but his close proximity tormented her aching body, and all she could think was that she could very easily have betrayed him a few moments ago. She *was* a child of the Devil.

On arrival, Richard carried her into the tent and dismissed the servants with brisk authority as he set her on her feet before him.

"I do not think you need a servant to undress you, when I am quite capable of doing it," he said in soft tones, and turned her around to unfasten the hooks down the back of her dress.

"You are fever-hot," he murmured, and swiftly bent to kiss her shoulders as the dress slipped to the floor. "Dear God, this is the moment for which I have waited so long. You are alight with longing."

Swept by the pain of her unfulfilled desire she leant back against him, sighing as his kisses covered her shoulders and throat, moving her palms against the strength of his thighs in the tight-fitting trousers.

It was more than he could stand. With something between a sigh and a groan he lifted her against him to walk with her behind the screen that protected the sleeping area from lamplit silhouettes visible to passers-by outside. Burning like a man in fever himself, Richard tore off his jacket and the last of her petticoats before lying her on the blankets beside the frail camp-bed, and dropping down beside her to take her naked body into his arms. His strength was that same strength she had just felt, his mouth as demanding. The caresses, the biting, seeking lips were there once more, and his hands travelled feverishly over her limbs that trembled with the ecstasy that had been denied her just now. There was no gentleness, just complete mastery that grew and grew until she was actually crying tears of joy as she gave everything he demanded, and drove him to demand even more.

She was beautiful—no brown sparrow, but a bird of paradise. He was enslaved, yet the enslaver. He was possessing her now, turning that ache into an agonizing rapture that rose within her like a great mountain as he climbed the heights with her, step for step.

"*At last, at last!*" he cried in triumph, and she knew, for certain, that she was a child of the Devil, as she moaned her surrender. Then, at the moment of supreme final commitment, his name burst again from her lips.

"Colley, oh *Colley!*"

She was suddenly brutally abandoned; cold and alone. The mountain began to crumble with a great roar, and she felt as if she were falling into a bottomless pit where no other person would ever find her. Fighting and struggling against fear she came to the surface of reality to open eyes that were drenched with tears.

Scarcely comprehending she saw a vague figure standing over her as she lay on the blankets. The faint glow of the lamplight behind the screen sheened his fair hair like a halo.

"*Richard!*" she whispered, aghast.

Next minute she was dragged to a sitting position by hands that dug into her shoulders and shook her savagely so that her head rocked.

"Has he been your lover?" he demanded with laboured sobs. "Answer me!"

Mute and terrified she was conscious only that the tears making a path down her neck and on to her left breast were warm against the chill that now filled her.

"*Answer me!*" he roared, and a palm came in a stinging blow across her cheek, and then again. "What is between you and that lecherous dog?" He shook her violently again, like a man possessed. "I shall have the truth from you, I swear."

Shocked out of passion as she was, it was a waking nightmare. The dim canvas surrounding her was strange and bizarre, and the numbness brought on by the blows on her face made her unsure where she was or whom she had been with just now. But there was no let up from the brutal attack.

"You are hurting me," she cried, as Richard's grip on her shoulders tightened until his finger-nails bit into her flesh.

"Hurt you? By God, I will break you," he swore in harsh panting tones. "All the time I have been holding back thinking you a timid, unawakened child, you have lusted after *him*. I should have known, should have guessed when you acted so strangely each time he was present. You were a virgin bride, so it has been since then. When did he first become your lover?"

"Never!" she whispered. "Never, never, never."

He struck her again across the cheek, "You are lying."

"*No!*" The brute he had become had stopped her tears, and almost stopped her heart.

"Then why . . ." he was fighting against overwhelming emotion to speak at all, ". . . . why is it that the first time I take you as I should have taken you from the first, you must pretend . . . pretend that I . . ." His voice broke completely, and he flung her down before going to stand by the screen, gripping the top and bowing his head against the lacquered wood in an attitude of complete hopelessness.

Something inside Charlotte broke. Terrified of him, trapped in this canvas cone, naked and humiliated, she clutched at the blankets in a feverish attempt to cover herself, and it all spilled from her like a torrent.

"He said I was a brown sparrow and she was a bird of paradise. He laughed—said the garrison was expecting a beauty and would get a . . . a Bible-thumping blue-stocking." The memories were too clear, they began to hurt as much as they had then. She rocked back and forth clutching the blankets to her cheek which burned from the blows that had rained upon it.

"I tried to show him . . . I tried to show them all that they were wrong," she cried desperately, "but they all laughed. You were the only one who did not—the *only* one."

He stood still, bowed and unmoving against the screen, and it was all the more imperative that he should understand. Her voice rose, and her tears flowed again—but tears of despair, this time.

"On the night of the ball he came across the room straight to me. I was the last person to see him go, and I thought he . . . dear heaven, I thought he was . . . *claiming* me that night. How could I know . . . you have no idea what a female feels when . . . when she knows she is not beautiful or desired." The recollection of her romantic dreams, so impossibly ingenuous, added to her present humiliation. But she had to tell it all now to this man in order to drive them away forever.

"The next morning Amy told me the truth," she said with rising hysteria. "It was so cruel I can never forgive her. All the way from Calcutta . . . beneath my innocent eyes . . . they had . . . they had played their vile game. *They* are the lovers!"

For a minute or so she sat with the blanket pressed to her mouth, her body quivering convulsively, staring at the man in the attitude of crucifixion.

"I could not stay in that house with her—that same house where she had . . . been with him. But I had nowhere to go. There was no one to whom I could turn . . . except you. Since then I have tried not to speak to her or to him—you know that. But tonight . . . tonight . . . out on that verandah he came and . . . and . . ."

Her voice faded into a terrible silence, and she looked up at him through eyes puffed with weeping. Then, he turned to her, face haggard and white in the flickering lamplight, and dark hollows for eyes.

"My God . . . *my God*, have you any idea what you have done to me? You have taken my whole life. For you, I gave up my freedom and the right to shape my own destiny. I surrendered the privilege to follow my own ambitions and desires, to seek far-off goals. I sacrificed my independence, my friends, and the pleasures of a bachelor. I have shared with you my name and everything I possess in the world. All this, *until the day I die. It is forever!*"

He stood so still, the voice coming from an apparent statue was all the more shocking. "Did you never for one hour, one minute, one second, give a thought to *me*? While you made your escape from your whore of a mother and that decadent charlatan who would sell his soul, yet by whom you are still infatuated, did it never occur to you that I was human? Did my deep love mean so little to you you did not even notice it?"

She was now as still and tense as he. He had vowed to break her, and was doing it with his every word now. She felt as cold as death.

"You have used me in the most heartless way known to women," he went on, in almost a whisper. "You have taken everything and given nothing in return. You have accepted my love and devotion, and yearned all the time for a man who mocks and despises you." He picked up his cloak and jacket. "You have stolen my life, and destroyed any feeling I have ever had for you. We are now tied forever in a limbo that will only end when one releases the other in death."

After he went out into the night she sat clutching the blanket, staring at the spot where he had stood, arms spread against the screen in an attitude of agony. The night wore away; the lamp guttered and died. She sat with shiny streaks on her face where the runnels of tears had dried, and her skin grew icier. She did not notice dawn break, or the birds begin to sing in the glorious blue promise of day.

Suddenly he was there before her, in full marching order with sword and gun-belt around his waist, water-bottle slung across his shoulder. His face beneath the shako was ashen.

"We are off," he said in a voice that came to her as if from a ghost beyond recall. "Before we left Meerpore I put my affairs in order. If I fall, you will have everything I own both in England and Russia, plus all I would have inherited. Have no fear, my family will accept my widow into their bosom with unreserved generosity, and love her as they think I do."

He turned and raised the tent flap, pausing in the bright triangle of sunlight to say, "Let us hope, for both our sakes, this war will prove to be long and bloody."

The tent flap fell behind his retreating figure, and Charlotte heard the distant commands of an army marching off.

· eight ·

THE BENGAL DIVISION of the Army of the Indus marched off a fortnight before Christmas 1838, knowing there was a long road ahead. Before Afghanistan they were charged with entering Scinde in an endeavour to win back the allegiance of the rulers to the puppet Shah Soojah, whom the British were championing. Alexander Burnes, now knighted and promoted to Lieutenant-Colonel, was posted ahead to buy the support of minor chieftains and smooth the way for the troops heading for Hyderabad, where it was hoped the sight of sixteen thousand armed men would encourage a bloodless surrender on the part of the influential Amirs.

Going to Hyderabad added another twelve hundred miles to an already formidable journey and, since it had been decided that the army must, in the main, live off the land they hoped to conquer, a vast herd of cattle was added to the tail of the fighting column and great numbers of camp-followers were added to those already engaged in order to cut grain, mill it into flour, and cook bread for thousands as they went along. Others were to pick fruit, slaughter the cattle, collect eggs, wring the necks of chickens, and make goat-cheese. Added to the grass-cutters, general cleaners, water-carriers, and pack animal drivers, *plus* their wives and families, the long line that straggled after the scarlet snake of soldiers numbered some thirty-eight thousand souls.

In view of the immensely long march to Kabul orders had been issued requesting the officers to limit their personal baggage to the minimum, but they were not fools when it came to personal comfort and, prepared though each one was to endure pain and hardship or lay down his life if necessary, there did not seem any point in roughing it when a dozen extra camel-loads would ensure them a few luxuries, at least. From all they had been led to believe it would merely be a triumphant procession through cheering grateful crowds, all the way to Kabul, and bottles of claret and a supply of good cigars to round off an elegant dinner in the Mess were surely essential. A few political wallahs like Colley Duprés "croaked" about hostile tribesmen and violation of agreements, but everyone knew they had "gone native" to a great extent and could not give a balanced opinion any more. As for Richard Lingarde and his engineer colleagues, it was well-known that their heads were so stuffed with facts and figures they made complications out of the simplest decisions—they were so busy with calculators and diagrams the Infantry had marched past before they knew it.

The departure of the Bengal contingent that dawn, therefore, was an impressive affair that took a matter of two hours to accomplish. Even after the last martial notes of the regimental bands had faded, and the last camel had lurched off squealing and protesting at the load on its back and the prods of the driver, the dust did not settle until well into the day. Those left behind felt desolate, and low-spirited as they surveyed the marks left on the ground by tents, cooking ranges, and horses. The sounds of an army remained somewhere in the zephyr blowing across the empty fields, like the sighing spirits of all those human souls who were destined never to see India again, and it did not seem possible they had gone.

The soldiers were high-spirited enough, however, and stepped out with enthusiasm, many of them convinced they would eventually come face to face with the Russians somewhere in Afghanistan. Promotion and glory were awaiting them, and if they should die it would be in a noble cause.

But one man riding with the soldiers that day was a mere shadow. He could ride forever and never feel more tired than he did then, he could face any foe and never feel more thoroughly defeated, he could fall for the sake of a hundred noble causes, but the one life he had had was already lost beyond recall.

For the first day or so Richard was mercifully numbed with shock, moving, eating, acknowledging his friends with automatic gestures. But feeling began to return and, when it did, he found the burden intolerable and resorted to drink to regain the numbness. As he rode, as he gave out orders to make camp, as he consulted maps and distances, he could see Charlotte's face in the distance, streaked with tears as she broke him apart; he could hear that ecstatic name *Colley* just as he attained what he had thought to be his ultimate possession of her. He felt once more that drive to strike her again and again until the word was beaten out of her mouth forever. The echo of that man's name lambasted his head with humiliating repetition until he felt dizzy and sick; the memory of her body that had been beautiful a moment before then treacherous in its nudity filled him with contempt.

Like the knives that had turned a fine man like Edward Kingsley into a pile of bloody rags, that one word had turned a timid, hesitant, beautiful creature into a naked slut in a bawd-house whose body had been used by others. The mere thought of her, of the weeks they had spent together now seemed empty and degrading. His pride, his self-respect, even his virility had been mocked by the sound of that man's name on her lips. Yet, she was like a great stone tied around his neck. For the rest of her life she would flaunt the title *Mrs Lingarde* and enjoy the comfort and protection it brought her.

At first he drank himself to sleep so that memories would not mock him during the welcome rest periods, but he soon found the long hours in the saddle gave him too much time in which to think, and took to carrying a bottle wherever he went. It was not surprising that his insobriety and the black temper it produced quickly became a subject for discussion amongst the other officers. They began avoiding him. But he was not aware of the true situation until Tom appeared at the entrance to his tent after they had made camp some five or six days after setting out.

"Ha, I thought I would come and smoke a cigar with you," he announced too heartily. "Or accept a glass of your excellent wine," he added with a pointed look at the bottle beside Richard's camp-bed.

In no mood for company, especially the brother of his wife, Richard remained where he was staring at the pointed canvas ceiling.

"Have you any objection, old fellow?" asked Tom undaunted.

With his head pounding Richard murmured, "There is an uncorked bottle of wine in that crate in the corner. The cigars are in the box on the table. You may take both with you as you leave."

Tom sat on the folding chair. "You only become quarrelsome in your cups, Richard, so I suspect you have had a bottle or two before that one." He leant back and studied his friend. "It is *they* who are allowed to go into a decline on parting, you know. We are supposed to be made of sterner stuff. I confess I am confounded at the way in which you are behaving."

Richard drew in his breath and said with quiet anger, "Then take your confounded self from my tent and leave me in peace."

Tom bristled. "Now look, my only reason for being here is because the other fellows are a little tired of seeing you mope around the place like a moon-calf—a love-sick girl. Quite a few of us have left our wives behind, but *we* are men enough to accept the situation. Are you so . . ."

Richard turned to look at his visitor, but Tom's face kept changing into Charlotte's, then Colley Duprés', and back to his own again.

"Get out!" he roared. "Get out before I hit you."

The blurred image stood up. "All right, make a fool of yourself, if that is what you intend, but I will tell you this,

Richard. That is not the only thing that is being said . . . and I do not care to hear the words 'faintheart' and 'false patriot' used in connection with a friend—at least, a man I thought was a friend."

Richard turned his leaden head on the pillow. "Damn you, I ordered you out once, Tom," he said with utter weariness.

"They—some of them—will not forget your dual blood, Richard, and you are playing straight into their hands with this. They will let no one forget you are half-Russian, if it seems advantageous to them."

With sweat on his brow, and the certainty that the wine he had just consumed was about to return in the most unpleasant manner, he rolled on to his side and demanded hoarsely of the whole world, "Where is justice—tell me that? I am suspect, yet he claims Russian, French, and God knows what other blood in *his* veins. He changes allegiance according to the price, and consorts with every villain who smiles his way. Yet *he* is the hero, and I . . . oh God, I am . . . I am . . ."

From somewhere in the sky came a disembodied voice. "Richard, *Richard*, are you all right?"

It was three days before Richard emerged from the fever that laid him low and caused delirium. He had been carried on a *dhoolie* during that time, and it took another three days before he was fit enough to pick up the threads of his professional life once more. Then, his weakness was replaced by cold dedication to work that prevented any form of relaxation. His rest periods were spent making diagrams and topographical surveys of every camp-site, plus a feverish study of Persian at advanced level. The other officers found him brusque and uncommunicative.

Tom was obviously still uneasy, but pretended nothing was changed and quickly stopped referring to those left behind in Meerpore. Richard was grateful, and the two young officers returned to something approaching the friendship they had enjoyed before marriage had split them up. They discussed the aspects of the campaign for hours on end, and argued over the detour they were making to Hyderabad,

Tom finding his friend very aggressive, as did everyone else, those days.

"Do you not think it is foolhardy enough to carry into Afghanistan an exiled king who is universally disliked by his subjects, without marching hundreds of miles out of our way to force his enemies to recognize him?" demanded Richard for yet another time. "What right have we to interfere in Scinde?"

"In for a penny in for a pound," quoted Tom gaily. "Think of the treasure to be captured in Hyderabad . . . and our share of the booty," he added slyly.

But the booty was unclaimed. Sir William McNaughten, in one of the first clashes between politicals and generals that marred the campaign, stepped in with unequivocal orders to leave Scinde and head for Afghanistan without further ado. The matter had been settled by diplomatic pressure and armed strength was not needed. The disappointed and puzzled troops were turned from their goal and marched off towards the Bolan Pass with nothing to show for their wanderings.

Richard was extremely angry, and made no secret of his opinion on the way the campaign was being conducted. The Bombay contingent of the Army of the Indus had arrived in the Scindian port of Karachi and was marching up to join them but, since neither general knew where the other was, it was going to be a matter of luck if they happened to meet before arrival in Kandahar, their first objective in Afghanistan. Richard claimed that too many people were running about on spurious errands while the wretched soldiers were worn down by excessive and unnecessary marching.

"Political officers are galloping all over the country in wild attempts to enhance their reputations, whilst we are changing direction at their slightest whim," he complained heatedly to Tom. "This is a military campaign which should be controlled by generals. Here is Sir Alexander Burnes dashing off to appease the Chieftain who controls the Bolan Pass and its surrounds—which should have been done long before this— a fellow called Eastwick is busy in Hyderabad bullying the Amirs, McNaughten is countermanding our orders left, right and centre, yet I have just been told to make a topographical survey of our new route to the Bolan Pass because it seems no one saw fit to reconnoitre the ground we are to cover. People like Duprés are paying lakhs of rupees to wily chieftains who treat them to feasts and native women, whilst the poor soldier is left to cover mile after countless mile on foot." He flung down his shako and ran dusty hands through his hair whilst Tom looked glumly at him from the chair.

"I tell you, Tom, they are so confoundedly obsessed with their own importance they have no notion of any army's role in such a campaign. One would not believe they were, a lot of them, military officers once. I grant they are excellent fellows in the main—Pottinger, in particular, for his action in Herat—but the military should be credited with the knowledge of how best to take themselves from A to B—and the best route from Ferozepore to Kabul is *not* via Hyderabad!"

"We all know that now," said Tom with depression. "Here we have been on the move for two months and are not a step nearer Kabul than we were when we set off. I, for one, would as soon have stayed that time with my wife. What say you?"

For answer Richard picked up his shako and went out into the blazing sun towards his own tent without a word. He spent the drug-hot afternoon poring over calculations and references until he was drenched with sweat and his head was ready to burst. It was the conviction that disaster was certainly ahead that fired his blood with angry heat, not the wasted time he could have spent with his wife. He would gladly march the length and breadth of this great continent if it gave him good cause to remain away from her.

Within a few days Richard was kept fully occupied in the construction of a bridge of boats across the River Indus which was wide and swift-flowing. For the engineer officers it was a challenge they met with great skill and whilst the column halted for a week or more, the sappers felled trees, sawed planks, forged nails, manufactured cables from a sisal-type grass and rounded up enough boats to anchor at regular intervals across the rushing water, under the direction of their British officers.

It was complicated and taxing work supervising such an operation, but Richard threw himself into it with all his considerable talent for his profession and gave no let up. It was what he loved doing and he did it supremely well. He stood on the bank often ankle-deep in mud, giving directions to his men, going out on a raft to inspect the lashed beams or the firm anchorage of one of the boats—it needed only one to break away whilst being crossed for the whole construction to collapse and swing in the current. He walked around beneath the sun supervising tree-felling, rope-making, and the collection of stones to act as anchors for the boats, sometimes lending his own hands to demonstrate how the work should be done and encouraging the sepoys who did good work. They grinned and worked the harder, for Lingarde-sahib was well-liked by his men. He never asked them to do anything he would not do himself and his punishments, like his praise, were always well-deserved.

The work went well, and all the officers were proud of the bridge when it was finished. From the natural resources of the countryside they had forded a river with a road of planks that must be stout enough to bear the passage of around fifty thousand humans, the same number of pack-animals— mostly camels—heavy artillery, ammunition and baggage waggons, and the heavily-laden cavalry. If some of the camp-followers had their doubts, the engineers had not. They knew it was first-class.

Richard stood on the bank gazing at the completed bridge with a heavy heart. It was finished, and he was exhausted. Against the advice of his fellows he had watched every minute of the construction, sweating heavily in the constricting scarlet jacket and fighting lethargy as his brains almost melted beneath the tight black shako, but he had put *himself* into that piece of engineering. For eleven days he had sublimated all other thoughts beneath the need for work; now it would be hours of riding and marching for day after day when the body ached and the mind was prey to thoughts designed to destroy him. For hour after sun-soaked hour he would return to the torment of facing the truth of his life, the humiliation of knowing he had been used as a substitute for another man's passion, that despite all he had striven to achieve in his short life he was regarded as nothing against a swashbuckling middle-aged voyeur who owed his success to no more than a smooth tongue, a good seat on a horse, and a gigantic self-assurance.

In the echo of such sexual and physical failure he heard far too often the doubts of his courage in battle ringing in his head. He saw the natives in the villages through which they passed, and hatred was in their eyes. These people did not hesitate to mutilate and torture others in ways that made an Englishman sick with revulsion. When the time came he prayed to be killed outright—as did any man in this army— cleanly and decently. With that prayer ever constant in his mind, would he find himself holding back or leaving his friends to be hacked to pieces while he stood away to organize the scattered remnants of a company? Engineering was something in which he excelled; in all else he appeared to be found wanting.

For some time he stood riding out his black mood watching the swirling water gliding past and under his bridge that now seemed a futile attempt to prove something to himself, then he pulled himself together and slowly turned back towards the encampment. His tread up the embankment was slow, his eyes on the ground just ahead of his feet. He looked up quickly, therefore, when a pair of tooled sandals, slim brown ankles and the hem of a bright *sari* appeared before him.

She was small and beautiful, with large dark eyes soft with concern.

"Richard—sahib."

A surge of pleasure and disbelief rushed through him from the pit of his stomach.

"Luana!"

Her tranquillity calmed his churning thoughts and tense muscles, so that his eyes smiled into hers with the light of past pleasures shared with mutual generosity and esteem. "What are you doing here? You are not a vision, are you?"

"Please?"

How well he remembered that lilting questioning word whenever he perplexed her with his conversation. Suddenly he wanted her, wanted to draw her against him in a display of virility that would subjugate her and prove, unquestioningly, his own ability to hold a woman in thrall. Overwhelming desire for a renewal of that past satisfying relationship thickened his throat as he asked, "What are you doing here? When I passed the village, you told me you were living with your brother now."

Her lashes lowered, but there was no hesitation from her. "My brother comes with the army as *dhobi*. I come also."

He knew what she was telling him, and it increased his longing for this girl of brown beauty who had made his uncongenial life in India bearable.

"It was wrong of you to come with your brother," he told her urgently. "There is great danger ahead." He put his hand against her back and moved slowly along the green riverbank, taking her along with him away from the curious eyes of those near the bridge. "You must go back home. I will hire someone to escort you."

She kept her lashes lowered, but there was a softness in her voice that charmed him with its overtones of sensuality. "I came with my brother because you are here. I shall stay, Richard-sahib."

Under a shady tree he stopped and held her by the shoulders, facing him. The warmth of her dusky skin was against his palms, and he thought, yet again, that he had never seen such complete beauty in miniature, from her worshipping, uptilted face to the feet he had kissed many times on their more erotic nights of passion.

"Luana . . . I am married. Such things are not possible now, you know that."

She stood meltingly submissive beneath his hands and smiled, as she always had when knowing his resistance was low.

"The Memsahib is not here . . . and you have great need."

He swallowed, but said as firmly as he could. "It is different now. You must go home, Luana. Do you understand?"

She nodded and turned to walk from him, the brightness of her swathed Indian dress staying within his sight for a long time as the thudding protest of his heartbeat drove him back into his black mood.

Yet he drank with moderation, for once, and when she slipped into his tent soon after he blew out his lantern that night Richard let out a sigh of thankfulness that she had ignored his words. It was short, violent and desperate, her hands setting his body afire and restoring sanity to his thoughts, yet what had always left him relaxed and spent, this time turned a knife in a wound with such anguish there was wetness beneath the girl's fingers-when she stroked his face with loving caresses.

The bridge lived up to its constructors' confidence, and the entire Bengal division duly tramped or trotted along its five hundred yard length to the opposite bank. There lay ahead an unknown stretch of unfriendly country which must be crossed in order to reach the entrance to the mighty Bolan Pass, and it proved disastrous.

The meat supply driven on the hoof from Ferozepore had all been eaten during the abortive detour, and all hopes of "living off the land" as had been carelessly dictated by those in charge of supplies were soon crushed. Since no one had reconnoitred this stretch they could not know that the soil was so thin and poor as to yield hardly enough grain to feed the poor inhabitants of the villages—certainly not an army of such vast proportions—and the water shortage was even more acute.

Before long the situation was serious, and the urgent needs of the army incurred enmity between villagers and soldiers who drained wells and tanks dry in their effort to quench their thirsts and those of their beasts, besides raping the fields for supplies of grain and fodder. The camp-followers were reduced to quarter-rations, and the soldiers to half. Horses began to grow thin and ill, oxen suffered pitiably, and camels died off in hundreds because they were useless in mountainous country which did not allow them to graze.

On the tenth of March, three months after leaving Ferozepore, the advance army reached the entrance to the Bolan Pass, in a state of semi-starvation and weakness, having lost half their baggage through lack of camels to carry it. They were to lose most of those remaining whilst negotiating the pass.

Richard's first sight of the entrance to this enormous chasm seventy miles in length filled him with awesome fascination. Even his mind, trained to turn a map into an accurately contoured picture, had not envisaged anything quite like the narrow split in a towering, cruelly precipitous mountain range that suggested it might suddenly move together like a crevasse in an ice-field, crushing the travellers between walls five thousand feet high.

When they set camp he and Tom Scott made the short excursion to the entrance with a sensation of approaching the road to the underworld, and stood for several minutes just looking at what they must face on the morrow.

In order to see the sky it was necessary to turn one's head right back and look vertically up the sheer grey rock rising with unquestioning supremacy over everything and everyone winding like ants along the boulder-strewn track riven by the River Bolan in gurgling flood. From where they stood it was only possible to see ahead for fifty yards or so before the chasm twisted in another direction further into the heart of the mountain.

Tom shivered. "Seventy miles long, did you say? I do not look forward to being sandwiched between those gigantic walls for all of a week."

"More than a week, I assure you," said Richard, unable to take his eyes from one of Nature's most awesome creations. "If a river flows through there you can rely on the track being blocked quite completely at more than one point with boulders brought down by melting snows. Where it *is* possible there will, at least, be loose stones large enough to impede the progress of guns and waggons, besides parts of the track being washed away by the flow of the river." Taking his eyes away at last, to look at his friend he added, "We shall be lucky to emerge from the far end within a fortnight, and I predict there will not be as many as enter it. Water there will be in plenty, but forage is non-existent in such places. Our animals must carry their own food as well as ours—an impossibility in their weakened state—and it will take twice as many men to shift obstructions as it would if they were healthy."

"In God's name, you paint a black picture, Richard," accused Tom heatedly.

"An army going to war deserves to be told the truth. Fairy tales are more pleasant on the ear but soldiers are not small children. We have been fed fairy tales regarding this invasion, but I swear you will find the black picture I paint nearer the true one. That man Duprés has negotiated this pass in late autumn when the river is a mere trickle and when a small party of horsemen find it comparatively easy to pass through. A column of thirty thousand men with artillery and ammunition, tents and supplies traversing a way which certainly narrows to no more than several feet wide in places is a different matter altogether. In spring, when rivers are in full flood, it is madness."

Tom looked severely crushed. "I do not know how you can speak with such authority."

"I know my profession. Engineers do not fight, you know," he said with great bitterness, "We simply paint pretty pictures on maps and do vast calculations. We cannot compare with political heroes."

He remounted and rode off leaving Tom open-mouthed.

For sixteen days the column struggled, sweated and fought its way through the pass to emerge almost at the end of its tether. Each day they had set off before dawn by the light of flaring torches to face the arduous route ahead. Richard's prediction of boulders, blocked passages, and broken track proved all too correct, and the column turned into a straggle of braying, mooing, bellowing, neighing animals led by sweating, cursing men who slithered on the loose shale, cut their feet and hands on the cruel rock, and waded through the icy river more than a dozen times a day.

Where the passage was most severely blocked it took a tremendous effort to move the huge rocks by manpower alone. Richard was involved in more than one argument because he insisted that using explosives to clear the obstruction would only result in bringing down rock from above to make the situation worse, and endanger the troops. His superiors bowed to his decision, but went away grumbling about men who prattle mathematical theories when a good dose of gunpowder would do the trick.

Many animals died, particularly the camels, who were so hungry they ate a poisonous plant growing prolifically through the low sections of the pass. The numbers of sick and exhausted that had to be carried in *dhoolies* increased alarmingly, making the progress even slower. As if that were not enough, the hostile tribesmen that roamed the pass to pounce on travellers made no exception with the army. Stragglers were picked off with rifles and their animals or weapons carried off; the weak and starving camp-followers who fell by the wayside were murdered and robbed; messengers going ahead or returning to the Bombay column bringing up the rear never reached their destinations.

Anything after that nightmare fortnight would seem pleasant, and the valley leading to Quetta was enchantment itself. But enchantment had a false face. Sunshine, clean crisp air, green plains and sparkling rivers were no substitute for food, and arrival at Quetta brought the shocking intelligence that the Political Officers sent on ahead had been unable to arrange for supplies.

Colley Duprés had posted off to Kandahar, where he had friends of influence, and the Bengal contingent was persuaded to push on immediately to that city. If they must starve, better on the way to salvation than sitting in a dirty mud town within reach of the murderous robbers in the Bolan Pass. And so the men that had stepped out so bravely from Ferozepore before Christmas dragged and staggered throughout April towards Kandahar. There was not one, now, who was not beginning to doubt the noble intentions of their mission to Kabul.

The officers, better fed than the troops by dint of the fact that they had their own supplies, were nevertheless finding it hard going. Lack of forage affected them most forcibly, and many had to see an expensive charger grow thin and broken—even lame—on the journey. Richard had been unfortunate in losing a camel carrying the furniture for his tent, which had to be left in the chasm for want of a beast to carry it. He was reduced to sleeping on the ground and using the chest containing clothing as a chair or table, whichever need was most pressing. Thankfully, the tent was saved, so his relationship with his Indian mistress continued. Luana was his salvation; she restored his sexual confidence and absorbed the anger that lashed out at everyone and everything but mostly at himself. If she sensed that her role had changed, it did not show. She loved and served him as devotedly as always and, in return, he looked after her. When the camp-followers were reduced to eating fried sheep-skins to keep them alive, Luana was given a small parcel of food for herself and her brother by her English lover whenever she left him.

At Quetta it also became generally known that the march into Afghanistan was not likely to be the triumphant procession they had expected. Alexander Burnes had been right in his urgent advice to back Dost Mohammed as the rightful leader of the Afghans, for the chieftains of the territories through which they were passing spoke unanimously of the popularity of Dost Mohammed and the hatred felt by the people towards Shah Soojah, whom the British foreigners were determined to force upon them. That the tribes would oppose the army's progress every step of the way through Afghanistan was solemnly predicted. To an army of gaunt, starving sepoys and British soldiers the news was devastating. Had they not been told they were to be the saviours of Afghanistan? Had they not believed their foe to be the Russian invaders? Were they not told Shah Soojah would be cheered and fêted? Whilst anxious to cross swords with Russians they had no wish to tangle with the bestial warriors of

Afghanistan and, if they already had a much-loved and skilful king, why was an elderly exile being thrust on to the throne by people who did not even want to occupy the country?

The British soldiers grumbled as they had done for centuries, and did as they were told. The sepoys grew anxious, murmuring of mutiny and return to their homeland. The camp-followers only continued because they were afraid to go back through the Bolan Pass. The Army of the Indus was a broken one.

At Kandahar, which surrendered bloodlessly due to the desertion of the chiefs in the face of danger, the entire force rested for two months in order to recuperate and allow the crops in fields along the route to Kabul to ripen. Recover it did not. The dirty, insanitary city, the appalling heat and a monotonous diet of greasy mutton and overripe fruit soon had the half that were healthy down with dysentery and enteric fever, whilst it became increasingly obvious to all that the tribes surrounding Kandahar were a great deal more than unfriendly. Two officers wandering in the environs were set upon and slashed with knives. One managed to crawl away intending to fetch help, but the second was hacked to pieces within minutes. To Richard all the signs pointed one way, and his heated views on the whole campaign were to lead him into violent opposition with the one man who could turn him from a cool-headed professional expert into a stubborn, reckless man prepared to put his future at stake.

The direct route to Kabul from Kandahar led past the ancient and apparently impregnable fortress of Ghuznee—an immense stronghold in a commanding position, with walls eight to ten feet thick and up to forty feet high. It was the Afghans' pride and joy, and the obvious plan for the expedition was to make a detour. But the man leading the force had a fancy to capture the fort on the way.

A conference was called of all engineer and artillery officers—the experts on fortifications—plus the various political officers who gave their assistance whenever asked—and frequently when *not* asked. Feelings ran high immediately between the military men and the politicals, the former advocating the avoidance of Ghuznee, the latter pooh-poohing such timidity.

The gunners claimed it would take prolonged and very heavy bombardment to force a surrender; the sappers delared trenching would be equally lengthy, and mining a mammoth task. The other alternative was escalading with infantry—a costly operation in human lives on such a stronghold, especially if it was strongly defended. Colley Duprés, along with other politicals, declared it was not, and that was when the discussion became heated.

"It stands to reason they will have a strong garrison there," pointed out an artilleryman. "They know we are heading for Kabul, and Ghuznee is the most strategic point at which they can make a stand."

"*Zut!* Their pride and confidence lies in that great citadel. It is such that they believe no army strong enough to attempt to take it," said Colley with exasperation, having made the same point twice already. "We mount a surprise attack, for they will be expecting us to bypass it."

"And that is what we should do," said Richard in definite tones, still coldly professional, at that point.

Colley raised his eyebrows. "What . . . no stomach for a fight, Lingarde?"

Suddenly, amongst those men seated on upturned boxes, some on the ground, some standing to lounge against a tree, Richard saw only one figure, clad in the plain white Indian-style field uniform he adopted, and heard the soft, ecstatic voice of his own wife call out that name in the height of her passion.

"I do not believe in fighting for something that is *worthless*," he replied with derogatory swiftness.

Colley smiled in a humouring manner. "Worthless? You call an impregnable fortress worthless?"

"You have just now argued that we can take it easily, and at the same time call it impregnable," said Richard pouncing on the weakness of his argument. "I challenge your ability to make a reasoned judgement on this point."

It became a verbal duel between the two men, one bitter and vengeful, the other supercilious and mocking.

"I think I have rather more knowledge of the country than you, Lingarde."

"From your native friends? I wonder you put so much trust in their information. They are hardly renowned for their simplicity when it comes to intrigue—neither are they fools when it comes to fending off intruders. The cost in lives of capturing such a place will not be worth the doubtful advantages."

"There will be little cost to lives. I have it on good authority that the fort is only lightly manned."

"On whose authority—another of your native friends?"

"Gentlemen, gentlemen, this is getting us nowhere," intervened a testy major. "The point at issue is whether we should take the fortress or not."

"I beg to differ, sir," snapped Richard, really roused by now. "Surely, it is more the question of *whether it can be taken,* or not. My colleagues and I have been invited to give our professional opinions, which were practically unanimous. It would be very difficult, time-consuming, and costly in lives . . . and once taken would need a strong garrison to hold it. I cannot see any tactical advantages in taking such a place, in any case."

Colley shifted his position with negligent grace. "You are not being asked to understand the tactical nuances of this campaign, Lingarde, merely to follow orders involving your own particular skills. *You* will not be expected to seize the fort, my dear fellow. Leave that to the fighting soldiers. You have been invited here simply to advise on how best to clear a way for them. You are obviously not acquainted with the Afghan temperament. The fortress of Ghuznee is their greatest pride—ancient, symbolic of their might, and proof against any invader. The fall of this symbol of their greatness will crush them completely, and any resistance to our efforts to put Shah Soojah on the throne at Kabul will fade away on this proof of our greater might."

Roused even further by the suggestion that engineers were not fighting soldiers, and hating the man and all he stood for,

Richard lost his temper completely and faced an adversary, all else forgotten.

"An engineer not only fights, he builds bridges and blows up strongholds—skills which demand a higher level of intelligence than is required to gallop hither and thither with gifts for chieftains. Or to fill the ladies of a zenana with sighs," he added viciously. "What you have just said is the complete denial of the supposed nature of this expedition. The gentlemen of your branch of the service have steadfastly maintained that the restoration of Shah Soojah to his rightful throne at Kabul would unite Afghanistan into a strong, confident country that could resist Russian and Persian threats. Why is it, therefore, necessary to crush these 'gratefully united' people into a state of fear of our superior fighting power by capturing the pride of their country?" His blood was up and the words poured from him. "Could it be that you have all misled us? Are you confessing, at last, that we are a *conquering* army rather than a *crusading* army? Are you bringing into the open the fact that we are doing what we have been righteously accusing the Russians of attempting to do? Are you finally admitting that the Afghan people are perfectly happy with the king they already have, and are about to have thrust upon them a ruler they hate . . . all for some devious political reason for which the poor sepoy and trooper must sacrifice his life? Is *that* why Ghuznee must be stormed?"

Colley was shaken from his assurance, at last, and straightened up, narrowing his eyes with speculation. "A crusade never goes smoothly. A man should not embark on one if he cannot accept that some battles are inevitable . . . and it is well-known that you have reasons of your own for avoiding them."

"And you have financial reasons for encouraging them," Richard flashed back.

"*Mr Lingarde!*" exploded the senior officer present. "This is a tactical conference, not the tap-room of a low-class inn. I suggest you apologize and leave."

Still staring at Colley, Richard said recklessly, "I will leave in company with Major Duprés, in that case. Let it be abundantly clear to everyone present that there is more than one man here who has Russian blood in his veins—or so he claims. But there is only one who has served many masters."

"And as that man, I can claim superior knowledge on native matters," said Colley smartly, showing that he was getting angry by the tightening of his lips.

"By no means," cried Richard. "You have still not answered my questions. Now we have put all our cards on the table let us be *fully* informed and have everything clear, at least. Just why have we come into this country?"

Colley narrowed his eyes. "To settle it in peace and strength under a king who is sympathetic to *our* policies."

"Then we are going the wrong way about it," said Richard with such heat he rose from his seat and prepared to leave. "When fortifications are weak, one strengthens and reinforces them. It is of no use to reduce them to rubble and expect them to spring up invincible of their own accord. If we are asked to take Ghuznee—which we will, because our army is the best in the whole of Asia—we will find no peace and strength in Afghanistan. It will mean a long and bloody war. Think about *that* very carefully."

They thought about it, and decided to take Ghuznee. By a tremendous stroke of luck an Afghan traitor crept from the fortress as soon as he saw the British force appear and disclosed the one weakness of the fort—a gate that was practically unguarded—and the engineers stacked gunpowder bags against it under cover of darkness ready to blow at dawn, when the infantry rushed in. It was over very quickly at slight loss of life to the British force, and everyone set about telling each other what splendid fellows they were. They had been right to show the Afghans a thing or two; they were a miserable rabble of incompetent warriors who could take a tip from their well-trained expert victors.

The political gentlemen and the military commanders were smugly pleased with themselves, especially when their agents reported that Dost Mohammed in Kabul had seen the light and dismissed his army before fleeing across the Hindu Kush into exile. Hurrah, hurrah, was the cry from most lips, and it would seem that men like Richard Lingarde should stick to drawings and calculations.

Richard knew he appeared, on the surface, to be quite wrong, and suffered some further jibes from his infantry colleagues about his reluctance for battle, but nothing would shake his belief that the whole campaign was a grievous mistake. He did not have to wait long for vindication.

In early August Kabul was entered by the returned monarch, escorted into his capital by the triumphant army amid great ceremony. With bands playing, everyone in his most impressive uniform, and Shah Soojah adopting the accepted dignity of an ousted king regaining his throne, the Army of the Indus marched through the empty silent streets of Kabul watched by sullen citizens whose hatred-filled eyes gazed through the apertures of their mud houses. Not a cheer disturbed the noise of tramping foreign boots; not a hand waved in irresistible joy; not a head bowed before the monarch. The jubilant returning Shah Soojah was as unwelcome as his detested foreign supporters. The troops with orders to restrain the enthusiasm of the Shah's subjects, looked from the corners of their eyes and tightened their grip on their rifles. Far from defending the king from rapturous crowds they prepared to shoot down murderous, angry hordes.

Within a month even the most optimistic realized that the puppet king would immediately be slain by his mutinous citizens once the British left Kabul, so what had been intended as a mere "triumphal march to restore the rightful ruler to his loving loyal subjects" before withdrawing to India, became a semi-permanent occupation of a country that was a sore embarrassment to those who had no wish to occupy it. The Army of the Indus had marched in and now dared not march out again!

To this end, the Bengal division of the force was detailed to remain in Kabul until further notice. The remainder went back from whence they had come, heartily glad the duty had not fallen to them. The sepoys in the Afghan capital settled unwillingly into makeshift and comfortless quarters with the gloomy prospect of a bitter Afghan winter coming on, and no hope of seeing their families again for another year, at least.

For the British officers and the men of the British regiments it did not seem quite as bad. They were no strangers to snow and cold weather—albeit not experienced for some years—and as most of their families were in England, anyway, it did not seem a lot lonelier in Kabul than at Meerpore and the other Indian stations they had left. Even so, the prospect of treacherous villains haunting the streets after dark, a robber's knife in the back at any time, and Dost Mohammed with his horde of vengeful supporters loose in the mountains surrounding the city, ready to descend on his former capital at any time, were all great deterrents to accepting their lot with any kind of good grace.

To Richard, delay in Kabul meant delay in facing the inevitable obligations of his disastrous marriage, and he watched Colley Duprés ride back to Meerpore with the returning contingent, having finally come to terms with what had happened on that night nine months before. Those nine months of marching had seemed like a lifetime and passions had died within him now.

While Tom Scott gloomily contemplated indefinite residence in that hostile and uncongenial city of Kabul, hundreds of miles from his lively young bride, Richard acknowledged that he wished never to see his own bride again as long as he lived.

A week later, news reached him that Anastasia Lingarde had died during her return journey to Calcutta from the disease that had been slowly killing her for months.

Completely broken, Richard rode out into the surrounding hills against orders and risking attack from enemy tribesmen. He stayed out there for three days and nights, roaming as wild and independent as those boyar spirits she had hoped to join, and aware that she had said her private goodbye to him that morning knowing it would be her last.

When he rode back into Kabul, he was a changed man.

· *nine* ·

THE SPRING BALL in Meerpore was to be held by the military, as usual. The theme was one of the blossoms to be found rioting through the English countryside at that time of year. It was not very original, but the great grinning hares of two years before had not been forgotten, and the committee members found it difficult to arouse much enthusiasm for the event—or anything else, for that matter.

The atmosphere of that outlying station had altered in subtle fashion. Although new regiments had been sent up to replace those still in Kabul, a strange feeling of staleness had crept into the routine and the social programme. The cricket competition was doggedly pursued, but there was no fairhaired athletic giant to flash his bat and send the ball flying time and again with ease and grace. The races lacked the thrill of anticipation caused by a young infantry officer who rode his horse as he did everything else—with magnificent enthusiasm, but doubtful skill. Even Colley Duprés, that outrageous flirt with a charm that made people overlook his cosmopolitan ancestry, seemed to do nothing but ride back and forth on diplomatic errands and was seldom at Meerpore for longer than two weeks at a time.

The colour, the *dash* seemed to have vanished with the marching army seventeen months before. Perhaps it was that those men had had the sword of Damocles hanging over them for so long that they had acquired a bravura in everything they did, which their replacements did not possess. Or perhaps it was merely a sense of anti-climax and the presence of a large group of ladies who were living in a kind of limbo whilst their husbands were on indefinite posting to Kabul. These solo ladies were a great nuisance to the military, who wished to be rid of them but had to take reluctant responsibility for their welfare.

It was a most unwelcome situation for all concerned. The wives of officers in the new regiments resented the occupation of the best quarters by these husbandless women, and the ladies themselves resented the prolonged absence from their husbands. They had been agitating for some time for their menfolk to be brought back to India, and when told that Kabul was now regarded as a British garrison, demanded that they be allowed to go there.

Socially they were an embarrassment for, although the ratio of men to women was always badly unbalanced, a parcel of other men's wives was more unsatisfactory to bachelors than a drastic lack of partners. The temptation was there but could not be followed up! When it came to dinner-parties, hostesses racked their brains to make their numbers even in a way that would not give rise to gossip, speculation or emotional embarrassment on behalf of their guests. Yet the "Kabul Zenana", as they were called by irreverent young men of the station, could not be omitted from the social round of Meerpore. As for returning hospitality, the poor creatures found themselves tied in terrible tangles by convention, with no husband to protect them from vicious speculation.

But scandals there were, despite all that, and, although these enlivened dull routine and provided the station ladies with entertaining gossip, they made the plight of the "Kabul Zenana" even worse. The spiciest of these were the passionate "affaire" conducted between Mrs Calshott-Mayne, a ripe matron of forty-one, and a nineteen-year-old ensign who agreed to pose naked for a water-colour of the God Apollo she was painting. One thing led to another, which led to the ensign being transferred to an isolated outpost run by one ageing Company officer, where the young man most probably met with a fate worse than death!

Vying for prominence was the strange birth of a child to Mrs Scanthorpe, twelve months after her husband marched away from Ferozepore. The mother claimed it was a "delayed conception" and spoke with heated authority on the frequency of such cases in other parts of the world, but no one at Meerpore believed her. Neither, apparently, did her poor husband in Kabul, who put a pistol to his temple and pulled the trigger.

There were smaller scandals, like the case of Mrs Loosemore's habit of rushing from her bungalow at night screaming that she was being raped by half-a-dozen turbaned men . . . and there was Charlotte Lingarde whose young, wealthy and irresistible husband marched away seventeen months ago and abandoned her completely. If it was not perfectly well known that she had received no word from him the whole time he had been away, it was obvious from news in letters from Kabul that Richard Lingarde was openly contemptuous of a bride he had left after only four months of marriage.

The news healed many old wounds, and disappointed mamas hastened to add their support to the story that swept through Anglo-India and was believed by all those who were foolish or vindictive. Anastasia Lingarde, that Russian woman with the strange eyes, had been immoderately affectionate towards her son, the story ran, and had plainly held some kind of power over him that had held him in thrall to her alone. It explained his lack of interest in other females and his immense admiration for his mother. Now the woman was dead, and the evidence spoke for itself. Sir John Lingarde was a broken man who had abandoned his brilliant political career to return to England and live like a recluse on his Kentish estates, while Richard was now sowing wild oats with an extravagant and reckless disregard for his little dowd of a bride.

This attractive story glossed over the fact that the eligible young Lingarde *had* selected a bride in his mother's lifetime, but if it was mentioned at all someone soon explained that the wicked Anastasia had appeared on the scene at Ferozepore to win back her son's total devotion and break the frail bond that had mysteriously tied the handsome engineer to a quaint little creature whom no one seemed to want. Fortunately, the gossip-mongers chose to forget about the other Anastasia Lingarde.

*   *   *

Charlotte left the hospital building thankfully. Although so much had been done to improve it since the day she had first entered the low white building, it was still an odorous, unpleasant place where men lay in unrelieved agony sometimes for days. But the floors were swept daily, the urine tubs emptied night and morning, and blankets washed for each new patient . . . only because she checked regularly, Charlotte knew, but it *was* done. But the biggest triumph was the completion of the new kitchen built at the opposite end of the hospital and equipped with new cooking ranges. The meals appeared little better than before, but they were inevitably more wholesome now they were prepared away from the night-soil beds and the amputating-room.

Charlotte sighed as she reached the open air and sunshine outside. It was already nine a.m. Soon, it would become unbearable to be in those wards. With an absent smile of thanks to the syce who held her mare steady while she stepped on to the mounting block and settled herself in the saddle, Charlotte then set her mount's head towards the outskirts of Meerpore cantonment and the open plain that led to Ferozepore in the Punjab. She would not go back just yet. The days in that bungalow were endless enough, as it was, without rushing back to it the minute her duty was done.

She walked the mare, enjoying the freedom of gentle movement through the straight avenue that gave on to the wide splendid view of a plain grown green due to the waters of melting spring snows from the hills. The Hospital Mercy Group had diminished to two members—herself and Mrs Smethwyck—and the great movement for improved hospital conditions and supplies had stopped almost simultaneously with the death of Anastasia Lingarde. No one was trying to revive it, nor would it be revived until a woman of the same calibre who also had the same sphere of influence took an interest in the neglect of the army's sick.

Charlotte did all that was within her power in their cause, but admitted that it was as much for her own sake as that of the patients. Her hospital work was the only thing that had kept her from going under after Richard had left—that, and Aunt Meg's upbringing, her legacy of perseverance in the face of adversity. Strangely, mingling with those ordinary men, both black and white, had helped her to come to terms with maturity and her own place in life. The "parcel" had not been deposited with anyone else—there *was* no one else—so it had been opened up to reveal all manner of things inside that she had never suspected.

Breaking free of the cantonment buildings Charlotte kept her mare walking out across the wide exercise area. Morning parades were over, and she had the place to herself except for a distant cavalryman breaking in a frisky stallion. The hot breeze lifted her hair from her forehead and set the dark blue skirt of her habit flapping against her legs. The hem was fraying, she noted with a sinking heart. She would have to be measured for a new one soon, however much she might resist the need.

In Richard's absence she had spent as little of his money as possible, wearing her clothes until forced to replace them, eating as frugally as she had at Aunt Meg's, and keeping a minimum of servants. There was only one direction in which she did not practise economy, and he could not accuse *her* on that score of taking anything from him.

Looking across the distant plain that was already beginning to swim with heat-haze, she tried to picture her husband and failed. Always the memory hung in the distance, unwilling to approach, refusing to be recognized. She had written two letters to him since he left, and received none whatever from him. She had not really expected an answer to her words of sympathy and genuine sorrow on the death of his mother, but she had believed he could not ignore the news that he had a daughter, safely delivered and named Anastasia, as she believed he would wish. For some months now she had lived in hopes that the reply had been delayed on its journey, but finally had to acknowledge that Richard had rejected his child as totally as he rejected his wife. That little Anna, as she was called, had been conceived on that fatal night of parting was no fault of the child's, and Charlotte burned with possessive

· 215 ·

anger that overrode all other results of that terrible farewell.

She was well aware of the gossip surrounding herself and Richard, and would have been deaf if she had not heard the "asides" referring to the shocking excesses being practised by some officers in Kabul, including one who appeared to be making up for lost time with a vengeance. Having grown almost immune to emotional pain she survived the barbs and sly pity of others, putting all her love and protection around her child who was the only good thing to come out of her journey to India. That love and protection had increased when a cholera epidemic had taken a great number of children, including Tom's son of five months, yet left Anna untouched.

But Amy's grief had been so great it had completed the healing of the breach between the sisters-in-law, and Charlotte's pity for a bereaved mother had led her to "share" her own baby with the girl who had been the indirect shock cause of Anna's existence.

Through that new relationship Charlotte learned the news of those still isolated in Kabul because of the need to protect Shah Soojah who was to have ruled over a settled and united Afghanistan. Tom wrote to Amy as he had always written to Charlotte, in dramatic, exaggerated style, putting his thoughts on to paper as rashly as he voiced them and forgetting the recipient was unlikely to follow the military and political intricacies of the situation. Fortunately, Charlotte could and explained it to Amy as simply as possible.

If Tom mentioned anything about Richard Amy never read it out. But he sent personal messages for Charlotte, which Amy passed on, and for herself, which she did not. So Tom could be commenting on Richard's behaviour along with everyone else. Charlotte did not face her sister-in-law with it, and Amy always behaved as if nothing was amiss. The red-haired girl had learnt the lesson of inner pain herself and become more understanding.

Amy was at the bungalow when Charlotte returned from her ride, playing with Anna as the child sat amidst piled cushions on a cotton blanket spread upon the floor.

"Have you noticed that she always picks up the blue block first?" asked Amy, looking up as Charlotte entered the room. "That surely indicates intelligence at such an early age."

Charlotte smiled faintly. "I think it is because the blue one is slightly smaller and therefore easier to grasp."

Amy shook her head in disbelief. "You are the only mother I know who does not think her own child is perfection itself."

"I know another," said Charlotte without thinking, then to cover her words swiftly bent to scoop up her baby and kiss the soft cheek with acute tenderness. "I do not wish you to be perfect, my dear," she whispered against the downy head. "Just *loved*."

The bearer brought cool drinks with unerring timing, and the two young women sat in long chairs with their feet up beneath the swaying *punkahs,* Charlotte still holding the baby against her.

"You do look so tired, Charlotte," commented Amy after a minute or two. "I am certain that hospital work is wearing you down. Can you not abandon it? All the other ladies have, except for Mrs Smethwyck."

"All the more reason why I should continue," returned Charlotte, relishing the cool lemonade, the movement of air caused by the *punkahs,* and the heaviness of her growing child as Anna lay against her breast playing with the buttons of her blouse with chubby fingers. "I cannot leave poor Mrs Smethwyck to cope with it alone, after all these months. Besides, I enjoy helping those poor men down there. You have no idea what it is like for them."

"Nor do I wish to have," said Amy smartly. "I fear I have to admit you were right when you told me at my engagement party that I would not be seen on a battlefield for all the riches of a nabob."

Charlotte sat quietly for a moment or two, while the swinging *punkahs* squeaked with a slow, monotonous rhythm.

"Did I really say that?" she asked, at length, thinking of

how she had stood at the end of the verandah determined not to let Tom's friend witness her in tears after her disastrous performance before the bachelors of Meerpore.

"That, and a great deal more . . . all of it quite true, you know," came the answer. Then, after a pause, "If you had been a matron you would have been dubbed eccentric and loved on the spot. It was because you were so very young that we all resented being told that we were shallow, frivolous creatures."

Charlotte gave a bitter laugh. "The wisdom of the world at seventeen-and-a-half, that is what I thought I had." She turned her head to look at the other girl's vivid face, sharpened by sorrow but still very pretty. "Do you know, Amy, even the sepoys down there know more of wisdom than I."

Amy looked away through the half-lowered tatties to the other officers' bungalows along the neat row. "Put a sepoy in an English village and he would be completely lost. I think you should not belittle yourself so, Charlotte. There are not many females here who would have come through these past seventeen months as you have. It cannot have been easy."

Unable to sit still after such a comment, Charlotte got to her feet, cradling Anna against her as she also gazed out at the row of identical bungalows.

"I saw the *dak* horses had arrived as I passed the Guard House."

"A day early!" cried Amy, rising quickly. "Why did you not tell me the instant you came in?"

Charlotte forced a smile as she turned to her sister-in-law. "It takes at least four hours before anyone attempts to distribute the letters, my dear girl, and that is a long enough process in itself. If there is word from Tom you will not be given it until after tiffin, you know."

"*If* there is word from Tom? Of course there will be," was the cry.

With a swift kiss for Anna Amy snatched up her parasol and left in a flurry of skirts. But Charlotte was left standing by the window, knowing her only link with those in Kabul was the sight of the *dak* horses that had brought the letters on their last stage of the journey from that wild country. Her arms tightened around Anna, and she whispered against the baby's soft head, "Papa is very busy, dearest. He has a great many important things to do. But . . ." her voice thickened as she brushed Anna's hair with her lips, ". . . one day he will *have* to return . . . and he will love you as deeply as I. *I swear it,*" she promised vehemently.

Kabul, capital of Afghanistan, was no more than a poverty-stricken sprawl of rudimentary flat-topped houses in sun-baked brick, the inner city consisting of a maze of filth-strewn alleys that were too narrow to allow sunlight to penetrate their dim meanderings. The haunt of vengeful citizens, human flotsam, and uncleared garbage, the city was also regularly hit by minor earthquakes which were prevalent in Afghanistan. Yet the soil was extremely fertile, and the wealthier citizens owned beautiful gardens, the inner court-yards of their unprepossessing homes being a surprise and delight to the unsuspecting visitor. But the one vivid gem in a dull city was the great Kabul bazaar, renowned throughout the country for its fantastic display of merchandise of every possible kind, and the hub of trade for all foreign merchants who brought the riches of their countries to offer the customer. The din of the normal bustle filling the alleys between stalls was soon increased by soldiers and camp-followers from the invading army, excited by the delights to be found, and bent on souvenirs to take back for families and friends.

The commanding sight of Kabul was the enormous towering battlemented palace known as the Bala Hissar, residence of the Amir, his court and his favourites. Fortunately for the occupying force, the situation had made it imperative for them to be quartered within the fortress which, standing high on a hill above the city, enjoyed the fresh, exhilarating air of such altitude.

As the weeks of occupation had worn on, much of the initial pessimism and depression had vanished. The citizens accepted the inevitable, and tentative overtures of friendship were made between conquerors and conquered. The British leaders and instigators of the invasion of Afghanistan began to lean back and dazzle themselves with their own brilliance.

Titles and promotion laurels were handed out to Sir William McNaughten, who had dreamt up the plan, to Lieutenant-General Sir John Keane, commander of the Army of the Indus, for the taking of the impregnable fortress of Ghuznee, and to Brigadier Robert Sale for leading the storming party. Lieutenant-Colonel Sir Alexander Burnes was appointed British Resident, Assistant to McNaughten, who was to be known by the glorious title "British Envoy and Minister to the court of Shah Soojah-ool-Moolk, Amir of Afghanistan". The remainder of the officers, troops, camp-followers and military hangers-on who had tramped, fought and suffered during the nine-month journey stayed as they were.

Since Kabul offered little by way of entertainment the British, as was their custom, instigated their own. It was not long before racing was underway, with band-concerts, theatricals, the inevitable tent-pegging, game-shooting, and cricket following in natural sequence. When the winter began the British invaders earned their first real respect and admiration from the long-robed, fiercely independent Afghans, but in an unexpected and not totally flattering way. As invincible warriors they had been greeted with sullen resentment, but when they donned ice-skates and glided gracefully over the frozen lakes, the watching Afghans gazed with awe upon such wondrous and magical skill.

Another of the British officers' skills, neither wondrous nor magical, had quite the opposite effect. The ladies of Kabul found the pale-skinned gentlemen in scarlet coats quite as beautiful as their conquerors found them and, the Afghan men being overwhelmingly homosexual, seized every opportunity to enjoy the delightful bounty while it lasted. But the Afghans had a dog-in-the-manger attitude towards their women, and many breasts burned for the moment of vengeance which they knew would come. The fact that the worst offender of all was the British Resident, Alexander Burnes, did not help the standing of the white men one jot, and the orgies held by him and his close cronies grew wilder and more reckless as month succeeded month and everything seemed quiet on the battle-front.

But, although Dost Mohammed had fled to Bokhara, where his supposed haven was verging on imprisonment by the chief who fancied ruling Afghanistan himself, and his vast horde of supporters in the surrounding hills would not move without him at their head, there was no sign that Shah Soojah was growing any more popular or making any attempt to rule his subjects. A mild man, as Afghans went, the puppet Amir seemed content to run his court in the Bala Hissar and remain within its protecting walls. Indeed, he was too terrified to let his protectors leave, for Afghan rebels under the leadership of various chieftains were constantly attacking outlying forts held by tiny British garrisons, which suggested that the nation had not yet settled into the peace the British plan had claimed to bring. In addition, the Russians finally made their suspected attempt to gain territory by launching an invasion across the opposite frontier of Afghanistan in a bid to seize Khiva. The force perished almost totally in the icy terror of a plateau swept by winter storms.

It was seen to be essential to maintain military might in Kabul and, since the Amir was agitating for his zenana and family to join him from India, it was necessary for the troops to have a cantonment before they were ousted from the Bala Hissar by several hundred women and children. Work began on a permanent home for the Kabul garrison just outside the city. Those detailed to supervise the erection of the cantonment never knew who had masterminded what they considered to be the greatest piece of short-sightedness and crass stupidity they had yet encountered, for the chosen site was a patch of swamp towered over by hills to the north and south, and surrounded by orchards that restricted the view all around the area. Worse, the commissariat and arsenal were to be situated in a small fort a quarter of a mile beyond the cantonment perimeter in full view of a dozen or more similar empty forts easily accessible from the hills. The site was defenceless and indefensible.

There was an immediate outcry from engineer, artillery and other junior officers, who pointed out not only the inadequacies of the site but the very real dangers in terms of defence. The cool response was that the garrison was merely one of occupation, not aggression, and had no need to defend themselves from those they were administering. Loud and long the arguments between military and civilians continued, growing more bitter and insubordinate until promising careers were at stake. Then, like Alexander Burnes, everyone felt it wiser to bow to the inevitable and give his support to higher authority which refused to bend. Only one man stood his ground: Richard Lingarde.

But the senior military officer at that time, Major-General Sir Willoughby Cotton, was the same general who had been visiting Meerpore on the evening Richard had had his quarrel with Refford and Colley Duprés. Cotton had a good memory for faces, especially those of intractable subalterns, and in view of that disgraceful affair in Meerpore, the outspoken and cowardly attitude taken by the young man over the taking of Ghuznee, the Lieutenant's dissolute behaviour in Kabul, and the removal from the scene of Lingarde's two eminent and influential parents, the confrontation soon ended in a court martial. The accused was relieved of any command during the building of the cantonment, and lost two years' seniority.

The first was due to expediency, since the young engineer had stubbornly declared he would have no hand in constructing a death-trap, and the second was not too harsh. Since Lingarde was wealthy enough to buy any rank he wished when it became available for purchase, it simply meant others would be offered the opportunity first. But the court martial itself would do his career no good, and it was also generally felt by the administration in Kabul that a stern eye should be kept open where that particular lieutenant was concerned. He was going to the dogs and needed steadying up before it was too late.

The court martial made no noticeable difference. Everything Kabul offered the British officers was seized by Richard. His love of athletic pursuits was exercised to the full. Abandoning his linguistic studies and engineering manuals he raced his various horses with such disregard for life and limb some of his fellows began refusing to enter if he was riding in the same race.

He hunted wild life in the environs with the same recklessness, shooting any creature that moved or flew and riding back to his quarters with his "bag" slung across his saddle like so much bloody skin and feathers.

He took up the sport of tent-pegging, and was soon beating lancer officers, which made him very unpopular. Similarly, he upset the artillery with his marksmanship, which he displayed in challenges to anyone who would take them up. He fired at targets, empty champagne bottles, cigar-tins, even coins. But when he proposed a competition to shoot apricots off a beggar-boy's head, no one would take up the offer. He did it, just the same, earning the disgust of some and the secret admiration of others. He earned the boy's total hero-worship, which he did not want, and celebrated his success by getting drunk on raw spirits and making the boy as paralytic as himself by sharing the liquor with him.

Indoors, Richard was equally energetic. Joining in and instigating some of the wilder capers of junior subalterns, he soon gained as doubtful a reputation as on the outdoor field. His wealth allowed him to gamble with high stakes, and his gaming partners were soon reduced to those who were richer than or as reckless as he. He drank very heavily, even by military standards. Although he never grew aggressive or objectionable in his cups, it was almost as if he viewed those around him with contempt, which seemed worse.

Only when it came to women did he appear to draw the line and leave the Afghan beauties alone. But he had his Indian *bibee* living openly with him, despite several strong recommendations by his superiors to keep the affair more discreet and get the woman out of his quarters. The sexual drive had to be satisfied, everyone agreed, but the man was newly-married and was offending the notions of good taste by treating the Indian woman as if she were his wife, openly flaunting the creature as the object of his passions with scant regard for the little bride left behind, who had now borne his child.

· 223 ·

When Richard had first heard that Charlotte was *enceinte*, by receiving the congratulations of several of his fellows who had been told the news in letters from their wives, he had greeted it with a feeling of violent bitterness. Oh God, what twist of fate had decided that he should sire an offspring on that fatal night? Now, he would have *two* stones around his neck, *two* others bearing his name, *two* who had the legal right to demand a share of everything he had, everything he did.

As his gaze wandered over the half-finished buildings of the cantonment he was forbidden to design, he told himself his child would be like that—ill-advisedly conceived, unattractive, unwanted . . . and an object of his complete contempt.

The cantonment was finished, and there seemed no reason why the wives of those forming the Kabul garrison should not now make the journey from India. Orders were circulated advising that any man wishing to have his wife and family join him should notify his superiors before the next *dak* left for India the following week.

This concession brought an immediate lifting of spirits at the mere thought of ladies arriving to organize a normal station life, although many a lecherous heart sank at the prospect of a "parcel of tabbies" arriving to put a damper on the erotic delights they were presently enjoying. Tom Scott, however, was overjoyed, and burst into Richard's quarters on the day he heard the news, a smile of delight across his good-natured features.

"At last!" he cried, flinging his shako on to the carved wood table and nodding to the bearer's silent enquiry as to whether the sahib wanted his customary drink. "You have seen the orders, of course?"

"Yes."

Too excited to notice Richard's lack of enthusiasm, he went on heartily, "With luck, and provided the transport wallahs do not take their usual excessive age to arrange things at the other end, they could be here with us by midsummer." He dropped into a chair and took the glass from the tray offered him, drinking deeply and with relish. "God, I can scarce believe it is true!" He leant back gazing dreamily into the distance. "To see Amy again, to have her beside me every day. How she must have suffered when the poor little fellow died, and I was not there to comfort her. I know she is better off than some, for she has the Judge and her mama to stand by her and give her protection . . . but a mother is no substitute for a husband, you know."

"A physical impossibility, I agree," murmured Richard.

Tom sat up abruptly, colour tinging his cheeks. "Damn you, Richard, here am I speaking of the death of my son and all you can do is mock me."

"No," he replied swiftly, genuine regret filling him. "Tom, the death of anyone is tragic, I know only too well. My remark was not aimed at . . ." He broke off and shrugged his shoulders. "You know me better than that, surely?"

It was a moment or two before Tom said, "I once thought I did." He sat forward, his usually merry eyes intent on his friend, his pleasant face perplexed. "Where has it gone wrong, Richard? I know we had that hellish dust-up over the rackety way you have been going on, but . . ."

"I understood we had said everything on that subject," put in Richard brusquely, snapping his fingers at his bearer to bring him another drink. "You agreed that a man's affairs were his own, did you not?"

Tom's mouth took on an obstinate look. "And you agreed a fellow was entitled to speak up on behalf of his sister."

"And so you did," Richard replied, narrowing his eyes. "That affair was months ago. What has it to do with the death of your son?"

"N . . . nothing at all," stammered Tom, as he frequently did in these days when Richard confronted him inexorably. "But, dash it, Richard, you just now said I should know you too well to . . . Well, the truth of it is, I do not."

"Do not what?" demanded Richard, not giving an inch.

"Know you! I mean . . . well, naturally I *know* you . . . but . . ." He tailed off miserably, never the most eloquent of men or the most perceptive.

Sighing, Richard ignored the servant standing obsequiously beside him with a glass on a tray, and said, "Tom, do you remember a long ago conversation we had about Eldred Pottinger?"

"Eh?" spluttered Tom, unable to follow the drift of the subject.

"You hotly decried the fact that we were not sending a relief force to Herat on his behalf, and asked me to promise to come to your aid if you were ever in a similar position."

Tom was frowning in concentration. "But that was merely . . ."

"Do you still believe I would come, in such an event?"

The frown remained as Tom looked his friend over slowly. Then he nodded. "Yes . . . yes, of course I do."

Reaching out for his drink Richard leant back with the glass in his hand. "Then, that is all that matters between two men, surely."

Tom gave up, since it was easier to do so than continue a fruitless subject. But Richard had forgotten his presence in the memory of the continuation of that conversation which had returned to him out of the blue. In answer to Tom's promise to do the same for him, should the need arise, he had laughingly said: *You will be a very welcome sight . . . so long as you do not bring your sister with you.*

Five days later Richard received a summons from a Major Spalding—a minor official in the Kabul administration—who was not only a Company officer but a dyed-in-the-wool opponent of Queen's officers being allowed to serve in India. A large blubber of a man with face whiskers of ridiculous proportions, he had been given the task of arranging the transportation of the memsahibs from India to Kabul, and was making it a marathon and highly complicated business.

When Richard knocked and entered the office, Major Spalding was poring over papers and lists. He kept his junior waiting while one fat finger traced a line across a simple map from one large dot to another, then pondered over the distance with great gusting sighs.

He glanced up. "Oh, it is *you*." A scowl settled over the folds of his face as his scrutiny returned to the large sheet of vellum. "Damned guesswork, if you want my opinion. If I were to believe this it would be unthinkable to bring ladies on such a journey!" He threw down his pencil. "Drawn by a bloody numbskull, I should imagine."

"It was drawn by me," said Richard. "And as it is the only one we possess, you will have to do the bloody best you can with it."

The huge bulk stiffened, and sweat broke afresh on the forehead of the Major. "If you were in *my* army, sir, I'd kick your backside so hard you would be out of the door and halfway to the Bala Hissar by now . . . and that damned native woman you keep would find her sahib greatly inhibited for some weeks."

With tightening jaw Richard replied softly, "I am sure she would soon find consolation with the officers of *your* army, sir. *Sekundar* Burnes might not have the time or stamina to oblige her himself, but I understand he acts as procuror for his friends."

Spalding gripped the desk hard in an effort to prevent further un-military exchanges over which he could not exercise the privilege of rank.

"How you have survived as long as this is beyond my understanding, Lingarde."

"Yes, I am sure it is, Major," was the swift double-edged reply. "But if it was not to clarify my map, what was your reason for asking me here this morning?"

Slowly, certain he had somehow come out badly from the encounter, Spalding embarked on the business at hand, knowing he was still not on firm military ground. It was a personal matter over which a subordinate could not be disciplined.

"I have not yet received your application for permission to have your wife and daughter brought down to Kabul."

"I have no such application to submit."

Apparently ready for such an answer, the Major went on without a pause. "Are you seriously saying you do not wish to be joined by Mrs Lingarde and the child you have not yet seen?"

"If that is how you wish to put it," agreed Richard carelessly, gazing through the window aperture at the peach blossoms rioting over the trees in the nearby orchard and thinking how impossible it would be to see attackers creeping up on the cantonments through those trees.

"You are the only man from Meerpore to decline the opportunity."

His gaze swivelled back to the hairy face. "What bearing does that have on my wishes?"

"None whatever," said the Major in rising tones, "but it is felt by more than a few men here that it is something of a slight to your wife."

"Is it?" demanded Richard, his own voice rising. "Then I will thank them to cease concerning themselves over another man's affairs and put a little more thought into those of Afghanistan, which they appear to have forgotten, of late."

The fat man stood up and, although tall, found he did not quite come eye-to-eye with his junior. "Mr Lingarde, I do not like you," he rasped. "I have not liked you since we first met at Quetta. I think I shall never like you . . . but I have been instructed to tell you that you are most urgently recommended to add your name to this list if you wish to save what is left of your career."

With the paper and pen thrust towards him across the desk, Richard looked across at the other man with disparagement. "Oh come, surely even in *your* army, Major, men do not expect females to come to their rescue in military matters, or fight their battles for them."

Sweating freely and trying to hold on to his control, Spalding almost choked out, "So you will not write your application?"

"No." He returned to his study of the peach blossoms. "And you just now admitted it was unthinkable to bring ladies on such a journey, much less children."

"You . . . you worthless young dolt! You are on the path to ruin, and this will send you helter-skelter down it."

Suddenly, Richard wanted an end to the interview and this unforgivable interference in his private life. God in heaven, did he have to shout to the world that his greatest wish was never to set eyes again on the woman who claimed his name, and try to forget that he had fathered a child by her? Blazingly angry, he poured out all he could not say in a bitter attack on something of which he *could* speak. "From the start of his farcical military adventure I have made it plain that I felt it a terrible mistake to set foot on Afghan soil. There are graves in their hundreds along the route we took to get here, and we are still here because there will be worse turmoil and slaughter if we leave than there was before we came. If that is not proof enough of my theory, the pitifully small garrisons we have at Ghuznee, Kandahar, and Jalalabad—the feeble protection we offer the Khyber Pass—are constantly under attack by groups of tribal rebels. Our messengers and supplies only get through because we pay extortionate ransoms to the mountain bandits—and even then some are attacked." He thumped the desk in his anger. "They hate us. By God, any fool can see they are waiting for the slightest opportunity to hit back and revenge, when it comes, will be bloody and unmerciful." He flung out his hand towards the window. "Look out there! I faced a court martial rather than have anything to do with this . . . this shameful tactical error. We sit here like grouse on a smooth lawn during the game season. Now, those in command are concerning themselves with matrimonial affairs of their junior officers as if it were some peaceful garrison in England, instead of a highly explosive situation that needs only the match put to it to begin a slaughter on terrible scale." He took a deep breath. "I would not ask *anyone* to join me here. To bring women and children into this death-trap is sheer irresponsible blindness on the part of everyone concerned . . . and each man has a free choice in the matter, has he not?"

All the Major could manage was an outraged nod.

"Then I have no application to submit. With your permission I will retire to my quarters."

He strode back through the sprawl of the cantonment

buildings, throbbing with anger, impotence and despair as he looked up at the towering hills around him and imagined swarms of armed tribesmen screaming revenge on the hated infidel invaders. Knives slashing and slashing at white flesh until it became red pulp. The old memory put nausea in his stomach and tingling weakness in his thighs as he jumped up the steps into his quarters, roaring for his bearer. In a mood of savage energy he flung off his uniform, walked into his bathroom to have several buckets of tepid water thrown over his heated body, then emerged with a terse instruction to his servant to fetch Luana, at once.

She came swiftly in a loose robe which dropped to the ground as he pulled her against him with a fierceness she did not resist.

"Richard-sahib," she whispered. "When the madness is upon you it is better to let the devils out."

Dragging her down upon the day-bed he groaned, "*My* devils will not go."

"Yes . . . yes, they will go."

Already, her hands were moving over his body in ways that only women of the East understood, and the erotic challenge swept him with the need to meet it to the full. No matter his great strength against her frailty, his size compared with her miniature beauty, his savagery over her gentleness, she made no protest throughout the storm he rode out, but incited him further, renewed the challenge each time he triumphed, and gave with unending generosity for as long as he demanded.

When it was over she took up towels soaked in fragrant lotions to cool their bodies, then poured the fiery liquid he always needed and handed him the glass. He lay spent and empty as she performed her ritual, then stroked her long black hair with lethargic gratitude when she lay beside him again with her dusky face against his chest. The devils had been banished, for the moment . . . but he knew they would return.

The two young women faced each other across Mrs Shilton's drawing-room, Amy flushed and lacking in her usual self-assurance, Charlotte a pillar of rigid, humiliated fury.

"I would not have believed you could do such a thing, Amy! All these months—after I helped you to nurse poor little Charles, comforted you during your grief, shared Anna with you—all these months have counted for nothing?" she demanded in ringing tones.

"I did it for the best," said the red-haired girl in a miserable attempt at defence. "I had no wish to hurt you further."

"Hurt me! Do you not see what you have done by your silence?" Charlotte put her hands to her temples. Her pulse thudded there as loudly as the monsoon rain on the roof and verandah outside. "I could have written to him, pleaded my case, explained that little Anna was robust enough to make the journey."

"I . . . I believed you would hear it from others, in any case."

Charlotte gave a bitter laugh. "*They* would only speak of it behind my back. Can you not see how they must have relished the titillation of wondering if the dissolute Lieutenant Lingarde would send for his neglected wife, or not? Well, now they know the answer." She took hold of the back of a chair to keep her hands from shaking. "You have played right into their hands by keeping from me all that Tom told you in his letters regarding the cantonment and quarters for married officers. I have depended on you for news, you knew that, even if you did not make it apparent, but you deliberately kept me in ignorance of this."

She gripped the chair and fought the tears that had threatened her from the moment she had realized the truth. "Have you any idea what it feels like to be the only one not mentioned on that list, to hear the laughter and excitement of everyone else and know it shuts you out in the most heartbreaking manner yet? *Have you?*" Looking at the other girl, slender and pretty in lilac muslin, she saw again a pert creature on a horse, speaking words that destroyed her dreams. She had done it again with her silence. "I see now that your friendship was a sham. You have not changed, Amy."

It was too much for the girl's volatile temper. Amy crossed the room to stand by the chair Charlotte gripped, her eyes flashing and the colour in her cheeks growing deeper.

"I am the only person who knows why you flung yourself into Richard's arms at a time when he was under some kind of absurd welter of protective pity for you. I suffered your punishment by silence for six months, but I have never divulged the facts to anyone . . . not even Tom. Your mama remains free of scandal, and the whole world remains ignorant of your reasons for rushing India's most eligible bachelor into marriage." She was unable to remain still, and walked with agitated steps to the fireplace in that gloomy salon whilst the rain thundered down as if the end of the world was approaching. "There are many who would say I had been a friend, indeed . . . and I kept from you the news that wives would be allowed to travel to Kabul for that same reason."

"For friendship's sake?" cried Charlotte. "Friendship to whom—those ladies of the station who do not give a jot about you, or to Richard Lingarde, a man you failed to captivate and whom you are pleased to see repenting the fact?"

Amy swung round to face Charlotte, her temper completely lost. "I must remind you that you are in my father's house. I will not be spoken to in this manner by someone who blames me for the disaster of her marriage. Do you truly believe it would have made any difference if you had known from the beginning? You appear to be the only person in Meerpore who is surprised that your name is not on that list."

"I was the only person in Meerpore who was unaware there *was* such a list," Charlotte flung at her, her throat tightening.

"Well, do not blame me for that, I beg of you," retorted Amy sharply. "It is not my fault if your husband has come to his senses, at last. The marriage was the biggest disaster of the season, everyone knew. I should think you would have more pride than to expose yourself to his further contempt by wishing to join him. Go to England with Anna, as you should have done long ago." Putting out her hand Amy tugged at the silken bell-ribbon to summon the bearer with Charlotte's cloak. "It is beyond my comprehension why you are making such a disgusting fuss over it. It is not as if you have ever loved him, is it?"

Defeated Charlotte walked out past the angry girl and took her cloak from the servant, before putting the hood up over her small day-bonnet and allowing herself to be ushered out into the deluge where her mare had been brought round from the stables and stood restless beneath rain that descended like a solid wall.

It was madness to venture out into such weather at all, but Charlotte had been in the grips of a kind of madness from the moment she had discovered the existence of that list from Kabul. Her name was the only one missing: it was something she could not accept.

The rain beat into her face blinding her so that she had to continually dash her hand across her eyes in order to follow the path that had turned into a mire of reddish mud. The pall hanging over a place that held few happy memories for her added to the desperation in her breast as she moved slowly along the deserted ride, urging the reluctant mare into the storm.

Amy's words still rang in her ears, all of them true, she had to admit. But what was done, was done. It was the future she wished so desperately to fashion, and her only hope of that was to get down to Kabul. She had been waiting and hoping for news that the army of occupation was returning, but if the wives were going down there to join the garrison it could be there for years. She would *not* wait like a package in the "lost parcels" office, remaining unclaimed as year succeeded year. Neither would she return to England to live with the grieving Sir John on estates that would be Richard's eventually.

The disaster of the season, Amy had called the marriage. Charlotte had known that from the moment she had opened her eyes from ecstasy to discover a brutal betrayed man cutting her from his life with words and blows. But there was one thing she would never accept and was prepared to fight for with any weapons. The arrival of that list had totally disarmed her!

The long rows of houses stood silent and seemingly deserted as she advanced along the main avenue between the residences of those of greatest importance in that northern station and, suddenly, she glimpsed a faint ray of hope in the greyness all around her. Yet it was only after sitting motionless in the saddle for some minutes whilst the monsoon downpour wet her through to the skin and set her shivering that she resolutely turned the mare's head towards her goal and urged the beast forward.

Permission to go up to the small salon was given surprisingly quickly, and Charlotte followed the servant up the familiar staircase all manner of memories rushing through her feverish mind. Since the army's departure she had been to her father's house on a fair number of occasions, always in the company of other guests and at the express invitation of her parents. Anna had only been there once, for the christening party. Sir Rastin had no interest in babes—especially female ones—even though this one was his own grandchild. Felicia had just as little interest. They were noisy, odorous, demanding creatures who could be depended upon to pull one's hair or crush a gown abominably, in her opinion.

But Charlotte's relationship with her adulterous mama had undergone a subtle relaxation since the days at Ferozepore. With the guilty knowledge that Colley Duprés could so very easily have made her a sister-in-sin that night, the young girl had suffered the remorse of her strict upbringing. Mother and daughter had mingled socially in a semblance of unity which satisfied convention and kept Sir Rastin and Lady Scott's image intact by visual signs of responsibility for their daughter separated from her husband by war. Charlotte participated for their sakes, not her own. Tongues wagged ceaselessly about her already. It would not have mattered if the gossips had shredded her reputation even more.

Yet anyone who had watched affairs in Meerpore particularly closely would have noticed that Charlotte never went to the Scott residence alone, and certainly never without an invitation. It was a sad blow for gossips that the weather prevented anyone from seeing the drenched, shabby figure of a young girl go into the house that morning.

As she approached the salon Charlotte felt her legs weaken with nervousness. She had expected to be told Lady Scott was unable to receive callers. Now the interview was upon her she felt the chasm between them too wide to overcome, her mission hopeless, and herself a target for righteous retribution.

Felicia was seated on a *chaise-longue* in a dress of caramel-coloured silk that had a goffered collar standing up along the oval neckline. Around her throat she wore a velvet ribbon bearing a magnificent topaz surrounded by creamy pearls. Flames from the small fire in the hearth danced on the huge yellow-brown stone and put a becoming richness on a complexion that looked flawless and unmatchable.

For a moment Charlotte remembered the mobile Slavic features and vivid eyes of Anastasia Lingarde, and was pierced with sadness for her loss and for what she would feel if she were witness to what had befallen her beloved son. That superbly brave gesture Anastasia had made at Ferozepore was surely worth more than that! Shored-up by that thought Charlotte walked in with outward calm to meet her mother's impersonal greeting.

"I had not expected callers on such a day as this, I vow, but your presence bears out my practice of always being suitably attired for even the most unlikely event."

"Good morning," said Charlotte quietly. "It is good of you to see me."

Felicia's gaze was taking in the saturated gown of floral cotton, the muddied boots and hem, the hair that hung lank and dripping across Charlotte's shoulders.

"If you could see yourself now you would understand the sense of my stricture to you on never venturing out if there was the slightest chance of rain," she said. "I think I cannot ask you to sit down. These chairs have been recently covered with damask and will be ruined if made wet. But do come to the fire. You look dreadfully chilled."

Charlotte walked across to the comfort of the flames, and silence dropped between them, cutting them off in their separate and incompatible lives. Holding out her hands to the flames Charlotte stood for a long time wondering how best to say what she must, for she would not leave until her last hope had been explored to the full.

"You must be feeling quite desperate to come to me like this," said the quiet voice behind her. "Very desperate indeed."

All hesitation gone, Charlotte turned to face a woman she scarcely understood, yet shared the same bond she, herself, had with little Anna.

"Not all your strictures have gone unheeded, although it must have seemed so to you and . . . Papa . . . these last months. There has been gossip, and I am sorry if it has been injurious to your standing in Meerpore."

Felicia said nothing, just continued to sit with erect grace seemingly unmoved by her daughter's words uttered with such difficulty. But, once started, Charlotte was not going to be stopped by anything.

"One day on the budgerow you said to me that a woman had either to be beautiful or able to produce sons. Without those qualities she has nothing. Well, I am not beautiful, and I have borne my husband a girl child." She looked frankly at her mother. "I have accepted the conclusion of those facts."

"Is that why you spend so much time in that terrible hospital? It will make you even more like Meg."

Charlotte shook her head. "I go because it is something I desperately want to do. If you remember, I did it before my marriage . . . before my daughter was born."

Felicia nodded. "I think your aunt's influence was too strong to be banished by anything I might have said. She is to blame for the situation in which you presently find yourself. Her narrow notions of the world and its ways were responsible for your decision to use an escape route that could only lead to disaster."

They were interrupted at that point by a servant bearing a tray, which he set on the table before his mistress and departed.

"I ordered hot chocolate when you were announced," said Felicia pouring it into dainty cups from a long-spouted silver pot. "And I think you could safely embark upon one of those strawberry tartlets without ruining what is already a sadly shabby gown."

It was all so ridiculously frivolous and conventional—as if she were not standing dripping and drenched on the rug of a house from which she had run two years before in revulsion and anguish. Yet, it somehow gave her a vague glimpse of something in her mother that she had also experienced. A determination to hide all else beneath a façade of normality.

"Mama," she said impulsively, using the name she had stubbornly avoided for two years. "You also said something else to me which I have not forgotten, and which I have learned is all too true."

Beautifully curved eyebrows rose. "Oh?"

"You said it was possible for a married woman to be humiliated in a way her spinster sisters could never be."

Felicia sat very still, the steaming cups of chocolate forgotten as she gazed at the bedraggled girl. "Ah . . . poor child! You are learning what it is like to be a woman, at last."

"That list," cried Charlotte. "The one that has just come up from Kabul. I *must* have my name added to it, and you are the only person who can help me achieve that. I will never ask more than this one thing from you, but . . . *please* . . . arrange for me to join those going to Afghanistan. You do not understand how very vital it is that I should."

"Oh yes, I do, child. You would never have brought yourself to take this desperate measure if you were not at the end of your endurance. I think there will be no difficulty in arranging what you ask—quite the reverse, I should imagine— but I hope you realize there might be nothing more at the end of it for you than more humiliation."

· *ten* ·

THE "KABUL ZENANA" left Meerpore with spirits as high as those of the army that had marched away from the station two years before. But, also like that army, the ladies soon became aware that they had undertaken a journey of no mean proportions. In a long caravan of horses, mules, wagons, camels and palanquins, they set off escorted by a company of native cavalry officered by three Englishmen in the Company's service, and guided by a political officer called Bateson who had a terrible scar across his right cheek from a Mahratta knife.

The journey was difficult right from the start. Since that grand durbar in Ferozepore the great "friend" of the British, Ranjit Singh, had died leaving the Punjab in as volatile a state as Afghanistan. Sikh sirdars and princes were plotting and conspiring in the race to the throne, with the customary surplus of brothers, half-brothers, cousins, bastards and favourites laying claim to it, backed by ramshackle armies.

That last state in India through which the British had been allowed to pass freely in the days of Ranjit Singh was now swinging from friendly to hostile, according to whichever man held sway. The Sikh attitude towards the British presence in Afghanistan had undergone a change, also, it now being seen as an attempt to sandwich the Punjab between two strong territories of the white queen's expanding empire. That meant only one thing to some Sikhs with hostile and suspicious minds.

But, with Captain Bateson to ride ahead and smooth the way for the caravan of women, and the impressive cavalry escort riding beside them, pennants fluttering, their passage as far as the Khyber Pass was unmolested. There they rested for three days, whilst Captain Bateson rode ahead alone to negotiate safe passage through the tortuous pass with the chiefs of the bandit tribes. He earned the ladies' fervent admiration for his courage in riding unaccompanied into such a place carrying enough rupees to warrant his immediate slaughter by the first bandit he encountered. But he was known, as were many of the young political officers, by the tribes who held them in some kind of strange respect, and he emerged from the awesome chasm three days later, successful in his errand and suffering from nothing worse than a series of boils on the inside of his thighs that made riding an agony.

Charlotte gave the young man a poultice to relieve his condition, and earned his genuine gratitude. They had medical supplies with them, but no doctor. The medical orderly, who was thought to be sufficient to the situation, hardly knew what his medicaments were, much less how to use them. To Charlotte, the circumstance was a godsend, for she occupied herself with the task of tending to any amongst the party who had minor ailments such as she had treated many times in company with Aunt Meg.

There had been no difficulty over having her name added to that list from Kabul. The Meerpore military most decidedly did not want one odd wife left on their charge, and were also well aware that those in command at Kabul were more than anxious for Richard Lingarde to be joined by his wife. It had needed only a word from Lady Scott to Sir Rastin's secretary to the effect that an error must have been made, and Charlotte received by the end of that same day instructions on how much baggage and how many servants she would be allowed to take to Kabul with her.

Her farewell to her parents had been at a dinner-party given by them for the Shiltons and Amy, Mrs Smethwyck—the senior lady in the Meerpore party—and two bachelor officers along with Captain Bateson, who were accompanying them as far as Jalalabad on the far side of the Khyber Pass. Charlotte said a formal goodbye to her father, who seemed to have completely forgotten that brief period when they had almost grown close. But she managed a moment in privacy with her mother, and thanked her for what she had done.

"It was the merest nothing," had been the reply. "But it appears to have put some life back into you, at all events. I trust you will not regret this step."

"I promise you I shall not," had been her fervent reply.

Felicia had smiled with a trace of sadness. "So young, yet so certain? Well . . . perhaps all hope is not yet lost." In a sudden astonishing gesture she had taken the girl's hand and squeezed it. "Charlotte, I am forty years old tomorrow and entering the autumn of my life. Do not waste the spring of yours, I beg you."

Taken unawares Charlotte could think of no response, and her mother had continued in lighter vein, releasing her daughter's hand. "I trust you are intending to employ a sewing-woman, my dear child, for if you appear in Kabul in the gowns I have seen you wearing these past months, they will take you for a trooper's wife." Moving back towards the assembly of people she said in her usual manner, "I have heard there is an abundance of luscious soft fruit around the cantonment. Do not be tempted to eat such things except at the dinner-table with a knife and fork. There is no more distressing sight than a female with sticky hands and juice all over the cuffs of her gown. Aside from that, it is extremely injurious to one's skin, bringing a rash of blemishes which compel one to remain indoors for days on end."

The start of the march had been a glorious release for Charlotte from the life she had been living, although the route taken was haunted with memories of the other times she had covered the territory—with Richard in his strange teasing mood going up to Ferozepore, and the nightmare return after he had marched away. The other travelling women were pleasant enough to her, but she knew they were all longing to see the wicked Lieutenant Lingarde's face when his unwanted wife turned up on his doorstep.

She knew too, now, about the Indian woman he had in his household and who, if gossip could be believed, was in his bed night and day. In the wisdom of hindsight Charlotte had realized that Richard was a very physical man. There had not been many nights—except on the march—when he had not sought satisfaction from her. But instinct told her this Luana knew a man she, herself, had never glimpsed. That the woman would still be there when she arrived Charlotte was well aware, but she smothered her burning anger beneath the primary determination to face her husband unflinchingly when she arrived. Each time she thought of coming face-to-face with him her limbs turned to jelly and her courage took a severe set-back. But she went on, counting each day as one more weight on her side of the scales. He surely could not send her back once she had arrived. Even if he were cruel enough to have such an intention, a woman could not travel alone through country such as this, she knew. No, he was bound to accept her presence and make the best of it. Her heart thudded at the thought, but she quickly concentrated on something else, before she lost her courage completely.

Amy appeared to have accepted the situation, and the two girls were reasonably friendly again. But Charlotte noticed that her sister-in-law spent a great deal of time with one of the bachelor officers commanding the cavalry escort. Lieutenant Spence was a handsome young devil with blue eyes brimming with invitation, and Charlotte felt it was as well he would be turning back when they reached Jalalabad. A new escort was coming up from Kabul to take them on the last part of their journey, and it would be as well for Tom if his wife did not ride in flushed and radiant, her gaze straying to her dashing escort.

The negotiation of the Khyber Pass, even to ladies who had travelled the length of India, was an experience they found extremely taxing. Unlike the army that had gone before and tackled the Bolan Pass in the spring, they did not have to contend with rivers swollen by melting snows, but the tortuous track, the stony footing, the threatening sheer walls of rock rising each side of them, the heat, and the knowledge that eyes must be watching them the whole way through, made the week they spent in that great split in the mountains the worst of the journey, so far. Captain Bateson rode at their head with complete self-assurance, but they could not help feeling that the money he had paid the bandits might have been accepted with no intention of honouring their pledge.

Everyone felt relief when the caravan emerged into open country once more even though the series of plains was unattractive, barren and stony, intersected by rivers which were reduced to streams at that part of the summer. They headed then for Jalalabad, a British-held garrison that had twice been under attack by rebel Afghans since its occupation. The news was reassuring. Scouts reported no hostile horsemen in the vicinity, and Charlotte was probably the only female in the party who felt uneasy. Jalalabad twice attacked by rebels and scouts constantly looking for hostile riders? What had happened to the peace Shah Soojah was reportedly to bring to his country? She looked down at Anna and, for the first time, wondered if she had done the right thing to bring her child to such a place. Then, her heart leapt as she realized that it might have been for a very sound reason that Richard refused to have her name put on that list. Did he, perhaps, care enough to wish to keep his child from danger? All the way to Jalalabad that thought kept her in a glow of hope such as she had not had for many months. But she was to receive two shocks when she reached that British garrison.

The rest of one week was planned to stock up with supplies, refresh the animals and effect the changeover of the escort. The garrison officers had been turned out of their quarters which they had made as comfortable as possible, in favour of the ladies. Their pique at being crammed together in mud-walled rooms of small proportions was offset by the sight of a few pretty faces and fluttering eyelashes—even if they were destined for some other lucky fellow down in Kabul—and efforts were made to entertain their female guests in suitable and lively fashion.

For the travellers, weary and saddle-sore, the sight of this walled city lying in a lush green valley with trees and villages dotted all along it was extremely welcome. Closer inspection brought disappointment, for the town itself was dirty, poverty-stricken, and badly defended by the wall, which was crumbling so much it would not keep out a stampede of cattle, much less hostile tribesmen. Work was going ahead to reinforce the defences, but it was a mammoth task.

Even so, the comparative comforts of civilized living cheered the ladies well enough, as did the company of the officers of the small garrison, some of them old acquaintances who had marched off from Meerpore with the Army of the Indus. With the last stage of their journey in sight and so much news to exchange, the ladies blossomed, and a lively time was had by all—to the extent of dancing, and entertainment on the pianoforte a young lancer lieutenant had had brought from India by camel only the month before.

On the third day of their sojourn at Jalalabad, Amy came into the room she was sharing with Charlotte, just as Anna was being lulled to sleep by the old ayah travelling with them.

"Shhh!" warned Charlotte automatically, then noticed the expression on her face. Going to her sister-in-law quickly she asked, "What is it?"

Amy hesitated, glanced behind Charlotte at the Indian woman busy with the toddler, then said quietly, "You had best come outside a moment. I have two things to tell you which will be better overheard by no one."

Full of apprehension Charlotte followed the other girl along the rough gallery, up the crumbling uneven steps onto the flat roof. There was no shade there, but it was possible to feel the benefit of a pleasant breeze and enjoy a view of great beauty across the valley and encompassing hills. Sepoy sentries stood at intervals all along the battlemented walls and on the towers, watching for signs of movement out there in the heat-laden stillness, and they could just see the strolling figure of the officer of the watch as he made his way along the top of the walls.

Amy came to a halt and faced Charlotte with colour in her cheeks. "You once accused me of keeping silent on something that closely concerned you. I vowed I would never do so again." Pulling something from the broad sash around her waist she went on, "The new escort has just come in from Kabul, bringing letters. No," she said quickly, "there is none for you . . . but I received a long one from Tom containing information I intend to tell you, this time."

Feeling her skin begin to rise in goose pimples Charlotte realized why Amy had never mentioned the Kabul list to her. The next few minutes were going to be embarrassing for the other girl and humiliating for herself.

"Go on," she said through lips that did not want to move.

"Richard has heard that you are travelling with us, and has created such a protest the whole cantonment is ringing with it. At first, he demanded that you be taken back by the returning escort when they leave here. When he was told a single lady could not possibly be put in the charge of an entire cavalry company, he demanded to know who had had the effrontery to bring his wife on a journey he had expressly stated he had no wish for her to make." Amy twisted the letter between her fingers. "He made a violent physical attack on Major Spalding, seizing him at the throat and threatening to knock him down. When restrained and taken before the Commander-in-Chief, Richard so abused him with words on unwarranted interference in his private life, charging him with incompetence and irresponsibility in every aspect of his command at Kabul, he was placed under immediate arrest to await a further court martial."

"*Oh, no!*" whispered Charlotte feeling colder every minute.

"There is more," said Amy, determined on her course of honesty. "Richard broke his arrest, slipping past Lieutenant Hesketh, who was his guard, and riding out into the hills. A patrol found him two days later." Amy's colour increased as she said determinedly, "He was in company with his Indian woman and so intoxicated he did not even know who he was."

It was more than she could do to look at Charlotte any longer, and lowered her gaze to the letter in her hand before adding, "The court martial proceedings have been dropped, and Richard is in the hospital under medical restraint. Surgeon-Captain Michaels claims he is suffering from severe fever of the brain."

Charlotte walked across to the low parapet and clutched the hot surface as she stared out across the hills. *What had she done?* Wild thoughts of turning back rushed through her mind, but she had just been told they would not allow a single woman to go back with the escort. There was no alternative but to pursue her course, but the determination with which she had tricked her way into being part of this group now crumbled. She was courting further disaster. Hearing such news first-hand from Amy—details written by her own brother in a letter just received—was a hundred times worse than all the gossip she had heard in Meerpore about her husband's dissipation. It now seemed undeniably true that he had changed irrevocably from the man she had married, and this evidence hurt so much that her immunity to emotional pain flew on the breeze across this walled city.

She gripped the ancient wall as tears hung on her lashes, and was then hit by a memory of another occasion when she had stood in a similar position, determined not to let the person behind her see her tears. Gone was the hope that Richard had not asked for her and Anna because he felt it was too dangerous for his child to enter this wild country. He very definitely did not want them—his wife or his daughter—and was advertising the fact to the whole world!

"You said . . . you said there were two things you had to tell me," she managed, at last, keeping her eyes on the hills.

There was a pause before Amy said, "The political agent travelling with the escort to Kabul is Major Duprés."

At that Charlotte spun round, colour flooding her own face, and Amy answered the unasked question.

"It is quite true. I have just seen him."

Charlotte had thought of pleading indisposition to avoid dining with the officers that evening, but merely felt it was foolish to postpone the moment when she would be forced to acknowledge and converse with Colley Duprés. Since that night at Ferozepore she had not come face-to-face with him. He had gone down to Kabul with the army and, by the time he had returned, Charlotte had been nursing Anna and out of the social scene. Since then, he had spent much of his time back and forth to the Punjab in the general effort to ease a turbulent situation or, in company with others of his ilk, acting as messenger between Sikh sirdars who owned land on one side of the Khyber Pass, and Afghan chiefs who owned land on the other side, reassuring them all of British intentions and friendship.

The news that that particular man should have been in the area and asked to act as guide as far as Kabul had distracted Charlotte's mind from the greater worry of her reception on arrival at Richard's front door, and thrown her into a fever of speculation on how to cope with something she longed to avoid. Eventually, she decided to emulate Felicia and hide her feelings beneath cool calmness as if that passionate embrace had never taken place. But it was with a pounding heart that she dressed in a plain dark-blue silk dress and descended the well-worn steps, holding her bell-skirt free of her feet, in company with a spritely and glowing Amy in pale green taffeta.

The garrison officers dined in a small inner room of the large house normally, but due to the ladies' presence and the addition of the officers from both escorting companies, had arranged for the meal to be served in the courtyard, lit by flambeaux and branches of candles. On a fine night of star-filled clarity, any with romance on his mind would find it impossible not to fall beneath the spell induced by high spirits, good food and wine, and the call of sexual attraction which had, so often, to be denied.

Charlotte saw Colley the minute she and Amy walked into the courtyard from the dimness of the surrounding cloisters, and her heartbeat increased further. In honour of the occasion he wore white breeches, a purple-brocaded coatee girded with a gold sash and edged with a heavy border of blood-red stones scattered across gold lacing. Around his neck he wore a pale-blue ribbon bearing a huge ornate ruby scarab set in gold and diamonds.

Amidst a group of scarlet jackets he was certain to draw every eye. It was obvious that he was aware of the fact, for he looked straight across when the pair came into the light thrown by flambeaux. As their glances met and held Charlotte felt as weak as that moment he had released her before walking away leaving her on the brink of mental ravishment. But he turned back to the officer commanding the small garrison and went on speaking as if nothing had occurred. Charlotte looked quickly at Amy, but her sister-in-law was looking in an entirely different direction . . . and the dashing Lieutenant Spence was looking back with shameless invitation. In the morning, he would be riding back with the Meerpore escort, and he was making it plain he wanted some very pleasant memories to take back with him.

Charlotte suddenly felt sick. What weak creatures women were when all was said and done! It took a mere challenge in the eye of an irresistible man to forget all else but the excitement of pursuit and surrender. It happened all the time. Even Felicia, beautiful, poised and unapproachable, was a victim of it. She closed her eyes against the romantic scene, thinking: *When does one ever find a gentleman languishing helplessly after some female?* The answer came back loud and clear, making her feel sicker than ever. It was an anguished voice asking her: *Did my deep love mean so little to you you did not even notice it?*

"Are you feeling all right, Mrs Lingarde?"

She opened her eyes to find the political officer, Captain Bateson, looking at her in some concern.

"Oh, yes . . . I . . . it was the sudden brightness after the dim stairway." She forced a smile. "I fear the garrison is being very extravagant with candles tonight. Let us hope the gentlemen will not have to dine by starlight alone if the next supply caravan is set upon in the Pass."

He smiled back, which puckered his scarred cheek badly. "I think they will not care, ma'am. It is a long time since they have had such a party as this, and no prospect of another for months."

"We shall be sorry to see you go, sir," she said with honesty. "You have been a source of great comfort to us all with your confidence and knowledge. I wish you were leading us the remainder of the way."

He gave a slight bow. "I am flattered, Mrs Lingarde, besides being immensely grateful for your ministrations, *en route*. But you will be in safe hands with Major Duprés, I assure you."

She nodded and looked across at the man in question.

"Yes, I expect we shall. He has been negotiating with the Afghans for some time, has he not?"

"Oh, yes, indeed. There is no man more adept at penetrating the hostility of native chiefs. He has a reputation for it."

She was astonished to detect what sounded like sarcasm in his voice, but when she looked quickly back at him he was smiling at Mrs Smethwyck across the courtyard in response to her dignified nod of the head in his direction.

The evening became alive with laughter and voices, next minute, as the last group of ladies entered. Soon, it was like any normal dinner-party at a large station, and everyone but the watching sentries on the parapets and gates forgot he or she was eating mushroom soup, ham and pheasant, followed by soufflés, in an isolated fortress of a wild barbaric country.

Romance was in the air with a vengeance that night. Even Mrs Smethwyck looked flushed and youthful at the courteous attentions of the commanding-officer, and Charlotte noted, with astonishment, that Captain Bateson's scarred face had taken on a strange kind of fascination in the candlelight which had not gone unnoticed by Mrs Timothy, a timid young creature of nineteen who was married to a fifty-two-year-old major in Kabul. The girl, normally self-effacing, had a bloom on her cheeks that was most becoming, and her dazzled eyes held a look that most certainly should not have been there.

Then Charlotte glanced round to find Colley looking at her across the table as he had done on so many occasions on the budgerow, dark eyes afire with amused challenge, and she felt the colour rise in her cheeks as the old feeling assailed her. He raised his glass in mocking toast to her, but she turned away wondering desperately if she had looked like the hero-worshipping Mrs Timothy during that journey from Calcutta. Forcing the meal down her taut throat she punished herself further by acknowledging that Mrs Timothy would doubtless run off in fright if *her* hero attempted so much as a chaste kiss on her fingers, whereas she had surrendered totally in the arms of Colley Duprés, like a wanton offering her body unconditionally.

From then on the evening became something to be endured rather than enjoyed, and the whole time she was aware that she only had to turn to find him watching her with relaxed speculation. He was like a puppet-master, who knew he had her on a string until they reached Kabul and was taking his time in deciding how he would make her dance. But the puppet had learnt a few movements of her own, and the performance was likely to be a fiery one when it occurred.

The gentlemen dispensed with port and cigars since there was no withdrawing-room for the ladies, and the whole party sat on chairs that had been placed along the sides of the courtyard while swift-footed servants cleared the tables away. Tea was brought for the female guests, and the pattern of the groups began to alter as people chatted first to one then the other. Suddenly, Charlotte found Colley beside her in company with a man he introduced as Captain Petworth, commander of the cavalry escort that had ridden out to meet them from Kabul. Charlotte did not know the man, for he had not marched from Meerpore with the invading army, but he made it immediately obvious that he knew a lot about her—or fancied he did.

"I am delighted to meet you, Mrs Lingarde," he said with a knowing smile. "The Kabul garrison feared they would be denied the pleasure, but I see *you* were determined they would not."

It was insolence coated with charm, and she longed to take the smile off his fleshy face, especially when the two ladies with them tittered into lace handkerchiefs. She smiled back with every appearance of friendliness. "You are too kind, sir, but it might be as well to have at least one determined person in Kabul as, from what I have heard, there are not too many of them in residence."

The smile vanished, but his eyebrows rose. "You have had news from Kabul, ma'am? How very surprising! I had thought otherwise."

Doing her best to control her tongue she said as pleasantly as she could, "As a junior officer of cavalry perhaps you are not aware of *everything* that goes on under your nose, Captain. My father is Sir Rastin Scott, Political Agent for Meerpore, and receives dispatches that would not normally be discussed with a mere junior officer."

Captain Petworth's protuberant grey eyes glared at her as he realized it might have been better not to attempt to be amusing at the expense of Richard Lingarde's unwanted wife.

Colley decided to intervene. "Mrs Lingarde is an avid student of Indian affairs, Petworth. I am in a position to know because she is my most successful pupil." He turned to her. "I taught you a great deal, confess now, ma'am."

With heart thudding painfully against her ribs she looked up to meet his smile of amused scorn. "Oh yes, indeed, Major Duprés. But is it not true that a pupil often concludes his education by teaching his tutor?"

He leant back against the pillar with his usual careless grace, and said softly, "I await the circumstance with eagerness."

He had her at a nonplus, and she knew she had left herself wide open to score. But her silence left the field empty for new attackers. The ladies beside her decided to maintain the entertaining situation that had not been of their instigation.

"Mrs Lingarde is also very knowledgeable on how to treat the sick," piped one in high fettle. "You will find her forever in the hospital ministering to the suffering. If you should ever find yourself in such unhappy straits, Captain Petworth, rest assured Mrs Lingarde will be at your side with a sustaining broth immediately."

He brightened, re-armed by the words. "Ah, how comforting . . . and what a relief it will be for your husband when you arrive, ma'am. Are you aware that he is presently under lock and key suffering from fever of the brain?"

"Yes, sir," she snapped, her anger overriding her control. "How reassuring it must be for you to know that is the one affliction from which *you* could never possibly suffer."

Petworth stiffened, his stocky figure almost bursting apart the buttons on his tunic with his fury. "I see, ma'am, that you are not only determined, but have pretensions to wit."

"You fear a rival, sir," she flashed back. "Dear me, how faint-hearted of you, when you know you have most of the gaggle-tongues in Kabul behind you! Such lack of courage is hardly heartening when we know we shall be looking to you for protection on our journey."

He made a jerky forward movement that passed for a bow and said through tight lips, "Excuse me, if you please. One Lingarde in Kabul has been unpleasant enough. Two will make the place unbearable, I fear."

The two ladies drifted away with him, leaving Colley still leaning against the pillar with an expression of acute enjoyment on his face.

"You did not recommend that he seek the guidance of the Lord," he commented with a bubbling amusement in his tone.

She turned on him, still churning with anger. "I doubt even He would succeed in *that* case . . . as with you, sir."

He pushed himself upright to take two glasses of wine from a passing servant. "Ah, so you have progressed enough to admit there is such a thing as Divine failure!"

"There is no such thing as failure," she cried, the words coming to her out of the blue. "It is just that some people are less successful than others."

He gave her one glass and raised the other to his lips, murmuring, "The Almighty appears to have been less than successful where your young fool of a husband is concerned. He is going to the Devil by the fastest route possible."

Charlotte took a gulp of wine. "I am assured Richard will find you already there when he arrives."

The dark eyes narrowed. "You are learning faster than I imagined, my dear."

"But I think you may find that what I have learned is not necessarily what you thought you taught me, Major."

"No?" he asked with confident query, waving the glass to indicate the crowded courtyard. "If this place were empty and silent, save for us, we should discover the truth or not of that statement, would we not?"

To her shame and confusion she knew only too well what

the answer would be. In desperation she said, "I have a child now, sir. A daughter who needs my guidance."

He gave a careless shrug. "Another child of India? She will be offered on the marriage mart like her mother when the time comes." He raised his glass in meaningful fashion. "Teach her to drink at the 'fount of the Devil' at the earliest opportunity, or she will suffer the same fate as you."

Head swimming from the wine and the intoxication of his nearness, she said recklessly, "It was a fate you yourself recommended, if I remember."

He pursed his lips. "I did not fully understand the man. I saw just his virtue. His weaknesses have only recently become obvious."

"How well I understand how such a mistake can be made," she said vehemently. "I have seen only your weaknesses. Your virtue has yet to become obvious."

In an instant he became vital, alive and excitingly dangerous as he breathed, "I will soon show you that virtue counts for nothing, if my previous lesson did not entirely teach you."

Knowing she must leave, Charlotte took a determined but sensually reluctant step to end the challenge. "Still aspiring to be the Devil's advocate, Major?" she managed to say. "When you finally succeed I vow you will be a Major-General, at least." Starting to back away she added, "You must excuse me. I must go to my daughter. She is slightly feverish tonight."

To her retreating back he said softly, "And her mama. It is a long way to Kabul, and you cannot run away forever."

Trembling from something that was certainly not anger, Charlotte moved swiftly through the dim cloisters and up steps that had withstood centuries of warriors' rushing feet. But there, at the end of the passageway leading to her room, where Anna was in truth fretful and feverish, she saw a couple in a close embrace oblivious to all else in their darkened alcove. Recognizing Amy's green dress, she knew Lieutenant Spence would take back to Meerpore exactly the kind of memories for which he had hoped.

Once inside her door she leant back against it while tears she had fought earlier that day flowed freely down her hot cheeks. Dear, uncomplicated, trusting Tom was being betrayed, if not in body very definitely in spirit, for the sake of a pair of enticing blue eyes and a wicked smile. Downstairs the game was being played many times over. Even Mrs Smethwyck, who was forty-eight, seemed to be losing her head in the face of the Commanding-Officer's gallantry. Where had virtue flown?

It was all the fault of circumstance, she realized. A group of ladies who had been deprived of their husbands' attentions for a long time were locked up inside a fortress with a group of gentlemen who were lonely and threatened. Add a wondrous starry night, softly-glowing candles that revealed attractions paled by bright daylight, and the "fount of the Devil", and a dinner-party became a bottomless well of temptation.

She moved across to the window aperture which allowed the night air in and gave her a square view of the starry sky. She gripped the sill as she gazed at the heavens through blurred eyes, and asked God if they were all sinners, at heart? What had happened to all she had so fervently believed in until she had arrived in India? Were Aunt Meg and the Tamworths so wrong? Was she truly and indisputably her adulterous mother's daughter?—for she knew that if Colley Duprés walked in the room at that moment, she would be as willing a victim as she had been on that night long ago.

For a long, long time she stood trying to find the answers to the questions that pounded her brain, and finally concluded that the Lord was to blame for creating two different human figures, then making them infinitely attractive to each other. It was inevitable that sometimes the wrong pairs would meet and answer the call. Was it so *very* sinful, after all? Perhaps, as Felicia had once said, if no one else was hurt by it one could excuse human weakness.

But the starry night had forced honesty from her, and she lowered her head on her hands in despair. In her case, someone had been hurt—mortally hurt, as far as his love for her went. And then, in that ancient foreign room she finally admitted that *she* was unbearably hurt by an Indian woman who knew, body and soul, a man broken by what she had done.

When she finally moved to look down on the sleeping Anna, Charlotte knew it was not only for her child that she had been determined to get to Kabul. The line between virtue and sin was very fine, and sometimes one could be mistaken for the other. But how was she to prove that to a man who had abandoned one for the other?

They resumed the last leg of their journey four days later, but there was a listless air about the column. That week in Jalalabad had been like a desert fantasy. Indiscretions had been committed by some who regretted the fact, and others who did not, and the seven days of comparative comfort made everyone reluctant to embark on another long period of marching and camping. One hundred and three miles of endless hills and stony difficult passes still lay between them and Kabul, and Jalalabad held memories better forgotten. Everyone lacked enthusiasm and energy. Even Colley Duprés' dashing figure in the all-white field-dress he adopted whilst leading the long column of beasts and waggons failed to arouse the admiration to which he was accustomed.

Charlotte rode with Amy, as usual. She had said nothing to the girl about the embrace she had witnessed, but Amy had been very quiet since Lieutenant Spence had departed for Meerpore, and Charlotte could guess her sister-in-law's thoughts. Her own kept her equally silent.

Their way soon led through more difficult mountain passes and over rocky heights that soon had the column straggling into twice its length. The ladies grew depressed and irritable, finding fault with everything as a week lengthened into ten days and still they found the everlasting hills blocking their route. It did not help that Captain Petworth was a man of little patience, who not only earned the dislike of the two cornets but upset his female fellow-travellers by snapping back at them whenever they complained.

It was after one of the frequent squabbles in the ranks that he ordered a halt for an hour on a high plateau where a stream provided water for his company's horses, and tea could be made to refresh everyone who was tired and dusty after a stiff climb to reach the place. There was an immediate confrontation between the calvary captain and Colley Duprés, each maintaining *he* was in overall command of the column.

Charlotte thought they should air their grievances out of earshot of the sepoys, and took Anna by the hand to walk her across to the stream so that the child could trail her fingers in the clear water. Further along, the more indecorous of the women were cooling their feet in the stream, and further still the pack animals were being allowed to drink.

With the breeze lifting her hair and cooling her body through the silk blouse, Charlotte stood on that plateau looking in the direction in which they were travelling. By the end of that week they would ride into Kabul, and she would see Richard again. The elusive memory of him had returned clearly, of late, but it was only of an ashen-faced man standing in the entrance of a tent telling her that if he should fall in battle she would have everything he owned. Every time she looked at Colley Duprés that image rose up to accuse her. Now, as her gaze wandered over the banks of barren bluish hills striped with the silver glisten of water she grew weak with dread at how he would greet her unwelcome arrival. She had no doubt the military would see to it that his "fever of the brain" had been cured by the time she got there.

Bending swiftly she put her arm around Anna to draw her close. "Soon you will see Papa, my dear. *Soon.*"

Hardly had she finished speaking than the air was filled with deafening cracks, and screams that had her clasping the child tightly against her in instinctive protection. Gasping, she saw that the plateau had become a terrible confusion of running and leaping figures as women stumbled over their long skirts in efforts to get away, others grabbed their children with shrieks of fear, serving-girls and ayahs sank to their knees in attitudes of abasement, cooks and grass-cutters flung themselves beneath the waggons, sepoys slipped and stumbled out of the stream where they had been watering their horses and ran for the piled arms nearby, and a number of ragged loose-robed figures were emerging from over the crest to rush the waggons and baggage that had been removed from the camels and mules while they drank. Colley Duprés and Captain Petworth with a few of the sepoys who had not dropped their weapons were firing at the attackers and yelling orders across the confusion and noise.

Charlotte did the first thing that came into her head and dragged Anna into the stream, where she crouched protectively over her child in the icy water, her head just above the level of the bank as she gazed terror-struck at a peaceful scene that had been transformed into a place of death.

The attacking tribesmen had few guns, but they used their knives with fatal skill on those they encountered. Captain Petworth stood with ridiculous courage in the path of the mob, but he and his men had been taken completely by surprise and were scant protection for four times their number who were unarmed.

Some of the women ran berserk, terrified out of their wits, causing even more confusion by not stopping in one place. But it was quickly apparent that the attackers were after the baggage and guns, finding the running women just as distracting as the sepoys found them. Then, Charlotte noticed Colley making a dash for the waggons, firing as he went and bringing down two of the Afghans. At the waggons he began turning them on their sides, kicking and clubbing the camp-followers sheltering there into helping him form a barrier of defences, and gradually Captain Petworth formed his sepoys into some kind of order with all the rifles they had been able to seize, and fought his way across to join him.

One of the young cornets, who had been ordered to get the women to safety out of range or in the stream, collapsed suddenly with a knife in his back, and the other was shot in the arm by one of his own stolen rifles. Several of the camel-drivers and cleaners had been cut to pieces as they tried to run, and one of the ladies lay on the grass screaming hysterically at the sight of her own blood which ran from a foot cut by the sharp stones at the edge of the stream.

But the horrible sounds of human conflict which rang in Charlotte's ears were gradually fading. She could see how the methodical and organized defence by the minority of sepoys had overcome the haphazard attacks by those who outnumbered them. The Afghans were retreating with what booty they had captured while they were still alive to enjoy it. Then she saw a figure in a muddied all-white uniform spring up from behind the side-tipped waggons and rush after the retreating men, tulwar held aloft, roaring orders in a native dialect until some of the sepoys reluctantly followed, despite orders in English shouted by Captain Petworth which demanded that they stay where they were.

There followed a scene such as Charlotte had never witnessed before as Colley Duprés cut down the stragglers with great scything strokes until they fell in heaps of bleeding flesh, while half-a-dozen maddened sepoys shot or clubbed any that showed remaining signs of life.

"Stop, *stop*," she heard herself moan in horror. "For pity's sake stop!"

Then it was all over. The soldiers were running from the shelter of the waggons, Indian servants were rising from their praying positions, and the white women were emerging from the stream like so many naiads in drenched skirts, and with dazed expressions. Most of the children were sobbing, as was Anna, frightened by the noise and strangeness rather than the sights of death, which they did not understand.

Automatically soothing Anna with words, Charlotte walked with her to the young cornet with the knife in his back. It was obvious that he was dead even before she knelt beside his still form, and all she could think was of how he had danced with so much enthusiasm and pleasure at Jalalabad. Dragging herself to her feet she then carried Anna across to the other young subaltern, who was white-faced and holding his arm just below the shoulder.

Her ayah appeared at her side just then to take Anna from her, and Charlotte asked the boy to let her inspect the wound. It was bad. The bone had been smashed by the bullet and was sticking into his flesh in what must be an agonizing fashion.

Charlotte looked up into his stricken face with compassion. "I have had no experience equal to dealing with this, I fear. All I can do is bind the arm tightly with a splint so that it cannot move, until we reach Kabul and a surgeon. But what I am going to do will hurt you a great deal, I must warn you."

He tried to smile. "Well, I daresay it will, ma'am. But I do, at least, now know what it is like to be wounded and so that is one worry removed."

While she was busy with her preparations Charlotte was aware of activity around her as order and calm were restored. Above it all was the sound of Colley Duprés and Captain Petworth arguing heatedly about who held overall command of the groups, who had been given conflicting orders in the height of the battle.

With the medical orderly and Mrs Smethwyck to help her Charlotte did what she could for the shattered arm and, brave though the boy tried to be, he moaned with pain as she bound the limb and eventually fainted away. By the time she had seen her patient comfortably installed in a palanquin willingly surrendered by the owner, Charlotte realized nearly an hour had passed since the attack, and she was shivering from reaction in her wet clothes.

In the interim, sentries had been posted, and a decision had been made to encamp there until efforts had been made to ensure that the road ahead, which ran down between hills, was safe to follow. Fires had been lit and a meal was being prepared, but it was plain everyone was edgy and more in need of reassurance than food. The seven of their dead—the cornet, two sepoys and some camp-followers—had been taken away for burial, but Charlotte noticed several men in the loose robes of their attackers lying to one side, where Captain Petworth was laboriously questioning them in the only native dialect he knew.

Charlotte walked across to him because she noticed the

prisoners were bleeding profusely from wounds on arms and faces.

"I am no expert, Captain," she began, making him turn sharply, "but I will do what I can for these men with the medical supplies available."

He glared at her, still in the grips of battle-fever and the argument with Colley Duprés that had just ended.

"They are enemy prisoners, ma'am, and my responsibility. I will thank you not to interfere."

"But they will . . ."

"Go away, Mrs Lingarde," he said in savage tones. "Save your ministrations for your husband—if he will let you near him."

She turned on her heel and walked away, shivering even more than before. Her tent had been erected, so she went thankfully into its shade and changed her wet clothes with the aid of her servant, while the ayah reassured the memsahib that the little girl was dry, fed, and sleeping off the fright she had had. Charlotte's head throbbed, and she wished *she* could sleep off the fright she had had and forget the two Englishmen who had been victims of the shock raid—one dead, the other almost certain to lose his arm when he arrived in Kabul.

Amy came into the tent shortly afterwards looking pale and red-eyed. "I do not know how you could do it, Charlotte," she said, sitting on a rug. "And when the poor fellow began to cry out it was beyond my understanding how you could continue to hurt him so."

"Was it?" asked Charlotte wearily. "My upbringing, which you have so very often condemned, Amy, accustomed me to sights not normally seen by females of our station. But did you think it did not affect me to hear his cries? He would have been *screaming* once we began to descend that rocky path if I had not done what I did. Unfortunately, that brute Petworth will not let me do a thing to help his prisoners."

Amy looked shocked. "I should hope not! They attacked us."

"But they are still humans in pain. If Tom were wounded

in battle, would you not hope his captors would ease his agony?"

The pretty mouth tightened. "The Afghans have no mercy. They torture their wounded prisoners until they die."

Charlotte sighed. "They are barbarians. We are Christians, Amy, and pledged to help the suffering, whoever they may be."

Amy got to her feet in a flash of well-known temper. "What a pious little creature you are sometimes. I wonder you did not become a missionary." She swung in a swirl of skirts to leave the tent, and said as a parting shot, "I suppose you will tell me you plan to forgive Richard all he has done, and welcome his Indian mistress into your house."

Shaking, Charlotte said, "I think you had better go. You are plainly not yet over the shock you sustained today. And I advise you to ponder on whether Tom has anything to forgive *you* for, before you concern yourself with other people's affairs."

Blushing scarlet, Amy gave her a long frantic look before rushing from the tent. But the red-haired girl's words stuck in Charlotte's mind as afternoon turned into evening, and a tense hush fell over the small encampment. Could she or Richard ever forgive and grow close again? What of the Indian mistress . . . he surely would not continue the liaison once she arrived? But as he so expressly did not want her there, he might do so in the hope of driving her back to Meerpore.

The events of the day had so darkened her outlook she felt stifled in the tent. With Amy certain not to return to keep her company, and the long night stretching ahead with threats of even darker thoughts, she left the ayah watching over Anna and pushed open the tent flap to escape into the freedom of the open hill-top. Fires were lit all around the perimeter of the camp to highlight any stealthy nocturnal attackers, and the sepoys were posted all around in a smaller circle and behind boxes or crates on which to rest their rifles during the long night watch. The tents were pitched close together and looked like a bunch of strange yellow triangular plants, lit from within. The shadows of the occupants could be seen moving about inside, but it was unusually quiet that night.

Knowing she was safe provided she stayed within the ring of soldiers, Charlotte trod across to the palanquin where the wounded cornet lay bathed in sweat and moaning softly. She rounded on the medical orderly, who was lounging against a waggon in apparent unconcern.

"Have you nothing to give him that will help him?"

"No, ma'am," he replied sitting up slightly by way of respect. "We got no rum nor nothin'. That's for when we cuts 'em up, and no one was expectin' that on this journey."

"How typical!" she cried. "It seems to me that an army is never expecting *anything* from the way it organizes itself."

She marched on to the tent usually occupied by Captain Petworth, intending to ask him for brandy or similar spirits to give the boy. But his servant told her the captain–sahib was not there.

"Well, that is natural enough, I suppose," she stormed. "Why should he be where a person can find him when he is particularly wanted?"

Worked up by then into a rare mood, she strode off towards Colley Duprés' tent, trusting she would find the Captain in conference with the other man, but that tent was also empty. On the point of turning away she heard a sound that made the back of her neck prickle and her legs turn weak. It was a whistling swishing sound followed by a muffled scream, then another, and another, and another.

Fearful, yet compelled to see what her senses were imagining, she walked slowly towards the sound that was coming from behind the grouped supply-waggons, and peered round. Her blood ran cold. By the light of a nearby fire she saw the three Afghan prisoners, one of whom was tied facedown on to a wheel laid on the ground, spread-eagled in the most agonizing manner. Despite his wounds, his back was being lacerated by a whip wielded by a dark-faced tribesman responding to orders. The other two were held fast and forced to watch. The man in command was Colley Duprés, who was speaking in fast and harsh dialect, first to the victim, then the man with the whip.

Motionless with shock, Charlotte watched as the sufferer

shook his head and cried rapid, desperate words in reply. She realized that the men aiding in this atrocity were Colley's personal servants—nothing to do with the army or Captain Petworth's command. But he had claimed the prisoners were *his!*

Leaning in relaxed manner against one of the waggons, Colley shot a volley of words at the helpless man once more. His back was not much more than bloody pulp by now, but he again shook his head and gave a despairing reply. Then, before Charlotte's horrified eyes, Colley nodded casually to another of his men standing near the fire, who bent swiftly to shovel up several blazing logs which he dropped on to the raw flesh of the tortured victim.

Charlotte fled, the screams and the stench of burning flesh becoming part of a madness that flooded through her. But she was not so shock-maddened that her brain did not tell her she must find Captain Petworth, that he was the only one who could stop the bestiality she had just witnessed. *He* found *her* by walking into her racing figure as he stepped from a clump of bushes, looking white-faced and ill. With instant reaction he grabbed her by the arms and swung her round to face him. Then he realized who she was.

"Go back to your tent," he rasped. "You should not be here."

"*Neither should you,*" she cried vehemently. "You already know what he is doing to those men, that much is plain."

"It is none of your affair."

"But it *is* yours. Before God, I swear you are as bestial as he if you do nothing to stop it."

Looking as if he were about to be sick again, Captain Petworth mumbled, "He knows better how to deal with these people. He has been doing it for years."

Just then, another scream rent the air, and the blaze of light behind the waggons flared momentarily.

"*Do* something!" screamed Charlotte, seizing his arm and tugging at it. "Stop him, or I swear I will make your name resound all over India. You scorn me, but my father has great influence in political circles, and Sir John Lingarde still has a great many friends in high places. A word from me could break you for good, believe me."

Petworth swallowed, his face now a greyish-blue. "He . . . he outranks me."

"He outranks no one," she returned with sobbing passion. "His services are sold to the highest bidder or for the greatest glory. He holds no rank whatever, apart from a courtesy title which he thinks nowhere high enough. That makes him lower than the Untouchables."

Still the military man held back, swaying on his feet and breaking out in a sweat as the whipping sound began again.

"He will not take orders from me."

"Then shoot the prisoners," she demanded, feeling hysteria rise inside her. "You have sufficient courage to fire your pistol, I trust. Shoot them, put them out of their torment, for pity's sake." When he still hesitated, she shouted contemptuously, "Then give me your pistol and I will do it for you."

He strode off in zig-zag manner, as if dazed, drawing his pistol as he went. Charlotte followed knowing she would not rest until she knew the deed had been done. But it never was. As they reached the scene, Colley's men were just slitting the throat of the last prisoner.

He turned at the sight of the military captain, and the corners of his mouth curled up at the sight of the drawn pistol.

"Was that meant for me, or these sons of wolves?"

Petworth offered no answer, but his hand was shaking uncontrollably as he lowered the gun.

"They told me nothing, for my pains," Colley went on calmly. "They never do, of course, but it is always worth a try, and is the only way to earn their respect." He smiled sneeringly. "They would spit in *your* face, my feeble friend." He clicked his fingers to signal his men to drag away the remains, then turned back to Petworth. "My guess is that they were simply a small raiding party subsisting on the spoils from such attacks. I believe it will be quite all right for us to go on tomorrow."

Captain Petworth backed away from the blood-stained

· 263 ·

scene, and Colley then caught sight of Charlotte behind the army man.

"*Diable!*" he swore, his face darkening. "So you were responsible for this noble rescue that came too late!"

As she stared at that sensual face she knew her very first feeling of revulsion towards him had been the true one. He was ruthless, sadistic, loyal to no one but himself, and deserving of no pity when he eventually met a violent end. With loathing filling her mind and body, she realized there was no romance about a soldier of fortune; he was simply a man who lived for the glittering heights of existence and reached them by whichever method would get him there.

Horrified that she had ever let him touch her, had ever dreamt wild heroic dreams that idolized him above others; totally sickened by the bestiality she had just witnessed at his hands, she whispered through parched lips, "I see now that your association with the Devil is very close indeed. I have had no more instructive a lesson from you than this. It is one I shall never forget."

She walked away through the camp encircled by fires and watching soldiers, and it was only her ability to devote herself to prayer, as taught by Aunt Meg, that kept her from succumbing to the horror she had seen that night.

· *eleven* ·

RICHARD WAS RELEASED from his enforced sojourn in the tiny cantonment hospital only the day before the Meerpore party was due to arrive in Kabul, the surgeon declaring him fit. The "fever of the brain" that had assailed him had abated enough to prevent him from riding straight back into the hills with Luana and a case of wine for company. But he

did call for her the minute he entered his quarters and embarked on a sexual marathon to compensate for all they had
done to him in the name of medicine.

Shut up for hours at a time in a darkened room with wet
bandages around his head, he had grown feverish from the
effects of frustration and fury over the way his life was being
governed by fools in uniform and a self-centred, heartless
creature calling herself Mrs Lingarde. To counteract this fe-
verishness they had bled him, which had induced giddiness
and confusion resulting in further long hours locked in a
darkened room. His initial fierce revolt against such treatment gradually paled into smouldering acquiescence as he realized physical resistance was only prolonging his ordeal. But
he lay in darkness in the room that reached a temperature of
over one hundred degrees in the afternoon, keeping his mind
occupied with plans of revenge on everyone he could think
of.

Now, he was back in his quarters after a month of punishment in lieu of court martial still uncertain whether the military authorities had meant it to be that, or if they seriously
believed he was half-way to bedlam. After his physical release with Luana he had slept until late afternoon, then drunk
himself to sleep again around midnight after giving terse, angry instructions to his bearer to arrange for a room to be
made ready for the memsahib.

Then it was morning, and he knew the day he had dreaded
was upon him. Scouts rode in saying the column was climbing the long valley ascent which should bring them to the
cantonment by midday. Reports of the attack they had sustained a few days before put the whole cantonment into a
flutter of concern, in particular the husbands of those in the
party, and some resolved to ride out and meet their wives to
see for themselves that no harm had befallen them.

Tom Scott was amongst the number, and informed Richard of the fact, just before he rode off, booted and spurred,
with the air of a knight off to rescue a fair damsel. Tom had
enough sense to pretend that his friend was in no way concerned with what was, for him, a momentous day, and left
Richard standing in his sitting-room with a head that ached

from the effects of the past month, and spirits that were leaden.

For some absurd reason he had dressed in full uniform, as if for a parade, and was so emotionally tense he could not sit down and relax for the entire morning. He declined anything but water to drink. Knowing exactly what he intended to say to her he wanted a clear brain and a steady voice. But his resolution was broken when Tom informed him that the column's escort from Jalalabad had been Colley Duprés. He then drank several stiff brandies in a row, and the thunder in his head grew. So, she had had the breathtaking thrill of that bastard's company for three weeks! Plenty of opportunities for slipping from tent to tent on such a march as that. No wonder she had plotted to get her name on that bloody list! His fingers clenched around the glass until his knuckles were white then, in a return of his past month's feelings, he hurled it into the fireplace where the shimmering crystal fragments scattered all over the rug.

He heard the column come in amidst all the excitement and noise, the shouts of sahibs and the babble of servants' replies, the cries of greetings, and the high squeaks of children being held aloft by fathers who had not seen them for some time.

"Oh God," he murmured in despair, putting his head back and closing his eyes as if, by doing so, he would not have to see her when she came.

The welcoming ritual seemed to go on for a long time, and still he stood in the middle of that room until the voices gradually died away in different directions all over the cantonment. The silence was then almost worse than the bustle of a crowd, until he heard a voice just outside his window saying in strained fashion, "These are your husband's quarters, Mrs Lingarde. I . . . I daresay he has been called away on some errand or other. Is there . . . I mean, can I . . . I will call his bearer, if you wish."

"No, you have already been more than kind, Mr Chapman."

"Not at all. That is what the Duty Officer is for. Welcome to Kabul, ma'am."

"Thank you. I am glad to be here."

It was bravely said, and Richard had a sudden picture of a young girl in an over-sophisticated riding-habit saying with absurd hauteur, "Your determination to make my acquaintance is *très apprécietement. A bientôt,* Mr Lingarde."

His mouth twisted. So ingenuous . . . or so he had thought!

There was a rustle as the bead curtain was moved, and he turned to face the wife he despised. She stood just inside the room, pale and travel-stained in a dark-green habit, holding a toddler by the hand and staring at him with eyes grown huge with emotion, apparently unable to speak or move nearer. But all he could see was that young naked body streaked with tears as she had broken him apart.

The words of his rehearsed speech were forming on his lips when she bent swiftly and said to the small figure at her side, "There, *there* is Papa."

Induced by a gentle push the child began to walk jerkily forward, arms outstretched, a smile of innocence touching the rosy mouth.

"Pa-pa," she said wheezily, big blue-green eyes upturned to his face as she staggered and jerked her way across the room.

Richard stood mesmerized, everything flying from his mind but the stunned realization that he was looking at a miniature replica of his mother, from the flaxen hair to the oblique eyes, already strikingly lovely, fringed as they were with dark lashes. Why had he had the madness to imagine his own child would look like Colley Duprés . . . or even like the treacherous mother?

The little plump figure in white muslin was three-quarters across the room when she began to sway, steady herself, take two more jerky steps, then start to fall. Instinctively Richard dived forward and caught her up in his arms, lifting her against his scarlet jacket in a strong protective hold while she smiled angelically at him, with no fear of a stranger.

His heart was thudding as he studied the face so like the features of a woman who had lived so splendidly and died so tragically, and when the child reached with delight for the shining gold fringe of his epaulettes, brushing his chin with a soft cloud of fair curls, his heart turned right over and his throat tightened with love.

"Although she is named Anastasia Lingarde, she is known as Anna."

In some kind of bemusement he raised his head to look at the woman across the room whom he had completely forgotten. And there, still holding his child against him, he heard what she had to say without interruption.

"It is only because of Anna that I am here. I ask nothing for myself. What I did to you was unforgivable. I have had two years in which to reflect on that and suffer the remorse of my conscience. In those two years I have taken the barest minimum of that to which the name of Lingarde entitled me, and I have done nothing to dishonour that name."

It was at that point that his bewildered brain registered that her voice was trembling, but emboldened by determination as she stripped away the remainder of his aggression by admitting to all of which he had planned to accuse her.

"I used you to escape from my mother's roof. I sheltered under the protection of your name without any thought for you or your needs. I suffered from a foolish infatuation for a man who deliberately set out to turn my head when I arrived in India, and I sent you away to war with his name on my lips." She paused fractionally to gather more courage, then went on, "I intended to go away, back to Aunt Meg where I would never see or bother you again. But that terrible night left me with your child growing within me."

She moved slightly forward so that the shadows no longer hid the shine of her brown hair beneath the severe riding-hat.

"Richard, I have defied your wishes and hoodwinked the authorities in order to come here. I do not expect forgiveness or anything else from you but . . . but. . . " Here, her voice broke and she had to struggle to continue. "I cannot, I *will* not let our child be unloved, as I was. I *will* not let her grow up a stranger to her father, to be dismissed like a casual caller after sixteen years of separation. I *will* not inflict on her loneliness, disappointments, rebuffs and humiliations. I *will* not allow her to become a parcel, to be deposited with whoever happens to be prepared to take her."

There were tears sparkling on her lashes now, and Richard knew his claws had been drawn without his realizing it.

"I love Anna with all my heart. The circumstances of her conception are no fault of hers, and the sole reason I have made this journey is to make you withdraw your heartless rejection of someone who is part of you whether you like it or not. Someone who . . . someone who. . . ." She broke down completely at that point, putting her face in her hands and sobbing, "I *beg* you, do not punish her for what I have done to you."

Prepared for a pitched battle and disarmed by a diversionary attack, Richard reached out to pull the bell-cord for his bearer. Within a few moments, Charlotte had been assisted to the room prepared for her, and Anna taken from his arms by the ayah, who bore her off in the wake of her mother.

Richard was left in a complete turmoil of thoughts and feelings. Charlotte had been very clever, he saw that, teaching the child to go towards someone she called "Papa" and knowing he would be unable to resist a little creature so like her namesake. The tottering near-fall could not have been planned, of course, but once he had taken Anna in his arms he had accepted her as his own, and half Charlotte's battle had been won. Holding the little girl with tenderness as she had played with the bright fringe on his shoulders, he had lost the other half with humiliating speed.

He gripped the mantel as he downed another brandy and tried to make excuses for his annihilation. How could he have known Anna would be so heartbreakingly like his mother? How could he have guessed what it would be like to hold such a captivating little creature in his arms and know he had created her? All this time he had pictured a small monster of some kind—a grotesque female version of Colley Duprés, or a miniature of that blotch-faced travesty of his wife he had left almost two years ago.

But Anna was beautiful, entrancing, and his entire strategy was now balanced on her soft downy head. He had accepted the inevitable—that he had been outmanoeuvred by a woman determined to force herself and her offspring on him at Kabul, and his long hours locked in that hospital room had produced the ideal solution. He had meant to fire the salvo at her the minute she put her scheming face around the door, but his guns had been instantly spiked by a little voice saying "Pa-pa" and a tottering little figure falling joyfully into his arms. But it was those words that had hit him the hardest. Anastasia Lingarde had loved him with excessive unconditional joy: he could not reject her grandchild by withholding the affection she deserved!

Wearily he sank into a chair and faced the quandary in which he now found himself. In his desk was his written notification that put his commission in the army up for sale. With it was a letter to his father asking him to see that his wife and child were installed in the small house at Wentworth which had been left him by an uncle, and there was a third letter, addressed to Cousin Igor, telling him that he intended opening up the estates left him by his mother, and making his permanent home in Russia. Until he had had time to think straight, all three communications would have to stay where they were.

It was a long time before Charlotte could regain her composure. She had planned so desperately for so long, and pinned all her hopes on the chance that Richard had not changed so much that he would be proof against Anna's appeal. All through the long journey she had spoken to the child of the papa she would soon see, promising that he would be waiting to love her as much as her mama did. Yet, beneath her resolution she had been afraid—afraid of a man she last remembered striking her without mercy and swearing that she had destroyed him. The stories of the man he had apparently become in Kabul only seemed to bear out her fears that his violent manner that night was symbolic of his new personality.

On riding into Kabul that morning she had been sick with fear and despair, dreading the meeting with a man who had shown everyone so plainly that he did not want or respect her. The greetings and excitement all around her fortunately prevented most people from seeing that Richard Lingarde had not even adopted the false courtesy of leaving his quarters to greet her. Charlotte had not known where he lived, and might have stood a long time in the deserted square after the others had dispersed if the young Officer of the Day had not conducted her to her supposed new home, plainly embarrassed and sorry for her.

It had taken more resolution than she had ever had to summon to walk through that bead curtain holding her child by the hand, and it had wavered for one terrible moment as he turned to face her, and she had seen a man who looked a stranger. Instinct had come to her rescue, and she had sent Anna across to him with their future in her tiny hands. That she had stumbled at that perfect moment must have been Divine intervention, and the sight of Richard's face as he held his child in his arms had set Charlotte reciting all she had practised with so much emotion it had been her undoing.

Only when she was in the strange room, sparsely furnished and without even the touches accorded the merest guest room, did she realize Richard had not spoken one word the whole time. The thunderous condemnation, the bitter outburst, the violent manner she had expected had been nonexistent. In the exhausted aftermath of emotion she admitted to herself that she had even imagined him not meeting her because he was in bed with the Indian woman, to show his complete contempt.

In a mood of lethargy she allowed her servant to undress her and fetch water to wash away the dust of the journey. Then, as she was donning a pale muslin gown, a servant brought a luncheon tray to her room, which told her Richard wished her to stay where she was. Sighing, she sank into a chair. He could not put off the moment forever, but she was not really sorry for the postponement. It gave her time to recoup her strength, and she would need it all when he did decide to face her.

It was late afternoon when a servant arrived at her curtained archway to announce that the sahib would be calling on the memsahib within a few minutes. Charlotte rose hurriedly from the day-bed on which she had been resting, called her maidservant to contrive a speedy coiffure with her hair that had been loosened, and ordered the ayah to keep Anna out of sight. She did not want the child to take all Richard's attention, this time. She had played her innocent part with unqualified success on their arrival, but now Charlotte had to take centre stage in a scene she had never rehearsed, with an unpredictable co-star. Stage-fright assailed her as she heard his heavy tread approaching.

He knocked on the wall beside the archway, and the servant drew aside the curtain to let him enter before slipping away down the passageway towards the servants' quarters.

"Will you sit down and be comfortable?" Charlotte asked her husband in an endeavour to strike a gentle note from the start.

He ignored the invitation, standing only a few feet inside the room as if reluctant to enter it at all. Now that first encounter was over she was much more aware of things to which fear and emotion had blinded her then. His face was thinner, hollow-cheeked, and lacking the usual glow of health. His frame looked even more muscularly developed than before, but there was a weariness about the way he held himself, a suggestion that he was carrying a burden that was slowly driving him to his knees. But it was his eyes that startled her the most. Always striking, they now dominated his appearance and held her gaze, despite herself. Gone were the signs of the dreamer, the man with his sights on distant goals, the vivid flash of laughing gentleness. They were now fathomless, haunted, stormy betrayers of a man outwardly strong. His months of dissipation had taken their toll of him, there was no doubt, and had certainly given him no peace from the devils still rioting through him.

Immense sadness filled her as she felt, for the first time since they had parted, the true width of the gulf between them. There was no way she could approach him, and no way he would allow her near.

"Kabul is no place for Englishwomen, and this cantonment offers no protection whatever to the inhabitants," he began in a voice that was unlike any she had heard him use before. It was harsh, clipped, and aggressive. "Afghanistan is nowhere near as settled as some choose to believe, nor will it be until we depart with our puppet-king and allow Dost Mohammed to return. I am persuaded you already understand all that, ma'am?"

She nodded. All she could think was that he sounded like her father, who had spoken to her as if she were a visiting male subordinate.

"It is my intention to sell out and take up residence on my estates in Russia. You will be sent to England, where I have a comfortable manor on a small-holding. My father will see you settled there, at my request."

Her heart almost stood still. Dear heaven, he was going to send her back—out of his life forever! Anna meant nothing to him, after all.

"However," he went on with even more aggression, it seemed to her, "summer is almost over, and within a few weeks the mountains will be covered in deep snow. The passes become death-traps, even for the most stalwart of travellers. As . . . the child . . . has suffered the rigours of a long journey, plus an attack during which shots were exchanged, I have decided it will be necessary to wait until spring. In the meantime, I will be obliged if you will remain in this part of the house, out of the way."

He turned to go, and she had to keep him for a while longer, say something which would turn his dictate into a conversation. All her jumbled thoughts could produce was, "Have you any objection to my continuing with my hospital work here?"

He cast a storm-cloud of a look over his shoulder. "You will be wasting your time. The staff are all in need of their own treatment down there."

She persisted. "All the more reason why I should try to help, surely. Because of my knowledge I was of some use to Cornet Mayes when his arm was shattered by a bullet on the journey."

He paused in the archway. "They cut his arm off this afternoon. The boy is dead."

It hit her like a body blow. "Oh, *no!*"

Richard gave a short bitter laugh. "Why not? He was clever, loyal, and highly worthwhile. It is those the Almighty carries off first. Had you not realized that?"

The arrival of the memsahibs from various Indian stations transformed the life of the Kabul cantonment into a replica of every military station in India. The pair vying for priority were Lady McNaughten, who earned precedence through being the wife of the British Envoy, and Lady Sale, who did her best to vanquish her rival as senior military wife. She mostly succeeded, being of strong forceful character and prone to voicing her opinion very decidedly, even when not asked for it.

Before long, dinner-parties and *soirées* enlivened the shortening autumn evenings, and a ball was rapidly being organized. Some of the more daring, or more foolish, depending on how one viewed it, rode in the beautiful environs of Kabul valley on expeditions to beauty spots, and some even took picnics to the lush lower slopes of the surrounding hills and frolicked genteelly as if they were in England.

The arrival of the ladies also meant that the great Kabul bazaar enjoyed a rise in trade. They scoured the rows of stalls for rugs, ornaments, and knick-knacks to make their quarters more homely, and for lengths of cloth to serve as furnishings or gowns, embroidered Afghan sheepskin coats ready for the winter cold, and exotic jewellery. They delighted in the abundance of luscious fruits that grew around Kabul and were so cheap but, perhaps, regretted the equal abundance of wines made in the vineyards of the fertile valley, which their husbands so much enjoyed.

In some directions, the presence of females added decorum to the British contingent, but those set on debauchery, like Alexander Burnes and his close associates, did not mend their ways one jot. Nightly, his palatial house in the city itself rang with the sounds of the wild parties he held, and passing Afghans heard, storing away their feelings in the mounting cache of hatred. When Shah Soojah's zenana, which had remained in India when he left exile, arrived in Kabul soon after the British wives, the Bala Hissar became another source of sensual delights which the more reckless of the Britons exploited, and provided an absorbing diversion for an Amir who preferred to leave affairs of state to anyone who would take them on.

There was only a handful of men who were not surprised when violence flared up a few weeks after the women arrived, for there had long been signs that Shah Soojah's army was dissatisfied with the new Amir and his scarlet-jacketed infidel supporters. At the end of September word came in from political officers in touch with isolated forts that Dost Mohammed was about one hundred miles west and marching towards Kabul with a large column of supporters. Overnight, a regiment of Shah Soojah's troops deserted and rushed off to join them, hotly pursued by a regiment of Indian cavalry commanded by a British lieutenant.

When they all met up in a valley, the sepoys were hopelessly outnumbered in the resulting mêlée. But they had taken cannon with them, and Dost Mohammed had none. The invaders withdrew very speedily, and the sepoys returned to the cantonment well-pleased with themselves. However, at the end of October, the displaced Amir was sighted again a mere fifty miles to the north of his old capital, his supporters having been joined by tribesmen of the area through which he was passing, who had been awaiting the moment of retribution.

This time, Sir Robert Sale was detailed to head off the attackers, taking with him a strong force of infantry, cavalry, and horse-drawn guns, confident of putting to flight men who had run from a single company and several cannon only the month before. By November the two forces met head-on in a narrow valley, the cavalry coming upon the enemy ahead of the remainder of Sale's force.

The English commander immediately gave the order to charge. He and his English fellow-officers galloped full pelt at the Afghans, swords held aloft and yelling savage threats. Unfortunately, they were not aware that their sepoys did not relish tangling with the barbaric robed Afghans and had not even broken into a trot before they stopped completely, leaving their commanders to plunge with reckless courage into the hostile mob closing fast. Their gallantry ended quickly beneath the slashing knives of their foe, who continued to gallop over their bloody remains to rout the sepoys so that they turned and charged in the wrong direction.

Sale's force retreated to discuss the situation overnight, while gallopers were sent back to Kabul with the news of the disastrous initial skirmish. In the way such news travels ahead of its messengers, it was soon all over the cantonment together with rumours that all outlying garrisons were to be called in, and the whole army was to occupy the Bala Hissar in a concerted effort to hold Kabul.

Richard heard all this with disquiet, but no surprise, and told Tom as they were riding back through the city after visiting the bazaar one late afternoon that he had been predicting some such thing for a long time.

"This is only the beginning, I warn you. All the time Dost Mohammed is free we shall not be safe or allowed to leave this accursed country. He was a much-loved man. Despite his severe rule, he was as just as any sovereign one finds in this part of the world, Tom," he declared, drawing his horse to one side to avoid a ragged urchin he instantly recognized as the one from whose head he had once shot apricots. The lad swung a kick at the horse's front legs and spat viciously in its path.

"See that?" Richard demanded. "The news of our defeat is all over the city, also. Six months ago that boy revered me as a giant of a man. Now, he despises me—and who can blame him?"

"Now see here," countered Tom hotly. "Neither Fraser, Connelly, nor Broadfoot could have known their men would mutiny when ordered to charge. It is not *British* fighting-power that is to be despised, but those damned cowardly Indians."

Walking his horse in a weaving pattern through the narrow crowded street, Richard recalled that scene that now seemed a lifetime ago, when he and Edward Kingsley had sat beneath some jasmine trees and exchanged philosophies.

"Our sepoys are trained to behave like English soldiers, but the blood of India runs through their veins and the history of past cen-

turies shapes their actions when feelings run high. Fools forget that, Lingarde. When they are loyal show them you recognize what that loyalty has cost them . . . and when the day of reckoning comes, I hope to God I am not still here."

The poor devil had gone from the world—another intelligent, worthwhile human being—within several hours of that speech, but the words had remained with the listener ever since, and Richard now said to Tom, "Do you never think before you speak, my friend?"

Tom came alongside him as they broke from the city into the valley track leading to the cantonment, and said with anger, "What is that supposed to mean?"

Keeping his eyes on the sprawling military community which lay as defenceless as a kitten at the bottom of a well, he said, "Has it never struck you, Tom, that Indian soldiers are only here because we brought them? They have no quarrel with the Afghans: they probably think Russians are just another tribe of the Hindu Kush. The people of India had no burning desire to trade with Afghanistan, or any reason to force on their neighbours a king they did not want. It was *us*, Tom. *We* are the ones who see imaginary cossacks riding over the horizon, *we* who fear for our dominance in India, *we* who seek further riches and glory by extending our armed friendship with those beyond our frontiers." He paused to let his point sink in, then went on, "Can the sepoys be too badly blamed for showing unwillingness to fight our battles for us, and wanting to go home?"

Tom stared at him in stupefied disbelief, riding silently beside him along the track. Then he suddenly exploded. "By God, whose side are you on, Richard? Here are your friends—splendid fellows, all of them—being slaughtered, cut to pieces, because they were deserted by men who have sworn to obey and follow them, and you . . . you *defend* the cowardly dogs? You have done this before, if I recall, when Refford challenged your loyalty."

Wearily Richard pursued what he already knew was a pointless subject. "It is not *my* loyalty that is in question, you hothead. Look, if Napoleon had occupied Britain fifteen years ago, and you had been recruited into his army with

French officers commanding you, would *you* charge with as much gusto as they if they invaded Prussia?"

Tom was still angry and disappointed. "What have Prussia and Napoleon to do with it?" he cried with a frown. "Damn, Richard, I am at a loss to understand you, sometimes."

Richard sighed. "Then do not attempt to do so, my dear fellow, if it creates such confusion in your mind. But just ponder on the fact that when the British finally ride out of India for good, the native people will be left with a neighbour bearing long-standing resentment, whilst *they* will be safely halfway across the world."

"Ride out of India for good!" exclaimed Tom. "Why ever should we? You say such dashed strange things, at times, I am not surprised they shut you up in that hospital for a month."

"Oh, really?" Richard felt the beginnings of an attack of uncontrollable fury and tried to fend it off by responding without provocation.

But Tom, extremely tetchy over his friend's unwelcome attitude towards the mutinous sepoys, was well into his stride and unwisely added, "But I daresay you will take care they do not repeat the cure, for Charlotte is down there every day, and it is well known you do not care to be seen within a mile of your wife."

Before he could stop himself Richard was out of the saddle and dragging Tom from his horse, caught in the grips of the rage that assailed him from within and always ruled him while it lasted. He was vaguely aware of Tom's face covered in shocked bewilderment as he gripped him by the jacket at his throat and demanded that he apologize or face the consequences. But Tom was no longer bewildered. He was fighting mad.

"Apologize for speaking the truth?" he choked. "No, I'm damned if I will. It is time someone told you of your abominable treatment of your wife. Charlotte is my sister. I am entitled to defend her, whatever you may say."

Richard pushed him away with such force Tom staggered backward, almost falling as his riding-boots slipped on the dry dusty track. But aggression sent him after his victim to roar in his face, "Then it is a great pity you did not do so when she first arrived in India, instead of joining in the general condemnation of the ridiculous figure she cut. It is a great pity you did not use what few wits you possess to see that she wanted a champion, someone to stand by her against all odds. *I* would not then have been duped into taking on that role, and *she* would not now be in Kabul plaguing me further."

Retreating from Richard's determined advance, Tom licked the sweat from his upper lip with a nervous tongue. "You are plaguing yourself," he panted, slipping and stumbling backwards over the loose shale at the side of the track as Richard relentlessly pursued him. "If ever I saw a man intent on going to the Devil, it is you. It must be your damned mixed blood."

Those words lit the remaining fuse, and Richard launched himself at Tom, grabbing him around the throat and shaking him back and forth with all his strength until they both went down in the dust, rolling back and forth as they grappled with each other, one in a blind attack, the other in shocked defence of his life.

Richard was hardly aware of what he was doing. All he could see was his mother out on that plain at Ferozepore, speaking of communing with the wild spirits of her boyar ancestors for a while longer, and her soft "*Do svidaniya*" as he rode away, unaware that she knew he would never see her again.

It was almost like a continuation of those thoughts when an agonizing thump in his side caused him to double up, and a great jewelled tulwar sliced into the ground between his own body and that of Tom, only inches away. The thump in his side had been a hefty kick from a boot, and Richard lay gazing up at a man standing over him, reality returning fast. A citrus-yellow Indian coatee, white breeches, and dark-blue turban adorned the figure of the man he most hated and despised.

"Brawling like common troopers, gentlemen?" asked Colley Duprés with silken sarcasm. "Hardly the best way to impress the natives with our civilized superiority." He seized

the tulwar by the handle and jerked it from the ground, saying as he replaced it in the elaborate scabbard, "Neither is it
the way *gentlemen* should settle their differences."

"How would *you* know that?" flashed Richard, getting to
his feet.

The strong face darkened, and Colley said sharply, "Mr
Scott, I suggest you catch your horse and ride back to your
quarters without delay. If I report this disgraceful affair there
could be dire consequences, which I take it you would prefer
to avoid?"

Tom stood up, still dazed and uncertain how it had all
come about. He looked towards Richard, white-faced and
covered in dust.

"He has no authority over you, or anyone else in the
army," Richard told him, the white-hot rage he had felt towards Tom fading as quickly as it had come. He had recovered his wits much more speedily than his friend, and
was now prepared to do battle with someone who had been
the cause of ruining his life. "The title of 'major' has been
given him along with the rupees he demands for as long as
he offers his mediocre services to the Company. The moment a better and more profitable position offers itself he will
be off, take my word for it. He can do nothing to harm your
career, and you have no obligation to take orders from him,
Tom. He is no officer and gentleman, just a paid messenger
who has a glib tongue where native rulers are concerned."

That last was said to Colley's face, and Richard was not
surprised at the reaction it aroused.

"Orders or no, I suggest it would be prudent for you to
leave this minute, Mr Scott. This so-called 'friend' of yours
has been wanting a confrontation for a long time. Now
seems the ideal moment . . . although if he feels he has anything to settle with *me*, it will be done with courtesy and cold
steel."

"Now . . . wait a moment," Tom began, but Richard cut
him short.

"Clear off, Tom, this is a private matter!"

The young man went. Catching up with his horse a few

yards down the track, he mounted painfully and trotted off in the direction of the cantonment without a backward glance, leaving Richard standing dust-covered and dishevelled before the immaculate exotic man in native dress.

Colley opened fire. "You have gone out of your way to denigrate me and my particular talents on every possible occasion. Resentment, envy on the part of other men is something to which I have grown accustomed, but from you it is served as an insult. You are twenty years younger than I and have never yet fired a shot in combat. Who are you to sneer at me?"

"Since when has killing become a virtue?" countered Richard in chilling tones.

"Ha, virtue!" cried Colley. "I once described you as the most virtuous man in Meerpore, but it was not meant as a compliment." He was the one who sneered now. "You were your mama's darling, the dream of every scheming matron who wished to place her daughter in your reliable hands, the object of simpering females' adoration, the hero of the sporting scene, the successful candidate at every examination. You were so sickeningly virtuous it blinded everyone to the fact that you were useless as a soldier, that courage is the one thing you do not possess."

Stung by a shot that was too near the mark for his liking, Richard broke into rapid Russian that left Colley speechless and uncomprehending. He then repeated the words in fluent aristocratic French, which also left his adversary at a standstill.

"You are a charlatan of the worst order," he flung contemptuously at him in English. "And I am the one person you have chanced upon who knows it. It would not surprise me if you were the illegitimate son of a French serving-girl and a passing pedlar. You live by your wits and charm which, I will acknowledge, you have in abundance. But this time, you have had the misfortune to sell your services to people who have in their midst a man who makes you feel uneasy in his company, has you always watching your tongue because he registers every slip you make, whose mother knew your claims to Russian lands were lies, who understands more languages and dialects than anyone else in this cantonment and therefore knows every detail of how you treat the natives when no one else is around. I suggest it is *you* who is constantly denigrating *me* and all I stand for, Duprés, because I am the true representation of all you claim to be."

Colley smiled with venomous assurance. "Really . . . are you? Then why have you never had the courage to voice your opinions openly instead of making guarded criticisms of me . . . particularly whenever I recommend and support armed action. Whenever there is a vital decision to be made, I have noted that you have always argued the course of non-involvement. At Ghuznee, you refused to support the storming of it, and very cleverly absolved yourself from any responsibility for building this cantonment by forcing a court martial. No, Lingarde, you can call me the bastard son of whomsoever you like, but my credit with my fellows stands higher than yours. I will allow that you are truly the result of an Anglo-Russian marriage, but no one in Kabul—or British India, for that matter—would say that it has given you any greater advantage than looks that foolish females cannot resist, and a great inclination to leave responsibility to everyone else. Some also say it has made you sadly unstable."

Richard looked at him with disparagement. "They said the same of my mother. It is the comment of those who are envious, uncomprehending, or just plain dolts."

"You really are insufferable—a combination of British arrogance and Russian aristocratic self-glory."

"Yes, that is just it," cried Richard growing impatient of the cross-talk. "The Afghan people have both those qualities—or faults, depending how one views it—so *I* understand what they secretly harbour in their bosoms. I did not approve of invading their country, I did not approve of destroying their pride by taking Ghuznee, I did not approve of building a permanent cantonment—especially one which is defenceless—and I did not approve of bringing women and children into a highly dangerous situation such as we have on our hands: But I am proclaimed unstable, while you, who are supposed to 'know the native mind,' dash about in pretty clothes making the dangers a bloody sight worse and earning the admiration of the elderly fools in command here. That is, between the wild orgies in which you indulge in this city each night. The only difference between you and Burnes—a man I once used to admire—is that he is succumbing to pure lust, whilst *you* are most likely being paid by wealthy Afghans to sully the British image. You do everything else for money, why not *that?*"

Colley flung out his arm like a whiplash and struck Richard around the face with one of his white riding-gauntlets. It stung his cheek and must have left a weal, but he was too contemptuous to respond in the hoped-for manner.

"Very dashing and spectacular, Duprés," he said coldly. "But I only accept challenges from men my equal."

"So, you *are* a coward! I always suspected it," was the equally cold reply. "One of these days, Lingarde, I will see that you are *forced* to face the enemy. It will be the end of you . . . if you have not already done it by your own efforts."

Richard began to walk away. "Well, however it happens, it will be a source of great relief to you, Duprés."

"And to your little neglected dab of a wife," came the soft taunt after him.

He halted only fractionally, then went on to where his horse was nibbling the plants at the side of the track.

"Neglected . . . how could she be with you in Kabul?" he commented in lazy tones as he mounted and prepared to ride off. "But are you so unsure of your virility that you must take on both mother *and* daughter?"

He walked his horse in leisurely fashion down the track, but he was nowhere near as calm as he appeared. The "devils were on him" again, and he had only one desire in mind when he rode into the cantonment. But as he trotted past his own bungalow on the outskirts he heard his name called, and reined in automatically. Charlotte came from the house, flushed with excitement, holding her skirts up as she ran down the steps and across the small garden.

With such thoughts as he had presently in mind, the last person he wished to see was his wife, and he spoke in harsh tones.

"What is it that you must run after me in the street like a hoyden?"

She pulled up short just inside the gate, the leaves of an overhanging branch throwing light and shade across her face as she looked up at him in distress.

"I beg your pardon, but I thought you would not have heard the stunning news," she replied in tones so quiet he only just caught her words.

"What stunning news?"

She clutched the gate. "Dost Mohammed has given himself up as a prisoner."

He shook his head impatiently. "That must be complete nonsense! He has just defeated our cavalry, and Sale has been ordered to get back here as soon as possible to defend the city."

"No, Richard. Sir William McNaughten was returning from his ride this evening when a robed and bearded man ran from the rocks and threw himself on Sir William's mercy. It is truly Dost Mohammed, who has surrendered the fight for Afghanistan. It is all over."

Richard forgot his destination, and the sexual escape awaiting him there. The fight for Afghanistan all over? Could he have been so wrong yet again?

The astonishing surrender of Dost Mohammed put an entirely new complexion on the existing situation. The cavalry defeat was forgotten, and everyone then believed the sight of General Sale's fine body of men had terrified the Afghans so much they had realized victory against such a foe was impossible. When Shah Soojah urged that the prisoner should be straightway hanged, the British Envoy refused such barbaric action. Sir William found the Dost a dignified and cultured man, and magnanimously decided to send him into exile in India, a prisoner in luxury. In return for such clemency, the ex-Amir ordered all his sons to go with him. Only one defied his father. His name was Akbar Khan.

Peace appeared, at last, to reign in Afghanistan, and the occupying force once again regarded itself more as a friendly administration designed to help Shah Soojah in his rather lengthy job of settling in, than as foreign aggressors. Everyone relaxed. The end was plainly in sight, but winter had set in and nothing could be done until the snows and freezing blizzards ceased making the country impossible to cross.

This severe weather restricted outdoor activities a great deal, so social life of the indoor variety flourished—and not only the dinner-party kind. Several ladies found themselves *enceinte,* including Amy Scott, who was thrilled at the prospect of having her own child to care for once more.

One female who did not succumb to this condition and who knew why it was impossible, found those winter months unbearably trying. The Lingardes did not attend social functions, much less hold them, and only appeared together at obligatory military gatherings or on receipt of an invitation from the top echelons of the Kabul administration which could not be declined. On such occasions they arrived late and left early, spending the interim period as far from each other as possible. Richard Lingarde never danced with his wife, and only with those senior ladies duty obliged him to partner. Charlotte Lingarde always looked shabby and smelt of the potions she was forever mixing down at the hospital.

Without that tiny, inefficient hospital Charlotte would have found her position intolerable. With little social intercourse to occupy her, and the snow preventing long walks or rides in the tree-dotted valley, time dragged. Yet, all the time, the dread of the coming spring hung over her. Once the passes cleared and the road to India was traversable, she was to be sent to a manor in England while her husband went north into Russia, where he intended to stay.

During those dark months she alternated between hopes and fears, hating the boredom yet wanting the winter to go on. However, in some ways things had improved. Despite Richard's dictum that she should stay in her room out of his way, as the days had passed to weeks, then months, his habit of visiting Anna had grown from a brusque five-minute sight of her to whole mornings or afternoons of playing games, looking at picture books, and teaching new words. Charlotte always remained on the *chaise-longue* in the adjoining room, and Richard always ignored her. But she watched his growing passionate love for the little girl with excitement inside her. He had not then grown so heartless he could no longer be moved by affection!

Then, one afternoon, when she was lazily watching them through the archway something occurred which was more frightening than anything else since her arrival in Kabul. Richard handed Anna a small coloured ring, and when the child piped, "Thank-oo", took it and presented it again, saying encouragingly, "*spasibo*".

Charlotte shot up, trembling violently. "Why are you teaching her Russian?" she cried fearfully.

He turned startled, then said quite calmly, "She is one quarter Russian, and has Slavic blood in her veins. I intend her to be bilingual."

"*Why?*" It came out in agonized demand, due to her thoughts.

He scowled. "I should have thought the reason clear enough for anyone to understand."

He continued this practice. She knew it was useless to protest, but deep inside her was a seed of dread that replaced the earlier excitement. Anna had won her father's devotion, there was no question, but had Charlotte's determination to achieve just that worked against her? Was Richard planning to take his beloved daughter with him to Russia when he sent his unwanted wife to England? There would be nothing left for her if he did, yet she could no longer imagine him parting with Anna, never to see her again. Day after day she struggled with that terrible possibility, telling herself she would not let him do it, yet knowing there was no way she could stop him if he put the child up in front of him in the saddle and headed north.

But as time passed, she struggled with an additional torment. It was two years and two months since that night on which Anna had been conceived, and Charlotte had been sexually awoken, in imagination by Colley Duprés, and physically by Richard. Aside from its fatal consequences, that night had shown Charlotte that she was a very passionate and sensual woman. At Jalalabad, on the night of the starlit dinner-party she had known an overriding desire to surrender to Colley. It had probably been merely what all the other women had felt—a longing for sexual release, a physical ache for something denied for too long. Thank God he had not put her to the test, for now she could not face him without feeling loathing and disgust.

But it was not so with Richard. Daily his physical presence bothered her more and more. The sound of his voice as he murmured endearments to Anna set her pulse pounding, the muscular width of his shoulders as he bent forward to retrieve a toy, the strength of his thighs encased in skin-tight overalls, the gentleness of his hands as he played with the little girl all aroused longings that grew ever harder to control.

It was some time before she realized she was now seeing the man "every marriageable female in India" had always seen; now realizing that he was a person of great physical impact with a smile that could make one's heart turn upside down, and eyes that weakened one's legs with their changing expressions. How *could* she ever have looked at such a man and seen only a big brother, she wondered in despair, as she watched him adoring Anna as he must have once adored her?

Gradually, they had progressed to eating dinner together on those evenings that he was at home, but conversation was stunted and limited to affairs in India and other parts of the world. Charlotte was thankful that her knowledge of such subjects was as full as it was, or they would not have spoken at all. As she sat at the table opposite him and watched him with eyes now opened, Charlotte recalled nights on the budgerow when she had studied Colley in similar manner. But the girlish breathlessness she had felt on those occasions was nothing compared with the driving longing to be possessed by her husband, which consumed her almost daily.

She lay awake at night, her whole body throbbing for the touch of his hands, the sweet incitement of his lips, the gentle demand for possession that turned into complete mastery.

Even memories of his wonderful introduction to marriage with kisses on wine-wet lips, now aroused in her a fire of desire instead of the safe contentment she had felt at the time. She tossed and turned, knowing he was either drinking himself to sleep in his room on the other side of the bungalow, or was down in some hired room with Luana. The woman was no longer in the house—she had gone through to the servants' quarters on the day after she had arrived, and there was no sign of her—but it was quite apparent Richard was maintaining the liaison elsewhere.

But Charlotte's desire overcame her pride as the winter forced them to spend even more time indoors, and prevented her from going to the hospital for part of the day. One afternoon, she ventured into the room with Richard and Anna, ostensibly to show him how their daughter could now identify all the objects in a book, but really as an excuse to be near him and share the full delight of the transformation back to gentle idealist Anna managed to wreak in him. In reaching across for something Charlotte endeavoured to touch him, as if by accident. He merely moved further away.

Another time, her hopes were lifted when he curtly asked at dinner if she had no clothes other than drab outworn garments with tattered cuffs which she seemed constantly to wear. Thrilled that he had taken that much notice of her appearance she had answered that she had tried to spend as little of his money as possible, to which he had snapped that he did not wish the entire cantonment to think him a pauper and he would be obliged if she would rectify that impression at her earliest convenience. When, however, she sat at the dinner-table in a new glowing amber silk dress he appeared not to even notice she was there, so absorbed was he in a letter from his cousin, Igor, that contained reams of information about the estates Anastasia had left her son.

Desperation made her grow bolder. She began ordering his favourite meals and asking eagerly if he enjoyed them. Her maid was ordered to arrange Charlotte's hair in many different elaborate arrangements, the necklines of the newer of her gowns grew lower, she used perfume lavishly, abandoned discussion of the hospital, often broke into the smattering of Russian she had learnt along with Anna, chatted about the new baby Amy was expecting in the spring, and through it all faced the fact that she had fallen hopelessly in love with her own husband.

Finally, one day he looked up and said, completely without emotion, "If you can do nothing but waggle your tongue ceaselessly, and persist in making yourself a complete nuisance in my house, I shall return to eating dinner in my own quarters, alone and in blessed peace."

Unbearably hurt she had hit back immediately. "I only do it because you would not otherwise notice that I was here."

Getting from the table he had flung down his napkin in high anger. "You were never invited here, ma'am."

That night she lay wet-lashed in her bed, knowing it was useless. Anna had drawn from Richard all the love and gentleness with which he was naturally endowed, but whatever he had felt for his wife had truly been destroyed that night, never to return. When she heard him go out shortly afterwards the knife twisted in her, yet her inborn honesty posed her a question. Could *she* easily forget if he now came to her bed, aroused her to the heights of ecstasy, then whispered "Luana" just as she gave her all?

· twelve ·

SPRING CAME. THE snows melted to swell rivers that rushed down the mountains into the valley. It grew lush and beautiful once more, with blossoms on the fruit trees scenting the air that was clear and pure. The hillsides began to teem with wild life, and hunting recommenced. It was again possible to ride in the environs, take walks through the fragrant orchards, get out and about.

With spring came the usual restlessness. Young men were filled with the demands of their youth and burned to express it in whichever way was dearest to their hearts. Older men were more restless in their minds than their limbs, which no longer craved or could perform the violent exercise they once had known. Women looked infinitely more attractive when the spring months put a bloom on their cheeks and a sparkle in their eyes. They fell into a frenzy of homemaking when the sun once more lit rooms that had been dark and dreary through the winter.

The combination of all that was dangerous. Old men remembered how things used to be and longed for a return of the old life. Young men listened to their elders and knew it lay in their hands to restore their heritage. The women challenged them all with bright eyes full of speculation, and waited to see if their challenge could or would be met.

In the British the new season wrought the urge to end an unwelcome sojourn and return to the old life in India. They had no desire to spend another winter in Kabul. The older men found the bitter cold injurious to their health: the young men had tired of isolation from their fellows. The women wanted their comfortable life in India, where it was possible to travel, go to the hill stations for holidays, and buy all one wanted by way of luxuries. They also wanted to have their babies there, not in a small cantonment in the middle of a savage foreign country.

But it was forbidden them. The garrison had orders to remain until Shah Soojah effectively ruled his people, and this the Amir was making no attempt to do. The few measures he had taken since his installation on the throne were oppressive and thoughtless, making his subjects poorer through excessive taxation and hungrier through forcing inflated prices on foodstuffs.

With their characteristic calmness, the British simply heaved a sigh and resigned themselves to doing their duty for a little longer. A few of the more hot-headed young men—among them Richard Lingarde—once more attacked the subject of the defencelessness of the cantonment, and urged steps to be taken to build up the walls, bring the commissariat within the cantonment proper, and erect gun-emplacements at strategic points. They were told they were "croakers", alarmists who upset the morale of the garrison. Even when General Cotton (the man who had court martialled Richard over the subject once) was replaced by General Elphinstone, an ageing invalid unfit for such a command but who, nevertheless, proposed buying an extension of land that would make it possible to improve defences, the answer always came back the same; there is nothing and no one in Afghanistan against whom we need defend ourselves. The General accepted it, and nothing was done. Then, since the Kabul force could not visit their friends in India, the friends journeyed down to Kabul instead.

In the Afghans, spring wrought the urge to regain their independence. In this, the whole nation was in accord, men, women, and youths. They set about planning the realization of their desire without delay. In the higher echelons of command in British India, spring induced a fever of distrust and suspicion . . . of the Russians. Reports had been received of Russians spying out the land in Afghanistan, of Russians inciting loyal Afghan leaders to turn against the British, of Russians sneaking around the outlying forts in disguise—of Russians being worryingly Russian.

Things came to a head and demanded action when a report came through from Captain Bateson—the political officer who had guided the Meerpore ladies through the Khyber Pass—who was at Malkhan, a small fortified settlement north of Kabul, that a Russian traveller had been reported two days off from the fort and heading straight for it. The chieftain of the Malkhan area, who resided in the fort, had declared his loyalty to the British the minute Dost Mohammed had surrendered, and Bateson had been sent to him, at that time, to advise and guide him through the period of adjustment.

The chieftain, Mooji-Lal, was an excitable, eager, but very egotistical man, who loved power. Yet it was only when Bateson wrote that Mooji-Lal had thrown in his lot with the British because he would have lost consequence in the eyes of his followers if they had suspected he had been forced to accept domination by white infidels, that the truth occurred to anyone. Then, the prospect of a smooth-talking Russian spy arriving at Malkhan to whisper treachery in Mooji-Lal's ear became extremely alarming. With only a single political officer to support British occupation of the district, the danger was too great to be ignored.

Civilian and military leaders in Kabul held an emergency meeting. To send a small armed forced to Malkhan would be a grave mistake, they all agreed, yet Bateson's message had suggested that he saw this Russian "traveller" as a threat. The obvious solution was to send to Malkhan a spy of their own, someone who would not be seen by Mooji-Lal as a sign of British mistrust, but who would neutralize the effect of the Russian.

Colley Duprés was summoned, at once. He was the obvious man for the job—part Russian himself he would be able to question the visitor in his own language and understand anything the man might say to his servants or companions. He was also very experienced in dealing with native chieftains, and would handle Mooji-Lal in just the right way.

But, unknown to the Kabul garrison, Colley Duprés had come up against Mooji-Lal in the past and was not anxious to meet him again. He had particular reasons for staying right where he was, and had no wish to be sent out to deal with a Russian whom he most probably would not understand. Quick thinking had him outlining all the advantages of keeping him in the vicinity of the shaky Kabul Amirate, and providing the perfect solution to the problem.

Captain Bateson, he told his listeners smoothly, was a very capable man who needed no assistance on the political side. All he wanted was someone who could speak fluent Russian—a junior officer of no special talent who could be easily spared from Kabul. A man who certainly would not be missed, and who might benefit from the experience. A man who, if the worst should befall him as he travelled through the hills, would be of no desperate loss to the garrison . . . or to his wife and daughter. His listeners all thought of the same man, immediately.

Richard received the summons to report to General Elphinstone's staff captain one morning after he had slept badly. Prepared for another strong warning on his private life, he was in no mood for the meeting. As he rode slowly through the cantonment he continued his troubled thoughts of the night hours. Spring had arrived, and the passes to India would be open to travellers again any day. Now was the time to put into practice his firm intention of selling out, going up to Russia, and sending Charlotte on her way to England out of his life for good.

He would have no trouble selling his commission, cousin Igor had everything in readiness for his arrival, and he would be glad to see the last of his wife. But . . . oh, dear God, how could he send little Anna out of his life when she was now the only worthwhile thing in it? The solution was to take the child with him, but the route he planned to take north was too arduous. The civilized way to travel to Russia was by sea, but that meant going back through India again. Six more months with a woman from whom he longed to be totally free.

Charlotte had changed a great deal, he had to acknowledge. She was quieter, more peaceful and reflective. The eager, searching, bruised child had been replaced by a woman who made no demands on him, no longer aroused the compulsion to protect her from others. She talked intelligently on subjects few females understood fully—but she had always been able to do that—and worked untiringly in the little hospital with Mrs Smethwyck to encourage her. If she were married to someone else he would quite probably respect and like her. But she was *his* wife—a great stone around his neck forever—and had destroyed any respect or liking he could possibly feel for her.

Yet, she was the mother of his child, a fiercely adoring mother as his own had been, and he could not imagine her parting with Anna easily. What, then, was he to do? He could not face keeping Charlotte in his house, and could not face Anna leaving it. All winter long, as the little girl had become more and more precious to him, the snows had been his salvation. Spring now challenged him, and he shied from meeting that challenge.

When Richard emerged from the meeting with Elphinstone's captain he knew he had been offered a reprieve, yet that reprieve could also prove the most disastrous event in his life. That Colley Duprés had been behind his being sent to Malkhan he had no doubts, but that blackguard would remain in Kabul during his own absence, and what he had done once he could do again—with more deliberate intent, this time. Charlotte could give herself to whomever she wished, with Richard's blessing, but he would let nothing and no one touch his daughter. The mere thought of Duprés peacock figure petting Anna's chubby limbs, stroking her fair curls, or touching her golden-hued cheeks with his fingers brought a rush of hot blood to Richard's head, and a sick feeling to the pit of his stomach.

He turned to his quarters and left instructions with his servants to put together all he would need for a journey over the hills. It would be necessary to take a fair amount of equipment with him, because he had been instructed to make a topographical survey of the country on his return journey, with a view to making a map of the Malkhan area when he got back. He wrote several letters of the kind soldiers often write. The most important of these was a directive that, in the case of his death, his daughter Anastasia Margaret Lingarde should be placed under the guardianship of Sir John Lingarde, and should reside at Meakworth House in Kent until such time as she married.

He sealed the letter thoughtfully. That should ensure that Anna could not be dragged around all over the world in the wake of a soldier of fortune by a mother who was plainly still infatuated. Comments had reached Richard's ears concerning Charlotte's behaviour at Jalalabad, and how she had been seen entering Duprés' tent on the night after the attack on the column. Some said she had also entered the tent of Captain Petworth, but that was probably only spiteful gossip since she openly detested the man, and he her. Duprés was different, however. Whenever she came face to face with him now she was unbelievably haughty and offhand—the surest sign of a guilty conscience—and unreadable messages passed between the pair in secret glances.

Richard tapped the letter with his fingers as he brooded on the fact. Well, Duprés was welcome to Charlotte, but he would never get his hands on Anna, he had made certain of that!

He was busy all day, only going to Anna late in the afternoon for his usual visit. She was delighted to see him, running forward with arms outstretched for the usual long spinning hug he gave her, and chuckling with pleasure at the giddy thrill of it. As usual, she talked endlessly in a mixture of baby words and clarity that enchanted him and smote his heart as he saw the many expressions on her face that were echoes of her grandmother. He was similarly affected by the natural way in which she intermingled Russian words with English. She was going to be a magnificent woman!

That Charlotte was watching them from her adjoining room was not important enough to matter to him, and it was only when the ayah carried the child off for her supper that Richard turned in that direction to find his wife watching him from the *chaise-longue*. He walked to the curtained archway and stood there, leaning on one hand against the curve.

"I am going away tomorrow," he told her quietly.

Her face went white, her features grew rigid and astonishingly drawn, all in a moment. "*Tomorrow!*" she repeated, almost in a whisper. "Oh, no!"

"They are sending me to Malkhan," he said, puzzling over her reaction. "There is talk of a sly Russian attempting to turn the Afghan nation against their white conquerors. I have orders to stop him."

Looking almost ill, Charlotte put her hand to her throat as she gazed at him with eyes enlarged by some kind of shock. He frowned, despite the levity of his words. Why should she be so affected by the news? Had she been awaiting just such an opportunity? Had she and Duprés planned it between them?

Fired to anger by such thoughts, he went on curtly, "I have no idea how long I shall be away. A month, possibly— but do not count on it."

"*Count* on it?" she echoed questioningly.

"Oh, do not put on those airs with me, I beg you," he retorted spiritedly. "I am not taken in by them, I assure you. For yourself, you may do as you please with that pretty popinjay, but it will not be in this house. Nor will I allow him anywhere near Anna. Is that clear?"

She appeared to turn even paler at that, but he continued, his aggression mounting at his imaginings.

"If you will not give me your solemn assurances, I shall instruct the ayah not to let the child out of her sight."

"*Richard,* that is enough," she cried, rising from her chair in distress. "I know only too well that I count for nothing in your esteem, but this is insulting in the extreme."

He studied her slender figure in the dull green silk gown that lent an aura of dignity she did not deserve. "I did not ask you to come here."

She took a long deep breath as she advanced towards him, still pale but more in command of herself. "No, Richard, you did not ask me to come, as you so often remind me. But would you rather I had vanished out of your life forever, taking Anna with me? You are fond of speaking with absolute honesty, are you not? Do so now, when you answer that question."

He found the expression in her eyes disturbing, and turned away into Anna's room, saying, "I do not want Duprés anywhere near my child. That is honest enough, I trust."

There was no reply, and he could not stop himself from turning to discover why. She stood in the archway still, with tears on her cheeks. There was no crumpling of her features, or convulsive heaving of her bosom. Just silent distress that was more disturbing than sobs.

"I knew when I made the decision to bring your child to you that I was leaving myself open to your scorn and rejection," she said in tones of such infinite sadness, he was shaken by it. "I think you have treated me to both on every possible occasion. I told you when I arrived that I asked nothing for myself . . . and you have given me nothing."

"Which is precisely what you gave me," he said quickly.

"No, Richard, that is not entirely true, and you should be honest enough to admit it. I gave you gratitude and much affection. It in no way compensated for what you gave then so willingly and ardently, but it was all I was capable of giving, at that time . . . and never were you publicly humiliated by my lack of maturity, confess it."

He thought the conversation had continued long enough, and turned to leave, once more. Her next words stopped him.

"I had no pride when I cheated and begged to come here, Richard. I have had none all through this terrible winter. But I will not stand silent when you suggest I am nothing more than a jade, a wanton who cannot wait to consort with a libertine the moment your back is turned . . . and beneath your own roof. Even you have had the decency to conduct your amour with your Indian mistress elsewhere since I arrived."

He was about to swing round and retort when she appeared before him, her cheeks streaked and wet, her voice shaky with emotion as she said, "And I will not stand silent when you suggest you will give a native servant orders to keep me from exposing my precious child to a cruel and ruthless man who has never been my lover. I once made a terrible mistake from which you suffered, Richard. I have also paid dearly for it since, but I will let you treat me as a treacherous sinful wretch no longer."

Her tear-streaked face reminded him of that occasion too sharply, and he said in cold tones, "You have always been at liberty to leave."

"And take Anna with me?"

He felt a sudden fear grip him, and he seized her arms. "Are you threatening me? There is no way you can leave here whilst I am away. They need my permission and signature before you can travel."

Still the tears hung on her lashes. "She means *that* much to you?"

His arms dropped to his sides as he realized she had achieved her object. "You have been very clever, I see that now. But have a care your plan has not worked too well. This mission to Malkhan has only postponed my decision on what the future will be. The passes to India are now open, you know."

She appeared to be fighting a tremendous battle with herself, and he found he had to wait to hear what she would reply to his last salvo. It took him by complete surprise when she put a hand lightly against his chest and said pleadingly, "Richard, is there no way we could all three stay together?"

"Ha!" he exclaimed shortly. "We have been doing so these past six months. Has it been a success?"

"You were determined it should not be." She drew nearer and gazed up at him with an expression he thought never to see in *her* eyes.

"You are an extremely intelligent man, so you must see that my 'plan' as you call it, was not only to ensure that you loved your own child, but that she should grow up in the united love of both parents."

He glared at her. "You truly believed I would saddle myself with you for the rest of my days?"

Shaking her head gently, she continued. "No. All I had heard of your conduct here persuaded me that the love you had once had for me had truly vanished that night. But a man who is ruled by such deep passions is also quickly roused to one or the other. You fell victim to Anna the moment she tumbled into your arms."

"And you thought I would repeat my folly over you?" he snapped, angry with himself for remaining in conversation with her so futilely.

"On the contrary, I thought your total lack of feeling for me would enable you to see that only by staying together would we prevent unnecessary suffering. Any other course will lead to heartache for you or me, and unhappiness for the child we both love so much. But I see how wrong I was."

"So you have that much sensitivity," he taunted.

"Oh, yes. Your love died with dramatic suddenness, I will allow. But it is not for that reason you are determined we shall not stay together, Richard. It is because you are afraid of me."

"*Afraid?*" he repeated incredulously. "Afraid . . . of *you?*"

"Why else would you confine me to one part of the house, avoid all conversation other than political affairs, refuse to dance with me at social functions, and move away, as you have just done, whenever I draw near?" As she stepped nearer he found himself retreating instinctively. "Your love certainly died, Richard, but *something* replaced it . . . and all the time it is there you are afraid of me."

Struggling to keep on top of the conversation, he asked, "What has all this fantasy to do with Anna?"

"Everything," she replied fervently, stepping quickly up to him and putting a hand on his arm before he realized it. "Richard, there is not the least need to run away from me. Stand still and I will prove it, I swear."

Shaken to the core he pushed off her hand and moved away from an unwelcome proximity. "I leave at dawn," he informed her stiltedly. "As soon as I return arrangements will be made to settle this affair."

She seemed to crumple suddenly, and her voice was full of weariness. "Anna is a child, not 'an affair'. It is a future life you are controlling."

Ignoring that, he went on, "If I should not return, for some reason, I have made provision for my wishes to be carried out."

He began to walk away, but she cried urgently, "Is there an element of danger attached to this mission?"

At the doorway he paused and looked back at her. "Why, no, ma'am. Engineers do not fight, as you well know."

She put her hands to her temples as if her head ached. "So you remember my every word, and hold them against me."

"No . . . just one," he told her harshly. "And therein lie the answers to all those questions you posed a moment ago."

He stayed with Luana until an hour before dawn, when his bearer came to the room to warn him he must depart. She had been melancholy over his imminent departure, and he had not found the release he sought. Determined passion had left him exhausted and edgy throughout what remained of the night. For once, he felt no gentle compassion on parting from the girl, even though she was in tears at the thought of what might await him in the wild land around them.

But he was moved to violent feeling when he was faced with an unwelcome farewell from his wife, who appeared on the verandah like a wraith from departing night as he mounted his horse.

"I do not remember expressing a wish for your company at this ungodly hour of the day," he said brusquely, keeping his attention on checking that his choggle of water was hanging from the pommel, his spare ammunition was in its place inside the leather pouch, and his cloak was rolled and strapped to the saddle behind him.

Charlotte appeared beside the great brown stallion, looking up at him, her face pale in the half-light. "I simply wished to reassure you that Anna and I will still be here when you return."

He went on checking the tightness of the strap around his cloak. "I took steps to ensure that you would be. Spalding has my instructions regarding travel to India, which I placed with him yesterday."

She was silent for a moment or so, then said sadly, "There is no need to fight me. God knows, that is the very last thing I want."

He called to the two servants who were to accompany him with the baggage and supplies, and prepared to lead the three-man cavalcade off through the cantonment.

"Kiss Anna for me," he said as he drew away from Charlotte's side into the light cast by the candle-wicks in saucers that lit the entrance to the bungalow.

But she called after him, "Are you mad, riding out dressed in uniform? That scarlet jacket will be seen from miles off."

He gave a short laugh. "I am not a romantic soldier of fortune slipping through the country in the guise of a native. I am a representative of the white queen riding through a nation I have helped to liberate. This jacket will protect me, for it signifies friendship. Were you not aware that there is nothing and no one in Afghanistan against whom I need defend myself? That assurance has been given by all those of wisdom in command. Have a care, and do not doubt them, ma'am. They will have you court-martialled or shut up in a dark room with wet bandages around the head."

He moved off at the head of his servants and passed through the gate on to the road leading out of the cantonment at the north end. It was very quiet in that early dawn, but still he only half-heard a sound like stifled sobbing which he soon left behind.

It took all of eight days to reach the fort at Malkhan. The route lay through a network of hill tracks which were in a treacherous state due to swollen streams and boulders that had been brought down from the heights by melting snows. Richard remembered the Bolan Pass, and thanked Providence that there were three single travellers, and not an entire army that he had to see safely through, this time. It was arduous and uncomfortable, the temperature changing to extremes as he went up and down the hills.

His frame of mind changed just as excessively as he journeyed. One moment he was exhilarated by the beauty of the landscape and the feeling of communion he had with his mother in those wild stretches, the next, he was depressed, full of anxiety, riddled with suspicions of Charlotte and what she might be doing with Anna. She had been determined enough to get herself down to Kabul against all opposition; could she do the reverse? Her parents were influential enough to guarantee her special privileges and, since he had made it clear to everyone at Kabul that he did not want his wife's company, there was a possibility that the authorities would turn a blind eye where she was concerned, once more. If she should take Anna away from him . . . ! Yet, was that not what he was thinking of doing to her? All the way to Malkhan he made himself miserable over the problem which, at least, kept him from worrying about being ambushed.

The fort looked unimpressive after the great bastion at Ghuznee, and Richard wondered cynically what all the fuss was about. Malkhan was hardly of strategic importance. Did it really matter if a minor chieftain who occupied a crumbling fortress on a trade route listened to a Russian traveller with interest?

It was evening. The place looked melancholy and deserted in the amber glow of setting sun, and Richard was suddenly swept by acute reluctance to approach the gates—not only reluctance, but a sensation of fear that had no basis. He reined in and sat gazing across flat land at the putty-coloured walls which looked ready to fall down in the first strong wind from the north, at the gates, studded and topped with long spikes. It was an ordinary eastern-type fort with only two lounging men outside the gates, serving as guards. There was nothing to account for the feeling he had, yet it was so severe he broke into a sweat and a violent pain began in his chest to restrict his breathing, as he forced himself to press forward. Warning his servants to keep well behind him he drew his pistol and kept it hidden as he approached the gates.

The guards stared at him with sleepy uninterest, retaining their lounging positions, jezails cradled in one arm even when he arrived before them. Nothing could have been less alarming—or lax—yet the feeling of fear, danger, revulsion was stronger than ever. To counteract it Richard shouted at the guards in tones of brave authority, trying several dialects with no success, then finding they responded to Persian.

Mooji-Lal was already aware of his coming, they told him, shifting themselves sluggishly to allow the visitor entry through the small gate within one of the large ones. But Richard hardly had time to acknowledge that the administration of Malkhan could not be as indolent as appearances suggested before he was passing into the fortified outpost, where the fearful reluctance increased so violently he felt physically sick.

But his horse seemed unaffected by any psychic presentiment and carried Richard into a quiet, almost deserted square, which divided the actual fort from the hovels and market-stalls of the inhabitants—Mooji-Lal's subjects. There was the usual stench associated with squalor, but it seemed worse after the clean air of the past eight days and increased Richard's nausea.

The sun had vanished behind the hills and Malkhan was lit with that eerie reflection from the sky that suggested the death of a day, the passing of bright hours and the onset of sinister darkness. The back of his neck grew cold as Richard moved slowly further into the outpost, and the gate slammed shut behind him. It seemed much too quiet, far too deserted, and he cocked his pistol with a click that sounded unusually loud in that silence broken only by the slow beat of the horses' hooves.

All at once, Richard identified the feeling that assailed him. He was carried back over five years to a memory of Edward Kingsley's butchered body lying twenty-five yards ahead, and an unnatural silence after the noise of death. His grip on his pistol tightened as he scanned the dusk for signs of murdering hordes, and tensed himself to hear the sudden fanatical shrieks. His nerves jumped when he sensed movement ahead, but it heralded just one man in flowing robes, a wide, flat turban, and skin shoes that made no noise as he approached.

Richard reined in and awaited the bearded messenger, his apprehension not entirely dispelled. After the customary Afghan greeting the man gave a long speech in a language Richard did not understand and, when it ended, he explained the difficulty in Persian. Without hesitation the greeting was repeated in that language. Richard then relaxed and put away his pistol, although he remained in the saddle.

The man was Sansar, wazir or chamberlain to Mooji-Lal, and expressed his master's delight at the visit of so honoured a guest as he found within his humble walls. His coming was expected and welcomed, Richard was told. A room had been prepared, and Mooji-Lal wished his English friend to take advantage of all that had been placed at his disposal. If anything had unfortunately been overlooked in the way of hospitality, Mooji-Lal would be wounded if his guest did not ask for it.

Richard thanked Sansar for his welcome, recited the appropriate flowery reply, and asked to be shown his quarters so that he could remove the dust of his journey as he was not fit to grace Mooji-Lal's opulent residence in his present state.

It was all impersonally false and formal, and each man was sizing the other up throughout the speeches. It was plain the old Afghan was not impressed by Richard's lack of a long retinue of servants—two only were indicative of a lowly position on the social scale—and his dark gaze was searching the baggage tied to the spare horses with speculation on what the visitor might have brought by way of presents.

Richard, on his part, was noting the signs of decadence on the lined face of the wazir, the eyes that did not reflect the friendliness of the greeting, the cruel downward tug of his fleshy mouth. A man of few virtues, he felt, and wondered if the friendship of Mooji-Lal, the man's master, was as warm as the British supposed. George Bateson appeared to have slight doubts, or he would never have asked for a Russian-speaking colleague. Richard determined to question Bateson on the present political climate at Malkhan as soon as possible. Not that he thought it mattered one way or the other, except to himself and the other two white men shut up in the fortress with the chieftain. The whole place was going to rack and ruin, and appeared to be surprisingly under-populated. It could hardly pose a threat to the great British nation.

Servants appeared at a clap of Sansar's hands to take the horses and direct the visitor to his quarters, the wazir apparently having decided Richard's consequence was not sufficient to merit his personal guidance, after all. But Richard was not prepared to walk off and leave his baggage where he could not supervise its removal, and matched Sansar's disparagement by indicating that he carried with him articles of such value they could not be left to servants to unload.

There was a moment when Richard thought they might have reached a stalemate, but Sansar was plainly uncertain what these "articles of such value" might be, and finally decided not to risk the withholding of gifts by an affronted guest. It might not help the relationship when the Afghan discovered that Richard had referred to his topographical equipment, but it won that particular point. The wazir waited while Richard dismounted, then led him across the square to the inner gates of the fort proper. They opened at precisely the right time, although it was not apparent to Richard how, or by whom.

Night had finally arrived by then, and the way was lit by flambeaux in sconces. The pale flickering light denied Richard a satisfying study of the courtyard, or fortifications rising thirty or forty feet above his head, but he saw enough to realize that Mooji-Lal followed the trend of eastern rulers by living surrounded by opulence whilst his subjects starved in squalor. As he stood while servants unloaded his baggage Richard could see fountains playing in an inner courtyard which boasted beautiful blossom trees, statuary, and pillars decorated by an artist with extravagant taste in colour and semi-precious stones. He began to revise his first impressions. Perhaps Mooji-Lal's chieftainship was more influential than he supposed!

The room to which he was shown within the north wing of the inner fortress was large, with stone walls painted pale green. There were rugs on the floor to brighten the room with colour, and a raised dais covered with furs and cushions to serve as a bed. In one corner was a sunken area with an outlet hole to allow water to run away. Several large pitchers stood beside it, and in the opposite corner was a large wooden chest with brass studs and bands across the lid. A small embrasure comprised the only window, and a screen stood across the entrance to serve as a door.

Richard was unhappy about that last. No way of locking himself in! He would find it difficult to sleep knowing anyone could walk in on him during the night, and he would worry about his equipment left there when he was out of the room. However, he said nothing of his fears as the wazir departed with the assurance that Mooji-Lal would cherish the delight of his visitor's company later that night when he had eaten and rested.

Richard was glad of the breathing-space. He was dirty, tired and hungry. He was also prepared to take stock of the situation before asking to see Bateson, or the Russian "spy". He stripped and stood in the sunken bath while one of his servants—a man called Wahab—threw pitchers of tepid water over him, then lay on the cushions for an hour or so resting his limbs and eyes until a tray of food was brought. It was unappetizing to a European, but he ate it doggedly knowing eastern personalities were quickly offended by refusals to eat what was provided.

It was eleven that night when a message was brought inviting Richard to meet Mooji-Lal. In that time, he had failed to find any sign of the two other white men supposedly in the fort, either by sight or sound. The remainder of the wing in which he had been placed would seem to be unoccupied. He tried to analyse the significance of that, but could only think he had been put in the overflow guest accommodation because Bateson and the Russian occupied the other rooms, or that he was too junior in rank to warrant a place in the main part of the fort. Either could explain why Bateson had not come calling yet. There was so little going on in Malkhan, the political officer could hardly have missed an event as momentous as the arrival of his colleague. He had expected the man to seek him out at the first opportunity but, as he donned evening mess kit, Richard realized Bateson would most probably be there to introduce him to Mooji-Lal.

The assumption was wrong. The chieftain was alone save for a clutch of youths Richard supposed were his bodyguard, so he was forced to adjust his approach to the man. As Bateson's junior he would have played a watching game, taking his lead from the political man with a wider knowledge of the Afghan's personality. But, alone, he would have to give an impression of confidence, experience, and friendship tinged with authority to a man he had had no opportunity to study.

He squared his shoulders and entered the room, closely followed by one of his servants carrying a bolt of silk and two sheepskins—the obligatory gifts when visiting in the East, and considered by Richard's superiors to be more than enough for a minor chieftain.

The chamber was vast, and he seemed to take a long time crossing it, his spurred boots making a ringing sound on the stone floor that echoed in the upper regions of a room that was more like a cavern. The walls were hung with silk of garish colours, and small studded chests stood against the walls each side. At the end of the room was an ornate arrangement similar to a four-poster bed that had grown wildly out of proportion, filling a space of twenty feet or more each way, yet barely two feet off the ground. Here, Mooji-Lal sat amidst outsize cushions and bolsters, watching intently as Richard approached.

But Richard was equally intent on the man who was playing host. Younger than he had expected—perhaps thirty-four or five—Mooji-Lal was strongly built and handsome in the aggressive and somewhat dissipated manner of his race. The features were bold and striking, but already showed signs of cruelty, self-indulgence, and sensualism, and his dark eyes, although piercingly alert, had whites that were yellowish, with the pink streaks caused by sleeplessness and unhealthy living. Twenty feet away the figure in the striped robe with a loose coat of intricately embroidered padded cloth looked impressive: close to he was all too plainly a man who had abused his strength and intelligence.

Richard stopped before the huge canopied dais and gave a formal bow as he offered the requisite greeting in faultless Persian. Mooji-Lal watched him throughout the speech, eyes glowing with a peculiar suggestion of excitement which left Richard feeling slightly uneasy. The feeling increased when, all formalities completed, the Afghan remained quiet for an uncomfortably long period, ending his silence with a great gusting sigh as he studied his visitor from head to foot.

When he went into the lengthy and elaborate reply that was demanded by protocol on such occasions, his voice was surprisingly gentle, lyrical and full of friendship—a cultured voice for a savage-looking man.

"Lieutenant Lingarde, I beg you to share my couch and my victuals," he continued, indicating some cushions beside him with a lazy wave of his hand. "Words cannot express my delight at the visit of another of my English allies. One's soul is a desert without an oasis if there is no friendship within."

Resignedly Richard scrambled on to the dais and tried to sit with some degree of comfort in his tight uniform, avoiding the risk of ripping the silk cushions with his spurs. Mooji-Lal seemed more interested in that spectacle than the presents offered by Richard's servant, and he found himself realizing why Colley Duprés had adopted the dress of the country, although it was beyond him why any European would live in the East from choice.

So, sitting in extreme discomfort beneath the limpid gaze of his host, Richard conversed for an hour in fluent Persian on a series of subjects introduced by the Afghan with surprising suddenness. They covered the glory of the surrounding countryside, the extent of Richard's personal wealth and influence, the perfection of the silk wall-hangings, the surrender of Dost Mohammed, the extreme attractiveness of Richard's uniform, the excellence of Malkhan fruit, the personal beauty of a woman allowed to rule the great British nation, the amount of physical exercise Richard took to maintain his muscular figure, the astonishing reverence shown by Englishmen towards their wives, the beautiful pale shade of Richard's hair and skin.

"Is it the normal colour of Englishmen?" he asked eagerly.

Tiring of the inconsequential nonsense, longing to stretch his cramped legs, and wishing he could escape the halitosis of his host, Richard seized his opportunity to get down to business.

"Well, sir, Captain Bateson has been at Malkhan for some months, and he is English," he said firmly. "Unfortunately, I have not yet had the good fortune to meet him. I hope to do so as soon as possible."

The change of approach did not suit Mooji-Lal. The smile vanished and he looked extremely petulant. "That will not be possible. He left several days ago."

Richard was astonished. "Left! Why?"

Mooji-Lal shrugged. "He did not say. Yes . . . yes, he went to buy horses."

"Horses! Why would he want horses?" asked Richard, completely mystified. "Did he not bring his own with him?"

"You must ask him when he returns," snapped the chieftain, stroking his beard with short angry movements. "I have not chosen to speak of him, but you."

"He is the reason I have come to Malkhan," persisted Richard, easing his position by putting one leg out straight in front of him.

Mooji-Lal grinned, revealing yellowed teeth. "I shall delight in your company while you await his return."

Thoughtful, and feeling somewhat heady with heat, rich food and the alcohol the Afghan was offering so freely, Richard approached the other subject he wished to tackle.

"Captain Bateson suggested that another traveller might have passed this way recently. A Russian explorer, perhaps."

"He is here still," came the quick answer. "It is wonderful indeed that you knew of this."

Richard fought the sleepiness that threatened him, and wished there was more air. "There is not much that escapes the notice of your friends, sir." He shifted again, finding the tight collar a torment around his throat and the gold-trimmed mess jacket restricting his breathing.

Mooji-Lal watched his every movement with his dark melting glance. "You wish to meet this traveller?"

"Yes . . . very much," said Richard, pleased that the offer had saved him from a long-winded approach to the matter. "I am part Russian. My mother was a member of one of that country's great families."

The statement brought about a feverish reaction in the Afghan, who knelt up and seized Richard's shoulders while he spoke with rapid excitement into his face.

"Of noble blood! I knew I could not be mistaken. That skin so smooth and golden like a ripe peach, those eyes like turquoise pools to reflect a man's desire, that pale hair the colour of an early sunrise, such beauty of form revealed by garments designed for all men to see and yearn to touch." His hand began to stroke Richard's thigh, high up and with unmistakable intention. "The fire of the Tartar races burns within you, I saw that at the start. What do I want with these boys surrounding me, when I find such perfection has come to me out of the desert?"

Shocked and horrified by what he tardily recognized in Mooji-Lal's whole approach, Richard was off the dais and out of reach before his would-be lover knew his intention.

This was something he had not foreseen, had never before experienced, and did not know how to handle. Wondering why on earth Bateson had not warned him, and with wild ideas of forcible rape held down by the man's homosexual bodyguard, Richard tried to master his repulsion enough to keep in mind the real object of his mission.

"Sir," he managed through laboured breathing, "your friendship is greatly valued, but I have to tell you that I have a wife and child in Kabul."

The Afghan shrugged as he studied Richard's legs encased in the tight-fitting overalls. "I have many wives—how else can a man acquire sons? But true delight lies in the love of a boy. For many years I have waited for a gift from the heavens, and I see it before me now."

"You must excuse me, sir," said Richard, manfully sticking to protocol. "I am tired after my journey and beg you to allow me to retire."

Mooji-Lal got quickly to his feet and slipped his arm through Richard's persuasively. "I will show you ways to sleep so that you will rise in the morning with the energy of three men, and the happiness of a whole nation. I will show you such joy, you will never wish to leave my side."

Putting safety before diplomacy, and certain it would not be long before he was heartily sick, Richard backed away.

"Your interest is most gracious, but the ways of my country forbid acceptance of your offer. I wish you a night of peace and the blessing of wisdom upon your awakening."

His spurred boots made an even worse commotion as he left at a very fast pace and headed for his quarters feeling he had awoken in the midst of sleep-walking. Once in his room, he rid himself of the food and liquor he had been obliged to swallow, refreshed his heated body with several more pitchers of water, and sank down on the cushions with his brandy flask. His two servants had been instructed to watch the open doorway, and in Richard's other hand was his pistol. He lay back groaning. That unlockable entrance had bothered him from the start, but he had been concerned for the safety of his life, not his honour!

The bizarre outcome of his meeting with Mooji-Lal took his whole attention for some while, and he wondered how badly he had blotted his copybook by refusing the man's overtures. It certainly did not augur well for his popularity during the time it took to interview the Russian and leave for Kabul once more. Then, his thoughts returned to the strange instance of George Bateson's decision to go off on a horse-buying trip just when the man he had requested was due to arrive. Still, it appeared the Russian was still at Malkhan and, since he was the reason for Richard's presence there, he would have to do without Bateson's briefing on the situation.

He began to relax and wonder what the Russian would be like. It would be good to speak of all the places he knew with someone who had recently come from there. His mind began to drift off on thoughts of distant estates, and memories of his cousins Igor, Sophie, Ivan and Mikhail, the twins, and little Natasha. Then, inevitably, he felt the old tearing sadness of his mother's death. He could see her still as she had walked into that reception like a boyar princess, defying the anti-Russian feelings running high against her.

Stealthy movement at the doorway brought Richard instantly alert and raising the pistol in defence. His servants were challenging someone, but above their voices he heard a cultured one speaking in French.

"Monsieur-Lieutenant, I regret this intrusion, but is it permitted for me to enter?"

The Russian—it could be no other! Richard rose and went to the screen, saying, "You have only to identify yourself, monsieur. One has to be cautious in savage lands."

"But, yes. That is why I visit under cover of darkness. I am Dmitri Feodorovich Verenchikov. I saw your arrival at dusk, but it was useless to come to you until Malkhan slept."

Richard pulled back the screen, feeling that the unreality of the evening was being continued as he invited his nocturnal visitor in. By the low light of the saucer-lights he saw that Verenchikov was of medium height, slightly plump with swarthy looks.

The man bowed and clicked his heels formally. "I am honoured, Lieutenant . . . ?"

"Lingarde . . . Richard Gregori Lingarde," he said, automatically following Russian custom by giving his full name.

"Well, monsieur, I will not say that I am glad that you are here for, much as I am cheered by your company, I regret the circumstance. You have been sent to find Capitaine Bateson, I suppose. I fear you will regret it."

"Regret it?" echoed Richard, finding the whole incident more than he had bargained for concerning this supposed spy.

Verenchikov walked further into the room. "He said nothing to me of leaving. Then—pouf! He has vanished overnight."

"Vanished—when?"

The Russian considered. "Three . . . four days ago. I sorrow to tell you that I believe he is a prisoner somewhere in this stronghold . . . if he is not already dead. I sorrow even more to tell you, monsieur, that there seems little hope that we shall not share his fate."

"What!" ejaculated Richard, feeling that unreality was fast turning into melodrama.

But the other man's face was grave and perfectly serious in the faint flickering light. "I will tell you frankly, monsieur, that I was sent here to test Mooji-Lal's loyalty to your countrymen and offer him promises from mine."

The voluntary confession of being the spy he was suspected to be took Richard by such surprise he could think of nothing to say in response. But he soon discovered the reason for such frankness.

"This man, this barbarous leader is playing a game with two great nations. There is no doubt he feels loyalty to no one but Dost Mohammed. We shall be kept here until he tires of the game and rids himself of us in the way that amuses him most. Of one thing I am certain—we shall not leave here alive."

· *thirteen* ·

THEY SAT ALL NIGHT in conversation, each man finding
in the other much that he admired. When Richard revealed
his Russian ancestry, Verenchikov was eager and excited,
clapping him on the shoulders and intermingling French and
Russian as easily as Richard did. Formality was dropped, and
the pair spoke of that great land to their north, and of people
who turned out to be mutual acquaintances in St Petersburg.
Richard admitted that he had been sent to "spy on the spy"
and they discussed their own countries' intentions in Afghanistan, both in agreement that it was a land better left alone.

That brought them back to the serious consideration of
their plight, Verenchikov having persuaded Richard there
were grounds for his fears. The Russian had been at Malkhan
for two weeks, during which time he had done his best to
perform the duty he had been ordered to carry out, but telling Bateson that he was surveying the area with the view to a
possible railway being laid some time in the future.

"I am thankful you did not put my engineering knowledge
to the test by being here instead of your colleague, my
friend," he told Richard ruefully. "The only method of transportation I understand is the horse. I am a captain of cavalry."

"But Bateson was suspicious of you before you even arrived. How could he have discovered that you were on your
way?"

"Pouf! That is easy. Those silent hills are full of watching
eyes. Did you not feel it as you passed through?"

Richard shook his head. "I had problems on my mind.
Perhaps it was as well, in that case. Who are these watchers?"

"Who knows? Not friends, I imagine. The people of Malkhan district who live in the isolated villages outside the fortress? Your guess is as good as mine."

"There seem to be very few people *inside* the fortress."

The Russian smiled. "In the morning you will see your error. They vanished like beetles into the wood when you approached. Mooji-Lal has known your every movement for the last four days."

"Four days? The same time as Bateson went on his supposed trip," said Richard thoughtfully. "Are you certain he could not have done just that?"

"And leave the field clear for me? Oh, no, my friend. Captain Bateson was very affable, although much more secretive than you, and I do not think he would leave the place without hint of his intentions, especially in view of what I now know concerning his request for you to be sent to join him. The English are much less devious than Russians, do you not find?"

Richard grinned. "With my parentage, where does that leave me?"

Verenchikov grinned back. "Full of Russian guile, but in an ingenuous English way."

Taking another sip from his brandy flask Richard passed it to his companion. "If Bateson is incarcerated in the fort it should be possible to find out where."

Verenchikov swallowed the brandy with relish and wiped his mouth with the back of his hand. "I have tried to do so for the past four days—thumping on walls experimentally, whistling half a tune and hoping for it to be completed, losing my way deliberately, sending my servants to lean against walls to listen for faint sounds. There was nothing."

"But why would Mooji-Lal kill Bateson? He had been at Malkhan since November and, according to his letters, felt safe enough."

"Yes, yes, when winter snow hampers movement one's enemies are content to be friends," commented Verenchikov getting to his feet and going to the embrasure. "Dawn is not far off. I should return to my quarters, I think." He turned back into the room, saying, "It would be better to keep this meeting secret, do you agree?"

That put Richard in mind of his experience with Mooji-Lal and tentatively asked if the Russian had been similarly accosted.

Verenchikov laughed heartily. "Fortunately, no, my friend. But I am nowhere near as beautiful as you, I can see."

"It was not in the least amusing," growled Richard.

"Ah, but think of this, my fascinating boy. When *I* am having my head sliced from my shoulders, all you will suffer is a fate worse than death."

With the departure of the lively Russian, the truth of his isolation hit Richard with violent force. He leant against the embrasure, staring moodily out at the infant day. What had really happened to Bateson? It was his duty to find out, but he could think of nothing that the Russian had not already tried.

Tired and restless he moved away into the room. What a hellish situation he was in! Duprés had vowed to force him to face the enemy one day, and this was how he had done it. It occurred to him that the man had chosen, not a military confrontation, but the kind in which he, himself, was eminently experienced. Was it deliberately done to show up the ineptitude of someone who had stood against his opinions publicly on too many occasions? It then occurred to him that his superiors might well have realized there was a chance that he might never return and had welcomed the opportunity to rid themselves of a trouble-maker.

And what of Charlotte? Had she felt the same? Was that why she had staged that tearful scene on learning of the mission? Had it been to ease her guilty conscience? Frustrated, full of gloom at the prospect of the next few days, he grabbed up a hairbrush and flung it across the room to ease his feelings. He could not attempt to escape until he had reassured himself that Bateson was not a prisoner somewhere beneath his feet, and it would take time to check. But if Verenchikov was right about the hidden eyes in the hills, escape was impossible without Mooji-Lal's blessing . . . and he was not likely to get that now!

Fruit, flat scones, and a jug of raw wine was brought to him, but no message from his host on what was expected of him during the morning. Verenchikov had described to him the situation of his room in the south wing of the fort, and also where Bateson had lived for the past five months and, while he ate his breakfast, Richard decided to go along to that room to see if any of Bateson's things were still there, or if there was any sign of why he had gone so suddenly.

Taking up his pistol he left Wahab and the other servant guarding his baggage while he stepped into the corridor leading around the fortification to the south. The noise immediately struck him, and he leant from one of the embrasures that gave him a view of the settlement outside the fort but within the crumbling outer walls. The square and market were now teeming with people—as if Mooji-Lal had the power to click his fingers and bring them out, then click again to make them vanish indoors. Malkhan was a thriving settlement, it seemed.

He had just withdrawn his head and begun on his way to the south wing when an unmistakable and shattering sound reached him. Rifle fire—hundreds of rifles—followed by those fanatical cries that made a man's scalp crawl. He began to run like mad along the stone corridor, drawing his pistol as he went, his boots slamming against the uneven surface with a sound that echoed in the deserted space ahead of him. Slipping and slithering around the corner, he went full pelt along the next stretch wondering wildly where everyone was. The fort appeared deserted.

But Verenchikov was emerging from an archway ten yards ahead, also with a drawn pistol, and they raced together in unspoken agreement for the steps leading to the battlements above. They broke into sunshine after leaping up the steps with great urgent strides, and Richard then saw where everyone was. Right around the top of the crenellated fort were men with jezails firing downward with ragged disunity. One risky glance over the edge was enough for Richard. There was a horde numbering ten to their one, surrounding the fortress of Malkhan.

His arm was seized and he swung round to see Sansar beside him, eyes wide with alarm.

"We are being attacked," he cried. "What are we to do?"

"Who are they?" shouted Richard above the din. "Why are they attacking?"

In a flurry of robes Mooji-Lal came up wearing the same look of alarm as his wazir. "I am being attacked," he wailed. "Because I made friends with the British I am being persecuted on all sides."

With vague thoughts of Eldred Pottinger holding the Persians at bay in Herat, Richard rushed past the two wailing men and began to organize the riflemen into an effective defence. From the corner of his eye he saw Verenchikov doing the same on the west side.

From then on everything merged into an impression of noise, confusion, heat, and dust as he ran back and forth encouraging the defenders with hoarse shouts, directing their field of fire, and dodging bullets, oblivious of the fact that they were not his own troops and intent only on a profession he knew well.

But, although some of the robed horsemen below withdrew to a safe distance, enough remained to make the defence desperate. He and Verenchikov conferred briefly, then decided to use the men in two waves—one firing and one loading alternately—as a more effective force, and Richard was running back to implement this when he saw that the outer walls had been breached near the gate he had entered only the evening before. With only two indolent guards outside he was not surprised, but it meant he would have to direct some fire to the south in addition now.

On the point of turning away he was attracted by movement in the courtyard below, and checked at the sight of Sansar hurrying to the inner gates of the fort proper where he signalled to the guard to open up.

"My God, he's going to let them in!" he breathed and, taking aim with his pistol, shot the man with a single bullet.

But he was too late to prevent the gate from being opened, and the attackers streamed in to disappear below the spot where Richard stood. He ran back to warn Verenchikov, and yelled at some nearby men to go with him to defend the top of the steps. They ignored him. It was then he realized that all attempts to fight had stopped. Fury overcame caution.

Swearing and cursing he began to manhandle the man nearest him, who appeared to have turned into an immobile and uncooperative pillar of resistant flesh.

"Damn you—*fight!*" he roared, then began picking off figures that appeared on the rampart from the steps leading up to it, killing with one perfect aim each time, and reloading to kill again. But it was only when he had just one bullet remaining of the few he had taken up that morning that he realized he was the only man left who was firing.

Swallowing hard to ease his dry throat, and sensing that the whole situation had drastically changed, he slowly looked around him, pistol still raised. The attackers who had been swarming up the steps a few moments ago had frozen into a tableau, and all the way around the battlements it was the same. Suddenly, it was deathly quiet. All eyes were on him as men stood motionless where they had been active before. Then he saw Verenchikov, pistol dangling uselessly at the end of its lanyard, held helpless by four of the Afghans he had been commanding.

It was then that fear rushed into Richard with all its pounding ferocity, and he realized there was now only one enemy in the minds of these people—himself. As he stood there beneath the merciless sun, a white man in a scarlet jacket surrounded by hundreds to whom he was a symbol of infidel tyranny, he thought of Edward Kingsley, Basil Summerford, and all those of his countrymen who had died slow, agonizing deaths at the hands of these barbaric people.

They began to move, to close in, and he knew he could not face the fate they had in store for him. There was one bullet left in his pistol. He would die cleanly, whatever they might do to his body afterwards. But, on the point of lifting the pistol to his temple, he heard Verenchikov cry out for mercy as one of his captors raised his tulwar with every intention of slicing off one of the Russian's hands held out by another Afghan.

Richard fired his last bullet, but it killed the man with the tulwar, not himself, as he started forward in instinctive defence of a man he had known so short a time. The tableaux were broken at the sound of the shot, and Richard just had time to witness the swift death of Verenchikov as one of his captors slit his throat with expertise, before he was surrounded by dark faces and darker eyes full of hatred as a battery of curved knives were raised above him. In a flash, he knew that every man *must* be afraid at such a moment. It was no sign of cowardice, but of human frailty.

His own fear of those slashing knives was not to be ended quickly, however, for a loud command broke across the swift violence, and his murderers responded immediately. They fell back slightly, and Richard saw Mooji-Lal, robe flapping in the breeze, smiling as he gave his orders from ten feet away. Richard could understand none of it, but it was plain from the chieftain's expression that he had special plans for his prisoner.

Helpless, fearful, and praying for courage to withstand the coming ordeal, Richard felt waves of giddiness sweep over him as one huge Afghan took out a curved knife and advanced on him. But Richard could not stop from flinching as the knife flashed past his right ear, doing nothing worse than slicing off one of his gold-fringed epaulettes. That evidence of fear pleased everyone watching, and he could not stop the same thing from happening when the knife flashed again, taking off the other epaulette.

He then faced the dreadful fact that his captors intended to derive the greatest enjoyment they could raise before the torture. Nothing was more satisfying revenge on an arrogant conqueror than slow, savage humiliation. He now envied Verenchikov, whose body lay in a pool of blood further along the rampart. He now knew the answer to that which had plagued him for several years. The instinctive noble gesture did not save a man's life: it was empty glory for which he would now pay dearly. And so he did! Methodically every embellishment on his uniform was sliced off by the knife wielded so expertly—the insignia of rank, the gold braid, the ornate cuffs and buttons and, finally, the jacket itself was cut to ribbons so that it hung like rags on his body that was now shaking uncontrollably from the tension of waiting for the final cut that would slash his flesh in the same manner. But he remained outwardly unscathed as he was seized amidst a great roar of cheers from those surrounding him, and stripped naked except for his underdrawers.

What followed was plainly Mooji-Lal's special punishment as a rejected lover. Richard lost count of time as he was manhandled into the courtyard and held down as chains were fastened around his ankles and wrists, then forced to shamble along behind a proud Afghan on horseback who ensured that the pace was more than his prisoner could manage, shackled as he was. When Richard finally fell and was dragged along in the dust through the gates and into the outer square, the entire population had turned out to watch and enjoy the spectacle.

The horse stopped amidst market-stalls. There, Richard was hauled to his feet and chained to a post beside a counter displaying fly-blown meat. Dazed, convinced the end was nigh, and praying it would be merciful, he could only believe they meant to carve him up to add to the meat already on display. But that would have meant too brief a period of enjoyment for his captors.

He remained chained to that post until the sun went down, without food or water, the object of vituperation by the people of Malkhan, to whom he was represented as an example of the white infidels who had invaded their land, dethroned a beloved ruler, and destroyed their great fortress of Ghuznee. To their curses, the people added physical expressions of their hatred, spitting on him, throwing stones and mud; showering him with rubbish of all kinds until his pale hair was matted and dirty and his white skin was darkened by filth.

When they came for him at dusk he was streaked with sweat, on his knees, and mumbling incoherently all the nonsense he had recited to keep sane. They offered him water in a bowl, and jeered when he was forced to drink it like a dog. But he was in a world of his own which offered him greater torment than they could give.

His mother had spoken that unforgettable morning of her boyar ancestors who had refused to surrender, their pride being so fierce they had turned bandit rather than give up

their possessions, their women, and become slaves of conquerors. Today he had shown fear. He had been degraded,
his body humiliated, his pride scorned, and all through those
hours when the sun had beaten him into the ground, and the
people had abused his helplessness he had known how she
would weep to see what had become of the son in whom she
had taken such pride.

They put him over a mule, where he dangled in darkness
for a dizzy interminable period until he was pulled upright
and thrown bodily into blackness, which exploded in his
head as he thumped against a solid floor.

When consciousness returned he was shivering and cold,
but his skin was burning. The blackness was total, although
there was air coming in from somewhere in cold draught. He
tried to move out of it, but it took three attempts before he
could stand the pain that movement brought to his limbs.
Gradually, on hands and knees, he crawled along to explore
the confines of his prison, hoping he might come across
George Bateson in that cell. But there were only rats for
company in that area ten feet square—rats and other vermin.
He huddled in a corner away from the air inlet, shivering as
if in a fever, and trying to think with calm reason. Had
Bateson suffered the same treatment? Was he still alive somewhere in another cell? What were they planning to do with
him and Bateson, if the latter were not already dead? He
could not guess the answer, so moved on to something more
positive.

After a time of confused recollection he realized the attack
that morning must have been staged with the permission of
Mooji-Lal himself because, despite the supposed "victors"
overrunning the fort, the man still retained command. And it
had been his own wazir who had opened the gates to the
attackers. It pointed to Mooji-Lal having sold his people to
an ambitious neighbour who had probably promised him
that their combined strengths would defeat the British demand for loyalty. In permitting the mock attack, Mooji-Lal
would have ensured his people did not guess at his treachery
and, under cover of the assault, had very likely rid himself of
personal enemies within the settlement. Along with Richard

there had been quite a number of other prisoners suffering the punishment of chains and shackles, although none had shared the humiliation in the maket-square

He also realized that, as his approach had been tracked for four days, Mooji-Lal had waited until his arrival before going ahead with his plan. He most certainly would not have wanted to risk the chance of an Englishman somehow getting back to Kabul with the news that Malkhan had turned anti-British and now housed a large rebel force. The fact that Richard did have that information was his death warrant. That he would never leave the fortress again was his thought for the long night ahead.

But night never ended in that cell. Wherever the air came from, the source must have been subterranean and let in no light whatever. Richard only knew when it was daytime on the opening of a metal door, which revealed two men outlined in the pale light beyond. They dragged him to his feet and took him out into the growing light that suddenly burst into brilliant sunshine when the corridor led into the courtyard of the fort proper. Dazzled, Richard had a vague impression of a row of men, shackled with chains, as he was, standing in the courtyard while Mooji-Lal and another robed chieftain walked up and down inspecting them.

Richard was thrust into the row somewhere in the middle and stood swaying in the sudden warmth, wondering what was happening. It soon became clear. Walking down the line towards Richard, Mooji-Lal stopped before one man, nodded to his regal companion, and guards seized the poor wretch to drag him out, force him to his knees, and behead him with one great blow from a tulwar.

All around Richard the others set off a great wailing cry for mercy, but he could only stand in sick horror as he realized why he was there. Then, Mooji-Lal was standing before him, looking him over from head to toe with his fiery gaze. So this was to be the end of his life. Thirty years gone with one blow! It would be quick and clean, yet he cried out inwardly for life. There was so much he had left undone, so many goals he had never reched.

Mooji-Lal's hand reached out and cradled Richard's chin in

a grip that forced him to look the man in the eye for as long as he wished.

"So, not quite as beautiful as before, my noble boy, but those eyes . . . ah, those eyes! I cannot bear that they should close just yet," said the Afghan in soft, caressing Persian. He added an incomprehensible aside to his companion which made them both laugh, then they passed on to select a second victim from further down the line.

The other execution having taken place the prisoners were taken off one by one, and Richard was plunged back into darkness in his cell once more. Food and water were brought as the interior of that hole became cruelly hot. There was a mess of some kind which he had to eat with his hands, and he was foolish enough to use some of the water to wash himself down. He never did so again after the thirst of that first day.

It was only possible to count time by the heat or cold within his cell, by the arrival of the meagre food and water, and by the daily execution routine. Two heads rolled every day, chosen on the whim of Mooji-Lal. Each day he stopped before Richard, deliberating for longer and longer, making gestures of a homosexual nature, and enjoying the cat and mouse game.

By the twelfth day Richard still felt no assurance that he would be passed over for some other poor devil. One morning the game would suddenly end . . . if he had not already died from fever, starvation or insanity. The line was getting dangerously short of victims, and food was no longer brought to that black cell.

Amy's second pregnancy was not going too well, and Charlotte spent a great deal of time with the fretful girl. Tom, was not the best of prospective fathers, having neither the tact nor understanding necessary for that temperamental period in a woman's life. Of course, Amy did not possess the ideal qualities to cope with discomfort and inactivity. "Rest," to Amy, was tantamount to being deprived of all pleasure, and her petulance led to many a quarrel with her bewildered husband.

When Charlotte arrived outside the Scott household one afternoon she encountered her brother just leaving, and he immediately unburdened his aggravation on her.

"If you can get a smile from Amy, I'll kick a monkey," he began. "Dash it, Charlotte, all I did was tell her of Mrs Canford's shocking new riding–dress with skirt slit so that it shows more than her ankles, and she was at me like a fighting–cock, feathers all on end! What is a fellow to do? If I ask how she is I am making a tarradiddle over nothing, and if I try to amuse her I am an unfeeling wretch. I tell you, I would sooner face the enemy than an ailing female."

His frank open face was so glum Charlotte could not help laughing. "Poor Tom! You never had much sympathy with my cut fingers or grazed knees during school holidays at Aunt Meg's, if I remember."

"What has that to do with anything?" he complained, looking more bewildered that ever. "Amy has not cut her finger. All she is asked to do is sit still and be waited upon all day—which I would have supposed any female to enjoy no end."

Charlotte put her hand on his arm. "Not when her husband regales her with tales about seeing other females' ankles, etcetera. You are a ninnyhead, Tom. Put yourself in Amy's place. Would you welcome her thoughtless prattle about the boldness and dash of a fellow officer, if you were tied to your bed?"

"Eh? Well . . . she has already told me how much she admires Captain Fanshawe's seat on a horse, and the manner in which Lieutenant Matherson excutes the steps of the quadrille, so this other handsome follow she admires so much will be just another to add to the list."

She laughed and squeezed his arm. "You are set on being gloomy, I see. Leave Amy to me for an hour and I guarantee she will forget Mrs Canford's shocking riding–dress . . . and I would advise you to do the same as quickly as possible," she added with a twinkle.

Tom kissed her cheek. "You are the best of sisters, Charlotte. I'm dashed if I can understand how Richard . . ." he broke off, collecting himself just in time.

But Charlotte used his slip of the tongue to ask, "Is there any news of him yet, Tom?"

He shook his head and steadied himself as his boot slipped on the step. "I promised I would tell you the minute I heard anything."

"Even if it is bad news?"

He looked at his feet. "It will hardly come to that."

"But it is over three weeks since he left. Surely he would have sent a message by now if he was able to do so," she persisted.

Tom decided to move off. "He is most likely on his way back, anyway. Ten to one that nonsense about a Russian spy is a hoax." He laughed rather forcibly. "I should not care to be the first person Richard encounters on his return."

"I should," she breathed watching her brother walk away to his stable at the side of the bungalow.

Amy very soon emerged from her irritable mood brought on by her husband's tactlessness, but the subject of sexual attraction lingered on even after Charlotte assured her sister-in-law that Mrs Canford had looked excessively common in her daring new dress.

"But it is only natural that gentlemen will look at her ankles if she displays them, Amy," she continued, arranging sprays of fruit blossoms in a vase. "They would hardly be human if they did not." She came round to sit beside the couch and looked at the other girl candidly. "We are equally weak, are we not?"

Amy flushed and seemed too confused to speak for a moment or two. Then she said quietly, "One is brought up to devote all one's attention to pleasing young men by every available means. After marriage, it is hard to stop the habits of a lifetime." She looked down at her clasped hands on the cotton blanket. "What I am trying to say is that it is possible to love one's husband dearly, but still find pleasure in a laughing eye, a handsome face, or a . . ."

"Or a dashing lieutenant on a journey through wild and dangerous countryside?" asked Charlotte with a gentle smile.

Amy looked up quickly. "You have never mentioned a word to Tom?"

"Of course I have not! You have kept my secret for much longer, Amy." She glanced out through the window towards her own house further on the outskirts of the cantonment. "I have news of Lieutenant Spence, as it happens. He is coming to Kabul."

Where Amy had been pink before she was now completely rosy. "Oh, no! How can you possibly know that?"

Charlotte understood only too well the joyful dismay on Amy's face. Had she not felt that way herself on many occasions?

"I had the surprise of a letter from Mama today. My father has been obliged to journey to Calcutta, and she does not fancy remaining alone in Meerpore for such a long time. Since she has not seen her granddaughter for nine months she has taken the notion of journey to Kabul for a visit that will coincide with the advent of her other grandchild. In company with other ladies who have now decided to join their husband here, and several visiting officers—one of whom is Sir Alexander Burnes' younger brother—she is probably well on her way by now. The letter mentioned that my father appointed as her personal escort a young lieutenant who seemed anxious to see the countryside beyond Jalabad."

Amy put her hands to her cheeks. "Charlotte, what am I to do?"

"You ask *me* that?" She stood up restlessly, and walked to the window where she could see the Bala Hissar brooding over the sunwashed valley. "The evidence of my mismanagement of marriage is presented for all to see. I have discovered that the one I yearned after is not at all what I imagined him to be, but the realization has come too late to save . . ." She swung round to face Amy. "I beg you not to follow my example of foolishness, for it leads to great unhappiness." Crossing the room she took Amy's hands in a pleading clasp. "Temptation is there to be resisted, believe me. That is one of the things Aunt Meg taught me that is truly wise. You are fond of Tom, in your own way, and he of you. Do not allow anything to spoil that. There will be a child to consider. I would not wish the poor infant a childhood such as mine . . . or a mama like my own." She sighed

· 326 ·

heavily. "It is all too plain why she is really coming here. She does not give a fig for babies."

Lady Felicia Scott arrived in Kabul a week later, complete with a bevy of servants, six camels laden with baggage, and three horses. The McNaughtens were set to play host, but she immediately expressed her wish to rent a place of her own where she could entertain her family and friends as she pleased. It was very easily arranged for a person of such consequence, and Tom assisted his step-mother's removal to a bungalow with ample rooms and the best view of the valley. It was intended for visiting V.I.P.s, of the male variety normally, but no one could deny that Felicia Scott fell into the category.

Charles Burnes moved into the Residency in Kabul city, occupied by his distinguished brother, and other members of the newly-arrived party, including Lieutenant Spence, found quarters with friends or relatives. Fortunately for Amy, the young man who caused such agitation in her bosom was sharing a bachelor apartment on the far side of the cantonment and, when he heard of her condition, contrived to stay on that side.

Charlotte was torn by indecision over her mother's arrival. They had reached a strange kind of understanding during her last days in Meerpore, but Charlotte found herself fighting the old revulsion because she knew the true reason for Felicia's visit and also knew the true character of the man her mother had followed at the first opportunity. So she did not go out to meet the caravan as it came into the cantonment, deciding that there would be crowds enough to hide her absence and she was unwilling to stand unnoticed while those large blue eyes searched for Colley Duprés.

But Felicia's presence revived old wounds and brought several new ones as Charlotte considered her own position anew. She was still a parcel ready to be sent off to England when Richard returned. She had chased after him no less obviously than her mother was doing with Colley—the fact that Richard was her husband made the act no less undignified—and had almost begged him to allow her to remain with him in the future. But her ardent pleading, her daring challenge to his emotions on the day before his departure had left him angry and suspicious of her, that was all . . . and he had spent the night with Luana. She tried not to think it might have been his last night on earth, but not all Tom's reassurances would persuade her that the absence of any word from him for over a month was not extremely alarming.

What if he should not return? Her heartbreak would demand that she go back to England and live as Aunt Meg did, absorbed in useful work, a figure of fun to some, an object of pity to others. Yet, there was Anna to consider. From the day Charlotte had discovered that she was to have Richard's child she had been determined it would not have a childhood like her own. Had Anastasia been still alive, the answer would have been to take Anna to live with the Lingardes, where she would have been cherished and adored. But Sir John was now a lonely, broken man in a manor in England.

The other alternative would be to remain in India with her own parents. Anna would not receive any warmth of affection, but would have the benefits of gracious living, a life full of social intercourse and the natural advantages of her birth. She was the child of a union between members of two very influential and cultured families, whatever the relationship between mother and father afterwards, and should be given her birthright. That had been Charlotte's only motive behind the journey to Kabul. Her present consuming love for Richard had come later. She must not let it govern her concern for her daughter.

Knowing that Anna's future might rest with the Scotts, if her worst fears for Richard proved right, Charlotte felt compelled to call upon her mother several days after her arrival, yet the knowledge that Felicia had come in pursuit of her ruthless and barbaric lover put loathing in Charlotte's mind at the thought of the meeting. Full of unhappy indecision she struggled to come to terms with the conflicting feelings she had on the matter.

At Ferozepore on that last night, and at Jalalabad,

Charlotte had been a willing conquest to Colley, saved only from emulating her mother by circumstance. She understood too well the force of sexual temptation, but she had been an *ingénue* in one instance, a cruelly rejected wife in the other. Felicia was beautiful, sophisticated, and wrapped in luxury. It seemed degrading, in her case . . . and Charlotte had always been cornered by Colley against her will. She had never shamelessly pursued him under the guise of family love, as Felicia had just done.

Charlotte was now wise enough to admit to herself that Colley Duprés would most probably always have had the power to arouse physical excitement in her—despite her new deep love for Richard—if she had never witnessed the terrible cruelty to the Afghan prisoners that night. The memory still haunted her, and the sight of his turbaned figure now only filled her with hatred and contempt. It was because of that she found it so difficult to face Felicia. Surely her mother could not know the real man beneath the Oriental élan or she would never let those hands touch her, those eyes gaze upon her body!

Each time she reached that point in her thoughts, Charlotte bowed her head in despair. Enough of Aunt Meg's teaching remained to make her deeply ashamed of Felicia's adultery, and of her own past infatuation with such a man. How could she have been blind to Richard's worth and dazzled by self-indulgent bravura? How *could* she have whispered that name in her ecstasy and broken a man to the extent Richard had been broken? How could she face her mother without revealing her true feelings?

Charlotte's dilemma was solved by a chance meeting with Felicia the very next morning as she left her bungalow to go down to the hospital. Her mother, superb in a deep blue riding-dress with lace and velvet frogging, was setting out for a quiet canter through the valley with an escort of gentlemen to whom no one could take exception. Colley Duprés was nowhere in sight.

Noting with amusement that there was not a cloud in the sky and no more than a zephyr blowing, Charlotte watched

· 329 ·

the cavalcade approach. Felicia reined in and her gaze revealed her opinion of Charlotte's outmoded gown in yellow striped cotton.

"My dear child," she exclaimed in her husky voice, "you were on your way to call upon me and I am about to ride out and take the air. How very vexatious! Should you care to take a light tiffin at twelve? I will see you then."

It had been handled expertly and given no rise to gossip about strained relations between mother and daughter. It also constituted an invitation Charlotte could not refuse.

"Thank you. I shall bring Anna with me."

The lovely eyebrows arched. "Anna?"

"Your granddaughter."

"Ah . . . yes, to be sure. I cannot wait to see the child again."

The party rode off leaving Charlotte as confused as before over her attitude towards her mother. She turned and went back to her bungalow to warn the ayah that she would be taking Anna out at noon, but it was an unfortunate decision.

Going around the side of the building where she knew the child and her nurse would be enjoying the fresh air and early morning sunshine on the back verandah, Charlotte came upon Richard's bearer in earnest conversation with a young woman who appeared in some distress. It was a moment or two before shock realization hit Charlotte. The girl could be no other than Luana come to enquire after her sahib-lover!

Not much more than twenty, the Indian girl was strikingly lovely, with the exquisite bone structure that gave some women of her race an appearance of aristocratic pride and dignity even when they washed clothes at the side of a river, or swept the floor of a mud hut. It was all too easy to see why Richard was attracted: the girl possessed the same air of exotic depth of emotion as Anastasia Lingarde had revealed. *This* girl would never whisper another man's name in the midst of passion with Richard!

Violent jealousy raged through Charlotte—an emotion more painful and overruling than any she had previously experienced before over the liaison. She saw that lithe, perfect body his hands had caressed, the long black hair that had tumbled across his own nakedness, the dark burning eyes that had gazed into his as he entered her room to seek escape from a wife he despised. She saw the gold bangles and ear ornaments, the bright sari of best quality cotton embroidered with coloured silks, the soft slippers on graceful feet, and knew an overwhelming urge to fly at the girl and tear the things from her. On that terrible night Richard had accused her of taking his name and all he owned. Apparently he did not mind sharing it with this creature!

Shaken and humiliated before someone who knew the truth about her, a paid seductress who knew Richard better than anyone on earth, Charlotte stepped forward and said in imperious tones, "Leave my home at once, and never come here again!" Turning to the bearer she added, "I will have no one coming here when I am away. *No one.* Is that clear?"

Richard's manservant bowed, Luana bowed as she departed, but it was Charlotte who felt inferior to them both. It had been there in their eyes—derision, contempt, mockery?

She did not go to the hospital that morning, after all. The unconquerable jealousy triggered off a renewal of her hopelessness regarding the future. She sat gazing from her window realizing how much she hated that cantonment, the surrounding hills, that brooding fortress overlooking her bungalow. Richard was right. It was like being a kitten at the bottom of a well—but it was not an encroaching enemy that rendered her helpless. It was Richard himself.

She did not take Anna when she wended her way through the rows of military buildings to the large bungalow occupied by her mother. Felicia really had no interest in the child, and Charlotte felt instinctively that conversation would take a serious turn better dealt with in the absence of a small girl. It came as no surprise to learn that Lady Scott was still dressing and asked her visitor to wait a few moments. They extended into a quarter of an hour, and Charlotte had exhausted her study of a spacious room furnished with an astonishing amount of Felicia's own possessions. Surely she could not have brought all that with her from Meerpore!

But she had, as she confirmed with some surprise that Charlotte should wonder at it, when she finally arrived in the sitting-room. They ate at once, Felicia making no comment on the absence of her granddaughter. Conversation over the light meal of cold meat, bread and butter, fruit and wine was confined to details of Felicia's journey from Meerpore, and her disappointment in Kabul.

"I cannot see how one could live here in any reasonable degree of comfort for longer than one month," she declared as they left the table to take tea in the sitting-room. "It is hardly surprising that the residents are so dowdy and dull."

"The winter was long and very trying," Charlotte told her. "We have only been able to walk abroad for a few weeks." They sat opposite each other in long chairs, and she decided to abandon the light, impersonal chatter that had covered the restraint of their meeting. "Shall you not stay here above a month, then?"

Looking elegant and cool in chartreuse-coloured muslin, Felicia showed no sign of recognizing the pointedness of the question.

"If one does not find things agreeable, one alters them to suit. I intend to entertain and use the facilities to their best advantage. I must say that I had not realized how very pleasant it was to ride in the cool of early morning through a valley of blossoms."

"Did you not find it *très fatigue?*" asked Charlotte, trying again to draw her mother out.

The eyebrows rose. "My dear child, I would not attempt if if there was any risk of undue exertion." She sipped her tea delicately. "I dare swear it is vastly more amusing than a morning spent in the hospital."

"I will not argue with that," said Charlotte recognizing the first signs of seriousness. "You doubtless also found better company than there is in the wards. That was a distinguished escort you had this morning."

Felicia studied her for a moment or two, her back perfectly straight against the cushions, her head poised beautifully above her creamy shoulders.

"It has been failure, then? I did warn you of the risk."

Nonplussed by Felicia's swift change to something so

painfully personal, Charlotte took refuge in lies. "You should not base opinions on gossip."

Her mother smiled in a faraway manner. "Ah, vicious wildfire that gathers heat as it spreads! Have you been near a looking-glass lately? It does not require gossip to know you are at your wits' end."

It was finding Luana at her door, facing pity from such a girl as her that had brought a bout of weeping prior to setting out that noon. Her mother's criticism coming on top of that caught at her raw nerves.

"You are wrong. He has accepted his child and lavishes love on her. That was my object in coming."

"And who will lavish love on you?"

Suddenly, the relationship that had been so enigmatic and painful was bursting to be fully explored, come what may, and Charlotte heard herself say, "Not one person, if the trend continues . . . and I have no intention of taking a lover, if that is what you are about to recommend."

There was a short silence as Felicia sat apparently lost in the past, then she said quietly, "You had the love of a worth-while man once, and threw it away. I think you have finally learnt the truth of what you have done, but it appears to be too late." She turned her head to gaze out over the blossom-filled valley. "I did not have the opportunity to marry young love. My mama lived her life through me and my beauty from the moment I was born. A plain woman who married late in life through desperation, she was determined that I should be trained for the brilliant marriage my looks would undoubtedly bring. My heart went to Italy with a young man who died there in poverty, but Mama continued to scheme and plan.

"I was taken everywhere, paraded before anyone of influence or wealth, petted and fussed, instructed on what to say, whom to flatter, when to smile. My life was taken over by Mama: my feelings were never once considered."

She sighed faintly, and Charlotte hardly dared breathe in the midst of such startling revelation of a true identity.

"My beauty attracted a buzzing hive of suitors all anxious

for the honey. There were some with whom I could have found tolerable happiness, but Mama would not have it. I was auctioned to the highest bidder." She turned then, and came out of the past into the present. "Your father was a cold, austere man from the start. His wife—Tom's mother—had been a sill, feeble creature whose only virtue was that she produced for him four sons. So, he had his family and plenty of heirs, but his position demanded that he have a decorative hostess for social occasions. His need was somewhat pressing, since he was leaving for India, and Mama made the match without asking my feelings."

She put her cup and saucer on the tray with elegant grace. "I was eighteen; he was forty-nine. I knew nothing of a man's demands, and he did not bother to explain beforehand. We sailed for India two days after the wedding, and I was *enceinte* for most of the voyage. You were born in Calcutta two months after we arrived. When you were three, Rastin was taken seriously ill with a child's complaint which he caught from you. As a result, he lost his manhood."

Charlotte sat motionless, shaken to the core. It was like looking at her own life from the other side of a mirror.

"He took an aversion to you and all children. I was sent back to England to find a home for you with one of his relatives. Meg was the only one prepared to bring up a little girl. I was immediately summoned back to India where I was needed at his side. Sea travel does not suit me, and two six-month voyages within a year and a half left me very low and unable to fulfil my social obligations. It was then I discovered he had also taken an aversion to females, in particular, those who possessed extreme feminine charm. It is not easy to accept, at the age of twenty-two, that there is no more in life to look forward to than the patronizing orders of a husband who needs nothing more than a highly-trained hostess. It is even harder to accept that all hope of affection, or even kindness, has gone."

Felicia got up and went to stand behind Charlotte's chair, holding the back of it as she said with a touch of unusual warmth, "Perhaps you now understand something of that last, my dear. However, I endured it for many years and tried to hide it from the outside world. You will think me extremely wicked when I admit that I even prayed he would die prematurely, before I became too old to find happiness."

She came round to stand beside her daughter, but her gaze was fixed on the past as she said, "Then, one day as I walked through that great house in Meerpore, I came face-to-face with someone who revived a feeling I had long thought dead. There has been no gossip, I have seen to that, nothing to hurt Rastin's career . . . and one cannot betray something that does not exist."

She sat slowly on the chair beside Charlotte and gazed into her daughter's eyes. "It is a passing thing, I know. I am getting older every hour, and one day he will go away never to return. But, while it lasts, he gives me back my pride, my lost youth, all the things Rastin ground beneath his heel throughout those interminable years. You have only ever seen it as disgusting and treacherous, but he has been my salvation. I will not voluntarily surrender it."

Caught up in the sadness reflected in her mother's face, Charlotte nevertheless caught herself saying urgently, "But . . . but do you know what he is truly like?"

Felicia rose and walked away to stand in the doorway leading on to the verandah. "I do not care what he is truly like. He may be lecherous, fickle, glory-seeking, vain and selfish—but when he is with me he is mine for a while. That is all I ask of him."

On the verge of speaking of the Afghan prisoners, Charlotte realized she could not mention such things after all. Who knew why men behaved as they did, what rioted through them, at times? But Felicia had turned to face her, all introspection gone.

"But Colley is not your salvation, you know. Richard is. He is legally tied to you, and loves your child, you say. If you do not win him back, there will be no chance of happiness for you, ever. He is a young man with a great capacity for love in all its forms. Your humiliation could continue for years and years. I faced rejection, but was never broken by another woman, as you are. My dear, listen to me, I beg you," she said with sudden ferocity. "You will never regain his affection with dowdy gowns that smell of hospital stews and herbal remedies. He is virile and sensitive. Give him beauty to surround him, and love that is unconditional. The rest will then come. Charlotte . . . I urged you into marriage with him because I wanted you to know youth as I never knew it. Do not abandon it so soon."

Charlotte was overwhelmed and unable to speak in reply to a woman who had revealed herself too suddenly and too honestly. Even when Felicia reverted just as suddenly to the woman she had always appeared to be by rhapsodizing on the virtues of a certain lotion guaranteed to clear the complexion of unsightly blemishes brought on by the eating of too much fruit, Charlotte sat still caught up in the unexpectedness of that day.

But the day had not finished with her, by any means. On leaving her mother Charlotte was unable to forget the words: *give him beauty to surround him, and love that is unconditional.* Luana had done that, without a doubt. She, herself, had never been beautiful—could never be. But she could give him love if he were in the right frame of mind to receive it, and it would certainly be unconditional, this time. With that thought in mind she decided to call on Amy, who had discovered a wonderful sewing-man who could make anything one wished from a scant description. It would help to look as nice as possible when Richard returned.

The request had hardly been made when Tom arrived home, out of breath and looking very grave.

"Ah, I hoped to find you here, Charlotte," he began without preamble. "Johnson said he went to your bungalow and then to Lady Scott, without success."

"It is news of Richard," she said, fear clutching her with strong fingers. "Bad news!"

"Well . . . it is not encouraging, I fear."

She rose from her chair beside Amy, the little samples of materials in her lap scattering all over the floor. "Tell me the truth, Tom. I have been expecting it, you know."

He frowned and shook his head. "We have no idea what the truth is. One of Richard's servants—a man called Wahab—came into the cantonment this afternoon after making his way alone from Malkhan. He says the fortress was overrun the day after they arrived there, by a strong force of rebels. He slipped away in the confusion when he saw they were taking prisoners. There was no sign of Captain Bateson, but the Russian was certainly there and came to Richard's room during the night. According to Wahab, they seemed on friendly terms and organized the defence of the fort next morning, until someone opened the gates and let the enemy in."

Charlotte swallowed and tried to sound calm. "So, Richard must have been killed."

"Not necessarily. Wahab saw them take Richard prisoner, but they killed the Russian there and then," he added, his voice deepening. "There is every chance that he—and Bateson, for that matter—is still alive. A decision has just been made to send a company of sepoys with a detachment of artillery. They leave first thing in the morning."

"Oh, thank God," she whispered, almost in tears. "Thank God they are making every effort to save them."

"Not a bit of it," replied Tom with sudden savagery. "They would not send them for that. It is only because they are affronted by Mooji-Lal's change of face and wish to teach him a sharp lesson. It is also not very comfortable to have a large number of rebels assembled in a fort a mere eight days away." He twisted his shako around in his hands for a moment or so. "The fact is, I have asked to go with them."

Charlotte's tears would not be held in check then. "Oh, Tom . . . *dear* Tom! Thank you."

"You *what?*" came a voice from the other person in the room they had forgotten.

They turned to find Amy flushed with anger.

"We . . . we had an agreement, Richard and I . . ." Tom tailed off and shrugged impotently. "Dash it, I have to go, Amy. He has been my friend for years."

"Friend!" she cried. "You are forever quarrelling."

"That? You do not understand friendship between two men," Tom retorted stubbornly. "If I were at Malkhan Richard would be there like a shot."

"*He* has nothing to keep him here," snapped Amy, her

voice rising. "You appear to have forgotten me—your wife. Is not your first duty to me?"

Tom flushed angrily then. "I am growing a little tired of that approach from you. I cannot do anything that is not somehow tied up with *your* wishes."

Amy grew tight-lipped and very stiff. "It was not *my* wish to become *enceinte* soon after my arrival here, it was not *my* wish to lie here day after day while everyone else is enjoying the spring sunshine, it was not *my* wish to be used as an excuse by your step-mother so that she could come here in pursuit of . . ." She stopped short there, but her eyes flashed dangerously as she flung at him, "I am about to give birth to your child, sir. I demand that you remain by my side."

"Oh, do you?" he responded with fire. "You are married to a soldier, let me remind you. Duty must come first."

"But this is *not* duty!"

"You had the other child without me by your side."

"Precisely. That is why I demand that you are here this time."

Charlotte could stand no more and went across to take Amy's hand. "I am here to help with the baby, and husbands are always in the way at such times. *Please* . . . if anyone can save Richard it is Tom."

Amy snatched her hand away, wrought up to hysterical pitch by now. "*Save him?* No one can save him if he has fallen into the hands of those savages. You know as well as I it would have been better for him if they had killed him at the outset. This way he will die slowly and in terrible agony. Tom will find nothing remaining of him but . . ."

Charlotte fled from the bungalow, hands pressed against her ears.

In the first few days of his captivity Richard dwelt for hours in the realms of his ancestry, reliving the wonderful weeks amidst his Russian relatives, recalling the wild and beautiful countryside not unlike Afghanistan where they had all roamed with the carelessness of the very wealthy. Talking to Verenchikov in the mixture of French and Russian adopted by aristocrats had brought it all back so very clearly, and the total darkness of his cell offered no distractions to his mind pictures.

He saw all their faces as they had been then—young, unformed by experience, confident of their future. A great yearning to be back there had obliterated other thoughts, and he roamed along paths of fantasy that had him choosing that half of his heritage, going to the military academy with Igor, and serving the Czar with pride and devotion. He would have married a dark Russian beauty with a touch of eastern exoticism and a passionate nature, living with her on estates teeming with pheasants and livestock, kissed by the hot sun in summer months and racing across sparkling snow in winter.

Throughout those suffocating days and freezing nights Richard had crouched in a black corner and escaped into the exciting world of what could have been. He travelled beyond all frontiers of love and pain to reach the pinnacles of existence before it was taken from him forever. And all the time, his mother had been very close, sustaining him, lending him strength so that he would withstand his ordeal.

But when fever laid him low, the daily ritual of beheadings was becoming a serious threat to his sanity, and that short daily excursion into brilliant sunlight after constant darkness rendered him blind, all fantasy flew and he knew he was sinking fast. Then, and only then, did he begin his real fight for survival . . . and it was not his mother, but a little girl in Kabul who still had her life before her that he kept in his mind when the temptation to succumb assailed him. Yet he could not think of Anna without thinking of Charlotte, the mother of the child, who had been so determined that he should see and love the little golden-haired girl.

Over and over again he heard her impassioned words as she had stood just inside his room that first day: *I will not let our child be unloved, as I was. I will not let her grow up a stranger to her father, to be dismissed like a casual caller after sixteen years of separation. I will not inflict on her loneliness, disappointment, rebuffs and humiliations. I will not allow her to become a parcel to be deposited with whoever happens to be prepared to take her. I beg you, do not punish her for what I have done.*

For the first time the real meaning of those words hit him. Charlotte had been describing her own life with those few pleading sentences! He remembered then how she had been when she first arrived at Meerpore, how everyone had laughed at her comic attempts at sophistication and her unsuitable clothes. He remembered why he had championed her, and how she had blossomed beneath his friendship. *Loneliness, disappointments, rebuffs and humiliations.* Had she really suffered all those, yet managed to bounce back the minute just one person showed her some kindness?

Hour after hour he struggled to keep his mind on Charlotte because Anna was dependent on her. He recalled that day at the waterfall, when they had skimmed pebbles across the water and she had forgotten her silly pose for a while. He remembered her, white and desperate, asking him if he still wished to marry her. *A parcel to be deposited with whoever happens to be prepared to take her.*

Then he forced himself to think of that last night in Ferozepore, and her sobbing confession of passion for a man who had played on her unsophistication whilst all the while making adulterous love to her mother. *I beg you, do not punish her for what I have done.*

He suddenly saw Anna in years to come, living in a mansion in Kent with an elderly, embittered grandfather, and a mother grown bleak, silent and defeated. If he did not return, his daughter would become an echo of that quaint little creature he had first come across on horseback, dressed in an overlarge black riding–dress, tossing her head in its ridiculous hat and speaking about *les poules*. Anna would be laughed at and pitied. There would be gossip about the father who had disappeared in the middle of Afghanistan in 1841, and *les poules* would patronize the wife and daughter he had openly rejected. Men would abuse Anna's lack of protection—men like Duprés, who would play on her sensitive emotions for their own amusement, knowing they need fear no irate father.

All those thoughts lived with him as days passed beyond his ability to count them, and he clung desperately to the faint thread of remaining life. When he grew too weak to pace his cell, he crawled on hands and knees so that he would not lose the use of his limbs. When he could no longer crawl, he forced himself to move arms and legs every few minutes. The one thing uppermost in his mind was to stay alive for Anna. She needed him: she must not become a parcel, as Charlotte had been.

He grew filthy and covered in bites from vermin in his cell. Around his wrists and ankles there were festering sores where the chains had rubbed his flesh raw. His hair was long and matted: he had a beard that harboured lice. Each day Mooji-Lal taunted him on his appearance, feeling the body that was slowly wasting away and deriding the fact that his fine limbs were skinny and weak, his fair skin was darkened by dirt, his bright hair was crawling with bugs, his striking eyes could no longer see . . . and each day the Afghan deliberated longer and longer on his choice of victim, staying beside Richard in cruel uncertainty until he sagged with weakness in the hold of the two men now needed to keep' him upright. But, day after day, he was thrown back into the cell to survive another twenty-four hours . . . and contemplate the fate of the child he loved so dearly.

It was in the midst of a memory of a bright-haired little figure stumbling across the room for the first time, to fall into his arms, that the door was opened and he felt himself hauled to his feet to be dragged outside. His legs would not move despite his efforts to make them, and he was pulled along, legs trailing the ground, until he felt the sun hot on his bare torso and knew he was back in the courtyard once more. He saw nothing but the dull red that signified he was no longer in pitch darkness, and heard only the faint moans of his fellow-sufferers.

He was held erect with a cruel grip beneath his arms, but felt too dizzy and ill to register much else. Even when the voice began speaking near him it was a little while before he realized it was Mooji-Lal. That was all, however, for he was no longer able to understand the Persian words he had learnt so painstakingly in Meerpore. The voice went on and on in mocking tones while he hung there between his two guards. Then, suddenly, he was being dragged forward, pushed on to his knees, his head thrust forward into a bent position.

His slow heartbeat increased painfully. So, it had come, at last. He had fought for life in the vain hope that rescue would come. But he had known all along that it would not. It never did. One subaltern at an outlying fort was expected to die for his queen and country with courage, upholding the traditions of his ancestors to the last breath.

They let go his arms, and he put every ounce of strength into staying there without collapsing. He would die with dignity. They would not chop him up as he lay squirming on the ground, like a helpless worm.

So he knelt there, head bent, waiting for the death-blow and regretting so much that was now too late to put right. It seemed an eternity before the tulwar fell, and the effort to remain in that position became a cruel penance. He saw nothing but dull red, heard no sound at all, and waited for sudden death to come slicing through the air.

It became a nightmare as he realized Mooji-Lal was playing his last sadistic waiting-game, but strength came to him from the determination not to give the Afghan his final chance of humiliation. He would remain steady on his knees until his persecutor tired and gave the word. Stay he did, and although the sun beat mercilessly on his back, his tongue began to swell with thirst, and the expectation of that blow grew into a terror of waiting, he did not waver or fall.

"Good God, it must be Lingarde! No . . . careful! I should not touch him. It is possible that he is already dead and they have left him like that as a warning to us."

"Poor devil! Look at the state he is in."

"What did you expect? He has been in their hands for six weeks."

"But . . . why leave him here like this in an empty fort?"

"I take it as their idea of contempt for the white infidel."

"Stand back, damn you! What is it, Henry? Oh . . . dear God!"

"We have found your friend, Tom. But he looks so damned grotesque I am afraid to touch him. Knowing those barbarous devils it is possible they have dismembered him and he will fall to pieces the minute we put a hand on him."

"I . . . well, I will soon find out, because I do not intend to leave him as he is any longer. It . . . it is *inhuman!* If I ever catch up with them I shall take my revenge for this, I swear."

Richard tried to speak, but his tongue was too swollen. He tried to move, but his iron will had made him hold that position for so long he could not now relax. He tried to see Tom, but even the dull red had gone and been replaced by blackness. But it was enough to know that he was there.

"If ever I am in such a situation, swear you will come to my rescue, Richard, I promise to do the same for you."

"You will be a very welcome sight . . . so long as you do not bring your sister with you."

• *fourteen* •

THEY BROUGHT RICHARD back to Kabul in a litter attached to one of the horses. He was weak, incoherent and blindfolded, but his grasp on life could not be shaken.

George Bateson's body had been discovered in a disused well, along with that of Verenchikov. The British political officer, who had lived for five months at Malkhan under the belief of friendship, had been dreadfully mutilated either before or after death. That atrocity, combined with the ordeal endured by Richard Lingarde, dictated the decision of the officer commanding the relief column, the same Lieutenant Matherson whose prowess at the quadrilles Amy so much admired.

Urged on by Tom, the young man used the prerogative allowed the man-on-the-spot to overrule his orders by dint of greater knowledge of the situation. The fort proper had been vacated by the rebels when the relief force had been sighted: the settlement itself was poverty-ridden and worth-less. In the opinion of Henry Matherson and Tom Scott there was nothing to be gained by occupying the fort and, since there was no Mooji-Lal to woo back with friendship, it took the two subalterns very little time to decide on destroying the fort and returning to Kabul.

With the interior well alight, and the crumbling towers toppled by well-placed cannon-shot, the small force em-barked on its return journey four days after arriving. The residents of the settlement watched them leave taking the man they had showered with curses and filth, and knew they should have killed him as he stood chained to that post. They stood against the background of a smoking fort, watching the scarlet jackets until they were dots in the distance. Their eyes were already seeing them broken and bleeding upon the ground. Only when all the infidel invaders lay dead would there be peace in Afghanistan.

The tale told by the returning column caused great anger in Kabul. Richard Lingarde became a hero overnight, with Henry Matherson and Tom Scott only slightly less so. But the events at Malkhan also stirred up once more those who were constantly accused of sabre-rattling. Was this not fur-ther proof of Afghan resentment and hostility? Did it not point to very definite intentions by rebels to drive out the white invaders as soon as the moment was ripe?

No, the authorities insisted stubbornly. There was nothing and no one to fear in Afghanistan. Mooji-Lal was clearly un-stable, and the last had probably been seen of him now—which was a good thing. Of course, it was regrettable that Captain Bateson had been murdered, but he had been a man well-acquainted with the native mind and knew the dangers of his profession.

The affair had the cantonment agog for a week, then the residents resumed their round of summer pursuits in the con-fidence that all was well. But for Charlotte, the incidents at Malkhan had a profound effect on her that would last a life-time. The agony of waiting nearly three weeks to hear the outcome of that rescue mission had almost broken her com-pletely. She had returned to the habits she had acquired from

Aunt Meg, praying for long minutes on end, reading from her bible to take comfort from the words, and trying to ease her own distress by tending the distress of others, in the hospital. Even in the face of Amy's petulance and vindictiveness, she kept a still tongue and smiling face, hoping that the Almighty would put his blessing on one who was meek, as the book said.

Amy's anger over Tom's desertion of her at a time when she needed his slavish devotion had brought forward the birth of twin sons. One died that same night: the other was sickly and had to be put to an Indian wet-nurse because his mother was unable to nourish him sufficiently. The experience left Amy frightened and unforgiving towards the husband she felt had been the cause of it all.

When Tom returned, he was informed of his wife's intention to take her son back to Meerpore and her loving parents just as soon as he was strong enough to travel. Towards Charlotte, who had assisted at the unforgettable birth and cosseted her afterwards, she showed just as much hostility. For the sake of a man who had treated her with the greatest possible public contempt, who had openly flaunted his Indian *bibee*, whose rackety behaviour was the talk of Kabul, Charlotte had begged her brother to go into danger and risk leaving a widow with a fatherless child. It was too much for any woman to forgive!

With Richard alive and back in Kabul, Charlotte was reasonable enough to see her sister-in-law's point of view and respect it. She would probably feel the same in such a situation. But it did not stop her from feeling overwhelming love and gratitude for Tom, who had stood by his word to a friend, revealing all the stalwart and unshakable loyalty his personality contained. It must have cost him something to ignore Amy's condemnation, but he was an uncomplicated man who saw a situation unclouded by emotional shadows or intangible complications. To him, Amy had plenty of people to help her through a natural situation of life, whereas Richard's life might have depended upon the arrival of a friend in an unnatural and bizarre situation.

Charlotte agreed that Tom had been right to go. His presence in Kabul would not have saved the dead child, or improved the health of the surviving one. But, by all accounts, Richard had responded only to Tom's voice in that semi-life to which he had been reduced, and was sustained by that close comradeship that transcended minor disagreements all the way to Kabul.

Richard had been taken immediately to the small hospital, and Charlotte would never forget the heart-breaking sight. However, he soon showed agitation at being confined in the small room, and doctors gave ready consent for Charlotte to nurse her husband in his own home. With her knowledge and capability the patient would be in good hands, and it was generally felt that it might bring an improvement to the broken marriage.

Charlotte was determined that it should. She looked upon Richard's rescue from death as a sign from the Almighty that she had been given a second chance. That, plus the fact that Richard was completely dependent on her, and her alone, persuaded her that she held every advantage towards winning him back.

Tom tried to spare her the full facts of Richard's ordeal, but the entire cantonment soon buzzed with the terrible story, including the heart-rending circumstance of the relief force entering a deserted fort to discover a filthy bearded half-skeleton kneeling like a grotesque statue in the middle of an empty courtyard, waiting to be beheaded. Charlotte had wept wildly at the thought, and longed to drive the memory from Richard's mind with love and physical passion. Strangely even the sight of his emaciated body and haggard face that revealed all he had resisted with such strength of purpose, had the power to arouse desire within her. As he slowly recovered his wits and strength her longing increased daily.

At first, she had to feed him with a spoon whenever he surfaced from feverish bouts of sleep. When he insisted on eating the invalid foods himself, she guided the spoon to the bowl for him. His sight slowly returned in a room that was dimmed by tatties during the bright daylight hours, until he was able to distinguish whoever was in the room with him.

During the first days he called constantly for Anna, and Charlotte was uncertain whether to let the child see her father in what would seem a frightening condition to a child. But Richard grew anxious and feverish, so she took the little girl to his bedside and cried with him as he stroked the pale curls with a bony hand that was movingly gentle and reverent. Anna *was* frightened when she saw someone she did not recognize as Papa in the bed, but his voice was familiar and the loving gesture reassured her. After that, she went every afternoon to be with him for a while.

It was after the sixth of these visits, when Charlotte was straightening the crumpled sheets on the bed that Richard said quietly, "I believe you are right. The child needs both parents with her if she is to be happy."

It was so unexpected, so full of possibilities, so enigmatic that Charlotte felt weak with suspense. The wrong word from her now could shatter the fragility of that remark. She looked at him in the dim light, unsure whether those striking eyes could see her or not. They were turned in her direction, but there was no sign of confirmation that they witnessed her nervousness.

She continued smoothing the sheets. "Anna certainly missed her papa. It was most noticeable."

"Well . . . a military man has often to be away from his family. But it is still my intention to sell out and return to my home." Almost as an afterthought he added, "We must have some discussion on the subject, in due course."

Heart thumping madly she replied as steadily as she could, "If that is what you wish, Richard."

But he said no more on the subject for a week or more, and Charlotte grew afraid that it had been spoken impulsively or as a result of fever. However, the aggression that had ruled his attitude towards her appeared to have vanished, and there was a definite and constant new gentleness that reminded her of the man she had married.

As time passed he grew stronger again and physically more challenging to Charlotte's exhausted emotions. She had not been alone with her mother since the day of that astonishing revelation, but she had not forgotten the lesson to be learnt from it. *Surround him with beauty and love.* She took great pains with her appearance, and loved him with tender care . . . but nursing him did not satisfy the craving for fulfilment within her. She found the need for him tormenting her more and more as she sat beside the bed, listening to all he had to put into words, her eyes now fully open to his attraction.

He spoke a great deal about his mother, and twisted the sexual knife even more when he said, "I realize now that I went to pieces after her death, which was not worthy of her. She faced it with courage, as she had faced everything else in life . . . but I love too few and too dearly. I could not accept that she should be taken when worthless creatures remained."

Swallowing hard Charlotte said, "But did you not see that in her short lifetime she made a far greater mark than most in a full span of years? She will be remembered long after the others are gone. I . . . I wrote to you of that in my letter."

He looked up and there was no doubt that he really saw her. "I wish I had read it."

On other occasions he spoke of Russia and his childhood there, giving Charlotte an insight into his great love for that country and his relatives, besides showing her how strong was the Slavic side of his nature. There seemed to be a great need in him to talk and talk of his past and those he had once known. Charlotte was not certain if he really wished to tell her, or if any listener would have done equally well, but she gloried in the fact that he spoke with warmth and generosity of such personal things where he had discussed only political affairs with her before. But, much as she cherished every moment with him, it was of the future she wished he would speak, not the past.

Then, out of the blue, he said one afternoon, "Yes, Russia is a beautiful land of extremes, Charlotte. I think you would like it there."

She was folding a nightshirt and her hands stilled as she decided to force the issue. "Is it still your intention to go there when you sell out?"

He took a long time in answering. "I think we cannot decide on that until we are back in England."

Resolution fled. Running to him she knelt beside the bed and looked up fervently into his face. "Say it is not a whim. We *are* to stay with you, Anna and I? You truly mean it?"

It was too sudden. He seemed almost startled and avoided her eyes. "Was that not what you intended when you made the journey to Kabul?"

She sank back on her heels, deflated. "Only if *you* wished it that way."

He nodded and closed his eyes wearily. "It is the only way. I cannot have my child turned into a parcel."

The word startled her, made her heart beat faster again. "A . . . *parcel?*"

His eyes opened again after a moment or two, and they seemed full of sad haunted questions. "Is that truly how you always felt?"

"I . . . yes," she whispered, marvelling that he remembered what she had said and wanting more than anything to go into his arms.

But he seemed to tire at that point and went to sleep. Charlotte sat for a long time beside him, exhilarated yet full of yearning. The future looked brighter than it had for a long time, but it was all for love of Anna, not herself. Unable to contain her feelings any longer she reached forward and kissed his lips very gently several times. But it only increased her yearning and, before she knew it, she was lifting the sheet to touch his body with fingers that trembled.

Two and a half years melted away as she remembered the times she had snuggled against him in gratitude rather than passion, the times he had asked and she had not understood. She recalled so clearly those days on the march to Ferozepore when he had tried every means to awaken her fully—the laughing, teasing invitation from a drenched man to be kissed or deposited in the river alongside him, an inebriated, stimulated would-be seducer who hit his head on the lantern hanging from the tent-pole, the intense young husband asking: Do you never wish to tease *me?* He had suffered then what she suffered now, and she knew painfully well how he must have felt when fulfilment was shattered by a name. Suppose he had cried out for Luana in his fever? Could she have gone on nursing him?

She got up and walked away to her own room. Most probably Richard's bearer had taken the news to the Indian girl. Charlotte supposed she must also have suffered until he returned safely. After all, she had been wife in all but name to him for two years—and before that. But Charlotte knew she could not let any woman share Richard with her in the future. Since she could not demand that he give up Luana, there was only one alternative. She must make it happen as soon as possible.

Richard made no attempt to hurry his slow recovery. It was not just the ordeal at Malkhan from which he had to readjust, but the last two years of his life. It could not be rushed.

Once he was certain his sight had not been permanently damaged he relaxed and took each day as it came, letting thoughts and recollections wander in and out of his mind quite freely and unemotionally. He was strong enough, however, to banish nightmare thoughts of Malkhan each time they threatened to take possession of his mind.

His one weakness was Anna. It was impossible to remain unemotional over her, and he believed he had actually cried when she had come to him the first time and her little hands had patted his in a childish gesture of comfort. Where Charlotte was concerned he did not know how he felt. That was one aspect of his recovery he had no wish to hurry. Her life in England plus her hospital work made her a wonderful nurse, and he was content to regard her as such, for the present. Somewhere along the road during his imprisonment at Malkhan he had accepted that they must stay together, at least until Anna was happily married. Beyond that he had not ventured, and a month slipped by before he realized that, having made that decision, he must think seriously of the consequences—of their future.

Since there was a likelihood of at least twenty years of to-

· 350 ·

getherness to consider it was essential to arrive at a definite and steady relationship, but it was at that point that he baulked, every time. He just did not know what line to take, and it seemed easier to let things slide.

Tom visited him regularly, a man noticeably maturer, a thinking man rather than the hot-head he had been. The bond of masculine comradeship between them had strengthened further, and that somehow helped the relationship with Charlotte by, drawing all three together.

At the end of two months Richard was reasonably fit again, but those weeks of mental torture had left deep scars that nourishment and devoted nursing could not heal. As soon as he felt able to ride Richard went through the cantonment to the little place where he rented a room for Luana. He had sent messages through his bearer to reassure her, but still she knelt before him, kissing his hands and weeping with relief.

It was then he realized, with a shock, that he felt an involuntary revulsion so strong that he had to stand away from her. He stood staring at her beautiful face, her slender perfection of body, her miniature dusky feet that had aroused him sexually on so many nights, and saw only the echo of Mooji-Lal in her dark eyes and brown skin. She reached out to him, sensing that he was not pleased with her, and his skin crawled with the memory of Mooji-Lal's dark hand on his body as he sagged between two guards. She was the same girl for whom he had felt great fondness, the mistress who deserved his deepest gratitude, the same meek temptress who had given him utter devotion . . . yet he knew he could never bring himself to touch her again.

Shaken to the core, he spoke briefly of his continuing commitment to her welfare, then left quickly before the stifled feeling that small native room gave him grew beyond containment. He rode for half an hour in the valley, coming to terms with feelings that were beyond his control, then returned home to find Tom awaiting him. His friend took one look at him, then vented his wrath.

"When Charlotte said you was gone riding I could not believe you would be so foolish, Richard. Look at you! If you are anywhere near fit enough to go careering all over the valley, I'll kick a monkey."

Richard smiled faintly as he took off his hat. "Your turn of phrase has not improved one jot since the day we met, my friend. But I will admit I feel a little done-up now."

"Ah!" pounced Tom fiercely. "There you are, you see? Dashed if I have ever come across such a bull-headed fellow as you."

"It would be of more use to cease insulting me and pour me a drink," Richard pointed out, sinking gratefully into his chair.

Tom hesitated. "Does my sister allow it?"

"No, but that is what makes it so damned enjoyable. Have you never crossed Amy and felt well-satisfied with yourself?"

Somewhat to Richard's surprise the joking comment brought a gloomy response from his friend. The open face clouded and a frown creased his brow.

"Of late, even that pleasure has gone." He poured two glasses of wine from the decanter in Richard's sitting-room and handed one to his host. "Females are deuced unpredictable, do you not find?"

"Only the intelligent ones," Richard replied cautiously, hoping he was not to be the recipient of a confidence of a marital nature when he still had not completely recovered from the shock of the morning with Luana. He appreciated what Tom had done by volunteering to accompany the relief force and, like him, could not see why Amy should be so unreasonable over it. But he had enough problems of his own with which to grapple.

Tom sat astride a chair and gazed unhappily at Richard over the back of it, his wine untouched in the glass. "The fact is, he doesn't seem all that attractive to me. His constitution is sickly, and he looks more like a yellow wrinkled doll than my son," he said heavily. "Dashed if I can get up any enthusiasm for the creature. Amy is always pressing me to hold him, but I confess I find no pleasure in it at all." He sighed. "If he was like your little Anna, now, it would be different altogether."

"Anna is nearly two years old," Richard pointed out, still occupied with thoughts of his own. "I daresay she looked much like Adam when she was born." But he knew in his heart that she would have looked beautiful from the start, and a strange regret that he had not been there blotted out his unease over Luana.

"I suppose so," conceded Tom cheerlessly. "Amy feels certain Meerpore will be more beneficial to his growth and nothing will persuade her otherwise." He glanced round at the door, then back to Richard to say, "Charlotte ordered me not to bother you with such things, but there are signs that all is not well in Afghanistan. That affair at Malkhan appears to have been just one amongst many. Reports are coming in from politicals ranging all over the country that Dost Mohammed's supporters are gathering in large numbers and plainly preparing for armed attack." He shook his head sagely. "I have come to share your pessimism. They are out to make a fight of it, Richard, take my word. Even in Kabul city we are now riding in pairs because it is no longer safe for a single man to enter those dark streets."

Richard sat forward with interest. "Is it not, by jove? What have I always said, Tom? And you accused me of uncertain loyalty?"

Tom's face darkened with shame. "No one could doubt you after Malkhan. It would have been so easy for you to fall in with Mooji-Lal and save your life."

"You do not know his terms, my friend. But enough of that. What is the attitude of Elphinstone and McNaughten now?"

"The same as before. There is nothing and no one in Afghanistan to fear," quoted Tom.

"The devil! Are their heads made of wood and their eyes as blind as mine in that courtyard?" raged Richard. "By God, will they never admit it until these hills are swarming with vengeful rebels? Does Bateson's murder mean nothing to them?"

Tom drank a long draught of his wine, then said, "Not only Bateson, I fear. Another of our politicals has been murdered at Khelat, and two of our officers who were hunting in the distant hills were attacked by a wild gang who appeared from the rocks. That insufferable fellow Petworth crawled away wounded to safety, but I am sorry to tell you Henry Matherson was cut to pieces. They brought in his remains only this morning."

Richard felt genuine sadness. Matherson, besides being the man who had led the relief column to Malkhan, had been a likeable and conscientious officer of great popularity amongst his fellows. But sadness turned to anger as he thumped the arm of his chair and demanded of Tom how men of intelligence could allow murder to pass unavenged, and unremarked.

"That is not all. They manage to discuss with airy disregard the fact that several of our supply-columns have been set upon and looted, while a number of our messengers have vanished in the passes without trace. It is no longer certain that the protection we have been buying from the tribes dominating the great passes can be relied upon. I tell you, Richard, I shall not allow Amy to set out from here under present conditions, however much she may wish to go. Why, my step-mama has postponed her return to Meerpore on the advice of Duprés, who understands the trend of native thinking better than most."

"Because his mind works the same way," said Richard savagely. "There is no more devious or cunning a man in this cantonment."

"That is a very sweeping statement," said an amused female voice from the doorway. "Who might he be?"

Tom turned to Charlotte and said, "Richard's arch enemy, Major Duprés."

Richard could have shaken him. Charlotte coloured very slightly, but carried it off very well by saying, "I have not heard the latest *on dit*. What has the scoundrel done now?"

"Advised Felicia to remain in Kabul while the situation is so unsettled," Tom informed her, oblivious of the slight air of tension between his sister and her husband, "I think no one could condemn him for that—even Richard."

Cheeks back to normal Charlotte said, "You have not been discussing the present worries with Richard? I did particularly ask you not to. It is too bad of you, Tom."

"Oh come," protested Richard, trying to sound nonchalant. "I am quite sturdy enough to hear the proof of all my prophecies that were judged so wild and cowardly a year or so ago." He drained his glass. "Who knows, someone might some day admit that this cantonment is the most ill-conceived death-trap ever built by men who are supposed to have military minds."

"And you might admit, sir, that you have been taking wine against express medical advice." Charlotte came across to him, the sunlight catching the sheen of her gold silk dress as she moved. "Do not attempt to deny it, for you have just tossed back the remainder before my very eyes."

"You know my opinion of doctors," he said, scowling at her. "And one glassful will not hurt me."

"With my brother to set a deplorable example, it would not have stopped at one, I'll wager," came her calm reply as she gently took the glass from his hand.

That small act had a strange effect on him. The fingers that accidentally brushed his were cool and beautifully pale in colour; the perfume that wafted over him as she turned away was fresh, clean, and hauntingly like something he remembered from his past—night-scented stock in a peaceful, dusk-filled garden. He closed his eyes momentarily, so strong was that memory of home, and he visualized lush lawns, dew-shimmered roses and aromatic apple-blossoms, white-painted cottages, beehives in a neat row, and women with white skins dressed in starched country cottons that smelled of sunshine and lavender.

He opened his eyes again, and something stirred fractionally in him as he saw the lines of worry etched on Charlotte's face—a face that contained no hint of Eastern passion, no expression of sadistic pleasure, no promise of erotic mystery. If only he had met her in England, away from arrogant hawk-faced men; away from jasmine trees, purple hills, and strange discordant music; away from heat, thirst, and the relentless, burning sun—away from Colley Duprés!

She turned to meet his gaze whilst the thought was still on him, and the faint blush returned to her cheeks. "I did not mean to act the shrew," she said hesitantly. "I know you have a strong dislike of such behaviour. It is simply that I . . . we *all* . . . are concerned for your swift recovery."

He sat unable to tell her there had been anything but censure in his gaze, and Tom got to his feet rather noisily.

"She's right, Richard. I am to blame for encouraging you to go against orders, so I shall now go from one scolding to another. I promised Amy to be back for tiffin at least fifteen minutes ago."

The speech brought a smile from Charlotte, as it was meant to do. "You two gentlemen are certainly to be pitied for the uncomfortable time you have of it! Go along, Tom, and take this little parcel to Amy for me—two flannel vests for Baby Adam." She went with her brother on to the verandah and stayed several moments talking before kissing his cheek as he went off to his waiting horse.

Richard watched the scene with the faint sense of excitement still on him. Nothing had prepared him for that sudden longing; for a sensation he thought gone forever between them. But when his wife re-entered and asked briskly if he was ready for tiffin, he wondered if that brief moment had ever occurred. He nodded and rang for water to wash with, while she went off to summon the bearer.

Over tiffin, which they had taken to eating together since his return from Malkhan, she seemed troubled. "Poor Tom looks so unhappy these days. I think things are not going too well with him."

"Yes," he agreed quietly. "He is apparently unattracted by his son, and reads all kinds of meaning into the normal masculine reaction to new-born infants. They are never in the least fetching, are they?"

"*Fetching!*" exclaimed Charlotte indignantly. "They are the most wonderful exquisite creations of nature . . . and I do not know on what authority you base your pronouncement. At the birth of your own daughter you were . . . not . . . there," she finished with slowing dismay.

Knowing they were on thin ice, Richard said, "No more was Tom. Military men are often away at such times. It is a professional hazard."

He almost heard her relieved outlet of breath. "Yes . . . it is."

But although they spoke then about Mrs. McCutcheon's forthcoming *soirée*, Richard was acutely sensitive to the spark of awareness she had aroused that morning with the touch of her fingers, and the clean sweet perfume of her nearness. Throughout the meal one word kept echoing in his head— *parcel.* How could anyone have treated a lonely child as such?

He watched his wife covertly as her hands moved about the table, serving him with anything he needed. A variety of expressions crossed her mobile face as she talked with commonsense and intelligence on all manner of subjects, and he could not associate that word with the girl he saw.

Through his reverie came her voice, and he realized she had asked him a question. "Eh? I beg your pardon, I was miles away."

She was immediately concerned. "Please, Richard, do not think of that terrible place. It is over and done with."

"No, it was not Malkhan, but something very different," he reassured her quietly. "What were you saying?"

For a moment he thought she was going to brush it aside, but she decided to repeat her question. "Did Tom speak to you of Amy?"

"Only indirectly. He claimed that females were unpredictable."

She folded her napkin very carefully, then looked up at him with great earnestness. "There is gossip about her and Lieutenant Spence. I could not help but hear it."

"Ah . . . *les poules,*" he said without thinking, then was astonished by her reaction.

Colour bloomed in her cheeks, making her surprisingly attractive, whilst her eyes grew luminous with something he recognized with shattering clarity. It was there in full—desire, passion, fire, the yearning to be possessed. The girl who had lain in his arms with another man's name on her lips was now offering him all he had wanted then. There was no artfulness, no flirtatious teasing. Her face, her eyes, her body, her mouth were all telling him boldly that she was his for the taking. All he had to do was say one word, reach out a hand, answer her optical question with a glance of acceptance.

Shaking slightly he got to his feet saying something vague about the advisability of not listening to gossip, then excused himself on the pretext of inspecting his stables. He did not look back as he left the room, but the silence within it was almost unnatural.

High summer brought more and more alarming signs of unrest to those willing to accept them, but General Elphinstone, once a masterly and intelligent military leader, had become an ageing, indecisive invalid concerned only with his debilitating health. He had on his staff some brilliant young officers whom he was constantly consulting, only to disregard their advice and ask the same thing of anyone who happened to be handy. In truth, he knew himself incapable of the command by dint of ill-health and lack of enthusiasm for it. When his gout and rheumatism grew so severe he had to be lifted into the saddle bodily, he requested to be relieved of his post. The request was granted, but it took time to appoint and send a replacement, so Elphinstone remained to blunder and bungle his way through the summer days.

Sir William McNaughten, on the other hand, was fatally convinced of his own ability, and boasted openly of the Kabul administration which had successfully settled Afghanistan in peace and serenity. He would allow no one to say otherwise, tolerate no criticism of the British occupation that was dragging into its third winter.

He was backed enthusiastically by Alexander Burnes, who had once heatedly and determinedly opposed the removal of Dost Mohammed. But, having decided he was up against a brick wall, Burnes had not only joined the opposition, but ensured that he was one of its most prominent members.

The coveted envoyship was still out of his reach all the time McNaughten remained in Kabul, but there were sure to be honours awaiting the administration when the force eventually returned to India. Ambition had overcome his principles, and many thinking men felt it was sad that the former explorer had let power and the temptations of Kabul go to his head. A brain that was extremely shrewd seemed not to recognize the danger ahead—especially for himself. But he was in company with the head-in-the-sand brigade, of which there were many.

Richard talked to other men like himself who grew more and more worried over reports of tribal movements in the hills, plus a swelling population in Kabul and other Afghan cities. It was known that Akbar Kahn, the one son of Dost Mohammed who had refused to go into exile with his father, was inciting rebellion and gathering together a large army. British troops had been stoned in the great Kabul bazaar as they shopped and, since the attack on Petworth and Henry Matherson, officers seldom rode out in groups of less than half-a-dozen when they went hunting.

But Richard made no headstrong attacks on policy or passionate condemnations of senior officers. He was still officially on sick leave and spent most of his time reading, studying maps, and consulting the engineering manuals he had put aside for two years. He no longer indulged in reckless sporting contests, or rode death-defying races that put in danger the life of every other rider as well as his own. There were no more exaggerated shooting feats to show off to everyone what they already knew was superb skill . . . and he was never glimpsed, at night, going to his Indian mistress.

Everyone was glad about the improvement. He was a hero, after all. There was no doubt he was the most attractive man in Kabul, and Charlotte was very lucky to have ensnared him. Although it was certainly her nursing ability that appealed to him now, she did seem to be making an effort to improve her appearance. Some days she looked almost fetching, in a church-mouse kind of way, but when her husband was fully fit again she would have to look to her laurels, the gossips all agreed. His suffering at Malkhan had added to his fascination, and there would always be females ready to console him.

Richard was well aware of that. He found himself surrounded by ogling and gushing women who had avoided him before he went to Malkhan. He dealt with them rapidly but politely, and walked away full of contempt for their fickle-mindedness and lack of intelligence. But he could not dismiss the growing challenge of his wife. They were companionable, having returned to a routine which meant they ate their meals together, played with Anna in happy company, and sat after dinner, he reading, she engaged in embroidery, or talking of music, art—anything they found interesting. But their togetherness ended when the lamps dimmed, and each night he saw the longing in her eyes as he spoke his brief adieu.

It was a problem that bothered him as continuously as the more general one of growing danger. With things as volatile as they were he could not risk travelling across Afghanistan and through the treacherous Khyber Pass with a woman and child, yet summer was swiftly passing, and all too soon the winter weather would cut them off in Kabul for some months. To get on the move would shelve the more personal problem for some months: staying as they were increased it. Commonsense told him they could not live together until Anna married, and stay as they were. By now he was beginning to feel the strain. It was weeks since he had visited Luana, but the aversion remained with him. His financial protection of the girl continued, but each time he thought of going to her all he could see was Mooji-Lal.

Aside from that uncontrollable reaction he accepted that he could not continue to keep a mistress if he was determined on his daughter having a warm family life. But, if he had no other sexual outlet he would have to find satisfaction with the woman pledged to provide it. It was not necessary to love her—many men had no fondness for their wives. It would be sensible and convenient. It was the obvious thing to do. But he could not do it.

Charlotte was an enjoyable and peaceful companion, these days. She laughed a lot and devoted herself to making him comfortable and happy. At twenty-one she had matured into a woman of quiet good taste with an interesting personality. He liked having her in the room, sitting quietly whilst he read. He enjoyed her wit and acuteness more and more as time passed. He glimpsed a fiery heart temptingly within reach beneath the outward calm. He read quite clearly what was burning within her. But, at the end of each day, he went to his own room leaving her with the hope still in her eyes.

For three months it had been like that. It troubled him increasingly as Charlotte doubled her challenge in every way known to a woman. He was taken unawares, delighted by something he had never suspected of her, painfully aroused by teasing, sensuous overtures. But he walked away from her every night to pace his room restlessly.

Unable to face Luana, unable to go to his wife, Richard wondered desperately if he had become impotent, lost the impulse to take a woman. But his quick unconscious responses to Charlotte's verbal teasing suggested the opposite. The impulse was very definitely there: it was physical obedience to it that was so difficult.

He was returning from the Officers' Mess after a regimental dinner late one night, with that thought heavily on him, not at all obliterated by the amount of liquor he had swallowed in an attempt to forget it for a while. He had said farewell to his fellows and was on the path leading to his bungalow on the outskirts of the cantonment, glad he had not to face Charlotte that one night, when he encountered another horseman riding in the same direction, who rounded a corner just as he approached it. The rider wore a turban and a skirted Indian coatee with white breeches, and Richard's stomach tightened with anger at his first sight of Colley Duprés since the affair at Malkhan.

"Good evening, Duprés," he said quietly, making the man turn sharply in the saddle. "Do you think it is wise to ride abroad on such a moonlit night?" He fell in alongside the great black stallion favoured by the soldier of fortune. "Ah, but of course, this road leads not only to the hills but the residence of my mama-in-law, does it not?"

The broad-shouldered figure tensed. "I would advise you

to strike such remarks from your conversation, Lingarde . . .
unless you have become enough of a man to accept a challenge from me."

Richard laughed softly with no humor. "The devil! You
have pretensions to honour? Have a care, man, or you will
be fighting duels in every city of the East . . . or is it your
practice to defend only your fair-skinned mistresses?"

Immediately, Colley's horse was across Richard's path
forcing him to halt, and the voice that could adopt silken
seduction or menace said, "I knew we had not finished when
you ran away from our last confrontation. I suggest we settle
this, once and for all."

Richard gripped the pommel, aware of the silence of a
heavy summer night broken only by the sounds of distant
revelry in the city. Burnes holding another party, he supposed.

"Yes, let us settle it, by all means. Let us put all our cards
on the table. *All* our cards. For instance, you will not deny
that *you* persuaded the military that I was the ideal man for
the mission to Malkhan."

"So you were."

"Your motive was twofold," Richard continued, ignoring
that. "Firstly, you knew you did not have the qualifications
for it—qualifications you have boasted of so often. Secondly,
there was every chance that I would not return. You would
have been rid of me for good, and your reputation safe, until
the next man who could prove you wrong came upon the
scene. By then, you would probably have been serving some
dark-faced princeling once more."

Duprés' horse stamped impatiently, jerking his rider from
side to side. Against the moon, Richard could only see the
outline of a light-coloured turban and a dark blur for a face.
He had no idea of the man's expression.

"I know Mooji-Lal," came the quietly savage words. "He
is ruthless and not a little unbalanced. He killed Bateson and
the Russian—why not you? There is only one reason why
you would be allowed to survive . . . and that fully explains
why your little drab of a wife has never been fulfilled."

Like a match applied directly to gunpowder the implication of those words exploded in Richard the hatred of a man who had been the cause of all his suffering and humiliation of the past two years. That uncontrollable fury that took hold of him when defending his own now rocketed through him unchecked, and he leapt at Duprés like a man possessed, gripping him around the throat as they both toppled from their saddles to land on the ground between the horses.

Richard's anger was silent and deadly as he rolled over and over with his struggling unprepared opponent, tightening his hold around the man's throat as he attempted to knock Duprés senseless against the stony ground. He was unaware of kicks from Duprés' boots, the scratching of sharp-edged rocks, or danger from the stamping hooves of frightened horses milling around them. All he wanted was to destroy Colley Duprés as the adventurer had hoped to destroy him, socially and bodily.

Every thump of the man's skull, minus the elaborate turban, was for a separate instance. One for Charlotte, one for Anna, who had been conceived to the sound of his name, one for Sir Rastin Scott, who had been cuckolded beneath his own roof, one for the supposed Russian blood he had dishonoured, one for the senseless taking of Ghuznee, and three for Malkhan.

At that point, Richard realized what he was doing, and that Duprés was very still. He returned to his senses as abruptly as he had left them. Chest heaving, breath rattling in his throat, aching with rage, he knelt astride his opponent and felt for his pulse. Thank God it was there, faint but steady, still. Panting and suddenly very cold, Richard got unsteadily to his feet and looked around the moonlit cantonment.

In some bungalows lamps were burning where other officers had returned home and were smoking a quiet cigar before turning in. But there was no other movement on this outskirt of the military settlement. The night was cold with a great moon and brilliant myriads of stars above. Patrols were not due to pass this way for another half an hour. He could not leave Duprés until then.

Up ahead a light was shining in Felicia Scott's bungalow,

and it told him what to do. He had no love for a woman who betrayed her husband with a worthless peacock scoundrel. She expected her lover tonight: she would have him!

Catching the horses, he lifted the unconscious man and threw him over the saddle of the stallion before mounting his own and leading the other along the path towards Lady Scott's rented bungalow. As they neared it, her mares whinnied their delight at the smell of an approaching stallion, and Richard then dropped the reins to allow the beast to carry its burden unerringly to the stables where the syce would be on guard.

With malicious satisfaction Richard had stripped Duprés of all but his underdrawers, his only regret being that he could not chain the man to a post and let the natives throw stones and filth at him. But his fastidious mistress might find him less than enticing, in his present state.

Entering his own bungalow shortly afterwards Richard found that his burst of murderous rage had left him leaden and introspective, as it always did. Pouring himself a stiff drink he decided against ringing for his bearer. He had seen himself in the looking-glass and had no intention of allowing the servant to exercise his considerable crafty curiosity so that the story could be spread around the cantonment by morning.

He was dabbing several small cuts on his hands and face when a soft voice cried, "*Richard,* whatever has happened?"

In the looking-glass he saw Charlotte standing there in her nightgown, with the long brown hair rippling over her shoulders. The candle held aloft showed she had walked through dark corridors to reach his room, and the light from the flame made her eyes glow as they stared at him in incomprehension. He knew, at once, that she had intended *this* thing to be settled tonight, once and for all, as well. But he was unprepared for another fight. He was off-balance, at a disadvantage because he had been cornered in his own room. He could hardly walk away, this time.

"What has happened?" she repeated more insistently.

"I took a toss as I was returning home," he replied carefully, straightening up and putting the cloth down on his washstand.

"But you look terrible!" She came across the room to him, eyes extra large with apprehension and nervousness. "Your uniform is covered in dust, and there is blood on your shirt. Why, you are cut and bruised around the face." Only a few feet away by then, she added, "A superb rider like you— how did you come to fall on a clear quiet well-lit night like this?"

"Faber stumbled, and I had been imbibing too unwisely." He moved away from her instinctively. "It is nothing, I assure you."

"Why is your bearer not here to assist you?" She followed him across the rug.

"I am not yet ready to go to bed."

"Then let me tend those cuts."

She was already on her way to the washstand when he stopped her. "No, I thank you. I am a grown man and a soldier, Charlotte. I have no need of a nurse any longer."

She stood as still as a statue, looking at him with the same expression she had worn when walking uninvited and unwanted into his home, holding his child by the hand.

"Then tell me what I am to do," she whispered brokenly. "You refuse to touch me, and now will not let me touch you. It has been well over two years, Richard, and I am not made of stone. I have abandoned pride and modesty, all to no avail. If it is your intention to make me beg, I will go down on my knees this minute."

His throat seemed to have dried up completely, and he half-closed his eyes in distress at what she was implying. But he could not take those few steps towards her, try as he might.

"It . . . it would be better if *I* came to *you*," he managed somehow. "You know how servants see everything that goes on."

It was plain she did not know what to do, whether he meant what he said or was simply dismissing her.

"Tonight . . . you mean to come tonight?"

It was a querulous, desperate question from a girl who could be so courageous, and he hated himself for being unable to do more than nod in reply.

Softly gliding in the long white nightgown she went off, leaving him with the inevitability of that nod. The room seemed silent, as if waiting to see what he would do, and the great clock in his sitting-room ticked with the sound of a hundred such clocks.

There was no escaping, this time. What she had said to him before he left for Malkhan was true. He was afraid of her—afraid of feeling again the deep love that had been destroyed so cruelly. He was afraid of exposing himself again to the anguish he had felt on that night.

He sank down in the chair with his head in his hands. It was impossible for him to embark on a loveless passion with her. He was not the kind of man who could kiss and run, or he would have conducted numerous flirtations during his days at Meerpore. His nature demanded that he committed himself fully and forever, unless something beyond his control broke that bond . . . and he was dreadfully afraid to revive something that had hurt him so unbearably.

At first, he had succeeded by pretending Charlotte did not exist then, when she arrived at Kabul, kept her at a safe distance bodily and emotionally. He knew it was useless to go to her room. It would be humiliating for them both. All the time he expected her to cry out "*Colley*" in her rapture, he would be incapable of doing what she asked . . . and he knew that would happen tonight. He broke out in a cold sweat. How could they hope to stay together when the mere thought of holding her naked body against him conjured up memories of a tent in Ferozepore, and rain beating on the canvas as he felt his life break apart?

Getting to his feet in desperation he stood with clenched fists, staring at the archway, seeing her in the soft nightgown, candle held high. If she were an unknown wanton in a bawd-house he could keep her occupied all night. But he *felt* something for the wife who had crept back into his life and, until he could love deeply and freely again, he could not produce passion on request.

That was what he would have to tell her. It was the only way to settle it, at present. He was tired and emotionally raw after his tangle with Duprés. He needed more time. Yet he could not bring himself to leave her waiting for a man who did not come. The least he owed her was to speak honestly now. It might be hurtful, but less so than staying away.

The decision made he went quickly, just as he was in his dusty dishevelled uniform, and his knock on the wall beside her bedroom archway was firm enough to disguise his reluctance.

There was no reply, so he pushed aside the curtain and went in with forced determination. Then he stopped short and drew in his breath. The room was lit with branches of candles so that it looked cosy and inviting, and Charlotte stood with a shawl over her nightgown beside a table containing a bottle of wine and two glasses. The words he was about to say fled from his mind as she smiled gently and said, "I think you will find my wine tastes like the usual sort, Mr Lingarde."

The tent at Ferozepore vanished and was replaced by a vision of their honeymoon room, where he had approached his fearful child-bride. The memory caught at his breast sharply as she moved towards him with two filled glasses, banishing one night with the happiness of another. He gazed helplessly into her eyes that had turned suddenly beautiful with soft desire, and sipped his wine with trance-like movements as she did the same. Then, she went on tip-toe to kiss his mouth with wine-wet lips, and his head swam.

"There is no need for this, I swear," she whispered, making that far-off night come vividly alive again with the words he had then spoken to her. "I shall never demand from you anything you cannot freely give."

She knew! She understood. He did not have to tell her, see the contempt and pain in her eyes as he admitted he was too vulnerable to be her lover. Her face looked golden and smooth in the candle-glow, and her hair had been brushed into shining beauty his fingers could not resist. Hesitantly he reached out to touch a long tress lying across her left shoulder. She moved closer until they were almost touching, and

he could smell the perfume of her nearness. It took him even
further into that night so long ago when love and desire had
been such precious, gentle things.

They drank more wine, and she kissed his mouth again
with lips that were sweetly wet and tender. Coaxed to a chair
he sat while she re-filled the glasses, then climbed on to his
knees to curl up with her head just below his chin. Slowly
she undid his thick jacket, murmuring that the buttons dug
into her face, and the feel of her warm cheeks through his
shirt made him slide an arm around her slender body in the
nightgown.

The heady wine coursed through his veins making his
head spin after the madeira and port he had consumed earlier
that evening, but he continued to drink it and began to return the wine-laden kisses with which she teased him. When
she asked huskily if the wine was to his taste, he replied that
it was the best he had drunk in a long time. She poured
more, and he emptied that glass, also. Her hand began to
stroke his cut cheeks and his bared throat with butterfly caresses, then her fingers curled into his hair as she whispered
passionately, "Richard, I think I could never bear to be
parted from you again."

Feeling exhausted, bruised and distinctly dizzy, he tried to
tell her that he had no intention of going anywhere, but the
words refused to be formed. Her face was now swimming
about before his eyes, and the whole room appeared to be
tipping from side to side. There was a tinkling sound as he
let the glass slip from his fingers and tried to sit upright. But
Charlotte was coaxing him to his feet and leading him towards the bed. It looked wonderfully inviting, so he dropped
on to it gratefully. After that, he was vaguely aware of his
clothes being removed and her warm curves pressing close
into his arms, demanding nothing more than to be held
there. Then, the events of the evening overcame him, and he
drifted off into pleasant darkness untroubled by dreams.

He awoke to sunshine dimmed by lowered tatties, and
knew by the bugle-calls ringing across the cantonment that
the morning was well-advanced. He was just recalling where
he was, and why, when there was a swish of skirts and

Charlotte walked in, dressed for morning, her face pale and shocked.

"So, you are awake, at last," she said in tones of throbbing accusation.

He cautiously raised himself on one elbow and looked her over from the pile of shining curls to the small kid boots peeping from beneath her crinoline.

"Is something amiss?" he asked softly.

She stared at him for a moment or two, breathing hard. "A most unusual circumstance has occurred. Major Duprés is in the hospital this morning recovering from an attack he claims was made upon him by two hostile Afghans. His face is contused and most dreadfully cut about. He was half-choked to death, and pummelled in the chest before being knocked unconscious. He was found, stripped of his outer clothes, by Mama's stable-boy when his horse trotted in with him hanging over the saddle. It is now all over the cantonment as to why the stallion should know its way to that particular stable, even when uncontrolled."

She paused, as if waiting for him to comment, but he stayed silent in the face of her strange attitude of condemnation. Duprés had got out of his predicament very nicely. Richard was content to leave it like that. But Charlotte was not.

"Major Duprés' discarded uniform was found on the path not far from this bungalow."

He considered that for a moment, then said with casual tones, "Dear me, these Afghans are growing dashed audacious!"

To his astonishment she turned away, shoulders heaving, head in her hands, sobbing softly. After a moment, he threw back the sheet and went across to turn her into his arms.

"What is this?" he asked with gentle amusement.

She looked up at him, desperation written on her face. "There was no need for that. I love only you, I swear."

He pulled her closer and murmured against her hair, "I know that . . . now."

She clung to him as her tears subsided, and he presently held her away, smiling. "No longer a termagant? Then, in view of my naked state, do you not feel you are a trifle over-dressed? That gown is most attractive, but what I have in mind will be much more enjoyable without it."

She looked up at him, joy dawning on her face. "You have crushed the life out of this gown, so I am obliged to change it. But it is mid-morning, sir. What will *les poules* have to say about your very improper suggestion?"

Fingers already busy with the buttons of her dress he said, "They will be far too busy discussing Duprés' experience at the hands of two Afghans . . . and since when has mid-morning passion been improper?"

Breathlessly, she whispered, "Aunt Meg would not approve."

"Aunt Meg has never seduced me with wine, madam," he murmured, bending to kiss one of her breasts. "Now is the time for you to reap what you sowed last night, my dearest Lottie . . . and your aunt would approve of that maxim very heartily."

· *fifteen* ·

THE EAST INDIA Company was suddenly aware that its bold, brave excursion into Afghanistan had become an enormously expensive folly. Their puppet, Shah Soojah, was certainly still friendly towards the British occupation, but he sat in luxury in the Bala Hissar, surrounded by his court, his women and his private army. After more than two years he was no nearer ruling his country than he had been at the start. Some reported that he never would, despite Sir William McNaughten's assurances that everything was going splendidly.

The Kabul garrison had become a luxury the Company could ill afford, yet dared not recall. As the summer of 1841 began to fade, McNaughten was informed by his superiors that he must make sharp economies. Being a single-minded man very proud of his own achievements, there was only one answer he could see to such a request. Each year, he paid the Ghilzai bandits who controlled the passes to India a large bribe to ensure safe conduct of supply-columns and other missions en route to the garrison. He cut the amount by half immediately.

The Ghilzais were savage independent people who lived in the border regions and felt no strong allegiance to anyone but themselves. The halving of their income was guaranteed to bring reprisals, at the best of times. In this case, it led to their closing all routes to India, and discovering a close affinity with their Afghan brethren, who were all set to rise against the British.

McNaughten took it all very calmly, considering that his small force was now effectively cut off and surrounded by hostile rebels. He had recently been rewarded for his services in Afghanistan with the governorship of Bombay, which he intended taking up as soon as he could get away, and had no intention of allowing his peers to believe the situation was not as he had described it. Accordingly, as the second of his economies, he decided to kill two birds with one stone. By sending General Sale, with an entire brigade, back to India he would be reducing the cost of his garrison and teaching the Ghilzais a strong lesson on attempting to defy the might of the East India Company. Sale had orders to clear the passes as he went.

The brigade was attacked three days after it set out, and had to shoot its way all the distance to Jalalabad where the General, wounded in the leg, wisely decided to stay. It had come home to him that the extent of Afghan hostility had been grossly underestimated, and there was no chance of attempting the Khyber or any of the other passes, with the numbers he had remaining. He sent word to this effect back to General Elphinstone in Kabul, who was now left with a dangerously small garrison in a country where the day of vengeance had arrived.

Meanwhile, in Kabul itself, which had gradually filled with rebels from outside, plans were being made to end the occupation by infidels. A group of minor chieftains had assembled there to organize the uprising, none with any real talent for command, but each with pride that had smarted for too long. Damped-down aggression now burned openly. Troops were set upon and beaten almost to death: some were found with their throats slit in the numerous dark alleys of the inner city.

In the outlying forts it was the same story. British officers were murdered; their tiny forces of sepoys slaughtered to a man. At the fort of Churrakur, Eldred Pottinger, the hero of Herat who had been rewarded for his outstanding services by the paltry promotion to major and another isolated command in a fort, had reportedly been wounded but miraculously escaped from the outpost into the wild countryside. Chances were, he would die unmarked as another young political whose brilliance was prematurely dimmed in the cause of his profession.

In the cantonment there was, astonishingly, a high percentage of normal behaviour from those whose innately phlegmatic attitude refused to believe the end was nigh. Social life continued unabated, and two scandals were currently enlivening the boredom of approaching snow-bound winter months.

Amy Scott was making no attempt to repel the ardent advances of Lieutenant Spence, who was still in Kabul because Lady Scott remained, and he had orders to escort her back to Meerpore. Young Tom Scott appeared unable to settle the matter, either with his wife or his fellow-officer, and went around looking perpetually bewildered and worried. His step-mother, the one person who should have been able to banish Spence and read Mrs Scott a stern lesson, was the subject of the other scandal—one so juicy and shocking the whole of India was certain to rock with it.

Since Colley Duprés' beating by the Afghans, sharp minds had been busy with the question of why his horse should have gone to Lady Scott's residence with unerring instinct, when he appeared rarely to go near her. It took very little time for past events to take on a new significance. The grandmother, who had come to Kabul ostensibly to see Anna Lingarde and be present at the birth of Amy Scott's child, showed no interest in the Lingarde toddler and was out riding when the Scott twins came into the world. Other things like the swift marriage of little Charlotte Scott which had coincided with a marked coolness between mother and daughter, even though it was known the beautiful Felicia had engineered the marriage herself, plus the hostility between the Lingardes and Major Duprés very soon revealed a possibility that was not only titillating but hinted at broken careers and social casting-out.

Felicia Scott put an end to speculation and malicious whispers by being seen everywhere in his company, speaking openly of her great admiration for him, and declining the opportunity to set off with Sale's troops as ample escort and protection for a female traveller. She had no intention, she said calmly, of returning to live in an empty house in Meerpore when her dearest friend remained in Kabul. She began to entertain on a lavish scale, with him beside her looking even more exotic with the marks of the attack still on his face. Everyone accepted her invitations out of curiosity, then found it impossible to cut the woman after doing so. Felicia admitted her immoral liaison with the same impeccable style with which she did everything, and the members of the garrison were beguiled into accepting it before they could stop themselves.

Charlotte was deeply distressed, at first, and blamed Richard for bringing to light something that had been kept so secret for a long time. But he was unrepentant, saying it was time Duprés was seen for what he was, and if Sir Rastin saw fit to block the man's career, it would only be his just deserts. As for Lady Scott, there was much for which he held her mainly responsible, and he could not see that it would do her any harm to stew in the juice of her sins for a while. Charlotte did not feel justified in telling him what her mother had revealed to her, in confidence, and marvelled at the strange set of standards, maintained by gentlemen. Really, they were sometimes quite incomprehensible!

She went impulsively to her mother's bungalow one morning, but Felicia was about to lie down with a lotion on her face and hands. She rendered their interview very brief, with a smiling confession that she was greatly relieved that the whole thing was out in the open, at last.

"It means I can enjoy every possible minute with him now," she said from the archway of her boudoir, "and it really does not matter any more. You know, of course, that none of us will ever return to India. You have won your Richard back, and I am glad of it. Live to the heights, my dear, and be grateful for every day from now on."

She had gone in to lie down then, and Charlotte had walked away strangely moved to tears. There was something fine about Felicia Scott, after all. Her courage might be shallow after the brand shown by gentlemen, but it was there. But she was also struck by her mother's disturbing fatalism. Had Colley told her something Richard was keeping back?

Walking slowly home Charlotte looked up at the hills surrounding her. In the heights to her left was a small detachment on the look-out, under the command of a brigadier who showed his opinion of Elphinstone's ability by frequently taking his sleeping-mat to tactical conferences and slumbering upon it until they broke up. Also, at one of the many outlying forts through the orchards was an even smaller force acting as a forward post in case of attack along the valley. At the Bala Hissar was a whole army of troops loyal to Shah Soojah. Or were they? Suddenly, she wondered if they would rise up against him if Dost Mohammed's son, Akbar Khan, arrived at the gates with a multitude of rebels. Richard thought it a strong possibility unless the cantonment garrison moved in with them. He was urging that step now, before events made it into a hurried, desperate affair which meant leaving behind valuable stores and equipment.

She stopped at a spot on the road that gave a view of the valley, and gazed out towards the north where Malkhan lay. Richard had never spoken to her of what he had suffered there, but she knew it had been so terrible it had changed him into a man she loved with frightening depth. Without him her life would be over. Felicia had just suggested they were all going to die there. That thought, in itself, did not frighten her, but to die alone whilst he was somewhere else giving his life to defend her, not to be together at the end, was unfaceable.

Invaded by morbid fears, Charlotte suddenly envisaged the roads, the familiar buildings, swarming with dark-faced, bearded Afghans screaming revenge and hacking at panic-stricken women and children with their tulwars. And the men, out on the perimeter, fighting desperately against over-whelming odds until their screams and shouts were silenced, and they lay in bloody mounds of scarlet and blue. That was how Lady Anastasia Lingarde had once described Waterloo to her, but never had it seemed as vivid as now. She put her face in her hands to shut out the peaceful valley and the images she had conjured up from the quiet verdure.

"Lottie? *Lottie* . . . what are you doing?"

It was Richard swinging from his saddle and leading his horse across to where she stood. His face was full of concern.

"Are you all right?"

She put a smile on her face to fool him. "Of course, my dear. I had something in my eye. But it is gone now."

"Where have you been?"

"To Mama's." She forced a laugh. "I was allowed three minutes of her time. She was about to rest with a lotion on her face."

A scowl crossed his sun-browned face. "She has to look beautiful to keep him, and it must grow increasingly difficult."

"Richard, that is unkind," she protested.

He smiled down into her eyes with all the wickedness of expression he could muster, when he chose. "I declare there are lines and wrinkles appearing on your cheeks now you are come of age." He sighed theatrically. "Ah me, I am wed to a matron."

"Wretch!" she cried, and put out the tip of her tongue at him. "It is really too vexing that gentlemen undoubtedly grow more handsome with the passing years. Always the object of extreme female flattery, here you are over thirty and still acknowledged the most fascinating man in Kabul. Small wonder females flutter their eyelashes at you, and their hearts beat faster when you salute them."

He took her by the waist. "And you, my sweet flatterer, what do you feel when I salute you?"

"That, sir, I shall keep to myself for fear of increasing your sense of consequence even further."

His exciting eyes lit with the sparkle of desire. "Then you shall pay a penalty for such reticence," he murmured, and drew her hard against him to kiss her with great intensity.

Taken unawares, she said breathlessly, "*Richard,* we are in full view of anyone passing along the road."

"When I did not kiss my wife, it caused comment. There should be none when I do," he said roughly, in what she termed his defiant tone. "And it does not matter any more."

Those words, an exact repetition of what Felicia had said, took all the lightheartedness from the moment. As he put an arm behind her and led her along the road towards their home, walking beside the horse that had carried him to Malkhan, she looked up at him searchingly from the curve of his arm.

"That is a curious remark. You speak as if we were all doomed."

He looked down at her quickly. "No . . . no, I do not believe that."

"But?" she prompted.

He frowned and slowed his steps. "But I believe we shall have to make a battle of it before we are assured safe passage back to India. And we must go back, Lottie. The occupation has been an expensive failure, no matter what the bull-headed optimists say. We should be strong enough to admit it and retire in good order before irreparable harm is done."

"How can we retire?" she pointed out. "General Sale was lucky to get as far as Jalalabad without being annihilated."

"Which is why we should remove *now* to the Bala Hissar," he said heatedly. "It is useless marching out into terrain in which they have every advantage over us. They are determined upon revenge. We must, therefore, lure them to Kabul where we have an admirable fortress from which we could hold off any numbers without difficulty, and reduce their strength by our command of the valley. Dithering here in the cantonment is senseless. It will take time to carry in all our supplies and armaments, and drag the guns within the walls of the bastion. It should be done now!"

She touched his arm sympathetically. "Would they not listen to you, this morning?"

His face darkened with anger. "They have another excellent excuse for dismissing my advice. I was informed that, since my commission is up for sale and my notice to quit Kabul has been accepted, I am no longer regarded as part of this garrison. In short, they consider me to have already left the army, and us to have gone from the area. It appears it was presumptuous of me to have offered advice, under the circumstances."

Knowing no words would be adequate, Charlotte remained quiet and deep in thought as she tried to match her steps to his long strides. Once their reunion had been complete Richard had put in motion all his plans to leave the army and start a new life in England or Russia. When it was known that Sale was leaving for India with a brigade of troops, Richard had arranged for them to accompany the force, along with several others anxious to get back in safety. Extra horses had been purchased, their furniture sold, belongings packed, and an open palanquin obtained for Charlotte to travel in.

But they were destined not to go. The day before departure Charlotte had begun to miscarry the embryo child that had been the instant result of their renewed passion. There was no question of her travelling and, three days later, the pregnancy ended. She took the disappointment well, her religious upbringing comforting her with the belief that the Almighty had his reasons for everything. She had been given Richard back, and they had their dearest Anna. Richard had been too thankful for her own recovery and too absorbed in the reports coming back from the marching column to show his feelings over the loss of something that had hardly touched them before going again. Perhaps he had not cared too much. Charlotte had the feeling that, like herself, he was too passionately grateful for what he had to expect more.

But the hope of now getting away was dependent on too many things, and they had had to buy back some of their furniture and unpack all their things. Charlotte vacillated between being glad they had not gone with Sale's column that had suffered attack, and wishing she were out of Kabul now it was so helplessly cut off. This new military attitude towards Richard was unforeseen. It was true that he was virtually no longer on the strength, that he held no command in the garrison, but he was still an officer in the Royal Engineers until his commission was officially transferred, and it was a very petty attitude that ignored sound advice from *anyone* in a dangerous situation.

It was a dangerous situation. Most people now admitted it and wondered how it would all end. Felicia plainly had pessimistic views, or was using uncertainty as an excuse to indulge her passion for Colley while they were unavoidably thrown together. Richard was visibly worried, and Tom seemed to have shelved the problem of his wife's flirtation while he fretted over military matters. In view of what Richard had just told her, Charlotte felt in need of a truthful answer from her husband, at last.

"Richard, what is our position if Kabul is attacked?" she asked quietly, stopping and turning to face him. "If you are no longer considered to be part of the garrison, are we to be left out of any plans for the protection of its members?"

He studied her in silence for a moment, then shook his head slowly. "Dear me, the penalty I pay for having an intelligent wife. You should leave all such problems to me, you know."

"Please, Richard," she remonstrated.

"Well . . . I believe I might just scrape through by offering my services as an interpreter, and you, my pretty," he added, flicking her curls gently with the reins he held, "could be counted a camp-follower, wench that you are."

She had to be satisfied, but consoled herself with the

thought that he would not have joked about it if he had been seriously worried.

But he did grow seriously worried the following evening, when a large body of horsemen was spotted riding towards the city, and messages were received from officers residing there that there looked like trouble brewing because a large selection of minor chieftains had arrived from various parts of Afghanistan, bringing followers and an air of aggression.

General Elphinstone was of the opinion that it was a mere storm in a teacup and did nothing. But Richard was so concerned he spent the night fully dressed and with his pistol handy, watching from the window of the bedroom he insisted on Anna sharing with them. The child slept peacefully, but Charlotte felt extremely alarmed by his precautions, wondering if he was being over-dramatic.

But when dawn brought sounds of rifle-fire, howls of vengeance from hundreds of throats, and the shattering thuds of the Amir's guns from the citadel, she knew he had merely been anticipating what his shrewd brain had guessed was coming. Rousing from uneasy sleep in a swift surge of fear, she looked across to where he stood outlined against the pale light from outside.

"Richard . . . what is happening?" she cried softly, careful not to awaken the sleeping Anna in the cot beside her.

He turned slowly, his voice heavy with regret. "Elphinstone has lost his chance. They have taken the city, right beneath his nose."

She scrambled from the bed and went to stand at the window, within the circle of his arm. They said nothing to each other, just gazed across the orchards towards Kabul, from where the tumult of crazed mobs floated on the still air. Thin spirals of smoke were rising, here and there, and over the whole hung a pall from the great guns of the Bala Hissar. Charlotte grew intensely cold and pressed closer against Richard's side. There was a truly awesome quality about the sight on a clear early November morning, and it was not something she could readily accept. How many times had she looked across at that great fortress, seeing it only as a walled bastion that witnessed her emotional despair over a marriage that could never be as strong and impregnable? Now it had become a symbol of aggression; a fortress that spit death upon those beneath; a palace of ostentatious protection for a man who was blind to the fact that there were others *outside* the walls.

"Oh Richard!" she exclaimed quietly.

"I hope to God Burnes and his brother are safe . . . and young Broadfoot, who also has his quarters in the Residency," he said, his eyes on the distant turmoil. "They have been receiving hints for some days past from Afghan friends who suggested it would be as well for them to remove to the cantonment. But Burnes is ever the optimist. He feels his credit with the Afghans stands too high for the prospect of personal danger. Three or four years ago that was probably true, but he has since turned his back on his great friend Dost Mohammed, enthusiastically helped to bring about his exile, and lorded it here with the wives of those who once revered his integrity and courage. The price of such folly might be paid in agonizing fashion, if he is not careful."

Charlotte shivered, thinking of a lone figure kneeling in a deserted courtyard, waiting for his head to be sliced from his shoulders by a man with a cruel twisted personality.

Torn between the desire for news and reluctance to leave his wife and daughter in a bungalow right on the outskirts of the cantonment nearest the city, Richard could not settle to eat breakfast that morning. Charlotte tried to persuade him that it would be better to do so, and forced down a cup of tea and two slices of bread and butter as an example. But she betrayed her sense of fear by refusing to let Anna go off with the ayah, as usual. The little girl was only too delighted to be allowed to stay with both her parents and looked upon it as some kind of celebration, chattering happily in a mixture of English and Russian, apparently undisturbed by the noise only a short distance away.

During the morning there were messengers galloping madly about the cantonment, and great activity around the various gates was obvious from Richard's scrutiny with his telescope. His agitation grew so great that Charlotte finally begged him to go off in search of news, assuring him that she would be quite safe all the time there were soldiers riding back and forth outside the bungalow.

But Richard never departed, because Tom came galloping up like a madman and almost threw himself from the saddle before running up their steps. Charlotte and Richard met him on the verandah, both anxious to hear why he had come, and he was so worked up he could not speak for a moment or two.

"Burnes has been murdered," he announced in a voice charged with emotion. "Young Broadfoot was shot trying to hold back a mob. Then, they rushed the Residency and put the stables and outbuildings to the torch. One of Burnes' native friends offered to lead him and his brother to safety dressed in Afghan robes, but once they reached the garden, he betrayed them, pulling back the robes and announcing in triumphant tones whom he had delivered into their hands. The pair were hacked to pieces. The Residency is destroyed."

Charlotte and Richard just stared at him, each taking in the implication of his words. But Tom was grappling with additional information that he seemed almost unable to tell.

"He . . . he apparently sent a note to McNaughten at dawn, telling him they were under attack and asking for troops to quell the rioting. No attempt was made to send anyone at all."

"*What?*" roared Richard so loudly it made Charlotte jump.

"No troops were sent," confirmed Tom, chest heaving, face pale. "Captain Sturt of the Engineers—old Sale's son-in-law—offered to discover the state of the situation, and Elphinstone finally agreed to send him with a message to Shah Soojah, asking *him* to investigate the disturbance and act accordingly."

"*Disturbance,*" cried Richard, in the same tones. "Good God, man, there is a full scale attack going on in Kabul. That much is obvious from here."

Tom nodded shortly. "Sturt never reached the Amir. He was stabbed three times by a man who ran out from a house as he neared the gates of the palace. His escort brought him back, amidst further attacks, and he is now with his wife and

Lady Sale, choking to death from a serious throat wound."

He stood in deep distress as Richard pronounced his genuine regret over Captain Sturt, whom everyone knew and admired as a dedicated and talented man who had been one of the sabre-rattling brigade all the time he had been at Kabul.

Charlotte, however, found herself growing colder and colder. The military implications hung in the background as she visualized the vivid human tragedy of all Tom had said. She had not known Sir Alexander Burnes well, and had found him too full of his own importance, besides deploring his reputation. But he had had his years of pure brilliance, and she found it unbearably sad that he would never now have the opportunity to recapture it and use the talents God had given him for the benefit of mankind. In addition, the picture her imaginative mind conjured up of the Residency blazing, and two fine young men helpless beneath the slashing blades of tulwars wielded by maddened natives, could not but help freezing the blood in her veins. Two young men dying in the hope that their appeal for help would be met. Two brothers, gone in seconds, savagely and ritually. A mother somewhere would hear the news in six months' time—as she had heard of Hubert's death—and ask the Almighty why.

"Do you wish to hear the rest?" asked Tom, quieter now and heavy with depression.

"Yes . . . yes, come inside," said Richard, subdued by the shock of the news, leading the way into Charlotte's sitting-room in brooding silence.

He poured wine for himself and Tom, while Charlotte made herself comfortable in a chair with Anna upon her knee. She felt the unreality of the day closing in on her as the guns continued to fire in the city, and screams mingled with cries of religious fervour. Whatever was happening in those dim, treacherous streets: how many were falling beneath the slicing tulwars?

Her brother took a long draught of wine, then looked across at Richard, who had done the same. "We have lost the Treasury. They plundered the contents and burned the place down. Fortunately, the paymaster spent the night in the cantonment and is safe. McNaughten and his lady have just moved in. Elphinstone finally sent a tiny force of sepoys out, but they have come in again, sadly decimated and, I regret to say, against the order of their officer." Tom looked especially stricken over this, for he was inordinately proud and fond of his own sepoys. He attempted to make an excuse for them. "They had no heart for an attack launched too late and too ineffectively. I suppose one cannot blame them, in the face of Elphinstone's weakness and vacillation."

"But the Amir—did none of his troops turn out?" put in Richard angrily. "Burnes sacrificed his professional integrity to finally support that man. We also have two companies in the Bala Hissar. Did *no one* do anything in response to Burnes' appeal?"

Tom sighed. "The Amir sent out one of his regiments, with artillery. But you can imagine the complete disorder of troops trying to drag and site big guns through that maze of streets, Richard. Half of them were slaughtered. The rest retired to the fortress, obliged to abandon the guns. As for our companies up there, they fought their way back to the cantonment with some difficulty. The chieftains have command of the city and have won over most of the population by ruthlessly killing any Afghan who will not readily join in the surge of revenge against us. The Bala Hissar is virtually under siege. Shah Soojah is a prisoner within its walls—I dread to think what they might do to *him*, knowing their range of tortures." He stretched his neck against the restrictions of his tight collar. "It means we are completely cut off from the city now, and our hopes of defence within the fortress look to be gone. From all I hear, McNaughten and Elphinstone are busy all the time biting the ends of their fingers and wondering that it should have come to this."

"And the Amir—the man we placed on the throne and have been defending these past years—what is he doing to restore order?" asked Richard with heavy sarcasm.

"He answers every letter sent to him by McNaughten and carried with great risk by native gallopers, but it is not certain whether any of the replies are genuine."

"So we are lost?" put in Charlotte in steady, questioning

tones. "You have always said we are like a kitten at the bottom of a well in this cantonment. If the city is captured, it is all up with us."

The two men turned to her in surprise, having forgotten she was there, but when Richard answered he spoke to Tom, as if it had been he who had asked the question.

"There is still time to put up hasty defences and fire the orchards to destroy the enemy's cover, but our only hope is to fight through to the Bala Hissar. If the commissariat falls into their hands, we stand no chance. We could not last out a week."

The commissariat was lost the following evening, and the Kabul garrison was threatened with defeat by starvation.

During the next few weeks, hope and despair fluctuated daily, and the winter, like a freezing white angel of death, crept ever nearer.

The commissariat officers, whose protests over using an outlying fort to store provisions and supplies were never heeded, did not cry over spilt milk. They set out to obtain what extra food they could from friendly villages in the area, in secret and at great financial cost. But these purchases were meagre, and rations were drastically cut to the troops. Officers could no longer buy their provisions, camp-followers had to get what they could scavenge, horses were reduced to eating the bark off trees.

Small engagements were fought, resulting in expensive loss of life to regain control of a few forts outside the cantonment, only to surrender them again when Afghans rushed them in overwhelming numbers when sepoys mutinied and returned to the dubious safety of the cantonment, or the British officers decided they had no desire to sacrifice their lives for so paltry a cause. But, all the time, the Afghans worried at the cantonment, making small assaults on various points around the perimeter where they had crept through the orchards unseen, keeping the inmates rushing hither and thither to shore up the breaches and fend off surprise attacks, exhausting themselves in the process.

It was obvious to most officers that all the time the rebels held the Bala Hissar and strategic points in the hills around, the garrison was helpless. Lady Sale's son-in-law had barely got to his feet after his triple stabbing before he was bombarded with requests to build defences, throw up breastworks, or strengthen gates, all of which had been urgently recommended by himself and others, including Richard, since the place had first been built. It was now far too late. Not only was Sturt still very ill, his sepoy workers were so affected by the cold and lack of food, they worked so slowly that they never finished one job before being told to leave it and start something of more importance.

General Elphinstone's ill-health, too, was proving a disaster. Incapable of thinking anything out, he called constant councils of war which took every officer away from what he was doing when he was most needed. All except for Richard Lingarde, who was not invited to the discussions because he was not considered to be there any longer. Tom always reported the facts to his friend, however, and said the meetings were nothing short of uncontrolled free-for-alls in which everyone was asked for his opinion, Elphinstone invariably acting on the words of the last man to whom he spoke, whether he be a staff officer or the lowliest subaltern on the station. Tom remarked with bitter sarcasm that it was to be hoped the General had no cause to exchange words with his sweeper after that.

All the old sabre-rattling brigade of the past two years pressed most urgently for an evacuation of the cantonment and a concerted attempt to fight through to the Bala Hissar. Better late than never, they advised, and although there would be greater loss of life now than if it had been done earlier, it was the only hope of survival for the greater part of the force. As they were, it was merely a matter of time before they would be completely wiped out.

This advice was pooh-poohed by Elphinstone, who was supported in his opinion by McNaughten, and when an attempt to dislodge the Afghans from one nearby range of hills failed ingloriously, both men in command appeared to give up the garrison for lost and sat wringing their hands.

One small incident occurred in the middle of November

that was destined to turn into a happy chance for the future, and that was the surprise arrival of Eldred Pottinger and a fellow officer, both wounded, who had somehow managed to travel across wild country from Churrakur after that fort had been taken and the rest of the force killed. The hero of Herat was welcomed with relief by junior officers who knew him for an experienced and sound man on situations such as they were presently in. But even he could not persuade McNaughten to make for the Bala Hissar, nor inspire action in the ailing General.

Then, hot on the heels of Eldred Pottinger, there arrived on the scene Dost Mohammed's favourite son, Akbar Khan, complete with his own army and ready to lead the disorganized chieftains with immense patriotic fervour and a personality verging on insanity. As virtual crown prince he, above all other Afghans, desired the utmost vengeance for the humiliation of having his country taken from him. Yet, inexplicably, those in command of the British force were pleased that he had taken the reins, believing that it would be easier to negotiate with a man whose large family was in the hands of the British in India—a bargaining power, in fact.

By this time, December was well on. Snow was lying everywhere, with a freezing wind whistling through the valley to further afflict the starving troops. Firewood was almost non-existent, spare horses and camels were being shot for food, and all other provisions had been reduced to a supply for no more than four days.

Sir William agreed at once, therefore, when Akbar Khan took up the minor chieftains' earlier offer to negotiate that had failed through lack of determination. Both sides proved remarkably amenable to the proposed settlement of hostilities. McNaughten returned to tell Elphinstone that he had agreed to withdraw the garrison from Afghanistan through Jalalabad and the Khyber Pass, taking with it the small forces presently at Ghuznee, Kandahar, and Jalalabad itself. The troops were to be given full protection by Afghan tribal leaders, and the Kabulis would send in immediate supplies to cover the retreat due to start in three days. In return, Dost

Mohammed and his entire family were to be allowed to return and take up as they had before, and four British officers must offer themselves as hostages as a sign of the garrison's good faith. In essence, their lives were being spared on condition that they quit the country and restored it to how it had been before ever they arrived. The four officer hostages demanded constituted something of an insult, since Akbar Khan offered no sign of *his* good faith. But McNaughten felt that under the circumstances he could not hope for more than the rescue of his force and a peaceful withdrawal.

The promised supplies did not arrive, however. Instead came a cavalry officer with a letter from Akbar Khan, proposing an alternative solution that was his own personal brain-child, unknown to the other chieftains who had sat in on the previous negotiations. The letter suggested that the British remain until the spring, when they could effect their withdrawal without pressure and loss of prestige. During that time Akbar Khan was to be appointed Shah Soojah's chief advisor, ready to take over as Amir when the British left, and to be given a present of ten thousand pounds and a large annual income for the rest of his life.

These proposals allowed for personal ambitions to be satisfied by both negotiators. They also offered another advantage to them both. Akbar Khan wished to be rid of one of the chieftains who, in fact, was responsible for the murder of Sir Alexander Burnes. As a sign of the Afghans' good faith, when they all met the following morning just outside the cantonment to finalize the terms, Akbar Khan would have the villain seized and presented to McNaughten. The British could then do with him what they wished.

It was basically an act of treachery by Akbar Khan, and something of a *volte face* by McNaughten, who had already agreed the terms of the first settlement with all the chieftains. But it promised a salve to the bruised occupation force, and praise from his superiors for McNaughten for such an advantageous bargain. He agreed, by letter, and set in motion an unimagined catastrophe.

The following meeting, presaged by elaborate formalities

and the exchanging of obligatory gifts, took place within view of the cantonment in a snow-covered meadow. McNaughten was accompanied by three staff officers, and supported by a detachment of native cavalry which stayed unobtrusively in the background. But the chieftains, led by Akbar Khan, were supported by an unexpectedly large horde of openly aggressive Afghans, which seemed to disconcert even Akbar Khan himself.

All went well, at first, until McNaughten was asked by his fellow conspirator if he was still set on carrying out his part of the bargain they had made. On his affirmation, Akbar Khan's face darkened, he cried to his chieftains that here was the proof that the British word could not be relied upon, and ordered the envoy seized. McNaughten, seeing that he had been the victim of a plot, cried out for mercy. His three companions began to draw their swords, but they were seized by the chieftains, forcibly mounted on horses and galloped away from the scene, pursued by the mob of Afghans bent on revenge. One was pulled from the saddle and hacked to pieces. The other two got safely to the city where they were thrown into prison. The native cavalry turned and galloped back to the safety of the cantonment, where stunned onlookers appeared unable to do anything.

Sir William McNaughten's head was placed upon a pole and carried, amidst hysterical fervour, around the streets of Kabul, his hands were tied to poles and poked through the windows of the prison as an example of their coming fate to the two prisoners, his arms and legs were exhibited separately to anyone who was fascinated enough to see them. His trunk, along with that of the officer who died with him, was hung on a meat-hook in the bazaar, the subject of vilification for the once-oppressed citizens of Kabul, who chose to forget that they had been oppressed for centuries by whoever was in power.

In the cantonment that night there were no plans for reprisals against the act of treachery and savage murder of a British envoy. Every mind was too shocked, too weary, or too exhausted to think. Each member sat, hungry and shivering, gazing dully at the snow drifting down.

The Lingardes and the Scotts, sharing a bungalow now for greater warmth, were as silent as everyone else. The two women looked desperately at their children and agonized over their thoughts. The two men, usually so fired with ideas, faced the realization that thousands of souls were now in the hands of an incompetent, ageing invalid. They could see ahead only a monumental military catastrophe.

• sixteen •

EXACTLY THREE YEARS after it had set out with such swagger from Ferozepore, what remained of the great Army of the Indus was completely at the mercy of a handful of squabbling chieftains. Starving, gradually freezing to death, and sitting in an undefendable cantonment, there seemed no alternative to slow, methodical slaughter.

Rumours ran rife, gathering horror as they went. The strongest of these was that Akbar Khan intended to take all the women for the chiefs' zenanas, and to kill all the men except one, who was to have his arms and legs cut off before being placed in the Indian entrance to the Khyber Pass as a deterrent to any further invasion of Afghanistan by infidels.

Amy Scott, suffering from the depression that follows a difficult and tragic birth and trying to come to terms with emotions that had fastened on to a heedless admirer and turned him into all she had ever wanted, became almost hysterical at the news, convinced that Tom would ensure the mutilated man was Lieutenant Spence, or that Spence would nominate Tom for the ordeal.

Charlotte, equally afraid and full of dread, told Amy angrily that she should forget herself, for once, and think more about little Adam's right to survival from a catastrophe brought about by men who held his future in their hands. She also lectured Amy on increasing her husband's worries when he already had more than enough on his mind, telling her she should have more sense than to believe any British officer would allow his wife—or any other man's wife—to be handed over to Akbar Khan. Had she so little faith that she did not believe they would all fight to the death rather than surrender their families?

Of course that was what the men would do, but they were extremely worried about the situation. Richard and Tom talked endlessly about the possibilities and options open to Elphinstone. There were hopes that General Sale, at Jalalabad, could bring a relief force back to Kabul, but the passes were under snow and he would have to fight all the way. The same applied to help from the garrison at Kandahar. They would all be frozen or starved into capitulation before help could arrive. Time and the frozen winter were fatal enemies.

The Lingardes had moved into the Scotts' bungalow because their fuel lasted longer that way, and the horses kept warmer crowded into the same stable. Richard also felt Charlotte and Anna were safer there than in the bungalow on the outskirts, which would be amongst the first to suffer attack if the perimeter defences gave.

During the day the couples split, the ladies and children sitting together by the fire, the men going back and forth around the cantonment trying to discover the truth from mountains of rumours. Christmas Day was the most miserable any of them had ever known, and ended with an attack by the Afghans which was repulsed only after several hours of fierce fighting.

Richard felt more angry and worried than most of the men. He was no longer included in discussions or tactical conferences, no one in authority would listen to his views or accept his help, and he began to fear that he and his family would be left to stand alone against the fate which threatened them. Tom reported everything faithfully to him and tried to express Richard's views by proxy, but they both knew they were really in the hands of an eccentric, vengeful Afghan and a dithering invalid general, whose orders they would have to obey, whatever they might be.

Finally, Akbar Khan presented his new terms to Elphinstone. The army was to retreat, as before, but they now had to leave behind all remaining Company treasure, all their guns save six, and all married officers with families must offer themselves as hostages until such time as every soldier had been withdrawn from Kabul.

There was an immediate outcry from the married officers, some going so far as to say they would sooner put a pistol to the heads of their loved ones than allow them to fall into the hands of such a man. Aside from that, the terms were insulting and hazardous. How could an entire garrison defend itself with only six guns? It was a point of great military honour to defend the guns, at all costs, and to meekly hand them over amounted to utter humiliation . . . and no one believed the column would be allowed to move unharmed from a country taken by force of arms.

Since no military law governed the compulsory surrender of an officer's family, the clause was dropped from the agreement and four officer hostages offered instead. Daily the situation changed, plans reversed, and all the time the snow grew thicker and thicker. But no order to move off was given. One day's delay was caused by the decision to leave the sick and wounded in the city under the protection of one of the more friendly chieftains who vowed to defend them with his own life. Another day's delay occurred when Elphinstone, sticking to the letter of the agreement, ordered all the guns but six to be dragged up to the city where, of course, they could have been used to very great effect upon the cantonment, had Akbar Khan wished. But the Khan was in a mood of melancholia, for the time, and was busily trying to convince the hostages of his innocence of McNaughten's murder, sitting before them and crying for two whole hours as evidence of his sorrow.

Further delays occurred whilst the fate of Shah Soojah was discussed. The chieftains claimed that they wished him to remain as Amir, after all. There was no question of putting him to death, they assured Elphinstone, but he would have to be punished for the manner in which he had seized the throne: a minor penalty, such as the putting out of his eyes, should suffice to show there was no ill-feeling towards him. The Amir himself, now violently anti-British and wise enough to realize that a blind man could never rule a country, still preferred abdication and exile in India once more. So the chieftains offered to escort him, his court, and his army from the Bala Hissar once the cantonment had been evacuated, and the fortresses of Ghuznee, Kandahar, and Jalalabad were also empty.

Then, on the eve of departure, they were once again delayed when a message came from the chieftains to say they could not hold themselves responsible for the actions of the Ghuzees—religious fanatics pledged to kill every infidel and unbeliever of the Moslem faith unconditionally. His troops should arm themselves, Elphinstone was told, and were permitted to shoot back at these men should they attack along the route.

Richard, who had been suffering an agony of indecision on the least risk to the safety of those dependent upon him, exploded upon hearing that piece of information. He strode up and down the long sitting-room, unable to contain his anger or keep his voice low enough to prevent the ladies hearing everything he said.

"You see what it is, Tom," he cried, as his friend knocked the snow from his boots and walked to the fire to thaw out. "We are bound by a treaty to quit the country peacefully, and here they are tricking us into carrying arms and using them. Oh, I have no doubt the Ghuzees will be there to have their revenge, but it needs only one man to fire on us and we shall all be popping off to give the chieftains proof of our treachery, and a legitimate excuse to fall upon us with our own cannon. They do not mean us to leave here alive."

Tom looked at him somewhat flushed. "Watch your tongue, Richard. Is it your wish to frighten the ladies further?"

"The ladies are forced to be part of this affair: they will have to face the truth, when it comes. Tom, let us not insult them by pretending to them that it will be anything less than extremely hazardous, full of hardship, and entirely dependent on the whims of Akbar Khan and the steadiness of our own troops." He went across to the fire, thereby making the discussion a general one, and looked down at Charlotte and Amy sitting in chairs before the meagre flames. "I think you should know the facts, at this stage. Tom and I have kept things to ourselves during these days of rumour and vacillation but, since I heard that Sturt of the Engineers has now been instructed to make a breach in the ramparts large enough to allow passage of a column in full marching order, it can only be that we are off tomorrow. I cannot believe that even Elphinstone would order a huge gap to be made in our defences if it did not mean we are to go out before the enemy could come in." He held up a hand as Tom seemed about to protest. Then he looked directly at Charlotte.

"My dear, the world and his wife professed to know why your name was not included on the Kabul list two years ago. We both had our reasons for doing what we did, but it should be on official record that I did not consider it responsible to bring females and children into this cantonment. Finally, another of my pieces of doubted wisdom is being realized."

She looked back at him gravely, as she always did these days, telling him by the pain in her eyes that they had both made fatal mistakes in the past. But there was also determination written in her face—determination that they would never be parted again, come what may.

"I will tell you frankly that I seriously considered offering us all as hostages, at one time."

"*Richard!*" protested Amy, but he continued undeterred.

"I also advised Tom to do the same. You see, I am one of the few men in India who has studied the more unusual native dialects. Instead of galloping dramatically all over the country, or impressing everyone with dashing cavalry drill, I was engaged in the unexciting pursuit of study. As a result, I am conversant with Pushtu, which the Afghans use when they do not wish us to overhear their remarks, and therefore know that Akbar Khan has no intention of allowing us safe passage to India. If several friendly Afghans had not already warned us, I have heard it on the lips of those attacking us."

"But you have changed your mind about remaining?" asked Charlotte quietly, showing that she accepted his wisdom and judgement without question.

He nodded, switching his gaze back to her. "After much soul-searching. I have been a prisoner of a man like Akbar Khan. They can be very charming, persuasive and intelligent . . . but, at a whim, can abandon fine feelings and indulge in cruel practices that defy all pretence of sanity. The Afghans are fond of children, they normally respect white women. You might be perfectly safe, treated with courtesy, and sent unharmed to India with genuine regret at the parting. On the other hand, you could quite likely be separated from me immediately—your only means of protection and negotiation—and, in the event of my death, subjected to indignities to which death would be infinitely preferable. As for Anna, she could be reared as an Afghan and forcibly married to one of those devils."

He turned to Tom with a frown. "In the light of today's clear evidence of Akbar Khan's duplicity, I feel it would be better to face the fate that awaits us in the snow-bound passes. It is the better of two evils, and I would sooner take my chance with my own countrymen than in another citadel commanded by one of those sadists. Do you agree?"

Tom returned his look, perfectly understanding and remembering that deserted courtyard with a solitary kneeling man waiting for death. "My dear Richard, there has never been any question on what I must do. I have a company of sepoys to get back to India. I have always known it was my duty to attempt to do so."

Richard smiled faintly. "How nice to have one's duty so clearly defined! I have been told I may do as I think fit with myself and my family. How quickly one changes into hero then back again. I am never entirely certain which I am at any given moment, you know."

He was soon put straight on that point when marching orders arrived that evening and the Lingardes were informed that they might join the party of ladies, if they wished, with

Lieutenant Lingarde forming one of the escort—mostly men who were already slightly wounded or recovering from fever and sicknesses that prevented their taking their rightful places with their regiments.

Richard was philosophical about the news, but Tom flew into an unprecedented passion on discovering that the ardent Lieutenant Spence was also to form one of the ladies' escort, he being charged with the duty of taking Lady Scott back to Meerpore and no other. In vain did Richard try to calm his friend with the fact of another young lieutenant being included as protector for Lady Sale, her husband being at Jalalabad and unable to see to her safety and comfort. Tom refused to be soothed from his tantrum brought on by the mounting stress and worry of the past month, and Richard had to give up, inwardly deploring the fact that that particular young officer should have become the object of Amy's deep infatuation. Long after he and Charlotte retired that night they heard the Scotts arguing loudly enough to be heard up at Bala Hissar.

The following morning there was a similar confrontation between Charlotte and himself, which Richard had hoped to avoid by sheer numbers. With Tom obliged to ride with his regiment in the advance guard, Amy, baby Adam, and all the Scott servants were added to Richard's party consisting of Charlotte, Anna, Lady Scott, Lieutenant Spence, the Lingarde servants and Felicia's entire army of them . . . all told, upward of forty people. But Richard's hope was foiled by the late arrival of Felicia, Spence and the servants. Charlotte spotted Luana from the window, almost at once.

She turned to Richard, white-faced and condemning, and she did not have to say anything for him to know she was deeply hurt and distressed, besides being puzzled over a sign that there was still some link between himself and a girl he had forsworn since his return from Malkhan six months earlier.

"Say nothing you will later regret," he said softly and swiftly, conscious of Amy nearby, and tried to take her icy hands in his.

She drew back. Her eyes, already enlarged by apprehension over what they were about to undertake, were dark with fury.

"I will not have that woman with me. Have you not made enough public mockery of our marriage without showing that you also hold yourself responsible for your zenana?"

The word was flung contemptuously at him and hurt as much as it was meant to do. "Charlotte, please listen and try to understand," he urged in an undertone. "This is no time for misunderstandings. We are about to embark upon a journey during which we shall have to fight for our lives."

"*Our* lives," she pounced with vicious quietness. "Not hers!"

"Of course hers!" he cried, unable to keep his voice low any longer. "We shall be fighting for the life of everyone in that column. That is what soldiering is all about."

She backed even further from him, caught up in something of which he had never suspected her capable. "You may fight for whom you please, Richard, but you will do it otherwise than in my presence. I owe that . . . *creature* . . . nothing. I will not have her near me." She gathered Anna close against the skirt of her riding-dress, and looked at Richard in a way he would never forget. "For the sin of merely whispering a name, I was punished for over two years. Do you not think your sin vastly deserving of more than that? Yet you have received none from me, nor will you. There is no command for you in this army now, so you may go with her to the rear of the column with the other camp-followers and defend her with every drop of your life's blood, but I will not allow you to do it in the sight of your child."

Already racked by fear for his family and knowledge of what lay ahead, Richard knew there was no time for reasoned discussion of his actions. He took refuge in condemnation.

"You have always been proud of your belief in the word of the Almighty," he charged. "Where is it now?"

"Flown . . . in the face of your duplicity," she cried. "There is a limit to Christian forbearance, and mine has been reached. As to the Almighty, He has deserted us, that much has become obvious." Fully in the grip of despair she went on, "There is no reward for loyalty, no virtue in goodness. He protects the likes of her . . . as do you. If ever there is a lesson to be learned this terrible day, it is *that!*"

He stood in a state of complete mental exhaustion, unable to do or say any more. How could he explain to her that he owed Luana this last gesture? How could he make her see that the Indian girl had given him something for which he would be everlastingly grateful—something completely divorced from the deep love he felt for his wife and daughter? How could he say that Malkhan had made him recoil from the girl instinctively, and that he was trying to ease his conscience by offering her what little protection he could, along with his servants?

He had taken the young virgin girl as his mistress five years ago. She had loved him; he had used her to ease his loneliness. Because of him, Luana had attached herself to the army entering Afghanistan, and had made those first two years endurable for him. He could not now abandon her in the face of danger. Charlotte had no objection to the servants being included within his circle of protection, and they had done no more for him than their duty. Luana would die for him. Should he not recognize that fact?

He turned away helplessly. How could he expect a wife to understand the tie between sahib and *bibee*? How could he justify his action by telling Charlotte that they would probably all be dead within a few days, and never had there been a greater need for her Christian forbearance than now?

There was a shout from outside, and soul-searching gave way to action as Richard was exhorted to get his party on the move as the last of the advance guard was finally clearing the breach, and the ladies, with escort, were due to follow immediately.

He went out on to the verandah, feeling the immediate cut of icy wind and the pinching of his nostrils in the extreme cold. But the officer had galloped away to round up the other ladies, and Richard was left scanning the road for signs of Lady Scott and her party.

"Hell and damnation," he swore viciously. "That woman

even has to dress herself suitably when going to meet her Maker. Wahab!" He shouted to the man who escaped from Malkhan to bring the news of his capture, and told him to take a horse and ride to Lady Scott's bungalow to desire Spence-sahib to hurry. Then he called Charlotte and Amy to quit the house and climb into the *kajavas* on the camel ready for them, carrying Anna and little Adam in their arms.

In the tenseness of the moment, all that had gone before was forgotten and, once he had seen the women safely installed in the cramped panniers each side of the camel, Richard got on his horse, instructing the servants to be ready to move off with the baggage. He sat trying to hold his fidgeting mount while he fretted at the continued absence of Felicia Scott.

The minutes passed. Wahab returned to say that Spence-sahib was looking for more horses and would be a little while yet. Furious, knowing that delay could lose them their place in the column, Richard called out to the two ladies that he would wait ten minutes and if Lady Scott had not then put in an appearance, they would move off without her.

Charlotte immediately rounded on him from the basket in which she sat wrapped warmly in a *poshteen* and a shawl, and said that it was a sad day when a native girl was treated like a lady, and a lady like a servant-girl. He could go on, if he wished, but she would remain until her mama was able to join them.

Fuming still, Richard waited a meticulous ten minutes, then instructed Charlotte and Amy to return to the bungalow for warmth while he rode down to discover the cause of the hold-up. It took a few minutes to help them from the *kajavas* and back indoors then, unhappy at leaving them there unprotected, Richard rode like Satan down the long road towards Felicia's large rented bungalow, only to find the party now preparing to leave. Giving Spence a thundery look that spoke volumes, Richard told him tersely that extra horses, at a time like this, were no excuse for holding up a whole group, and that to consider bringing the amount of baggage already piled on to skinny horses and camels that were no more than skeletons was not much short of stupidity.

Felicia was, surprisingly, mounted on her favourite mare, now a shadow of its former glossy self. She wore a coat of expensive fur over her riding-dress, and a turban-style hat of thick cloth that gave her the appearance of a Persian dignitary's wife. Richard gave her a curt good-day, reflecting that he could not imagine her sharing a *kajava* and squashing herself into that uncomfortable mode of conveyance, so she really had no alternative but to ride. She appeared not to notice his brusque bad humour. Indeed, there was a strange faraway aura about her that almost suggested that she was unaware of what was going on around her.

Richard snapped an order at young Spence to put spurs to the beasts, and set off back to the Scotts' home knowing the amount of baggage and servants in the entourage would make speed impossible.

And so it proved. By the time the whole group had assembled, Richard was informed by a staff-officer that the ladies, with their escort had gone some time ago, and that there was an order from the chieftains nominated to accompany the column to return to the cantonment as they had not had sufficient time to prepare for the safety of the army. All movement was now halted while the source of the order was investigated, and also to allow time for the backlog to clear the hastily-thrown bridge of planks across gun-carriages which was holding up progress outside the cantonment.

Richard sent everyone indoors again, then plodded up and down the verandah, hunched into his cloak against the biting wind, knowing in his heart that hope was a vain emotion. For himself, he felt that the end had merely been postponed from Malkhan so that he could make his peace with Charlotte. That six months' extension had been worth the fight he had put up for them in that black cell. He was prepared to die now, but was tortured by the thought of his wife and daughter also being slain by those savage villains— Charlotte, to whom life owed a little kindness and colour after the pale emptiness of her childhood, and his beautiful child, Anastasia, who should be destined to emulate her grandmother, already taken too soon.

He leant against the pillar, staring out across the scene of dazzling white, and felt as cold as the wind that blew the snow from the trees in great flurries. He would let neither of them suffer. His pistol was loaded, and he knew he would find the strength to pull the trigger when the time came.

It seemed an age that they waited for an explanation for the order to halt. When it came it was more vivid than any words. The far end of the cantonment, where the Lingarde bungalow was situated, was suddenly full of the noise of firing and the sky above it began to cloud with smoke as buildings were put to the torch.

"*My God!*" breathed Richard, straightening up and feeling the blood run hotly through his veins. "It was a trap."

He rushed into the bungalow so hastily he knocked his shoulder badly on the door jamb. "Get outside as fast as you can," he shouted without ceremony. "They are breaking into the cantonment and setting the place alight. We must get through the breach and catch up with the advance guard. It is our only chance."

There was an immediate panic from the servants when he went into the back of the building to tell them to make haste, and he had to shout harsh orders to prevent a headlong rush in all directions. But some did not heed the authority in his voice and ran off up the road, just as they were, heading for the breach and what they took for safety.

That incident was multiplied five hundred times and, once outside and mounted, it was clear to Richard that the orderly retreat had turned into utter confusion, fear-crazed servants, camp-followers, and even sepoys fighting and clawing to escape the Afghans who were streaming into the vacated end of the cantonment, killing, looting and burning as they went. Cries and screams filled the air showing that many stragglers of the retreating garrison were being caught and methodically slaughtered before they could get on the move.

Richard looked swiftly around him and saw Charlotte, white-faced and clutching Anna face forward against her *poshteen* so that her small eyes and ears would not bear witness to the scene. There was no time to lose. Half the servants had gone, so there was no one to bring the camels with most of the baggage. The beasts would have to be left behind.

He shouted to Lieutenant Spence to get on the move leading the group whilst he brought up the rear himself. They all started forward towards the breach through which the entire garrison was now attempting to stream, but on the main track Richard thought he was in danger of losing one or more of his party.

The whole width of the road was filled with screaming, pushing camp-followers who, having no intention of forming the rear of the column, as was usual, were struggling to pass bullock-carts, laden mules, strings of camels, horse-drawn guns, cavalry troops, companies of marching sepoys, mountains of baggage, and packs of the wild dogs that always attach themselves to military camps. British officers on frightened plunging chargers were bellowing orders designed to check the wild confusion and panic that would bring fatal results, but their voices went unheeded. Richard saw one go down, with his horse, beneath an onslaught of crazed Indians, and disappear under the hooves of a company of native cavalry, who were unable to control their bolting mounts.

Ideals flew in the face of such mayhem, and Richard pushed his way through the personal servants in his party until he reached Charlotte, Amy, and Felicia, who was riding beside the panniered camel, yelling to Spence to take up the left flank as he took the right. His first duty was to the ladies. The rest must do the best they could in the face of chaos. To lose sight of that precious camel would be fatal . . . and all the time, the noise of plunder and murder grew louder and louder behind them, sending the crowd surging even faster.

Suddenly the snow-laden hills ahead took on an aspect of refuge, although Richard knew it was a false illusion. They had been betrayed by the chieftains, and up in those hills another horde would be waiting. But there were rocks, places to hide, and time to reorganize their defence. The advance guard had two of the permitted six guns, and Captain Sturt must surely have supplies of explosives with which to dislodge hidden gunmen. Up there they had a slender chance: in this cantonment they had never had even that!

With the sweat of his exertions freezing on his body beneath his clothes, Richard fought a way through the mixture of beasts and mankind, emulating Spence in striking with the flat of his sword any camp-follower who blocked his way by sobbing for help and hanging on to his stirrup for support. It was each man for himself, and when a man had ladies and children to protect no one stood in his way.

He could see the breach ahead now, and also a long straggling line across the snow-covered ground beyond that gave access to the first of the mountain passes they would have to traverse to reach the safety of Jalalabad. There were a few Afghans beyond the breach, hopping about and taking wild pot-shots at those on foot labouring through the deep snow. But they were too excited to be accurate, he noted thankfully.

They neared the breach, and there were several officers manfully trying to carry out what was a ludicrous duty, under the circumstances—namely, that of checking everyone who passed against the order of march they held in their hands. Richard did attract the attention of one, however, to indicate that he had brought out the ladies who should have gone with the rest some time earlier.

"Is that Lady Scott with you?" the man yelled above the din. "Duprés has just galloped down to her bungalow to find her."

His words reached Felicia and, incredible though it seemed, she pulled her mare round in that mêlée and was off, climbing the breached rampart and galloping along the top until she was level with another cantonment track, when she plunged down the slope and vanished from sight. It had happened so quickly Richard had no time to prevent it, but it took him no time at all to assess the situation and resist the natural urge to go after her. When Spence, looking like death, shouted that he would go back, Richard roared instructions for him to stay and defend Mrs Scott and her baby.

"She needs your protection," he ended in a tone that dared Spence to argue.

"But Lady Scott is under my charge," he protested miserably, wanting to remain with Amy, but obviously feeling guilty about doing so.

"Her life is her own," he said significantly, ". . . and Duprés is down there."

That was his last word on the subject, or he thought it was until he saw Charlotte's expression. Closing in on the camel he asked her savagely, "It is your mama or Anna. Which would you have me choose?"

She turned from him, but he saw the tears glisten on her lashes before she put up a hand to dash them away. He rode on silently wondering how she could care so much for a woman who had done nothing for her, but his decision was proved right within a few moments of leaving the cantonment. A shot from one of the Afghans loitering gleefully outside the ramparts hit the camel and brought it to its knees, bellowing in pain and of no further use. There was nothing for it but for each officer to take up a woman and child on his own horse, for the spare animals, along with the baggage, had been left way back in the confusion.

Because Anna was a plump child, Richard took her up before him, and Charlotte behind, clinging to him as he headed slowly for the river they must cross. One look told him his only choice was to ride through the freezing water, for the hastily-constructed bridge was already beginning to break up beneath the onslaught of waggons, beasts and impatient thousands trying to cross without due care. Those waiting to use the bridge tailed back for a quarter of a mile across the snow and, as afternoon was well-advanced by then, were liable to be overcome by darkness before they crossed.

Richard had just indicated to Spence that they should ford the river, as others were doing, some distance along the bank, when Charlotte suddenly shouted in loud, distressed tones:

"*Major Duprés!*"

He was beside the bridge, trying to prevent people from overloading a purely temporary construction, but he heard the voice and turned. Then he came running over, his face dark with emotion.

· 403 ·

"Where is she?"

"Gone back for you. We were told you were at the bungalow," cried Charlotte in shocked tones. "Dear heaven, she is back there looking for *you*."

"I did go . . . three hours past. *I* was told she was with you." It sounded desperate, angry. "*Diable,* if they catch her . . ."

He was gone, vaulting on to his horse with brilliant timing and galloping back across the snow, the flying hooves of his stallion sending clods high into the air.

Richard said nothing. He was busily trying to calm Anna, who bumped up and down with excitement and chattered non-stop in distracting bilingual sentences about the great adventure she was having. But Charlotte tightened her arms about his waist and leant her head against his back, seeking comfort from his strength. She remained that way as he took the horse into the icy water and made no sound as the river rose up above their legs to penetrate to the skin. Anna, with her feet up on the horse's neck, was dry when they emerged on the far side, but Richard felt his overalls and boots start to form ice soon afterwards, and Charlotte's long skirt and boots must have done the same.

He stopped for a moment until Lieutenant Spence, with Amy and Adam, caught up with them, and looked back at the cantonment. Fires were blazing everywhere and sending smoke up to hang as a dark pall over the place where his own bungalow had been. The withdrawal had become a humiliating hounding from a city that would not bow to conquest. These were people with whom it was not possible to credit western attitudes and standards. *The history of past centuries shapes their actions when feelings run high. Fools forget that, Lingarde.* The words of murdered Edward Kingsley came back to him after seven years.

The next few hours of slow plodding in the wake of thousands more in similar plight were passed in silence. They all had too much on their minds for conversation. Now they had cleared the cantonment, Richard had time to think of the consequences of their hasty departure. Their tents and clothing had been on the pack-animals: provisions had been left behind with the servants. There was no certainty that they would get through or find Richard in the darkness. Light was already fading, and only half the force had yet left the cantonment. There were blankets strapped to his own horse and that of Spence, but unless they could trace their baggage the appalling prospect of spending the night in the open faced them. But he would surely be able to find places for the two females and the children in one of the regimental tents. Tom would see to it that room was given up by members of his own company, so it was essential that he find him as soon as possible when camp was made for the night.

The great, cumbersome, disorganized column halted that night a mere six miles from Kabul, the rear-guard not having even quitted the cantonment before nightfall. It was small wonder that some twenty thousand souls, six times that number of beasts, and countless tons of supplies and equipment could not efficiently and swiftly vacate the military settlement whilst under attack and subject to confusion of orders.

But Richard was horrified when he caught up with the advance section and discovered that there were orders to encamp within such easy distance of Kabul. It was dark as he picked his way through hundreds of men scraping hollows in the snow in the hope of finding some protection from the wind that had got up with the onset of night. It was strange and still on that ice platform as the sound of voices was immediately whipped away on the wind, and he strained his eyes to avoid stepping on dark shapes on the ghostly white ground.

He found Tom without much difficulty, and told him the reasons for their delay which had had the poor man sick with apprehension. They both went back immediately to join the two women and Spence, all shivering in their clothes that had frozen solid after being immersed in the river. Tom thanked the young lieutenant with sincerity for his services to Amy, all hint of jealousy or aggression gone. It was not the time for such things. The children were exhausted and had fallen asleep in their mothers' arms, so the three men set to to dig little "nests" which would reduce the effects of the wind as much as possible. It was a temporary measure, they thought, until all the baggage arrived.

No baggage arrived; nor did any food. The passing of the dark hours brought in just a few survivors of the rear-guard who told of the total loss of the commissariat, the baggage, and ammunition before it even left. All along the way they had found camp-followers and servants, frozen and starving, lying down in the snow to die. Many had been killed by Afghans before they could get away; the remainder appeared to have given up the ghost. The picture was black, and those thousands who had reached the camp successfully faced a bitter, hungry night with little hope in their hearts.

The Lingardes and Scotts had small bags of provisions with them, but everything had to be taken cold. There was no wood anywhere to light a fire, and too much wind for it to stay alight, anyway. Tea and coffee remained in tins, the dry, unappetizing food they ate being washed down with sherry or brandy, which warmed them by dint of its potency. Even baby Adam was given a sherry to warm his little body which could not be heated by vigorous movement as adult ones could.

They were all very quiet, in particular young Spence, and Richard took him aside after they had eaten in an attempt to put the boy's mind at rest. It reminded him once again of Edward Kingsley and himself, Spence being no more than twenty-two and unseasoned in battle, and himself now the experienced veteran.

"Under attack one has to make quick decisions, you know," he began with rough friendliness. "Almost always they have to be in favour of the safety of the greater number." He studied the young face, and eyes that had lost their wicked twinkle drastically fast. "Lady Scott had her own reasons for doing what she did. You would not have deterred her, just accompanied her into foolhardiness."

"It was my duty to protect her," said the young man miserably.

"Ah . . . duty. There are many kinds, the highest being that which is owed to God and mankind. At that moment of her unexpected abandonment of us all, I believed our duty was better served by assuring the safety of two young ladies and two children who have the right to expect more of life than this." He put his hand on Spence's shoulder. "Lady Scott disdained your protection in favour of Major Duprés. None of us could have known he was not there to give it. Mrs Scott, on the other hand, had a child to care for and needed the assistance you offered. Think, man, what would she and the baby have done for a horse if you had not been there to take them up with you?"

He saw the reason in the words, but could not help saying, "If any ill has befallen her, I shall blame myself."

"Then you are extremely foolish," Richard declared heartily. "Lady Scott has chosen a way of life few would copy. If she has also chosen a way to die, I cannot see why you should feel responsible. By the end of this week we might all wish we had done the same, and shared her blessed peace."

"You think it will come to that?" Spence asked apprehensively.

"Look around you, my dear fellow. Is the answer to that not obvious?" He took the young officer's arm. "Come, let us see if we cannot make the ladies and babes more comfortable with our cloaks as some kind of protection."

They went back to the others and tried to make some cover by laying cloaks over the "nests" and weighing them down with rocks, but the wind got beneath them and was in danger of blowing them away altogether. Spence, still worrying about Lady Scott, walked up and down moodily, speaking to stragglers as they came in long after midnight. Richard and Tom, holding their sleeping wives against them for warmth and wrapped in their cloaks, were unable to sleep. They sat shivering and silent for some time.

"I am sorry about your step-mama," Richard said finally.

"You did the only possible thing," murmured Tom, "and I'm glad you made that fellow stick by Amy. I have my two spare chargers with me, which will do nicely for tomorrow . . . but there will be an abundance of spare horses by the end of tomorrow, if I am not mistaken."

"Yes," agreed Richard unemotionally. "Tom, if I should fall, take Charlotte and Anna safely through to India and put them on their way to my father in Kent. My affairs are all in order: you will not find the duty complicated."

"Of course, and I rely on you to do the same for me. Tell her . . . well, I have never been much of a ballroom beau, and perhaps Amy is not fully aware of how much . . . how very much I . . ."

"Yes, I will tell her, Tom, never fear. But I think she is more aware of it than you imagine."

All such reflections were halted then as Spence came running up, waking Charlotte and Amy from their frozen slumber with his cries of excitement, and they all scrambled up as Colley Duprés rode up, his horse picking its way through sleeping bodies. Felicia was in his arms, wrapped in a sheepskin and very still.

No one spoke as Colley was helped from his horse by Richard and Tom, who then took his burden from him as he unstrapped a small tent from his saddle and began to put it up with the help of Lieutenant Spence. Richard looked at the pale blur of Felicia Scott's face, and was conscious that Charlotte was standing close beside him doing the same. He longed to put an arm around her for comfort, and could not. He tried to give her reassurance with a look, but she did not take her gaze from Felicia. He wanted to speak, but could not think of any suitable words.

Only when the tent was erected and they had all crawled inside the tiny space did Colley say brusquely, "She was knocked from her horse and trampled by the crowd. She was already dying when I reached her."

The silence that followed seemed to go on for an eternity until a small piping voice broke it with, "Papa, is the lady sleeping?"

"*Da*, Annushka," Richard said thickly. "We must all be very quiet so as not to awaken her." He took Anna closely into his arms and cradled her head in his hands, dread of what lay ahead filling his limbs until they grew weak. How could he bear to see this little golden-haired creature still and cold in the snow?

"Thank you for bringing her out of that place," said Charlotte suddenly. "She wanted to be with you at the end."

Colley looked up at her from his crouching position beside her and said, "She did not want to go back to Meerpore. When your father went to Calcutta she made up her mind never to see him again." He scowled darkly. "I think you did not realize what she suffered at his hands."

"Oh, yes . . . yes, I did," came the soft answer.

It was a private conversation being conducted in front of four other people, but it did not seem to matter. They had recognized that convention and social niceties were frivolous luxuries in the stark business of living. Richard watched the pair and felt no resentment at their closeness. How vain was the human male, until he was brought face to face with the basic truth of life.

They brought out candles, which they could now light without having them instantly snuffed out by the wind, and began to shiver slightly less as the heat generated by their closely-packed bodies made the night more bearable.

Richard, holding his sleeping daughter, watched Charlotte as she crouched beside Colley at her mother's side. There were no tears, but her expression was stricken as she gazed down on the face that looked intensely white against the black hair. Christian forbearance had not been abandoned by her, after all, that she could look that way on a woman who had condemned her to being a parcel for so many years. His throat tightened as he felt the full depth of his love for a little brown sparrow who had once been captivated and tormented by the man crouching beside her. Charlotte did not have his mother's exotic splendour, but she was as brave, honest and compassionate as that other woman he had loved so dearly.

It was a night of wind-lashed iciness that reached them even in the tent. Felicia Scott roused from her comatose state for only a short while and recognized Charlotte, who had not moved from her position the whole time. The words were faint, but Richard just heard them above the sound of the wind.

"I cannot lose him now, my dear. It is he who will lose me . . . and I could not have faced growing old."

She said no more, just looked away towards Colley and fastened her gaze on him until her eyelids drooped once more. Strangely, she looked as young and beautiful as Richard had ever seen her, and glowing with something like happiness. At four o'clock she died, and they all sat with her body, like a circle of frozen mourners unable to let her go. But they had no alternative until dawn broke and they could make some kind of grave for her beside the track.

Richard handed Anna over to Charlotte, who seemed to find comfort in the young life that compensated for the one just ended. But, as soon as he detected a paling of the darkness outside, he pushed his way through the small opening in the canvas to stretch his cramped limbs and get away from the scene inside. He felt leaden and depressed, shaken by too many emotions since yesterday morning. It was one thing to suffer oneself; it was double the pain to see loved ones suffer.

Hunched into his shoulders against the cold he walked forward, then almost fell over something lying in the snow right beside the tent. The iciness that ran through him then exceeded any outer coldness he had yet experienced, as he gazed down in horror at a face he had known, and touched so many times. Her hair was spread across the snow in stiff sheets of blackness, her graceful hands were now extended into rigid, curving claws, her legs stuck out in unnatural angles with the beautiful feet now encased in torn pieces of bloodstained rag that were as hard as metal. The exquisite features were grotesque in their frozen immobility.

He sank down on the snow, a pain in his head thundering against his eyes that half closed in distress.

"Oh, dear God," he panted. *"Luana!"*

· seventeen ·

THAT FIRST MORNING of the great retreat from Kabul revealed a horrifying number of Indians who had frozen to death as they crouched or lay in the snow in inadequate clothing and without food. There were also several Europeans who had died similar deaths a mere six miles from their comfortable cantonment bungalows, and ninety miles from the safety of Jalalabad. All along the route they had traversed with a piteous line of corpses lying in snow stained red where Afghans had fallen on the camp-followers—men, women and numerous children—and killed without mercy.

When daylight broke, the Ghuzees were amongst those still miraculously alive, and were either stripping the wounded naked and performing sadistic tortures upon them until they could endure no more, or leaving them to perish slowly and equally cruelly of wounds and sub-zero temperatures. In the face of all this, large numbers of native cavalry and infantry who had been quartered in the Bala Hissar as guards of Shah Soojah deserted and went back to Kabul in the hope of escaping protracted agony. Their British officers were dumbfounded by what they saw as complete betrayal. But military loyalty and discipline had fled, even amidst some of the European regiments. Demoralized, panic-stricken and with feet or hands severely frost-bitten, the troops had no sooner become aware that daylight had started a stampede of camp-followers determined to get at the head of the column where they would not be attacked, than they joined the stumbling, staggering flow of terrified humanity in a bid to avoid forming the rear-guard.

The track became a scene of utter pandemonium as soldiers, servants, women and toddlers who could scarcely stand, fought each other to stay ahead. No order was given to move off. The retreating Army of the Indus went of its own accord. The British officers, themselves frost-bitten and hungry, desperately shouted orders and tried to halt the rush, but were almost mown down by their rebellious subordinates, who had had enough of the men they believed had caused all their suffering. The Englishmen, who had taken great pride in their sepoys and, in many cases, had great affection for them, were shocked and distressed at the ineffectiveness of what had seemed, to them, to be a close bond of loyalty.

So, disorganized and completely incapable of ordered defence, the whole force moved on throughout a morning when the temperature never rose above freezing. Most of the soldiers were so cold they could hardly hold their rifles, much less pull the trigger, if required to do so. Each step took them a foot deep in crusty snow, and those who staggered accidentally from the track were soon wallowing up to their thighs in it. The beasts who had survived the night dragged painfully onward with their loads, halting frequently while heavy clods of packed ice were hacked from their hooves with chisels.

But it was not long before small parties of Afghans were seen on each side of the long, long snake of exhausted, retreating souls, some way off but moving parallel and maintaining the same speed. These men were not the Ghuzee bandits of the previous day, and those in command hoped that the promised escort had finally been sent by Akbar Khan to ensure their safety through the nearby Khurd-Kabul Pass.

Optimism was dashed when the Afghans suddenly veered and bore down on the rear-guard of the column, jezails firing and swords slashing at the helpless, numbed soldiers. Resistance was completely hampered by rushing, screaming camp-followers who pushed their way blindly through the ranks of soldiers trying to fire rifles that were frozen solid.

The guns were immediately captured by the gleeful Afghans, but a British subaltern led a heroic charge supported by a few artillerymen who rallied to the call, and took them back. Success was short-lived. In the confusion and mêlée, the horses pulling the guns were stampeded. One overturned causing the others to halt, and the Afghans swooped again to carry off their death-spouting booty. The only consolation for the loss was that the subaltern had successfully spiked the guns so that they could not be used.

It then became plain that there had never been any intention on the part of Akbar Khan to allow the retreat to proceed without attack and, when the Khan himself was spotted in the distance with a group of around six hundred horsemen, a political officer was sent across to remonstrate with him on his betrayal of the promise of safe conduct.

His reply was that the British had ignored his advice not to set out the day before, and only had themselves to blame. He no longer trusted them, and demanded three more officer hostages as guarantee against the column moving beyond the village of Tezeen until he had definite evidence of Jalalabad being cleared of General Sale's force. One of those three political hostages was Eldred Pottinger, a man probably more highly appreciated at that time by the Afghans than his own countrymen.

Akbar Khan's other demand in return for the protection he promised was that the force should not enter the Khurd-Kabul Pass until the following day to allow him time to clear the ice-bound defile of hostile tribesmen. Elphinstone, despairing, ill, and wishing he had never allowed those under his command to set out, agreed to the humiliating terms. Pottinger and two experienced colleagues were handed over, and the column was halted for the night. It was then only a little past midday, and a mere four miles from the previous night's camp-site. In vain, junior officers of insight and intelligence urged the General to push on through the pass, telling him they were being deceived all along the line and that Akbar Khan wanted the breathing space to get extra troops into the pass for purposes other than protection. But the old invalid was beyond changing his mind now he had made a decision, and some fifteen thousand remaining members of the column sank miserably into the snow with the prospect of eighteen hours of purgatory facing them. God alone knew what faced them after that.

Charlotte heard the order to halt with a feeling of acute

dismay. Everything was terrible enough already, and determination had only been maintained by a forward movement, by the feeling of leaving danger and the horrors of the previous day and night behind. Inaction created fear and despondency. Mind-spectres returned at the thought of sitting down to become another of those stiff travesties of human life she had seen all around the tent that morning. Movement, however slow and punishing, held off the possibility of becoming a statue of death, covered in ice and preserved in a ghastly posture.

Felicia's passing, that had seemed so tragic a few hours ago, now filled Charlotte with thankfulness when the ravages of the night became obvious. Colley Duprés had carried her body off, and neither Charlotte nor Tom had made any protest. Somehow, it had seemed the most natural procedure. Lady Scott, who had suffered extreme loneliness in life, would not be lonely in death. Accompanying her in that snow-field were some thousands of others who had died less peacefully than she.

It was with difficulty that Charlotte held back tears of apprehension and frustration on being forced to face hours and hours of doing nothing in the icy wilderness. Even the soldiers, exhausted though they might be, she felt certain would prefer to be on the move, would rather cover another mile, another few hundred yards towards their ultimate destination than sit in purgatory with nothing to interrupt their imaginings.

The whole force had become merely a mass of separate souls bent on personal survival. Even the officers, in many cases, had given up trying to command and concentrated on their own misery. The two tents remaining were given up to the ladies and the wounded officers. Fortunately for the Lingardes and Scotts, Colley Duprés' tent remained in their possession, and they took in two officers who were suffering from frost-bitten feet after spending the previous night in the open.

Charlotte's biggest concern was Anna, who was growing soporific under the effects of cold and hunger. Richard had been given some cakes by a fellow officer for his wife and daughter and at great personal risk had gone to the stream for water under fire from Afghans ensconced nearby. There being no wood, Richard, Tom, Spence, and the two frost-bitten officers sacrificed their pistol cases to burn, and hot tea was made. The liquid warmed their stomachs, the metal cups carried by all officers in their saddle-bags providing a means of easing the cold in hands and fingers as they curled around them.

Anna took the food and tea so fast she was immediately sick, and Charlotte again worried about the prospect of fever in the child. Little Adam Scott, less than robust to start with, miraculously appeared to thrive on tea-soaked cake and small drips of brandy from Tom's flask. There was little conversation as they all huddled together in the tent in such intimate proximity it would have been embarrassingly uncomfortable in normal times. But Tom and Lieutenant Spence appeared on easy enough terms, with Amy showing no signs of testiness towards Tom or especial favour to her admirer. As for herself and Richard, a relationship that was almost unemotional had sprung up between them in the face of the need to concentrate on keeping Anna alive and protected. Charlotte's anger over the girl Luana and Richard's apparent abandonment of Felicia had evaporated as the full import of what they faced had hit her. She now understood what he had done, but there was no chance to tell him so in that crowded tent. All she could do was lean against him in gratitude when he put a protective arm around her, and convey with a glance that her love was as strong as ever.

The afternoon crawled past, and darkness fell once more. All around the encampment fires began to spring up as the native troops desperately and insanely burnt their outer clothing in attempts to gain temporary relief from the agony of frostbite. A few officers attempted to stop them with words of reason, but gave up when someone threatened to add them to the fuel. They were choosing their own agonizing end, but a feeling was rife that every man would choose when he would die and no one was going to stop him.

Indeed, in that small tent there was an air of conspiracy against those *outside,* each person not so much thinking of his own welfare but just of those with the canvas walls. Charlotte had stopped being sorry for fifteen thousand people. Her world had become those six others and two children who huddled with her, eyes dull and thoughts fearful. But she did spare a thought for those women who were *enceinte*—there were three or four of the officers' wives in that condition—and told herself that the Lord, in His wisdom, had taken her own embryo child so that she was now better able to protect Anna. The teachings of Aunt Meg returned to her constantly during that night, and she found comfort from them.

Once, whilst awake in the darkness, she had reached up to touch Richard's cheek covered in rough stubble, but he had dozed into uneasy slumber and was not aware of the gesture. An intense pain filled her as she realized that she could very easily lose him shortly, and her heart cried out a protest. Had he endured the hell of Malkhan only to die now at the hands of the same people? For long hours she lay against his body, wrapped into his cloak and holding their child, regretting those lost two years. Love, she now realized, should be prized during every minute of every day.

That next morning, the 8th of January, sunrise threw pale light on a pitiful scene. Corpses lay everywhere, and several hundred others, in the throes of dying, pleaded heartrendingly for food, warmth and help. There was none to give.

Before any decisions could be made there was a concerted rush by those determined not to be in the rear, and hundreds of stiff-limbed Indians blundered through the confusion of prostrate bodies and frozen beasts, snatching anything that might be of use, making their way to the awesome entrance of the great pass and starting another stampede that paid no heed to military commands.

Charlotte, standing with Amy while the men struck the tent and lashed it to Spence's horse, heard the sound of rapid firing to the rear of where they had spent the night. News flew through the column that the Afghans were attacking in force, and those British troops and sepoys still amenable to command were ordered to the rear to hold off the enemy while the position was assessed by the commanders and political advisors. Amongst these was Colley Duprés who, with others experienced in dealing with native leaders, rode back and forth between Elphinstone and those handful of Afghan chieftains who had finally appeared for the purpose of escorting the retreat through the country.

The attack was beaten back, and a long period of negotiation to ensure no repetition meant that it was almost midday before they realized that the column had split in two, giving the enemy ample opportunity to come between and launch attacks on both halves. Orders to march finally filtered through, and Charlotte was lifted on to her horse by Richard, who handed Anna, wrapped in shawls, up to her. His face showed signs of the strain under which they had all been recently, but he said nothing, just touched her gloved hand momentarily as a message flared in his eyes to make the day bearable for her, then walked to his own horse.

Tom had gone to the rear with the fighting troops some hours earlier, so Lieutenant Spence helped Amy to mount and gave her the baby, who was crying from hunger. There was no question of waiting for Tom, or of trying to find out what had become of him, but they all rode off full of anxiety over his absence and apprehension for what lay ahead.

Keeping close within the circle formed by Richard, Spence and the two frost-bitten officers, Charlotte tried not to look at Amy's stricken face or at the corpses spread over the snow. She knew that no one relished entering the pass, that everyone suspected an ambush, but there was no choice. Now that the moment had come she felt steady but very cold—not the coldness of ice and snow but coldness of feeling, as if her destiny were about to be decided and all emotion was already freezing in defensive preparation.

They progressed slowly, the horses suffering from cold and starvation as much as their riders, and overtook many followers who had rushed off at sunrise only to collapse from exhaustion a few miles further on. Charlotte steeled herself against the sight of women crying for mercy and a helping hand from those who dared not offer it and, worse still, little brown-skinned children, almost naked, sitting in the snow too dazed and ill even to cry. But tears were on her cheeks almost without her knowing, and she clasped Anna to her in fierce protection against such inhumanity.

The entrance to the pass looked truly formidable as they approached. She had been through many such passes on the journey from Meerpore, but spring had added a softness that was missing now. The sides of the defile rose up a tremendous height on each side of the narrow way, which was consequently dark and gloomy because the winter sun could never reach the bottom of the cut. The mid-afternoon sky was grey and threatening, and Charlotte shivered as their small group passed into the shadowy defile.

There was a new kind of coldness now, dank and sinister, a coldness caused by a torrent rushing through the centre of the pass that even sub-zero temperatures could not still into ice. The roar of tumbling water filled Charlotte's ears, and her horse took fright, not liking the enclosed passage and finding the smooth ice edging the stream provided a precarious footing.

Twice the beast stumbled, and Richard put a hand on its bridle, speaking soothing words. But Charlotte felt her stomach tightening with unreasoning fear as they moved further in, rounded several bends, and shut themselves off from the open expanse they had just crossed from Kabul.

Beside the thunder of water there was a great echoing rumble of marching boots, clopping hooves, and grinding wheels as an army tried to condense itself into the confines that presented perilous rocks, thick, frozen snow on uneven winding tracks, and countless dousings in icy water as the stream crossed and re-crossed the narrow footway.

Charlotte felt her cheeks growing stiff with cold, and dread filling her limbs. She exchanged glances with Richard and saw the same thing reflected in those wonderful eyes of his. He did not try to humour her with smiles and false jollity: she knew that was a compliment and loved him all the more for it. Her boots and skirt grew saturated and stiff from dousing in the water, and progress slowed as those ahead negotiated tricky frozen sections, or guns and waggons stuck in the stream amidst rocks. Finally, they came to a halt behind a narrow section that was so choked with people and animals that for a time no one could move.

Then, suddenly, all hell broke loose as a screaming, yelling horde appeared in the heights above them, and Charlotte realized that the shower descending on them was a multitude of bullets from Afghan jezails. Before she could absorb the sounds of sudden death all around, before she could accept that men were dropping to the ground lifeless in their dozens, before she could acknowledge that there was no escape, Richard had pulled her and Anna from the horse and into a small crevice in the rocks which offered some protection from above. Spence did the same with Amy, and all four clung closely together with the two children pressed between them.

Above the tremendous din the chieftains were shouting from their saddles, and Richard cried in outraged tones, "Treachery all the way. They call out in Persian to hold their fire, and add in Pushtu, 'Kill them, kill them all!' They are betraying us to the last man."

Hardly had the words left his mouth than a new hazard arrived upon them without warning. From the rear came hundreds of terrified Indian men, women and children desperate to get through the pass and out at the far end, away from the death-trap. Fear ruled, and they surged through the tortuous defile pushing all before them, or simply trampling everything beneath their feet. They came, a tide of petrified brown faces that saw nothing, heard nothing but the evidence of their own panic, filling the space between the heights with an inexorable tide of humanity.

Before Charlotte could think, they were upon her, and she was dragged from Richard's arms and carried off in the tide, buffeted and punched, but holding on to Anna with arms like iron clamps. She cried his name, but her voice was swallowed up in the swelling volume of sound that now filled the chasm with screams, shouts, whinnies, thuds, cracks, whistles, grunts, the thunder of running boots, and the roar of water.

Sobbing with fear and effort she nearly fell over the long

frozen skirt, but that stumble brought her free of the forward push because she was elbowed aside whilst off balance and thumped face forwards against the rock, where another crevice offered slight protection. There she clung, unable to think, as the horde rushed past, as many falling to the ground as managed to pass her.

Soon, the rush slowed: the numbers thinned. The feet trampling the dead and dying grew fewer. But they were followed by Afghan horsemen who picked their way through the bodies, cutting the throats of the wounded and hacking with their swords at the dead in case any should have a slight breath of life left. By some miracle, Charlotte was unmolested, whether because of her white face or because she had a child in her arms, she would never know. But they killed without mercy any Indian woman and left brown children to die of slow, frozen starvation.

Then Richard was coming, pistol drawn, looking like death itself, riding one horse and leading another which were both strange to her. But, before she had time to mount, there was a flurry of rushing bodies once more, and she was separated from him by a dozen panic-stricken Indians being hunted down by Afghan riders slicing recklessly with their swords.

She slipped on the ice, put out an arm to save herself, and Anna was wrenched from her hold by the impetus of the crowd. Frantic, terrified, she clawed at the people around her, screaming Anna's name on a series of sobs. Then she saw the child, thrown to one side as they swept round a corner, but before she could reach her an Afghan rider closed in and swept the little bundle up to ride away with her.

"Richard!" she screamed hysterically. "Richard!"

He had seen: he heard. Like a man demented he spurred his horse into an impossible forward plunge that took him after the Afghan holding his daughter, but he had no chance to fire the pistol in that mêlée. Charlotte saw him draw his sword and gallop headlong into a group of the enemy that fell in with the rider taking Anna. But her vision was restricted by a fresh rush of camp-followers who knocked her from her place and took her along with them. Her last sight of him as they bore her around a corner was of a reckless courageous attack on those surrounding him before he went down and vanished beneath their slashing swords.

From then on she was a fighting clawing demon, screaming curses at those whom she could not pass, and sobbing Richard's and Anna's names until they became part of the entire thunder of hideous sounds in her ears.

There were soldiers around her now, sepoys led by Englishmen in scarlet jackets, who roared in Hindustani as they valiantly stood in the face of attack. She saw one sepoy's face explode into a mess of crimson blood, and another that broke into a grimace of agony as he fell screaming with his stomach a gaping hole.

"Oh, dear God, help me," she moaned, finding herself at last free of the crowd and able to go back for Richard.

But a scarlet jacket loomed, a voice in English said, "Mrs. Lingarde, you cannot go back there."

Then she was lifted bodily into a saddle and taken off, further away from her loved ones. She stared at the face, seeing only a pale shape before her, and begged in anguished tones to be released.

"They are there—they are back there," she moaned at him.

"They will come later," croaked the voice desperately. "You cannot go . . ."

The sentence was never finished. A dark hole appeared in the middle of the forehead, and the face twisted into strange contortions as it begun to fall away from her into space. And she began to follow it as the horse slipped, checked, then doubled up beneath her. Icy water lapped over her, but the urgent need to reach Richard had her struggling out of the stream and on to the snow-covered track.

She looked around wildly. How far had she travelled since Anna was taken from her? Each bend and twist looked the same. She began to run, heedless of the cold, the noise, the human flow in the opposite direction. A tremendous roar beside her set her swerving instinctively from a gun being fired at a group of Afghans in a natural rocky breastwork, and into the path of a bearded robed horseman who offered to take her up in his saddle to safety. An Afghan! Perhaps to take her to Richard and Anna? But he was knocked from his horse before her eyes and beheaded with one slash of a British sword before she found herself again hauled up by a man in a scarlet jacket.

"Charlotte . . . where is Amy? *Where is she?*"

She stared at a square face covered in brown stubble, blood-shot eyes and features she knew beneath the terrible expression.

"Tom! He took Anna. Richard is back there. I must go."

He held her tightly so that she could not get off the horse. "It is useless. They are all dead back there."

Why would Tom lie to her? Why would he say such terrible things? Did he wish to punish her because she did not save Felicia—because Richard had not gone back for her? It must be so for he forced her to stay on that horse with him, fought her desperate attempts to jump from the saddle, took her at a fast pace through an underworld of rock that was filled with the sounds of screams and groans, like souls roasting in Hell.

Pinioned tightly, deprived of her heartbreaking need to go back, to see their dear faces once more, to be with them at the end, Charlotte clung to her brother and cried aloud against the Almighty, whom she had tried to serve so well and who had cast her out when she most needed Him.

They broke suddenly from the defile into open space so white it was almost blinding, but Tom gave a sharp cry and fell forward across her, his weight almost knocking her from the saddle. The horse gave a scream barely seconds later and fell heavily, throwing Charlotte to the ground with such force she was temporarily stunned. But the coldness revived her quickly and she was up on her feet ready to go back, at last.

After two steps she halted. Streaming from the pass was a long line of staggering, bloody men, some dropping to lie still only a few yards from the entrance, others carrying or supporting comrades, yet others being hit by marksmen above as they went back for wounded friends. It was of no use to go back. Richard and Anna had gone. Beauty had vanished in an instant: love had ended as if it had never been. She was alone once more.

Turning away she went to Tom, who was pinned beneath the body of his horse and moaning in pain. She shouted to a passing Indian to help her move the carcase sufficiently to pull Tom free. His right shoulder was a mess of blood and bone, and there was a deep slash in his right thigh that must have been received before she had come across him. Taking great care they lifted him up and she and the unknown camp-follower began to move towards the survivors of that terrible day, who had halted on a high, wind-swept plateau. She trudged through the snow with painful, automatic steps, oblivious of others making their shattered way beside her.

Behind, in the pass, the echo of screams, moans and rifleshots remained. The Afghans were finishing off all those who clung to life. Ahead, less than half their original number were slowly assembling for yet another night of hunger and freezing endurance. For them, the agony must continue.

Men came to meet her; men she knew from a long time ago before she had entered the pass. Amy was there with baby Adam, both crying. A fair-haired young man took her arm and led her to a tent. He had sat beside Felicia's body that night, miserable because he had not gone back for her. But it was useless to go back. They were all dead.

Snow began falling, thicker and faster, like a moving fluffy blanket. It would cover them up, cover their staring eyes and gaping mouths. It would cover their torn bodies and broken faces. It would cover golden curls and little plump limbs. It would cover magnificent oblique eyes full of far-off goals which would now never be reached. It would cover up those she loved as if they had never been . . . and when the snow melted in the spring, there would be nothing left of her life save two piles of bones in a twisting, tortuous slash in the mountains.

She turned against Lieutenant Spence and clung to him, as if he somehow contained her sanity.

That night of January 8th 1842 was spent on an exposed plateau high in the hills. It was colder than ever before and filled with the cries of the wounded, who had to be left unattended, unsuccoured, and unmourned out on the snow for want of doctors, supplies and mere human sympathy. That night, everyone in the column was concerned only with staying alive himself, and keeping alive any who were dependent upon him.

By morning their numbers had been halved once more but, such was the pulse-beat of the need for life, many exhausted souls, including a number of troops, dragged themselves from the snow and stumbled off in the constant struggle to head the column. They were recalled by Elphinstone, who had received a message from Akbar Khan regretting that he had been unable to hold off the aggressive Ghilzai tribesmen the previous day, and promising food, tents, and stronger protection if the column remained where it was until he had had time to arrange it all. No one really believed him, but the officers were told to hold camp and their discipline was too strong to disobey. Their subordinates sat down again like automatons, beyond caring where they died.

Charlotte shared that feeling. She did not want to go on living: there was nobody left. All night she had lain awake in that cramped tent, listening to Tom's faint moans and those of four other wounded officers they had taken in. All night she had watched as dozens of poor wretches had invaded the canvas shelter fighting to get inside, fighting to snatch cloaks and *poshteens* from the occupants, fighting for survival. She did not wish to survive. Several times she would have gone out into the night if Lieutenant Spence had not prevented her. He had not slept, either, providing her with a calmness that kept her from breaking up, tending the wounded men as best he could, comforting Amy, and repelling the desperate invaders of their tent by flourishing his pistol.

By morning, two of the wounded officers were dead, a third nearly so. Tom was finally treated by a surgeon and his wounds dressed with makeshift bandages. Although in pain, he declared himself fit to ride a horse—except that he had none.

Lieutenant Spence went off to find horses for them all, if possible, but particularly for the ladies, and whilst he was gone Colley Duprés appeared at the tent with the news that the ladies and children, with the married and wounded officers, were to go over to Akbar Khan, who had guaranteed their safety personally, and proposed bringing them to Jalalabad one day's march behind the army.

"I am not allowing my wife, or my sister to fall into the hands of that villain," said Tom with surprising vigour for his condition. "Do not tell me any man has agreed to *that*."

Colley, looking almost like an Afghan himself in his native-style field-uniform, and with dark growth over the lower part of his face, frowned.

"There is no choice. Elphinstone has agreed."

"*What!* By what authority does he dictate what we should do with our families?" cried Tom struggling on to one elbow and setting Amy trying to restrain him.

"Eldred Pottinger's authority," was the short answer. "The Major advises that it is the only hope of sparing the wives and children further suffering and hardship." He looked around the tent, his dark eyes red-rimmed and lustreless. "Since all of you qualify for this offer of protection, I will tell you that there is no chance for the rest of us. The tribesmen have smelt blood. They are waiting in their thousands all along the road to Jalalabad, and even if Akbar Khan meant to protect us—which he does not—he would be powerless against the hatred of his countrymen. You either go to him and take a chance, or die along the route with all these luckless devils."

As no one said anything, he sighed heavily. "Elphinstone cannot allow Englishwomen—some with babes being suckled, others well advanced in pregnancy—to go ahead with the troops. He cannot guarantee them safety. Akbar Khan professes to. Is there a choice?"

Tom nodded slowly. "Very well. When do we go?"

"Now. A party of Afghans is here with horses, and they are impatient to be off." He turned to Charlotte and looked at her with a seriousness she had rarely known in him. "You once said to me that females did not indulge in adventures, and I replied that you were now in a country where adventure was its life's blood, and who could tell what would lie before you. I did not guess it could be this . . . or I would have told her to return with you to England immediately."

Charlotte remembered that day beside the Ganges. It was a lifetime ago. "She would not have gone . . . no more would I. I do not regret coming here, but I wish that, like her, I had died back there."

He shook his head. "No . . . no, never wish that. She lived for herself, you know, but you live for others. You must not give up now. There is more to you than that."

They were called outside to the waiting horses, and there was no more time for anything. The two wounded officers were lifted with surprising gentleness by the Afghans waiting to escort them. But, just as Charlotte was about to mount, young Lieutenant Spence arrived leading two horses that were so thin they could barely stand, and she knew that fair face with eyes that had twinkled with wicked youth would never smile again.

He took the news with brave calm, but his gaze flew straight to Amy, already mounted beside Tom. They all knew it was goodbye forever, but they murmured ridiculous phrases about meeting again soon and the party they would all have at Jalalabad. Then Charlotte reached up and kissed his rough cheek, because Amy could not and because, like herself, he was alone and bereft now.

They left the encampment, their countrymen, and those Indians who had served them and the army so well, to ride off to a small nearby fort where Akbar Khan was waiting to receive them. Charlotte rode in the line of women, many of whom were grieving—Lady McNaughten, whose husband had been murdered and dismembered, Mrs Trevor, *enceinte* and with seven other children, whose husband had been murdered along with Sir William, Mrs Sturt, whose popular and talented engineer husband had just died of wounds after going back into the pass to help a friend, Lady Sale, her mother, whose husband was wounded and in Jalalabad, Mrs Boyd, whose four-year-old boy had been snatched from her arms in that terrible defile, and Mrs Anderson, who had lost a daughter in the same way. But they all had someone left— a husband, child or mother. Charlotte had lost them all. Even Tom seemed unlikely to recover from his wounds without medical attention.

At the fort her loss seemed accentuated for there with the three officer hostages Pottinger, Lawrence and McKenzie (the last two having escaped murder when McNaughten was seized) was the Boyds' small son, handed in by the Afghan who had seized him. The Anderson girl had not turned up, nor had anyone any knowledge of Anna Lingarde. Mrs Anderson clung to her husband in her distress. Charlotte just walked away to a silent corner of the dark and dirty room to which one third of the party had been sent. The others were divided between two similar rooms in which there was nothing but the floor as a bed. She sank down in that corner and remained there until someone approached her with a small bowl of greasy rice and a mutton bone. There did not seem much point in eating it, so she left it where it was. It was still there in the morning.

That next day passed almost unnoticed by Charlotte, who remained in her corner, guarding her privacy. People spoke to her every so often, kind voices full of encouragement. But she was left as she wished to be. Pain began returning around mid-afternoon as it occurred to her that Richard had sat in a darkened room in Malkhan believing that he had lost everyone—his mother dead, his wife uncaring, his daughter beyond his reach. She felt his pain and despair with her own: she knew now what he had never spoken of when he returned to her. In such situations one realized the foolishness of human pride and passion. She had had so much within her grasp and not valued it.

Everyone and everything had been forced into firm slots created by her youthful limitations, but she knew now there were lights and shades to every relationship; grades of right and wrong in every situation. Felicia, in her determination not to dominate her daughter as she herself had been dominated, went to the extreme of shutting her from her life completely. Charlotte, believing a mother should be plump, cosseting and an example of impeccable virtue, could not accept the mama she found. Yet, with a little understanding on both sides they could have found a way.

As for herself and Richard, all their problems could have been prevented if they had abandoned pride and spoken honestly to each other. She had been too proud to tell him of her infatuation with Colley, and married him instead. He had been too proud to admit he was afraid of loving her again. Had they known it would end so soon, they surely would never have tormented each other so!

That night she ate the rice with her fingers, like everyone else in the room. They had so much with which to contend, she could not increase their worry by being unnecessarily ill.

They marched the following day, one day to the rear of the army. The snow was thicker than ever on the ground, and a bitter wind blew. Charlotte was given a horse. Amy, with Adam, shared a camel *kajava* with Tom, who was unable to ride because of his leg wound and shattered shoulder. It must have been a painful ride, lurching and bumping on a camel over uneven ground, but it was the only way he could move on with the rest.

They had gone only a mile or so when they joined the route followed by the army and learnt the horrifying truth. Bodies lay mangled and split open, stripped of their clothing and frozen into the postures of agony they had taken at the moment of death. The snow was drenched crimson and smelt so overpoweringly of blood it was difficult not to heave as they took their beasts carefully across the carpet of corpses, desperately trying not to trample on them.

There was no conversation as they passed the sites of numerous massacres, or wound their way beside living, jabbering camp-followers who had been left behind in that march of death. The cold eeriness of the scene was so awesome it seemed almost sacrilegious to disturb it with the rustling squeak of frozen snow beneath the plodding hooves. It was all the more unnerving, therefore, when a sharp female cry rang out across the stillness, and Charlotte turned her head to see Amy, just ahead, hanging over the edge of the *kajava* and moaning.

Lieutenant Spence lay, head thrown back, his body covered with deep cuts that had bled profusely to stiffen his uniform with darker red. His left foot lay a short distance from his body and his throat was a long crimson gash. In contrast, his face was youthfully handsome still, and those fatal blue eyes stared at those passing by as if with casual unconcern.

It dissolved Charlotte's remaining numbness and she rode along that continuous path of carnage knowing she could bear very little more. In her mind she saw Richard in that mutilated figure and all the others she passed. In the little brown abandoned children she saw Anna, and became obsessed with the embryo she had lost. She would have had a part of him; a child to replace Anna. She would have had *some* reason to live.

Her Christian beliefs fled. All she had learnt from Aunt Meg was false. It was *not* blessed to be meek and to suffer. She no longer accepted that His will should be done. What reason could He have for the past four days? If they had served His purpose, it was an unforgivable one.

For five more days they followed on the heels of slaughter until they were halted a mere thirty miles from Jalalabad. There, they were told by Akbar Khan that of the twenty thousand men, women and children who had set out from Kabul, one man only had arrived safely at Jalalabad. It had all come true, after all. The women and children had been handed over to the chieftains, and all the men had been killed save one. The only variation on that earlier vow was that he had not been mutilated and placed in the Khyber Pass. Dr Brydon had arrived, wounded, at the fort and survived . . .

The Jalalabad garrison no longer had any intention of going. Instead, it seemed to be planning revenge for a massacred army along with the force stationed at Kandahar. Akbar Khan was angry. The hostages would not be allowed to go free until *all* the British had gone from Afghanistan, and Dost Mohammed had been sent back over the border from India. He did not trust the British, he raged. They did not keep their word or their promises.

It was then, when told they were all to be taken to a fort as prisoners of one of the chieftains and travel with his troops and household wherever he had need to go whilst driving out the infidels, that Charlotte realized she had turned full circle and had become a parcel once more.

· *eighteen* ·

BY THE TIME the approaching summer made the hills and valleys beautiful with hot sunshine, blossoms, shrubs, and sparkling waterfalls, Akbar Khan's hostages had heard the full story of the tragic retreat from Kabul and all its consequences. As with any great military defeat, there were stories of personal heroism and courageous stands against the enemy that only ended when every man had given his life. The most memorable of these had been at a place called Gandamuk, when eighteen officers and the fifty remaining troops held a hill until there was no one left to fire a rifle or swing a sword.

General Elphinstone, wounded and also taken hostage by Akbar Khan under the pretext of summoning him for negotiations, died broken and bitter whilst in captivity. A request for the safe carriage of his body to Jalalabad for honourable burial brought Akbar Khan's generous agreement, but the disguised funeral party was attacked, the coffin broken open, and the body abused before it was finally carried into the garrison. Shah Soojah, the luckless puppet king who had not known how to rule, was murdered by a treacherous son of a Kabul chieftain whilst pretending to escort the exile to India.

Yet, although the British had been driven from Kabul and their puppet ruthlessly killed, there was still no peace in Afghanistan. The chieftains were all jostling for position, if not actually hoping for the throne, at least sizing up their chances of increasing their influence and territories. There would be a hiatus between two regimes, and now was the time to gather an army to protect personal interests. Assassinations or woundings of prominent leaders began to take place. Akbar Khan himself was fired upon and injured on three separate occasions. And the British were on their way back.

Defeated, but certainly not deterred, an avenging force had set out from India, battled its way through the Khyber Pass, and joined up with the garrisons of Jalalabad and Kandahar. Fighting now with gritty determination under leadership inspired by outrage and true British wrath over ungentlemanly practices, the force was sweeping through Afghanistan bent on retribution and the rescue of those handed over in good faith who had been made prisoner and dragged forcibly over the country for six months.

The party of women, children, and wounded officers had been marched hither and thither, sleeping in forts or villages, and placed in the hands of one chieftain after another, gathering numbers as they went. They ate Afghan food of the simplest kind, had no clothing other than that they were wearing at the time of going over to Akbar Khan, were crowded together indiscriminately and were alternately threatened and reassured. The chieftains who became their temporary jailors at the bidding of Akbar Khan varied from courteous men who felt genuine sympathy for British ladies and children suffering such conditions, to cruel, eccentric fanatics who withheld their food, gave them false bad news of their chances of rescue, and hurled abuse at them whilst their bodyguards flourished knives in their faces.

But they struggled on, trusting in the countrymen who had sworn to rescue them, and overcoming the privations and rigours of their nomadic life. A few of the men stilled their frustration and anxiety by sketching the magnificent scenery on any scraps of paper they could come by, others collected botanic specimens and pressed them between leaves. Some officers made topographical studies of the terrain, noting the position of hills and villages for future military use. Some endlessly discussed the campaign they had survived and argued over why it had failed. Others wrote poetry, or diaries of their day-to-day experiences.

The ladies were different. Whilst the menfolk did the worrying, they used their more adaptable natures to the full by making their situation as bearable as possible. Most had a husband or children to care for, so their prime concern, as always, was to nurse their health, see to their comfort, and offer sympathetic understanding when they chafed against their restrictions. For the women, duty was much the same wherever they found themselves.

Several babies were born in captivity, the mothers being found some corner of privacy in which to give birth to new life created by men now six months dead. Everyone felt the tragic blessing of such births, but none felt it as overwhelmingly as Charlotte. Two such births within ten days took her to crisis point, coming as they did so soon after the return of their missing daughter to Captain and Mrs Anderson.

Acknowledging that she had reached the end of her endurance, Charlotte walked from the foul-smelling room in the fort, out on to the hillside overlooking Kabul cantonment, now blackened and broken, whence they had been marched back by a circuitous route. Those burnt ruins below held such memories of those she had lost, and it seemed particularly cruel that her only escape from the fort should be dominated by that sight.

It had been raining heavily for most of the day, which had kept everyone inside in a stifling atmosphere of humidity. The weather had been bad for several days, and there had been strange rumbling in the earth that had frightened the children. Now, there was a break in the downpour, and she had come outside quickly hoping to have a short spell alone before the others decided to follow her example. But there was little refreshment from the heat to be had, since it was thundery and very close beneath the lowering clouds. Desperation for solitude and a place in which to come to terms with her thoughts kept her out there, however.

She wandered along the hillside away from the fort, the hem of her skirt growing saturated from the wet grass and tugged by the scattering of rocks half-hidden beneath the green covering. It did not matter any more. A sharp pain went through her as she remembered how she had once patched and mended her riding-dress so that she would not be obliged to buy another with Richard's money. All he had owned was now legally hers and hers alone . . . and she would give it all and anything else beside to have him alive again.

She came to a halt some distance from the fort. Gazing down on the place where their bungalow had once stood, she took from her skirt pocket several small phials that had been there since she left that cantonment—laudanum, enough to make certain she would never wake again. She had taken it from the hospital when it was revealed that they would have to march through the winter perils to freedom. It had been with some vague idea of soothing Anna, or helping Richard if he should be wounded, but for some days now she had realized she had in her possession the means of making the same choice as Felicia. The moment had come to make it.

She had been taught that it was a heinous sin to take one's own life, but all her religious standards had been abandoned some months ago. *We are all unanimous about what is sinful. It is when we come to goodness that we all have our own ideas,* Colley had once said to her. She had certainly had her ideas and fiercely defended them. To what end? Everyone had been taken from her, the only two people in the world she had ever loved had suffered agony and violent slaughter without even the comfort of Christian burial. They lay in some unknown place where she could not even place flowers or experience communion with their spirits. That was where goodness led.

As for sin, Colley Duprés seemed to thrive upon it. Along with several other political officers allowed by the Afghans to act as mediators between the chieftains and the British, he was still "galloping madly about" as Richard would have put it, taking messages to Akbar Khan, whichever chieftain was presently their jailer, and the various generals in charge of the avenging force. He had carried messages from Eldred Pottinger and other captive officers which gave secret information to their countrymen about the true situation around Kabul. Pottinger wrote in Greek, a language unknown by the Afghans, others used simple codes like dotting certain letters in each sentence or adding French words here and there in what otherwise appeared to be a harmless missive. The invading force used the same techniques, marking certain words in the newspapers they sent to political couriers, using expressions that would only be understood by Englishmen, or putting Latin postscripts to innocuous letters.

Oh yes, the careless acceptance of sin appeared not to have penalized Colley Duprés one jot . . . nor had Amy's selfishness and unkind tongue. Tom had now recovered from his wounds and, although his shattered shoulder had produced a virtual immobilization in that arm which would certainly affect his military career, he was alive and reasonably healthy. On top of that, young Adam had confounded everyone on the rough, open-air, nomadic life to the extent that he was now a plump toddler who was extremely popular with the Afghan guards, and the wives and womenfolk of the chieftains' households.

If that were not enough, along with her own tragic loss, Charlotte had ample evidence around her of virtue being a wasted commodity. The months of captivity for so contained a group had brought forth evidence of ugly human traits, especially in the women. One, a soldier's wife who acted nursemaid to two children, took an Afghan lover to better her own conditions, and profited even further by revealing the whereabouts of Lady McNaughten's jewels, and other objects of value owned by others in the group. They were all forced, at knife point, to surrender them. Other women used subtler ways to punish their fellow prisoners. Some had husbands or friends in Jalalabad who sent them money or small articles such as needles and thread, soap, medicaments, and lotions to help counteract the ravages of severe heat or cold. These women made no attempt to share such items, or help another in dire need of medicine or a mere needle with a length of thread to repair torn clothes.

As weeks had stretched into months there had also developed an astonishing snobbery practised by those of high rank, and the entire group had divided into sub-groups dictated by elements that should never have entered into a situation that was seldom less than potentially dangerous. The gentlemen did their best to soothe feminine feathers, but even they gave up in disgust when faced with tight-lipped females who guarded their luxuries with determined selfishness. Charlotte could not help thinking that Richard would have thought of some way of shaming them into sharing with others less fortunate. He had abhorred feminine silliness in all its forms.

Charlotte had stood aside from such things. She had no husband or child to consider; there was no need to fight for extras with which to nourish a baby, or needles and thread to improve the state of her clothes. But she saw Amy doing both and almost coming to blows with another woman who denied possessing anything extra. Tom did nothing about it. He seemed a broken man, these days, and found the almost exclusively female company difficult to stand.

Charlotte had spent many weeks nursing her brother back to health, and doing what she could for the other wounded. But they had a doctor in the group now. He had come in one day, sent by a nearby chieftain who had discovered him, wounded and frostbitten, in a village to which he had crawled from that retreat to slaughter. There had been others, other officers who had been carried off by Afghans during that carnage, either because their uniforms suggested they were of high importance, or because the volatile tribesmen had felt the urge to hand them over to Akbar Khan in the hope of future favour from him.

So the group of prisoners had grown larger as it moved from place to place, and men thought lost in the passes were brought in by those who found them lying helpless somewhere. Akbar Khan made it known that he encouraged this because greater numbers would increase his bargaining powers when the time came. But, although Charlotte had lived in hopeful anguish for many weeks, Richard had not walked one day into the fort . . . and the last of those isolated survivors had been handed over long ago.

Neither had Anna returned like three other children, who had been held in Afghan villages until the situation quietened. Hope had finally gone; even Tom and the wounded no longer required anything from her. That morning they had been told by their Afghan captor that the British advance had been halted, and the infidel soldiers had mutinied, killed their white officers, and were fleeing back to their homeland. Major Pottinger had assured them all that the opposite was true and had gone to see the chieftain to remonstrate with him on the brutal mental torture inflicted on helpless women. In return, he was accused of sending and receiving secret messages, denounced as a spy, and came very close to being executed on the spot. He had used his brilliant gift of diplomacy to placate his persecutor, and returned as calm and reassuring as usual.

Yet that incident, together with the birth of yet another baby in the early hours of that morning, had proved the turning point in Charlotte's fortitude, because she realized that she did not care if the report was true or not. If they were rescued, where would she go? Her father, already hating the female sex, would have to face the scandal of his wife's love for one of his own staff. She had nothing to give Sir John Lingarde now his granddaughter had gone. Aunt Meg? No, Charlotte could not go back there disputing all her aunt held dear. Religion had kept that neglected spinster from going under. With her back turned on her earlier commitment to God, Charlotte knew there was no place for her now in that cold, silent manor.

She saw that Felicia had been right to take what happiness she could find—sinful or not—and she had also been right to evade long, lonely years of growing old without her love beside her. Even in her youth Charlotte had never felt as lonely as she did now, had never felt as much of a parcel to be deposited first here, unwanted by each recipient.

Fingering the phials, she knew they contained her escape. In a matter of minutes she could close her eyes on that scene of destruction below, on the Bala Hissar that had brooded over her for a year and a half, on the country that had already taken life from her and left a shell. In a matter of minutes she could be beyond recall by those who did not give one jot for an unwanted parcel. In a matter of minutes she could ensure that she remained in Afghanistan with her loved ones. Her soul would roam forever without finding a resting-place, but it would find many others along the way, among them Richard's and Anna's. God had not wanted them, or He would never have destroyed them so cruelly and denied them the words of salvation. He had cast out the Lingardes. She would now cast Him out!

The phials dropped from her fingers as she fell to the ground, but they were still full. A violent movement of the ground beneath threw her off-balance to lie, all breath knocked from her, as the entire hillside seemed to heave and shift to the accompaniment of subterranean rumbles against her ear. Dazed, she realized the small tremors they had been experiencing recently had finally exploded into an earthquake of some magnitude. There was shouting, high-pitched screams. She turned her head instinctively just as part of the walls of the fort way behind her appeared to ripple before collapsing in a pile of rocks and dust, falling inward on to the courtyard favoured by the prisoners as a recreation area.

She tried to stand, but the ground shook and trembled too much. It was difficult to tell whether it was overhead thunder or the disturbance beneath that caused the continuous loud rumbling. There was a great deal of shouting coming from the fort, and she staggered to her feet knowing it was essential to get back to help those who might be trapped.

Trying to run across that rocky hillside that shifted frighteningly every few minutes, Charlotte's attention was taken by the hills surrounding her that appeared to be throwing up clouds of dust or toppling in the most amazing way. A wind had sprung up to tug at her long skirts and buffet her face; the heat and humidity had increased to such an extent it made her head pound and restricted her breathing. It had grown unnaturally dark, and the roaring echoed all through the Kabul valley as successive shocks assaulted the earth.

Stumbling up to the fort, Charlotte found concern and agitation everywhere. English and Afghans alike were desperately searching the dust-laden ruins for those who were not immediately visible, and masonry was still falling. The officers were all shifting stones with organized efficiency, whilst attempting to calm a mother who could not find a child or a wife whose husband was not by her side. The children were all terrified and screaming: some of the women behaved little better than their offspring.

In the darkness of the courtyard Charlotte found Amy by following the sound of her voice as she screamed at Tom to leave what he was doing and go to her. Once beside her sister-in-law, she sized up the situation and took Adam from the arms of the hysterical girl for his greater safety in that dreadful atmosphere of choking dust and heat, where everyone was trying to cope with something he had never before experienced.

Amy looked round wildly at her. "He does not care for us. He prefers to dig for Afghans," she cried shrilly at Charlotte's face. "Once already he has nearly died. Now he stands right beneath that wall that may topple at any moment. He does not care for us."

Across the shouting and children's screams Charlotte said loudly, "They are looking for some of our own number. Would you have Tom stand back while the others are behaving like gentlemen, you foolish girl?"

Just then, another violent shock threw them all against the wall, and some of the officers yelled at everyone to get outside, clear of the building. Charlotte grabbed Amy's arm and dragged her forcibly from the fort in company with the other women and most of the Afghans, and there they remained even when rain began falling heavily to drench them to the skin and plaster their hair to their heads. But they all fell terribly silent when the flat roof of one of the rooms they usually occupied collapsed with a great roar, and they stood staring across the windswept hillside unable to believe that such an ordeal should be added to those they had already faced.

"Tom is gone. I know he is gone," whimpered Amy. "He wished to punish me because of Rupert. Now I have lost them both."

"*Be quiet!*" Charlotte told her fiercely, remembering that corpse of Rupert Spence, bloody and frozen beneath their horses' hooves so long ago. "This is no time to indulge in selfish melodrama. They are both too worthy for such stupidity on your part," she added thinking how ridiculous it was for two drenched women on a shaking hillside to be shouting at each other across a terrified child whilst a drama was being enacted within that fort—a drama of life or death.

Amy rounded on her, the pretty red hair flattened like a bright bonnet by the rain that streaked down a face grown sharp and bony.

"*You* be quiet!" she cried with heedless passion. "It is not your husband in there risking his life. You have had no one to worry about these past months but yourself, so do not accuse *me*—of selfishness."

For a long second Charlotte stared at the other girl while the wind and rain lashed them both, then she put up a hand and smacked Amy very hard round her face. They continued to stare at each other until another tremor shook them, and the men came running out crying that all was well and the missing ones were safe in another courtyard.

The noise of voices broke the deadlock, and Amy, looking like death, whispered, "Forgive me. *Oh, forgive me, Charlotte.*"

Charlotte thrust Adam at the girl and began to run down the hill to the place she had been before, oblivious of the cloudburst. But she could not remember exactly where she had stood, could not see for the rain that beat into her eyes, could not think for the pain in her head.

The earth tremors continued well into the night, and the prisoners slept in the open to escape the danger of falling walls. They became soaked yet again when another severe storm broke in the early hours of the morning, but one of their number sat huddled in her *poshteen* and acknowledged that God had even taken away her means of ending what had become an intolerable burden.

Three days later, Colley Duprés rode into the fort with the news that Anna Lingarde had been found by one of his colleagues in a village near Kabul. She was being returned to her mother by the officer, who had bought her from the family that was looking after her with great kindness. Charlotte fainted at his feet.

* * *

August! Akbar Khan's hostages had been under guard for eight months and, despite raised hopes that kept them going from day to day, they were no nearer to freedom than they had been at the start.

Still at the fort above Kabul, they were visited almost daily by the several political officers who were now being kept in the city. From them they learned the true situation, that the army was on its way to release them. These reports contradicted the cruel lies told them by their captors, who enjoyed tormenting them with false boasts of having annihilated the British yet again, or threats of immediate execution if their countrymen made any attempt to reach them. There were also refinements guaranteed to break the nerves of those who had been weakened by close captivity, poor diet, and ill health. Threats to separate husbands from their families, withdrawal of rations, the seizure of their letters from Jalalabad, and trumped-up charges against various officers all added to the strain under which the group now suffered. And the earthquakes continued to add their threat to life.

Eldred Pottinger, now living in the Bala Hissar under guard, was attempting to negotiate between Akbar Khan and General Pollock, who was in command of the avenging force. With his usual skill the Major retained an air of command which, despite the fact that he was a prisoner in great danger of his life, greatly impressed the Afghans. In a desperate attempt to win the lesser chieftains' support, he agreed daily to their claims for land and concessions when the British arrived back in Kabul, and produced official-looking pieces of paper which he signed with great ceremony, knowing they were quite worthless. The British were coming back, but not to stay.

However, his constant communications with Pollock, who was already on the Kabul road, were hampered by missives from his superiors in India which told him not to interfere. Pollock also had messages from India. One of these told him to withdraw immediately before another disaster occurred. Since he was defeating the Afghans all along the line, the

General chose to pretend that the message had never reached him.

The numbers of the prisoners now increased further. Those political officers left behind in Kabul as hostages when the army first set out that January had been bought from the chieftain who had held them captive, and now joined those in the hill fort above the city. More were handed over, including nine officers captured at the fall of Ghuznee at the start of the year. Then the group heard rumours of a British officer being discovered in Kabul bazaar disguised as a native, possibly a Russian spy since he spoke a strange tongue. On hearing this Charlotte was thrown into an agony of hope that it could be Richard, but the mystery turned out to be nothing more than an Arabian trader who was so fair in colouring he could be mistaken for a European.

Since Anna had been returned to her so miraculously Charlotte had taken on a new lease of life. The weeks of captivity, although uncomfortable, exhausting and dangerous, could be faced with determination now she had a reason for surviving. She did not dare think of that day when she had fingered those phials. Anna would have been left an orphan, a parcel unwanted even more than the mother who had abandoned hope.

The little girl had been well looked after and appeared none the worse for five months with an Afghan family, although she cried heartrendingly on seeing her mother again. It had been some time before Charlotte could communicate with her own child. Anna now spoke Persian quite fluently and naturally, or she fell into a rapid mixture of English and Russian which was difficult to follow. But, although her joy at the return of Anna was inexpressible, Charlotte knew now that her love for Richard was a separate and precious thing that had not needed a child to sustain it. Anna's presence accentuated her loss unbearably, showing Charlotte that, even for the sake of her child, she could never bring herself to marry again. Richard was her one love, and his memory would always hold her in thrall.

There were days now when she smelt the snow in the

breeze that blew from the north. Unless rescue came soon they would be faced with another journey through snow-filled passes—a terrible re-enactment of the death march they had survived in January. But another evil threatened to add to the casualties of that ill-fated force when typhus fever attacked an officer who had been one of the original hostages in the Bala Hissar and had escaped murder by the Afghan mob on two separate occasions. Captain John Connelly died within two days of being taken ill—a man universally popular and one of three brothers who had perished in Afghanistan as members of that original brave Army of the Indus.

Charlotte was saddened by the thought of such fine young brothers being sacrificed in the same cause so far from their homeland and loved ones. But her concern became more personal when the fever spread to a great number of the group, and she feared for Anna. The little girl did not succumb, but several of the children did, along with one or two of the ladies. The officers seemed better able to resist it, but it killed a soldier and a three-year-old boy, who were both laid to rest with John Connelly in the corner of one courtyard, the headstones a constant sad reminder.

Everyone was filled with fresh despair, however, when Pottinger, plus the other political hostages held in Kabul city, arrived at the fort saying they had been banished from the Bala Hissar by a very angry Akbar Khan, who had broken off negotiations with General Pollock because he would not agree to his terms. As a result, the captives were to be sent on a one-hundred-mile march into the savage interior of Afghanistan where the British would never find them.

Pottinger explained that Pollock had orders to secure the release of the hostages unconditionally, since they had been handed over in good faith eight months ago and had since been ill-treated and forcibly marched for miles under inhumane conditions. The British considered that it constituted a flagrant violation of the rules of warfare, and there was no question of bargaining for their lives.

To be so near freedom only to find it snatched away proved too much for some of the women, who broke down and wept silently over their children. Amy, to nobody's surprise, created a scene of despair and frustration which called down curses on the head of General Pollock and all her countrymen, who were prepared to risk their lives for a principle. Tom found her difficult to handle, and came to Charlotte for help, as usual. But he had chosen the wrong time. As upset and desperate as the rest, she found herself telling Tom she had had her fill of Amy's tantrums and felt a strong inclination to tell her so. This speech developed into a catalogue of incidents since she had first met her sister-in-law in Meerpore, which showed that Amy was a spoilt, selfish girl who expected her prettiness to get her everything she wanted. She ended by telling Tom it was time he took his belt to his wife.

Next minute, she was apologizing because she could not stand the look on her brother's face. "Tom, you really must not expect me to be sensible at a time like this," she said, putting a hand on his arm. "I cannot see where this will all end."

He sighed heavily. "It will all come out right. But . . . but so many good people have been lost." He glanced up at her, a frown creasing his broad brow, and she thought how old he looked, these days. "I would give anything to go back to that day you first arrived in Meerpore, Charlotte. Life was good then. I was so certain of everything, you know. Amy was the sweetest and most wonderful girl, Richard was a splendid but rather studious friend . . . and my company of sepoys was the best in India."

Charlotte's heart softened. She knew how much it had cost Tom to know he had been taken off to comparative safety, wounded, whilst his men had been left to face massacre. Her brother had been an enthusiastic, headstrong warrior. The realities of war had hit him hard. With a useless sword arm his future career was in some doubt, and she knew he brooded on the fact that the invasion he had so heartily supported had been the failure Richard had prophesied. The glamour of war had vanished, for Tom, and he also felt the death of his friend very deeply. With his infatuation for Amy broken by disillusion, there was little ahead for him that spelled the kind of carefree happiness to which he had just referred. But he had survived. So had his wife and son. He was a great deal luckier than many.

"Tom," she began quietly, "has my lesson taught you nothing? You know, there was a time when Richard thought of me as a heartless, selfish wretch who was tied to him forever like a great millstone around his neck. He . . . he had cause to believe I had given my affection to another and had betrayed him. It took that terrible ordeal at Malkhan to make him attempt to save something of our marriage. Our last six months at Kabul were the most wonderful of my life, and I would give anything to remove those two years of pain and unhappiness we gave each other. I beg you not to waste what you may have in your grasp. Amy never was the sweetest and most wonderful girl. She has not changed, has not let you down. It is you who cannot accept your own disillusionment. Take her for what she is and adjust accordingly. She needs flattery, and Rupert Spence provided it. That was all it was: she had no real love for him. A strong man with determination could soon abolish all her self-centred nonsense. Make a fuss over Adam—you rarely do, admit it—and show that you have definite plans for the future that will need her fullest co-operation and support. So far in your marriage it has been she who has done all the demanding. It is time you turned the tables."

His face registered bewildered astonishment that such wisdom should come from the lips of a female, and Charlotte relaxed enough to smile.

"Dear Tom, you are the most transparent person I know. Amy is very fortunate, and it is time you made her realize the fact." She put her arm through his and began walking him outside the walls to the slopes overlooking the fatal cantonment Richard had refused to help build. "Do you remember those school holidays with Aunt Meg? Your company then was the only thing that brightened my life. Brighten Amy's in the same way."

They walked in silence for a while, lost in thoughts of their own. Then she said, "I thought of going to Richard's father. In the tragedy of Anastasia's death, he was forgotten by everyone, including Richard. He is a man who has lost all purpose in life. I know what that is like, Tom, and I think Anna is the one person who can give him consolation."

Her brother turned to her, taking her hands. "Richard asked me to see you safely on your way to Sir John if he fell in battle. It appears he had not entirely forgotten his father."

Foolishly her throat tightened and prevented her from speaking further. Then, before she knew it, she was against Tom, clutching his sleeves and crying the tears she had held back for so long. He held her close, and when she finally looked up she found his throat working and his eyes bright with emotion.

"If I could bring him back to you, as I did from Malkhan, I would give up the use of my other arm," he said huskily.

"I know . . . I know," she whispered, then tried to smile. "At least give me the pleasure of seeing you happy with Amy."

The opportunity was denied him. Amy's latest tantrum had been intensified by the onset of the prevalent fever. She died in Tom's arms the following evening as the sun was going down and was buried in the courtyard with the other victims of their prolonged captivity.

Charlotte, beyond feeling greater sorrow than she had already experienced, simply added several more years to her age, and took Adam into her care without hesitation. Tom lost the last of his simple philosophy of life, and with it the endearing warmth of his nature. There was a new ruthlessness in his attitude that suggested he had matured and come to terms with the truth that dashes optimism.

There was little time to grieve. On the following day they were told they must march away from Kabul, and anyone attempting to get to the city would be shot. Pottinger immediately protested to Akbar Khan, but the Afghan shouted angrily at him that the enemy was almost at the city gates and, since the English General would not bargain, the prisoners would not be surrendered.

At ten-thirty that night, they were all obliged to mount ponies or climb into camel *kajavas* ready to embark on the long, treacherous journey across the hills. It was heartbreaking to leave when their countrymen were so near. Entering their ninth month of captivity their resistance was low, and this action of Akbar Khan's was cruel in the extreme, in the face of the fever deaths. But his volatile personality left none of them in doubt that he was capable of murdering them all rather than give them up.

They departed, leaving behind the Andersons and Mrs Trevor with her eight children. Both women were so seriously ill with fever it was expected that they would shortly follow Amy to the grave, and Pottinger insisted that they be spared the further ordeal of such a difficult journey. One soldier, who was in the first grips of fever, had to go, however, and the poor man died along the way—one more soul to wander that wild country without commendation to the Almighty.

Charlotte rode in a *kajava* with Anna and Adam, and soon began to have fears that the proximity of the avenging army meant their treatment would worsen. Their way lay through narrow lanes overhung with trees, traversable by the camels but not the great panniers on their sides. The occupants of these were knocked and scraped by branches throughout the entire period, and found it necessary to curl up in painful positions to avoid a crack on the head or the danger of having an eye put out by unseen sharp twigs.

By crouching over the two children to protect them Charlotte was severely scratched on the cheek and one arm before they broke into open country once more. The men protested vigorously to the camel drivers who were plainly enjoying the discomfort of the infidel women, but they merely grinned insolently and continued on their careless way. Charlotte, like the other women, had been told to wear Afghan dress for the journey, since their way lay through country inhabited by warlike tribes who would probably attack foreigners. Their safety relied on their not displaying their true identity, they were told. The loose white robe and veil were better travelling clothes than their own, admittedly, but it gave rise to the fear that the disguise was really to hide them from British troops who might be looking for them. Dressed as they were, they could be spirited away, travel forever across Afghanistan and never be found by their rescuers.

This fear was increased when, on the following day, they were unexpectedly joined by thirty white soldiers and three officers who had been left behind in Kabul at the start of the original retreat because of wounds or sickness. It seemed to everyone that Akbar Khan was planning to keep all his European hostages well out of sight when General Pollock marched into Kabul—which he was certain to do at any time.

September! Still they marched. The paths were now no more than mountain tracks which could not be negotiated by camels, so everyone had to ride the surer-footed ponies. The children were shared out between the officers where a woman had more than one, or was too weak to manage one herself. Charlotte found it hazardous along precarious footways above sheer drops of rocky promontories with a child in her arms. Anna was now three years old, and excessively lively despite all she had suffered. It pointed to an indomitable spirit, and Charlotte dwelt many times on the pride Richard would feel in a child who not only resembled his mother in looks, but also in character. She passed the long weary hours in dreams of Anna's destiny, and the happiness she was determined Richard's daughter would have.

As the September days passed, however, it began to grow obvious to the men that the chieftain chosen to accompany them at the order of Akbar Khan was more afraid of the British soldiers than his Afghan superior. He did not relish being the man found with the hostages when the avengers caught up with them. Why should he take the punishment when he had not seized the women and their husbands in the first place? It soon transpired that the accompanying bodyguard shared his fears. They began deserting in twos and threes along the way.

The captives took this as a sign that Pollock was hourly expected in Kabul, and this was confirmed when the chieftain received a message from Akbar Khan ordering him to march the prisoners as quickly as possible further into the interior and hide them there, under close guard. It seemed to be another defeat when the chieftain called Pottinger to him and revealed the contents of the message. Everyone was leaden-hearted and pessimistic.

Charlotte was washing the two children in a nearby stream when Tom came running across to her with such a look on his face, her heart leapt. "They have retaken Kabul?" she asked, getting to her feet and letting the folds of her Afghan robe drop around her. "Is General Pollock truly in power there?"

"Better than that," he replied. "Pottinger has just come from the chieftain, who offers to let us go over to Pollock for the price of twenty thousand rupees. Pottinger and the other three politicals have given him a written personal guarantee of the sum, and we have all pledged ourselves to make up their loss if the Company will not meet it."

Trying to stay calm, she said, "What would we have done without Major Pottinger all this time?"

He managed a faint smile. "I remember once telling Richard that if a man with a name like Eldred Pottinger turned out to be of any help, I'd kick a monkey."

"When do we go?" she asked, unable to contain her excitement any longer.

"Wait . . . wait," he told her gently, taking her arms to hold her still. "It is not a matter of just walking away from here. A message is to be sent to Pollock's camp to notify them of our position. The local tribes have been bought by Pottinger and will support our cause. We are to be given arms to defend ourselves against any force Akbar Khan might send against us, when he discovers the truth."

Charlotte's excitement died immediately. "So we are *not* free!"

He shook her gently. "We are no longer captives . . . but it might be some days yet before we can count ourselves entirely rid of that treacherous devil."

She turned back to the children, hitching up the long robe so that it would not be saturated by the water in the stream. Freedom seemed no nearer than before. So much could happen before they linked up with their own troops. Akbar

Khan always seemed to have the upper hand, and she now had doubts of the chieftain's offer. Even Eldred Pottinger must realize it could be an elaborate plot to incriminate them all in an escape attempt, which would give him the justification for killing them.

"I will believe in freedom when I see a British officer riding towards me, backed by several thousand sepoys," she said tonelessly.

Six more days passed before a British officer rode towards them. He was not backed by several thousand sepoys, but by six hundred Afghan horsemen of the tribe Pottinger had won over to his side. The men, women, and children who had been dragged all over Afghanistan since January, had been subjected to hunger, pain, privation and fear, and had witnessed birth and death during their ordeal, stood silent and unmoving as it dawned on them that freedom was finally theirs. Emotion too deep to find expression ruled them all.

A private soldier in Queen Victoria's 44th Regiment of Foot had died of fever a few hours beforehand.

• *nineteen* •

AT FIRST, IT was no more than a vague impression of far-off visions and sounds. There was snow, horses in a long line, rocky walls rising high above him: shouts of men, laughter, and music of strange rhythm and tone. There was a peculiar swaying motion, moments of terrible pain that made him cry out, darkness that never really lifted. There was also a pleasant sensation of being in a cocoon of warmth from which emergence would mean more pain. He stayed within the soft padded enclosure.

Later, he was aware of being touched by gentle hands,

washed with liquid that eased the pain he found harder to elude, encouraged to drink some kind of warm broth. Female voices spoke softly, and gentle fingers were laid on his head that ached with leaden agony. He liked those times. It did not seem so lonely, or so abstract.

Then, the mist over his eyes began to clear, and the abstract became reality. He lay in the cocoon of warmth staring at a ceiling of dark stone that seemed to be part of the fantasy still. But it remained, solid and real. He puzzled over it for a long time. What did it mean? He closed his eyes again, trying to think, but it was still there when he opened them again a few moments later.

He must have been ill, he supposed, for he was possessed by the lethargy fever produces and appeared to have a beard of some substance. But where the hell was he? That stone ceiling was still above him. Swivelling his eyes slightly he discovered the whole room was made from dark stone, almost like an ancient castle.

He began to feel a strange alarm. A castle? Why should he be in a castle? Why was he alone? What had happened? He did not remember being ill. He lay staring at the stone walls surrounding him. A castle. Then he could not be in England: it must be somewhere in Russia. Where was Igor? Why had he left him like this for so long? The alarm began to increase. There was something very sinister in the situation in which he found himself.

Suddenly, the cocoon took on the guise of close bonds prohibiting movement, making him a prisoner. He tried to move and suffered severe pain all through his body. He lay panting, alarm turning to fear. Something had happened to him—something extremely frightening. It was as if he no longer had control over his limbs and trunk. Where in God's name was he, what was going on, why was he half-paralysed?

Breaking out into a sweat and breathing heavily he lay still, fighting fear by trying to think out the answers to those questions. There was no doubt he had been ill, suffered some kind of severe injury . . . but where? He racked his brains. There were horses. He could remember a long line of horses crossing snow. That was how he knew time had passed. There had been whiteness everywhere; now the rocks and grass could be seen on the hillsides through that whiteness.

How he knew that was not entirely apparent, because there were only two windows in the room, high up and very small with gratings across them. But he knew the snows were melting. That meant he had been moved in his comatose state from place to place. But by whom? That he was in Russia seemed certain—the snow and stone building proved that—but Igor would not leave him alone like this without someone beside him to soothe his fears when he awoke. The fears were very real, and so was the pain, particularly in his head.

In desperation he gazed around him again. His bed consisted of a pile of cushions and rugs on a platform raised from the ground only two feet or so. Rather strange for a Russian home. There was a small chest against the far wall on which stood a decorated bowl and ewer, and to his left was a low table. It was bare save for something small and golden that caught the light and teased his memory to identify it. Feeling there was some significance about the object, he struggled to raise himself in order to get a better view of it. Something told him it held the clue to the frightening situation in which he found himself, but movement increased fear to nightmare.

The loose robe he was wearing fell apart to reveal his naked body. He stared at it in horror as his skin rose in gooseflesh. The white skin was dreadfully disfigured by vivid scarlet and brown wounds that drew the flesh up in ghastly puckers. His chest and stomach were scored by a mass of gashes that were healing by means of tightening up and restricting movement of his muscles.

Blind panic took hold of him, and he lunged forward in an attempt to reach the golden object on the table. Falling heavily on to the floor he lay fighting pain and sobbing with effort. His right leg was completely useless. He could not move or bend it, and there appeared to be another very deep wound in the back of his thigh which gave him no pain whatever. Paralysis! Gazing helplessly at the walls surrounding him, he knew this was one nightmare from which he would never awaken.

Growing immensely cold, he made a superhuman effort to reach that table, certain the little thing upon it was the means of sanity. Crawling across the floor and dragging his useless leg in a marathon of endeavour and pain, he reached up and closed his hand around the thing he sought.

He gazed at the badge as he collapsed on to his back once more. Unconnected patterns began to drift through his mind as he studied the shape of the insignia; faces and voices sought partnership with each other. He wore such insignia on the collar of his uniform. Hazy memories of an old building of red brick followed on the realization that he was a military officer. A house . . . a school? Questions spun around in his head, confusing him further until he realized that, apart from knowing his name was Richard Lingarde, there was little else he could recall at will. Recollection came when it wished, and not at his bidding. It was more frightening than the terrible scars and made him feel unbearably desolate. He struggled back to the padded cocoon on the dais and reached it with thankfulness before dropping asleep from exhaustion.

When next he awoke it was to an extension of the nightmare. He was surrounded by dark-skinned girls in colourful skirted coats, with hair divided into a dozen or more braids that stuck out stiffly from their heads. With his heart pumping fearfully he wondered if he was going mad. These women were not Russian. Where had they taken him? Dear God, what were natives doing with him as a captive? Trying to struggle up, he found the old pain returning, and fell back helplessly, gazing at them in fear and distrust.

They saw his reaction and tried to calm him with smiles and by holding up a pot of ointment and bowls of scented water. Could these have been the feminine voices he remembered, the soothing fingers that took the pain away? They untied the padded bag in which he lay and began to remove the loose robe with every sign of gentleness. But he still experienced unease as they commenced work on the disfiguring wounds, lying naked and helpless as much from physical restrictions as mental ones.

Who were these women? Why was he their prisoner—for they had keys which must have unlocked his door? What, in God's name could he do to get back to sanity? What *was* sanity?

In the midst of the women's giggling ministrations, the door opened to admit a tall, dark-skinned man in full trousers, a long, belted dress, and a loose jacket trimmed with sheepskin. He had a black moustache and beard, strong features and large, soulful eyes. His teeth were sharp and yellowed as he smiled down at Richard.

But the sight of the man filled him with an overwhelming and inexplicable dread—not the kind he experienced when not finding the answers he wanted, but a scalp-prickling sensation that made him want to cry out against what the man intended to do to him. Accompanying that was an urge to cover himself. It did not make sense, this desperate need to hide his nakedness from a man when three women had been touching the most intimate parts of his body during their bathing and cleansing of his wounds. But it was so strong he had to obey, and drew the robe across skin that was crawling with revulsion as he gazed up at someone who was a complete stranger.

Yet Richard understood what the bearded robed figure said to him in what must have been a native language. The man expressed his pleasure at the recovery of his honoured guest and assured him that no request would be too great to grant. He had only to ask, and servants would be sent far and wide to obtain whatever he desired.

Richard kept his lips tightly together as he lay tense and trembling beneath his scant cover. The man sounded very friendly, yet it was that very friendliness that produced such dread. The fact that it did made Richard's helpless state even worse. Why should he be reduced to almost uncontrollable trepidation by a stranger in foreign dress who gave no outward sign of aggression, no visible cause for the feeling? How was it Richard understood the strange language and could have answered in the same tongue? What language was it, for God's sake?

In the face of silent resistance, the man gave up and departed, promising to come again the following day. When the women finished their treatment of his wounds, they gave him a plate of food and left him alone again, locking the door behind them. Richard lay clutching the padded bag with hands that shook.

A week passed. He had given up trying to force recollection because it merely left him frustrated and feverish. But he held that golden insignia in his hands, like a talisman, turning it over and over in the hope that it would touch some chord in his clouded mind. Then, when he least expected it, the faint floating impression of an expanse of wood with great billowing canvases above it told him he had once been on a ship, that he had spent a very long time on it.

Full of bubbling excitement, he told himself he must be in India, that land of great military achievement and expansion. Rushing in on top of that came memories, helter-skelter, of himself preparing for the voyage, visiting old friends to say goodbye, riding around the estate for a last time before leaving. Then his youth and schooldays piled in so fast he could hardly keep up with pictures that filled him with warmth and delight, like the reunion of old friends.

Suddenly, he was struck with dismay as it occurred to him that his mother would be suffering great distress over him, believing him to be dead because she had had no word from him. He was almost certain she was in Calcutta. That was where she and his father had been when he sailed for India. He remembered the pleasure he had felt at the thought of seeing her again on reaching those shores. A great longing to see her filled him. He was certain it was a long time since they had last met, although he could not say why he was so certain of the fact.

If he was a military prisoner something could be done to secure his release, surely. Had the authorities already tried to negotiate with the bearded man? It was essential to find out, and insist that he be allowed to send a message to his unit.

But where was it? That he was in India was plain, because of the ship and the dark-skinned people around him, but he had no idea how long he had been in the country. Long enough to learn the language, it appeared, and to engage in a battle in which he had apparently been badly wounded. He hoped he had dealt the enemy some punishment first.

When the women came in that day, he questioned them and found he could speak several dialects without difficulty. When he hit upon one they understood, the fact appeared to frighten them and they fled. He was left to anoint his own wounds, but he vowed to get outside that room, the door of which they had left unlocked in their haste.

But he was forestalled by the immediate arrival of the man he had come to know as Yakub-Jan. Pulling on the robe hastily, Richard experienced that same faint dread of a man who had been unfailingly courteous to a prisoner he treated more as a guest. This time, after a week of stubborn silence, Richard answered his greeting cautiously, then went on to speak of being allowed to write letters to his superiors, and to his mother. But this constituted a desire the servants were unable to fulfil, the foreigner explained, saying that the British had all been driven from the country and there was no way of communicating with them.

It was a thought so tremendous that Richard was driven to challenge the man for details, finding it impossible to believe the East India Company had been driven from India. But Yakub-Jan related his story with such apparent frankness it had a ring of truth about it. His countrymen had risen against the infidel, he told Richard, and there had been a great war. The soldiers had been slaughtered to a man. The women and children had been taken away to safety. The British had gone. Now, there was to be a new ruler, and it was important for men like himself, who owned vast lands, to have a strong army in the days to come. He wished to offer his guest the post of General to his troops. In the battle, Yakub-Jan explained, he had seen the exalted gentleman before him rush headlong and unafraid into a group of cavalry and fell several before being brought down himself. Such courage and military skill had so impressed itself upon him, he now honoured his former enemy and accorded him the ministrations of the women of his household.

Richard could not answer. It was all too much for him to absorb. The visitor left, locking the door behind him. But the imprisoned guest no longer wanted to walk from his room. The conversation had aroused a ringing confusion in his head . . . and a return of fear. Could so much have happened, such tremendous events, and been forgotten so totally? He could not believe he was the only white man left in India. He lowered his head in his hands despairingly. Yakub-Jan could tell him what lies he wished, there was no way of disproving them. He recalled the deck of that ship, and nothing more after that.

From that day on Richard concentrated on physical advances, knowing mentally he had come to a dead end. He soon discovered how to walk reasonably well with his right leg dragging. The wounds on his body were healing but leaving dreadful scars that tugged painfully at his muscles if he became too energetic. He would never play cricket again, that much was obvious, and he felt a sharp pang of regret that seemed a little extravagant, under the circumstances.

As soon as Yakub-Jan found his prisoner could walk about the door was left open, and Richard was given the freedom of what he discovered was a fortress in the midst of wild, mountainous countryside. The locked door must have been to keep people out, not himself in, for they were in the middle of nowhere. The weather had turned hot, and he walked outside the walls amidst sweet-smelling flowers where beautiful, exotic birds and butterflies abounded. He soon found he could ride a horse with skill, despite his stiff leg, and there were no restrictions placed upon him. But it was pointless to gallop off into a country he did not know without food or weapons to support such an escape.

Eventually, he stopped demanding that letters he had written should be delivered to his Colonel and to his mother. Yakub-Jan insisted he had no means of sending them, and Richard had nothing with which to bribe servants into taking them for him. He had no idea where to send them, in any case.

Although his inexplicable dread of his host remained, Richard's life was in no way unpleasant. Yakub-Jan talked to him for hours on end about military matters and treated him with kindness and courtesy. Knowing he owed his life to the man, Richard did his best to overcome his aversion that he did not understand, and was astonished, and somewhat relieved, when he discovered some weeks later that he was in Afghanistan, not India. He immediately bombarded the chieftain with questions, but Yakub-Jan declined to answer, saying it was all best forgotten.

It left Richard confused and more unhappy than ever about his own past but, although he now vaguely remembered a column of Indian soldiers, and himself riding with another Englishman he had found very likeable, that really was the end of his recollection. For several months now nothing new had come to him, and he resigned himself to accept that those years of his life were irrevocably lost. For years they must have been. Uncertain of his present age, he did know he was no longer an inexperienced boy.

Offered a choice of Yakub-Jan's women, Richard had at first felt a strange aversion to them. But, after a while, a very young and gentle creature, with small dusky feet that fascinated him, began to grow from handmaiden to companion, and then to mistress. That was when Richard realized he was no inexperienced boy.

He dressed in Afghan robes and spoke their language with increasing fluency. He ate their food and obeyed their customs. The mountainous environment gave him back his strength, and he grew to revel in the wild scenery and a landscape where he found an immensely strong feeling of communion with his mother. He prayed that affinity they had always had with each other would allow her to sense that he was safe and would eventually return to her. For, although he had grown resigned to his captivity without bars, he never lost the longing to return to his own people.

Hour after hour he studied the landscape, the movement of

the sun and the star formations. He watched those around him when they rode off to other villages, and chatted with the menfolk, gleaning valuable information that would give him the layout of the country. Fretting over the fact that he knew absolutely nothing of his position in a country whose terrain was a mystery to him, he tried to make maps from the facts he had obtained. Nearly always he ended in despair over the knowledge that he must have ridden through Afghanistan, studied maps, calculated distances, noted the hills and rivers . . . and it had all gone from his mind as if it had never been there. He prayed the blank in his mind would clear, but it never did. He could picture quite clearly that column of soldiers and a man with serious features and friendly likeable personality. But the memory always ended abruptly in the middle of that journey.

He waited and hoped for the means to escape, steadfastly refusing to become General of Yakub-Jan's troops. He gave military advice, when asked, but told his host time after time that he had pledged his life to his king and country, and could not therefore serve another. And all the time he wondered why the army authorities were apparently making no efforts to negotiate his release.

It grew colder again. Snow appeared on the higher slopes of the hills. Winter was approaching, and Richard had to abandon hopes of escape until the spring. By then, he would be enough of an Afghan to pass as one, if he travelled at night and no one saw the colour of his eyes and hair. He could dye the small beard he wore with dark earth, and a turban would hide the fair hair grown long over the deep cut in his head that must have been responsible for his confused condition. But nothing would disguise vivid blue-green eyes that were undoubtedly European. Meanwhile, he had all winter to draw his guesswork maps, and try to lay in supplies for a journey of uncertain length.

But Fate had other plans for him. One afternoon, on returning from a hunting expedition with some of Yakub-Jan's henchmen, Richard was told by his fearful mistress that a stranger had arrived at the fort—a man of her master's army to see Yakub-Jan. Richard's heart leapt. A British officer

· 458 ·

here? Had he come to negotiate for his release? With barely containable impatience he waited for a summons from the Afghan chieftain, knowing he would be barred entry to the man's apartments if he attempted to break in now, and his one fear was that the Englishman might leave without even seeing him.

When the summons came, Richard made his way across the courtyard with the hopping gait he was forced to adopt when trying to run, and he tried to calm the excitement within that would make him appear foolish and undignified to a fellow countryman. But he had never prayed so fervently as he entered the ante-room of the chieftain's apartments.

His hopes of a negotiating military courier were immediately dashed when Yakub-Jan greeted him in the small room, saying that he had a British guest who had been so surprised to hear there was one of his countrymen already enjoying the hospitality of the fort, he had made a request to meet him. It did not suggest the man had come to secure his release. Nevertheless, he represented a chance to plead his case, send messages, gain valuable information.

They went into the silk-hung audience-chamber together, and the pungent smell of food and liquor was immediately overpowering. The man was sitting on a pile of cushions, paying delighted attention to several serving-girls surrounding him, and he did not immediately look up at their entry. He was a well-built man of middle-age, with dark looks, dressed much as Richard was, except that his clothes were more ostentatious and ornate. He could have been an Afghan.

Yakub-Jan turned to Richard. "My great disappointment at your refusal to command my army, has been consoled by great good fortune. I am honoured by the presence of so distinguished a warrior. General Duprés, late of Mekhar Khan's army, Commander-in-Chief of Ranji-Lal's personal cavalry, and Aga of Sultan Mushteg's revolutionary force, has travelled to my humble abode in order to support my cause. He has graciously offered to train my army."

Richard was not really listening to the words. All he saw

was his means of rescue and return to his own people, and he was already stepping forward with his hand out before Yakub-Jan had finished speaking.

"How do you do, sir? I am Lingarde of the Engineers. I cannot tell you how good it feels to see another Englishman after all this time."

The serving-girls forgotten, the man stared at him, as if in shock, the colour leaving his face almost ashen. He ignored the hand Richard held out.

"*Diable!*" he swore viciously. "You!"

Taken aback by such reaction, Richard frowned. "Have we met before, General Duprés?"

"Of all the men to come across now it has to be you," went on the savagely soft voice. "We all thought you dead long ago."

Disturbed by the way things were going and sensing real aggression in the man, Richard lowered his hand and spoke with formal stiffness.

"You will have to forgive me, sir. Unfortunately, I have no recollection of my life from the time I arrived in India. It is a complete blank. If I have offended you in some way in the past, I apologize, but it is my very earnest desire to return to India. I trust you will not refuse to help me."

When there was no response, Richard went on. "My mother, Lady Anastasia Lingarde, will have been very anxious on my behalf all these months. I do not wish to put her through any further distress, as I am sure you will understand."

General Duprés took a long time to reply, then he began laughing softly as if at some exquisite secret joke. "*Mon Dieu*, you really have forgotten! I foresee a *situation très émoustillante*. I almost wish I could be there when you get back."

· *epilogue* ·

THE SPRING BALL was held at Meerpore, as usual, that year of 1843. The committee argued for days over the theme to be adopted until a Thespian subaltern discovered in the store-room of the garrison theatre some huge cut-outs of grinning March hares. These were immediately adopted as eminently suitable, in view of recent events.

In the way they had of making victories out of defeats, the British had revelled in the rescue of the Afghanistan hostages, and clapped themselves on the back over the successful re-entry of Kabul and the reprisals taken. The most effective of these had been the blowing up of the great Kabul bazaar, pride of the country, where Sir William McNaughten's and Captain Trevor's headless bodies had been hung on display as objects of vilification. As the pulsating heart of the city, the loss of the bazaar amounted almost to the destruction of the city itself. Ghuznee was destroyed, and other strongholds reduced to rubble. Akbar Khan had been forced to flee and was in permanent hiding for fear of retribution.

In order to forget the fact that Dost Mohammed was now back on the throne of Kabul as if the past four years had never happened, the Anglo-Indians thrilled themselves with the stories of those who had been the prisoners of Akbar Khan and endured the harrowing experience. There was an officer who, because he had wrapped the regimental colour around his body to get it safely through, had been mistaken for a person of great importance when wounded, and saved from slaughter by a chieftain who cared for him with great kindness until he was handed over to Akbar Khan.

· There were the children born in captivity to widows of the massacre, little mites who had the mark of adventure already upon them. Then there was the tale of a soldier's wife who took an Afghan lover and betrayed them all for her own gain. There was the bravery and endeavour of the political officers, who had made hazardous lone journeys between the captives and their saviours. There were stories of intrigue, and clever plans to send messages in code, and there were the personal diaries of those who had survived, already intended for publication.

But the most enthralling story of all was that of Lieutenant Lingarde, who had gone to the desperate rescue of his little daughter and been surrounded by Afghans in the terrible massacre of the Khurd-Kabul Pass. Counted amongst the dead he had been discovered almost a year later on the far northern border of Afghanistan, captive of a chieftain and remembering nothing of his wife or the child he tried so valiantly to rescue. Not only that, his mind had rejected any memory of his life from the time he had arrived in India in 1834—nine years of his life wiped away as if they had never been. Why, the poor man was not even aware that his country was now ruled by a queen!

Already the subjects of many a colourful story, the Lingardes appeared to be living up to their reputation. Some maintained it was a convenient pose he would be forced to drop on his return, others were convinced it spelled the end of a controversial marriage. There were others who were kinder and suggested it was the delayed result of that terrible affair at Malkhan. The sentimental sighed over the bizarre fact of the young officer being found by an adventurer who had abandoned his allegiance to the Company and gone where the financial and personal rewards were likely to be more advantageous—a man who had been something of a personal enemy, and whom young Lingarde had not known on meeting. How sad, they said, that his first thoughts had been for a mother he thought still alive. How sad that his wife and little girl meant nothing to him. How sad that such a handsome, athletic young officer with his career before him was apparently crippled in body as well as mind.

The army authorities told themselves they had been right all along. The fever of the brain which attacked Lingarde from time to time had mastered him, after all. It all came of having mixed blood, of course. Barbaric people, the Russians—and damned devious, besides. Russian spies had been reported entering Kabul to seek alliance with Dost Mohammed. They would need watching in case they attempted to extend their influence as far as the Indian frontier. Such a possibility was unthinkable and would have to be stopped.

Tom had broken the news of Richard's survival to Charlotte one morning in January, and she sat for a long time, stunned and full of anguished thoughts until she found herself saying, "The Lord does move in mysterious ways, Tom. Aunt Meg always used to quote that to me, and it has taken an earthquake to make me truly believe it."

He had not understood her words, but he understood her actions and held her comfortingly when she flew into his arms in a flood of uncontrollable tears. But it had taken some months for Richard to be escorted across Afghanistan, through the treacherous Khyber Pass, and a Punjab seething with hatred against the British, and Charlotte could do nothing but wait full of desperate apprehension over the coming reunion. Meerpore medical men had told her she must be prepared to accept a man who would act like a total stranger towards herself and Anna. On the other hand, there was a slight chance that the sight of her might bring it all back to him in an instant. Remembering the times she had wished she could begin her marriage again, without the terrible mistakes, Charlotte realized her wish could become reality. But what if Richard remained like a total stranger?

She found the weeks of waiting unbearable. She and Tom were living with Sir Rastin, who took little interest in them or his grandchildren, but had no objection to their sharing his home temporarily. Tom had fiercely resisted the Shiltons' claim to Adam, and asked Charlotte to rear him alongside Anna, in England where the climate was not as cruel to small children as the Indian heat. She had instantly agreed. Tom was to remain in the army. He already wielded a sword effectively with his left hand, and felt he would be needed in the war that was sure to come with the Sikhs of the Punjab. But there was none of the boyish eagerness for battle he had once had, and he had grown considerably quieter, of late.

That he would marry again before too long, she had no doubt, but hoped his new wife would be more loving and giving than Amy had been. Tom was made for happiness.

Tom had determinedly requested leave to ride out and escort Richard over the final part of his journey. They had come in to Meerpore an hour ago, and she was now waiting for Tom to bring to her a man who had been shocked and upset to learn that he had a wife and child of whom he had no recollection.

If Tom had hoped his friend would know him he had been disappointed. The note from her brother, sent ahead of them, told Charlotte he had found it something of a leveller to be faced with a polite young man who offered to shake him by the hand when introduced. His cautious words that Richard had been "somewhat knocked about" and that Charlotte must understand that he was a man who had suffered and bore the scars, increased her web of fears and imaginings until she was a mass of nerves at the thought of coming face to face with someone who was Richard, but would not look or act like Richard. What must she do; what must she say? How would she ever reach him?

So she waited on the evening of the Spring Ball in the small first-floor salon that was so reminiscent of Felicia. The evening was warm and still—so still, the faint sound of music from the ballroom carried across to remind her of things she would rather forget. With her mother seeming so close, and with memories of other dances, other people gone beyond recall, Charlotte felt as if the whole world was holding its breath along with her as she listened for the sound of footsteps on the stairs.

Then she heard them coming and she got to her feet with the idea of running from what she was about to face. But the influence of Felicia was so strong Charlotte was swept by thoughts of how she had always faced everything calmly, hiding her feelings beneath graceful dignity. She sat down again, compassion filling her. It would be even worse for him, having to accept a strange woman as his wife.

Tom brought Richard in, said he would be in the library,

if wanted, then went out again shutting the door softly behind him. That was when Charlotte found she had lost the power of speech. So certain had she been that the bond that had existed between them was strong enough to penétrate his blankness that it was like a great physical blow to realize she appeared a complete stranger to him. Aching to run to him, hold him, bathe his beloved face with her tears, she merely rose slowly from the brocaded sofa, as Felicia would have done, the folds of her rich claret crinoline falling around her.

He stayed where he was, just inside the door. With a tearing at her heart she saw the deep scar running across his brow to end just below his ear, the slight hunch of his shoulders that used to be so broad and erect, and the leg he held stiffly to one side. *Oh, Richard, what have they done to you?* she cried silently.

The silence in the room seemed to go on and on, whilst the strains of a waltz tune floated across the night to add a touch of normality that now sounded bizarre. They would never waltz together again.

"I . . . beg your pardon," came the dear familiar voice, at last. "This must be very painful for you."

She longed for the right words, the right actions, but Felicia had been forgotten and all she could think was that this was even worse than her arrival in Kabul. There had been *something* between them then, something she could fight. But how did one fight polite impersonality, how did one start again at the beginning of love when one had gone so deeply into it?

"They told me about Kabul, and so on," he ventured next. "It must have been a terrible experience for a female to endure . . . and a . . . a little girl, I believe."

It was more terrible than she had dreamt it could be, standing at opposite ends of the room after all they had been through. But when he began to move forward, she felt panic return. He dragged his leg as he walked and, as he neared, the light from the lamps revealed the ravages of illness and shock upon his face. She saw desperation written there as he searched her face with his gaze, hoping to find that which evaded him. His skin was beaded with perspiration which betrayed his tension in a situation he was doing his best to handle.

Her heartbeat slowed almost to stopping point as she realized the full implication of what had happened to him. How helpless he must feel; how dark life must appear. This marriage must represent as much of a prison as that fort in Afghanistan.

"I hope my appearance does not distress you too much, Charlotte," he said with a brave overture to what had to be faced.

She became aware she had been staring for too long, and he had misinterpreted her scrutiny. "After thinking you dead for over a year, how could the sight of you distress me?" she managed. "I think I shall never cease to gaze at you with thankfulness at my good fortune . . . and you usually call me Lottie," she added, finding the restraint almost more than she could bear.

"Then I must continue to do so," he said on a softer note than before, and as he moved his head slightly, the lamplight caught the brilliant blue-green of those wonderful eyes. Suddenly, she knew the rest did not matter—the scars, the heavy limp, the lack of recognition. He was the same gentle man she had first met, the sun behind him as he steadied his horse, and his hair standing up in a little shimmering crest on his crown as the breeze caught it. It would be all right. They *could* begin again. Her love was strong enough to break through all frontiers of love and pain.

She now stood calmly before him and sensed that he found reassurance in the fact that she had not thrown herself upon him, or shown repulsion at the sight of him. Relaxing visibly, he seemed to lower the barriers he had erected around himself.

"Well, Lottie, there will be a great many things you will have to tell me about myself. I trust they will not be too bad."

Making herself smile she said lightly, "My dear Richard, I must tell you that a wife can see no wrong in her husband. If you wish to hear the truth about yourself, you must ask your devoted friend, Tom—and I advise you to do so before the Meerpore gossips get busy. They like nothing better than to tear a person's character to shreds, and a man who cannot deny their words will be a scoundrel before he knows it."

She could imagine Felicia applauding her calmness and dignity, but it nearly fled on the four winds when, with a spark of interest lighting his eyes he said gently, "I hope I have been a good husband to you, at least."

Swallowing hard she said through a constricted throat, "Oh yes, my dear, the best husband in the world."